never
too
soon

TAMIKA CHRISTY

BOOK TWO IN THE ANAYA'S WORLD SERIES

Virginia

Published in the United States by BQB Publishing
(an Imprint of Boutique of Quality Books Publishing Company)
www.bqbpublishing.com

Printed in the United States of America

978-1-945448-43-0 (p)
978-1-945448-44-7 (e)

Library of Congress Control Number: 2019940435

Book design by Robin Krauss, www.lindendesign.biz
Cover design by Rebecca Lown, www.rebeccalowndesign.com

First editor: Olivia Swenson
Second editor: Pearlie Tan

ONE

There were no conventional seasons in the East Bay. Sweaters in June and flip-flops in October were standard. Some argued that the weather was quirky even before the effects of global warming had taken hold. Others claimed the weather had only gone wacky in recent years. Either way, the natives were accustomed to layering and keeping umbrellas and shorts on hand all year round. The Bay boasted mild but inconsistent temperatures, Indian summers, and local meteorologists who could never get the forecast quite right.

Despite the unpredictable weather, the six-figure median income, and faltering public education system, the Bay was *the* place to live. It was home to many start-up and global tech companies, bustling with development, a biker's paradise, and pet friendly—something about it seemed to appeal to everyone. And though rain or fog could always swoop in unannounced, the mild climate made for perfect running weather.

Lake Merritt was Anaya Goode's favorite place to run. Mornings were ripe with domestic engineers toting lattes and toddlers, singles trying to become un-single, and plenty of workout groups. Healthy living was fundamental in the Bay Area. From farmer's markets and vegan soul food restaurants to Trap Yoga and Booty Ballet, one had to try hard *not* to live a health-conscious lifestyle in the Bay.

"Finish those sit-ups!" a burly trainer urged as Anaya passed a boot camp near the lake's cascade stairs one crisp July morning.

"You wanna be sexy this summer? Wanna wear tank tops and tight dresses?"

Only two participants were actually doing the prescribed sit-ups. Another drank water from a bottle, while the rest stared off into space. From the looks on their faces, it was too early in the morning to be thinking about the rhetoric of taut triceps. Most of them probably just wanted a cup of coffee.

Anaya was an avid runner. In the last five years, she had completed four full marathons, a dozen half marathons, ran a six-minute mile, and had never had a running-related injury. When Anaya laced up her Asics, she felt like Jackie Joyner-Kersee. Running sustained Anaya's sanity when Aunt Deb tried to convert her to Scientology, rendered her sublime patience when Uncle Riley asked her to help him increase his credit score, and permitted her to enjoy the occasional guilt-free slice of key lime pie.

In addition to running, Anaya participated in fad lifestyle challenges that her friends never wanted to do. Last month, her goal was to drink a gallon of water a day. The month before, she had completed Whole 30 for the third time, and next week she planned to start intermittent fasting for two weeks. Wearing a perfect size two with enviable abs and thighs like a cyclist, Anaya didn't need to think twice about her weight. But she did.

As she neared the predetermined "finish" bench, Anaya lengthened her stride, her breath coming faster and arms pumping harder. After sprinting past the bench, she slowed and jogged back to it, reveling in the cool morning air. She looked down the path with sweet patience.

"Look at you," Anaya called out a few minutes later as her companion finally reached the finish bench and immediately rested his hands on his knees to catch his breath. She put a foot up on the bench to stretch and looked over at him. He glanced up, caught her admiring gaze, and winked with those long lashes. She blushed.

"No," Carl said, still panting. He stood up and wiped his face with his tank top. "Don't look at me. I'll look at you." He reciprocated her appraising look.

She pouted playfully. "So tell me. How do you feel? Was that better than our last run?"

She knew that five miles was four-and-a-half too many for Carl. She concealed her smile and remembered how Carl had replied the first time she mentioned she was a runner: "Running is at the bottom of my list of faves, along with beets and talking to my mom after she drinks a pint of gin. But if it means spending time with you, I'm in."

"It was a good run, babe." He was lying but he got an A for effort.

"Well, thanks for coming."

"You're beautiful, you know that?" he said in a soothing voice. She still blushed when he complimented her. Even after five years together, his adulation and flattery never got old, and every day, she found herself falling more in love with him.

She ran her hand over the loose bun that contained her dark brown curls and felt small ringlets sticking to her damp forehead. She covered her face. "Stop it. I'm a hot, sweaty mess."

"You're the sexiest hot mess I've ever seen." He gently pulled her hands from her face.

She could tell from his expression that he didn't think she was anything less than perfect. Carl was a wonderful boyfriend but had become so much more to her than that. He was one of her closest friends, and she trusted him with her heart. He listened patiently, he consoled when she was stressed, he helped out whenever he could, and he was never demanding or overbearing. Anaya often heard her mom's say "Love is patient, love is kind" whenever she thought of Carl. He was more than she expected in a partner, and even her two best friends approved of him in their own ways—Sophie called him safe, and Catie called him boring.

"You're sweet. You know that?" she told him softly.

"Shhh. Don't say that too loud." He pretended to look around. "I don't want everybody to know."

"You don't want anybody to know how sweet you are?"

He pressed a kiss on her forehead before adopting an offended expression. "Sweet? No way. If my boys found out that I was running around the lake this early on a Saturday morning, I'd never hear the end of it."

"If your boys heard you were out here running early on a Saturday morning, they would be jealous of how fit you're going to be." She leaned into him, running her hand over his ridged abs— her favorite part of his body.

"They would only be jealous because of who I'm running with." He winked.

"Stop it." She punched him playfully. Carl had told her on more than one occasion that his friends thought she was out of his league.

He gave her booty a playful swat then grabbed her hand as she tried to slap him away. "You ready for breakfast? I'm starving."

They leisurely headed to Lakeshore Café, the crisp morning breeze cool against their damp faces. Lakeshore was crowded. Families and businesses seemed to be moving into the area by the droves. When she was younger, Anaya and her mom would come to Lakeshore after Anaya's ballet class, and they'd run into other families they knew. They would see the same faces each week and were able to easily grab breakfast or tea without waiting in line. Now she rarely recognized anybody and the restaurant and coffee house lines were insane.

Luckily, a couple was leaving just as they entered the café and they snagged a table right away. They ordered their usual— black coffee and an egg white omelet for her, and orange juice and pancakes for him.

"What do you have on tap for the rest of the day?" Carl asked after the waitress had taken their order.

"I have to help Aunt Deb find a new financial planner and finish my report." Anaya rubbed her eyes wearily as she thought about the work and family obligations she had planned for the weekend. She liked her job as director of Housing and Community services for Alameda County. The pay was great, and it was good work, but the hours were long and her boss Wendy was a miserable bitch. And she had recently been assigned one of the toughest projects of her career.

If work weren't enough to drive Anaya mad, she had become the cornerstone of her family since her mom died six years ago—giving financial advice, resolving conflicts (except for the one between her and her sister Ava), and trying to hold the family together. Ever since she'd started working on the naval base project three weeks ago, her days had begun to bleed into each other—work, family, sleep, stress, repeat. She told herself it wouldn't last forever. No matter how bad things got, she tried to keep her head high, and her complaints at a minimum.

Carl furrowed his brow in confusion. "What happened to the last financial planner you helped her find?"

Anaya sighed. "Same as the one before that. She didn't trust him." She gazed out the window, trying not to think about work or family, and just enjoy the present. She watched two men walk by with three dogs and twins in a stroller. She smiled and turned back to Carl.

He leaned in and took her hand. "Hey, you wanna go to Sam's bowling party next week?"

"Huh?" Anaya asked, pulling away and grabbing a menu from the stand on the table, even though she could recite it in her sleep. *Bowling party? Isn't there an anniversary party coming up too? When do these people rest?*

Carl slid the menu away from her with an inquiring look. "Do you want to go to Sam's bowling party next week?" he repeated slowly. "It's his birthday and I'd like you to come with me." He smiled at her. "We haven't spent much time together lately."

It was no secret that Anaya and Carl's friends would never be close. She normally accepted his invitations because she knew Carl's friends were important to him, but Anaya didn't particularly enjoy spending time with them.

And no, she didn't want to go to Sam's bowling party, or any party hosted by Carl's friends. Faven, Bobby, Ricky, Sam, and Carl had been best friends since middle school and they were more like siblings. Faven's parents had paid for Carl's high school cap and gown, and Bobby's dad had helped Carl negotiate a good deal when he bought his first car. Anaya was glad Carl had such a strong friend base. She just didn't understand why *she* needed to spend so much time with them.

For Carl's sake, she'd tried to be nice, but even after half a decade and countless social gatherings, she felt like an outsider around them. And while Carl knew she wasn't close with his friends, she'd never quite figured out how to tell him how isolated she felt when she spent time with them.

"Um, okay." She fingered the rim of her water glass. "But you mentioned that Faven was having a party soon too." *Maybe I can get out of one of them . . .*

Carl nodded happily. "Yeah, her parents are having an anniversary party in a couple of months. We are invited to that as well."

Of course we are. She paused before saying, "Um, okay" again.

"You sure?" He reached across the small, wooden table and tilted her chin toward him.

No. "Yeah, I'm sure."

He raised a skeptical brow and leaned back in his seat. "If you don't want to—"

"No, it's cool," she lied, forcing a smile. "I was just thinking about the rest of my day." *Bowling party. Anniversary party. Ugh.*

Another bowling party meant more deep-dish pizza and beer. Anaya didn't drink beer and knew she'd spend the entire night warding off the usual remarks from the ladies: "I see why you're so skinny. You don't eat!" or "We are going to have to put some meat on those bones. Here, you can have some of mine." Hanging out with Carl's group tested her patience, and because of them she'd exceeded her simple carb threshold four bowling parties ago.

"Sweet. I'll let Faven know. She's been hounding me about a head count."

Super.

Faven and Carl were the closest among the group, and she organized all the group's gatherings and always managed to leave Anaya out of the details. The only person Faven seemed to like less than Anaya was her husband, Darren. Thanks to Faven's inclination to gossip, the entire group knew Darren cried after watching *Sparkle* and that he "lacked spontaneity" in the bedroom. After thirteen years of marriage and three kids, Darren still hadn't earned Faven's respect, so Anaya didn't hold her breath that they would become friends anytime soon.

"Cool." Anaya fiddled with her napkin. A little bit of dishonesty was preferable to creating tension between her and Carl—at least right now. When she wasn't so swamped with work and being hunted down by her family members to complete their personal tasks, she'd take time to talk to him.

Carl tucked a wayward curl behind her ear as the waitress brought over their order. Anaya immediately picked up her coffee, the heat on her hands calming her.

Carl began to cut up his pancakes. "The ladies will be happy to see you."

No they won't. "Are you sure about that?" She sipped the Jamaican brew. It felt like the warm cloths her mom put on her sore throat as a kid.

Carl furrowed his brow.

Anaya put her hand on his. "I'm just kidding. It should be fun." She laughed uneasily.

It wouldn't be fun. It would be slow torture, but Carl was her man, and sometimes you had to take one for the team.

She kept her hand on his and looked out of the window. In her hectic world filled with preparing tax returns for family members, handing out personal loans to her sister, fielding arguments between her aunt and uncle, and handling her ever-growing work responsibilities, Carl was her rock. Her shelter in the eye of the storm.

"You're stressed." He looked into her eyes.

"You're right."

"Talk to me." His gentle tone made her want to go back to his place and not leave for three days. But she didn't have that time luxury right now.

"It's just the same work stuff." She was tired of saying it so he must be tired of hearing it. "I've had to deal with so many non-emergency emergencies, and then there's Wendy, of course. This new project has everyone running around like mad. And even though we both work for the county, it's starting to feel like we are on opposite sides."

"Why don't you get out of there?" She'd heard this argument a thousand times before. "With your master's and your work experience, anyone would want you working for them."

She smiled at his familiar praise. "I know. I want to see this project through, and then . . ." She shrugged. "Then maybe I will start looking."

Behind Carl, a young woman with a grocery bag approached their table. Anaya didn't recognize her. Carl turned around to follow her gaze and straightened up when he saw who was coming.

"Hey, Carl!" The woman gave Anaya a nod as she stopped at their table, and then turned to Carl. Anaya leaned back in her chair. She was accustomed to other women being attracted to Carl. Who wouldn't be?

"Hey there, Zendaya," Carl said with a wide smile. "How are you?"

"I'm great." Zendaya pushed her straight dark hair over her shoulder. A gold stud in her nose glinted in the light, accentuating her bold features. "Fancy seeing you here. Do you live in the area?" Her voice sounded like she drank golden honey tea all day.

She's cheerful. And cute, Anaya thought, taking a small bite of omelet.

"Actually, I do. About a mile away." Carl seemed to sense Anaya's thoughts and took Anaya's hand. "Zendaya, this is my girlfriend, Anaya. Anaya, Zendaya."

Anaya extended her other hand. "It's a pleasure."

Zendaya's hand was as warm as her smile. "You're even more beautiful than the picture on Carl's desk."

Ah, so she's been in his office. "Thank you. That's sweet. So you two work together?" Anaya asked Carl. He had never mentioned this Ryan Destiny look-alike with her tiny shorts and neo-soul vibe.

"Not really." She laughed. "Carl is my nephew's social worker, and he's been helping me navigate the system so I can get custody. He's been a godsend." Zendaya put her hand on Carl's shoulder.

Anaya tilted her head and looked at Carl with a smile. "That's Carl. A godsend."

"Yes, he's come by the house a few times to talk to Tyrell and even showed up at his school once. He just goes above and beyond."

"Yes, he does." Anaya was still smiling at Carl. "Above and beyond."

"Well, I'll talk to you later, Carl. It was great meeting you, Anaya. I have to get going." Zendaya turned to leave, then suddenly spun back. "Carl, are you still going to the festival?"

"Yeah."

"Cool, we will see you there. I'm going to get Tyrell from practice now."

"Okay. See you guys soon," Carl said.

"She's pretty," Anaya said as she watched Zendaya maneuver through the crowd and exit the café.

"Who? Zen? Is she? She's a client, so . . ."

"So that makes you oblivious to how attractive *Zen* is?"

"Come on now. I'm not interested in her that way."

Anaya rolled her eyes. "Come on, Carl. She's gorgeous. Just because we're in a relationship doesn't mean you don't find other women attractive. Just don't act on it and we will be fine." She paused. "Seriously though, she looks young. Is she actually going to get custody of her nephew?"

"Yep. She's determined. Tyrell's a good kid, just born in unfortunate circumstances."

"That's admirable. Does Zendaya have kids of her own?"

"No, she just wants to do the right thing."

"Impressive," Anaya said. Her smart watch buzzed, and she looked down to read the notification.

"Don't tell me you have to go already," Carl said.

"Pretty soon." She hated to say it. She didn't want to revisit the "you work too much" conversation because it never ended well. Gone were the days of long lunches and half-day Fridays at County. Anaya was now responsible for a thirty-million-dollar budget and a staff of sixty and was currently in the middle of the naval base project—the biggest development agreement in county history, and during her career.

"It's a gorgeous day." Carl interrupted Anaya's thoughts. "The carnival Zendaya mentioned is for some of the kids who are getting permanent home placements. Can you come for a few hours? I want you to meet that little girl I told you about."

Anaya shook her head and finished eating her omelet. "Sounds fun, Carl, but I can't. I will come to the next one." She pushed her plate away. "You ready to go?"

"Actually, I'm not." He held on to her hands. "I'm enjoying you."

Anaya smiled and squeezed his hands. Carl's sweet sentiments echoed in her heart. She couldn't imagine loving him any more than she did. "I'm enjoying you too. And if I could stay with you all day, I would. As soon as this project is over, we are going to take a trip. I think we both need it."

He paid the bill, and they walked to her car that was parked in front of his condo.

"Do you want to come up?" he asked.

She glanced at her watch and groaned. It would be a miracle if she finished everything she needed to today. "I can't. I'm already running late." She turned to get in her car, then noticed Carl's glum expression. He tapped a rock on the ground with the tip of his tennis shoe.

Anaya put her arms around him. "I promise we will hang out later in the week. Last week was a little crazy."

"And the two weeks before that?"

She grimaced. He didn't know how much she'd rather be with him instead of working. She kissed him and got in her car. She wasn't going to ruin the morning with tension. "I will call you later," she said from her window.

"We gotta do better than this," he said, stuffing his hands into the pockets of his sweatpants.

"I know." She blew him a kiss. Anaya needed to change her priorities or she risked losing the best thing that ever happened to her.

TWO

Anaya drove down the street she had lived on her entire life. The neighborhood had developed during the zeitgeist of white picket fences and bungalow porches. Her mom had taken great care in keeping the house and yard impeccable and since her death, her dad Roscoe accepted the responsibility. The yard was still one of the best maintained on the block, secure behind the white picket fence her mom had loved.

She pulled into the driveway and saw her dad, Uncle Allen, and Uncle Riley sitting on the porch. Riley and her father smiled at her, but Allen seemed to barely notice she was there. *I hope it's not Aunt Marie again.*

"Hi, Daddy," Anaya called stepping out of her car and slinging a drawstring bag across her back. She walked over and gave him a hug. "Hey, Uncle Allen, Uncle Riley."

"Hi there, baby girl." Roscoe looked up and shielded his eyes from the sun.

"Hey, niecey," Uncle Riley said. Uncle Allen nodded and accepted her hug.

"Did you beat Carl around the lake again?" Roscoe's laugh sounded like gurgling water.

"Yep. Sailed past him like a champ."

"Don't show him up too bad," Roscoe joked. "He might not like that."

"Point taken." Anaya pointed a finger at her dad.

"You're looking more like your mama every day," Riley said.

"Thank you," she replied. It was a familiar compliment, but she still liked hearing it.

"Your mama was a beautiful woman. She was smart too," Roscoe said, looking over the yard.

"Yes, she was," Riley agreed.

"What are you guys up to?" Anaya asked.

Allen finally smiled and looked up at her. "Ah, just hanging out. We were supposed to go play a few holes, but your daddy got here late. Been at that nursery again." Allen laughed.

"We can still make it," Roscoe said, rubbing the back of his neck and avoiding Anaya's gaze. "We just got caught up talking."

She didn't know what Allen was teasing her dad about, but she smiled. She was glad her dad had the yard and her uncles to keep him busy.

"Well, you guys have fun," Anaya said as she headed into the house.

The interior of the Goode house looked exactly the same as when Anaya was growing up. The brown leather sofa still faced the fireplace at an awkward angle, the rubber fig plant, browning at the edges, overwhelmed the corner near the kitchen, and the wobbly leg on the coffee table was a constant reminder of cousin Marguerite's fall while trying to perform a dance move to prove to Aunt Deb that her size 18 frame didn't keep her from doing anything a size 8 could do. The house was full of memories—family spats, holidays past, a Warriors-Lakers divide, parental tirades. But as much as the Goode house appeared to be the same, the people who lived inside had changed drastically over the years.

Anaya headed upstairs and settled into her home office, formerly her brother Andrew's room. When he was tragically killed just before she started college, Anaya had decided to be a commuter student so she could support her parents and sister. Then her mom died right before Anaya started her master's program, and again, thinking her dad and sister needed her, she stayed home. Now almost thirty, she had never lived on her own.

Anaya shrugged off the familiar twinge of disappointment. By staying at home, she had been able to save her money and could now afford to buy almost any house she wanted in the competitive Bay Area housing market. She always used that reminder to ward off feelings of regret.

She looked at her seemingly never-ending list of tasks and decided to start by calling caterers to see which one was available to help with Roscoe's sixtieth birthday celebration in a few weeks. Next, she added a reminder to Monday's to-do list to look into an internship with the County's health department for her cousin Amber. She skipped over the job of finding a financial planner for Aunt Deb by editing cousin Marguerite's resume. She was starting to regret not going to Carl's house.

Her cell rang.

"Hello?"

"Hi, sister dear."

"Hey, Ava. What's up?" Anaya rubbed her chest, feeling a twinge of heartburn. She popped two Zantacs before leaning back in her chair.

"Not much. Blessed and highly favored," Ava said breathlessly. "How are you?"

"I'm good. Just trying to get some stuff done." Anaya could hear the boys yelling in the background and imagined the complete chaos of Ava's house. "Where's Joe?" She asked the question out of habit. Joe was always at the gym. Joe Carraway was a nice guy and loved Ava and the boys, but he wasn't always helpful.

"At the gym."

"I see," Anaya said. The fact that going to the gym seemed more important to Joe than finding a job to support his family never made sense to Anaya. *Nice pecs don't pay the bills.*

"I wanted to check on you," Ava said brightly.

Anaya was immediately suspicious. Ava was never overly concerned about anything except her children, healthy eating habits, cancer awareness, and keeping the Sabbath holy. She wanted something.

"Well, that's nice of you," Anaya replied. "I'm fine."

"You and Daddy getting along?" Ava asked.

That was a silly question. Roscoe was the mildest mannered person they knew, even when he drank, which he hadn't since their mom died. He was a loving and supportive father. Their getting along had never been an issue.

"Yes, we are," Anaya said. "How are the boys?"

"Doing great," Ava gushed. "Jeremiah and Hezekiah are running around pretending to be pirates, and Joshua is in his rocker. I just finished feeding them breakfast." Ava may not have had a dime to her name, but she didn't let anything ruin her mood. It was annoyingly refreshing. She and Joe were similar that way. "Joe had an interview yesterday, and I think this job is going to come through."

"Oh?" Anaya yawned. Joe had gone to more than a dozen interviews in the last two months, and he still didn't have a job. But Ava was steadfastly optimistic despite Joe's crop of failed interviews. In Anaya's opinion, something wasn't right. Joe wasn't the sharpest knife in the drawer, but he should be able to get another job besides being a part-time fitness trainer.

"And he helped his uncle lay carpet the other day, so that check will be coming any day now." Ava continued as if she were talking to herself. "I know our breakthrough is coming, I can feel it. God is so faithful."

It was funny how people changed. Growing up, Ava was the corporation-protesting, sustainability-promoting academic, determined to rid the planet of capitalism and carnivorous pleasures.

She didn't like hanging out with friends the way Andrew and Anaya did. She excelled in school, so Anita and Roscoe didn't worry too much about her lack of social life. They worried even less when she was accepted into all twelve of the colleges she applied to.

When their mom died, Ava deferred college for a year, during which time she found herself most comfortable at a local church. That's when her focus shifted to being "saved." Then she met and married Joe and morphed into a baby-toting, scripture-quoting, tofu-eating career student who couldn't keep a job or the required minimum balance in her checking account. Ava still believed in fighting the good fight but now she did so between pregnancies, Boy Scout meetings, and church auxiliaries. Their family lived off of Joe's meager earnings as a trainer—the only job he could hold—and Ava's part-time job. Joe and Ava earned enough money to pay the bills and very little else.

"What's the interview for?" Anaya started re-reading cousin Marguerite's resume.

"It's for a position at that new credit union downtown. Perfect for Joe!"

Anaya rolled her eyes. "Ava, has Joe worked in finance before?"

"Well, no, but he's good with numbers."

"Why did Joe quit his last job again? I thought they paid pretty well."

"They did, but they wanted him to work on Sundays."

"So?" Anaya waited for an explanation.

"So? So, we *worship* on Sundays. He can't go to work and leave his family to worship alone on the Sabbath. The Bible says, 'Forsake not the assembly of thineself.'"

Anaya closed her eyes. She would never see eye to eye with her sister on religion. "Can't you guys go to church a different day, Ava?"

"Ny, you know we attend church on Sundays," Ava said matter-of-factly. "Which leads to my next question. The boys are outgrowing their shoes and need a few other things. I was wondering if you could loan me some money."

First of all, asking for money had nothing to do with going to church on Sundays. Second of all, Anaya had loaned Ava two hundred dollars last month. Or was it earlier this month?

"Again? How much, Ava?"

"Six hundred dollars."

Anaya almost choked on her saliva. "Six hundred dollars! Are you shopping at Gucci?"

"No, silly. I also need to cover a few bills. We are a little short."

Anaya sighed. This was getting old. "So you guys don't have *any* money?"

"If you don't want to lend me the money, that's fine. The Bible says, 'Be of good cheer for I have overcome the world.' I won't hold my head down because my husband is seeking better employment. God is on the throne, so I know I will get through this."

Shut up!

"Ava, nobody asked you to keep your head down. But you need to do more to help yourself. You're smart. You can get another job."

Ava worked from home as a reservationist for United Airlines— twenty hours a week for the past five years. She mostly did it for the health benefits. She had considered getting another job when Jeremiah was a baby but found out she was pregnant with Hezekiah before Jeremiah could crawl. And in the spirit of consistency, she followed the same pattern with Joshua. The older boys were in pre-school, but Joshua still wasn't potty trained, so he stayed home with Ava during the day.

"You're right. I'm smart. I graduated summa cum laude, re-member?"

Yes, I remember. You won't let me forget. You won't let anybody forget.

"I remember Ava, but that's not the point. Faith is fine, but a job is better, don't you think?"

"I don't doubt my God."

Anaya realized she needed to change tactics. "Neither do I, Ava. But faith without work is dead. God is merciful and understanding, but you have to look for a job yourself. God doesn't do interview and resume skills."

"I will not worry about my future because God doesn't give us a fear of worry. If anybody should worry, it should be Aunt Deb because she uses those harsh color chemicals in her hair. You know hair coloring causes cancer, right? And you know all that psychic stuff she's into is satanic. Aunt Deb needs to go to the altar and pray that stuff off of her. And Aunt Marie? She . . ."

Ava continued her rant until Anaya sighed. "Ava, I have work to do. I will bring the money by in the next few days."

"Thank you, sister! You know I appreciate you. Hold on a sec, Ny." Ava's voice became muffled. "Hezekiah, honey, put that lamp down, you might break it." The one scripture that Ava never quoted was "spare the rod, spoil the child."

"Sounds like you need to get back to the boys, Ava. I will see you tomorrow."

"Wait. How is Carl doing?"

"He's good." *Cue her speech about marriage and fornication.*

"When are you two going to get married? You can't keep fornicating, Ny, you know that's not right. The Lord said it's better to marry than to burn."

"The Lord didn't say that, Ava, the apostle Paul said it. And you don't know if I'm fornicating or not," Anaya said. "You aren't in my bedroom."

"Well thank God for that." She chuckled. "But I know Carl is a man, and a man isn't going to go for too long without sex," Ava said firmly.

"Why do you always find a way to talk about my sex life? It's weird."

"I'm just trying to help save your soul, sister dear. You better stay woke."

"Carl and I are taking our time, thanks. We don't want a bunch of kids running around that we can't afford." Anaya cringed as soon as the words left her mouth. *Crap. Here we go.*

"The Bible says to be fruitful and multiply," Ava replied, overly bright.

"The Bible also says that if a man doesn't work, he doesn't eat." Anaya had prepared her own comebacks to keep up with Ava's incessant Bible-quoting. If Ava was going to dish it, she should be prepared to swallow it too.

"Spiteful talk, Ny."

Anaya resisted the urge to throttle her phone and replied calmly, "No. It's realistic. Don't criticize my relationship when you and Joe haven't figured out your lives either."

There was a pause. "What is that supposed to mean?"

"It means," Anaya said slowly, "that I'm writing you checks too often, Ava. I think someone in your house needs to get a job."

"We have jobs," Ava said, as if Anaya were missing the point.

"Your jobs are not enough," Anaya said. "Don't you want to be able to provide for the boys? They are growing and need things. I don't mind helping, but I can't be your supplemental income."

"I didn't ask you to be."

"Not in so many words."

"Wow. Look at you," Ava said. For the first time, her tone shifted from bouncy to sharp. "Calling out the splinter in my eye and ignoring the plank in yours."

Anaya couldn't believe what she was hearing. "You know what, Ava? Maybe I do have a plank in my eye, but you know what else? I can afford it. You can't get tweezers to pluck the splinter out of your eye without me writing a check for it."

Ava gasped. "Whoa, somebody's salty."

"Nobody's salty." Anaya sighed. "Listen, Ava, I really have to go. I'll see you tomorrow." And she hung up.

Anaya pushed her chair back from her desk and leaned back with a sigh, waiting for her irritation at Ava to pass. Her gaze floated around the room until it caught on a green A's hat hooked on the corner of the bookshelf, and she was swept away in a memory of simpler times.

✳

"Give it back!" Anaya yelled, chasing Andrew into the kitchen. He was too quick for her and rounded the island in the kitchen before darting around the breakfast table. As he turned the corner into the living room, his green A's hat fell onto the floor, and quick as lightning, Anaya snatched it up triumphantly. He reached for it, but she put it behind her back.

"Will you two cut that out?" Anita said from the dining room where she examined swatches in preparation for redoing the laundry room. She stood up to block their path as Anaya ran, squealing, away from Andrew's outstretched hands.

"Andrew took the remote control. I was watching *The Proud Family*, and he just snatched it from me!" Anaya yelled, her two pigtails flailing as she tried to escape her brother.

"The Lakers are playing, Ma," Andrew said. "It's the fourth quarter. I'll let her watch TV when it's over. Her show is all re-runs anyway."

"You can't just come into the living room while somebody is watching a show and change the channel without even asking them. It's rude." Anaya folded her arms.

"I did ask, and you said no." Andrew smiled. He was annoying but was still everyone's favorite. Even when he was being a television hog.

"Well then, you have your answer."

"Anaya, help me get dinner finished and let your brother watch the game," Anita said. "It will be over soon. Then you can watch your show."

"Yes!" Andrew pumped his arm. "Love you, Ma. And Ny, you know you're my favorite sister." He blew a kiss across the room, which she ignored.

"You always pick his side, mom," Anaya whined, following her mom into the kitchen. "Always."

"I'm not picking sides." Anita pulled some greens from the refrigerator. "Cut these up."

Anaya pulled out a cutting board and knife. "But it's not fair. I finished my homework and my chores before I started watching television. Andrew walks in from practice, probably hasn't done a lick of homework, and he gets to watch what he wants."

Anita sighed. "Life isn't fair, Anaya, and I don't want to leave this earth with you thinking that it is. You won't always get your way, and sometimes you have to give, even when you don't get anything in return. That's just the way life is." Anita walked over and held Anaya's chin in her hand. "You're strong and can handle more than most people. You understand? If you just do what you are supposed to do and don't complain, you will always get ahead in life. Some of us are required to do more and you, my dear, are one of those people. You have to be smarter and stronger than other people, but you will be a better person for it."

Anita kissed Anaya on the forehead and released her chin.

Anaya nodded and turned back to chopping. She didn't want to be a better person. She wanted to get her way like her siblings always did. It seemed like she was always the one who had to give, and she rarely got anything in return. She had to help her mom cook, do the majority of the chores, and always concede when it came to her siblings. Andrew was the fun favorite and Ava was "sensitive"—whatever that meant. As far as Anaya was concerned, her siblings were spoiled, and being the middle child wasn't fair.

The back door that led into the mud room next to the kitchen slammed, and Anaya saw her mom straighten her back and take a deep breath. Her daddy stumbled into the kitchen, the scent of alcohol strong on his body. Anaya kept chopping the vegetables, but also watched the familiar scene, a tight knot of worry in her gut.

"Hey, my beautiful wife," Roscoe sang out. He dropped his lunch bag on the floor and tried to kiss Anita, but she turned her head slightly. He moved to sit at the table but knocked one of the chairs over. Anita started a pot of coffee.

"Hello Roscoe," Anita said tightly, glancing in Anaya's direction. Anaya pretended to be focused on the greens. She didn't want her parents to get divorced, but if Roscoe kept coming home drunk, she didn't know what her mom would do. Anaya overheard her mom telling Aunt Marie over the phone that she was going to take the kids and move to Atlanta if Roscoe didn't straighten up. Anaya didn't know exactly what that meant, but every night, she prayed for Roscoe to straighten up.

"Smells good in here, Nita," Roscoe stammered. "You was always a good cook. I knew you was gonna make a good wife and mother." He leaned forward to try to kiss her again and almost fell out of his chair.

"Roscoe, drink this coffee." She set the cup in front of him. Before he could even reach for it, he closed his eyes and passed out, head down on the kitchen table. Anita sighed. "Anaya, help me get his shoes off and get him into the den before your sister and brother see."

It wasn't the first time Anita asked Anaya to help her cover up Roscoe coming home drunk. After Roscoe was snoring on the couch, the phone rang and Andrew yelled, "Anaya, telephone! It's Sophie!"

"I hate my parents," Sophie said as soon as Anaya picked up.

"What happened?" Anaya said. She listened to Sophie talk for thirty minutes about her parents missing another one of her dance recitals. There was no point mentioning how her daddy had just passed out. It happened all the time. She was strong. She could handle it. She could handle anything.

✻

The ding of a new email shook Anaya out of the memory, and she twirled her chair to face her computer screen. She squinted when she recognized the sender's name. *Now that's a blast from the forlorn past.*

She couldn't wait to tell the girls about this at brunch tomorrow.

THREE

"**D**o you like it?"

Catie frowned as Antoine fiddled with the change in his pockets. His indifference was exhausting. They had spent two hours looking at cribs, and Catie was ready to make a decision, but Antoine apparently felt it was more important to clink the coins in his pocket. She agreed that most of the beds were white, frilly, and overpriced, but it was about the process. This was for their baby girl, for goodness' sake. Their first child.

"Yeah," he said.

"No, you don't." Catie tried to control her irritation, but she was frustrated by what seemed like deliberate unconcern. Antoine knew that choosing a bed was important to her, and instead of being supportive, he was sulking and playing with the stupid change in his stupid pocket.

"I like it. I just don't know why you have to pick one that is so expensive," he said, his voice so low that Catie had to lean in to hear.

"This is the same crib Princess Charlotte had!"

Antoine looked around the posh boutique and put his finger to his lips. "Shhh. I don't care if it's the same bed King Combs had. It doesn't make sense to buy a bed that costs so much when the baby will grow out of it in a year."

"Don't *shhh* me! And yes it does. It's the best. I want the best for our baby, and you should too!"

"Fine. Buy it."

Catie saw the woman behind the register look over at them, and she turned her back to the snooping sales rep.

"Are you serious right now?" she hissed. It wasn't Catie's fault she could afford a luxury crib and he couldn't. He should be grateful instead of standing there looking like he was going to puke. He was so ungrateful and contrary. And his constant clinking of coins made her want to scream. "Are you really playing with coins while we are deciding on a bed for our baby?"

"Deciding? That would include discussion and compromise," Antoine said with thinly veiled sarcasm. "I suggested Macy's or Target, but once again you ignored me, and here we are at this hoity-toity furniture store with stuff that costs way too much." They were losing their battle with discretion.

"First of all," she held up a finger, "I'm *not* buying my baby's bed from Target. Have you lost your mind?"

Instead of rising to the fight, Antoine seemed to deflate. "Catie, buy the bed. You want it, so get it. And put your finger down."

"We are supposed to do this together." This was not how she had pictured crib shopping for their child.

"Together?" he asked.

"Together," she repeated.

"Buy it." He pulled out his phone.

Catie raised her eyebrows, spun on her heels, and walked away. "I'm not going to buy it if you're gonna pout."

Antoine caught up to her by the door. "Just get the bed, Catie," he said.

"You don't like anything that I like." She kept walking, and he groaned and opened the door for her.

"Have a great afternoon!" the clerk called as the door swung shut.

Antoine and Catie had differing opinions about family, finances, where to live, what to name the baby, and whether or not to go to church. The additional conflict of choosing a luxury crib was the icing on the cake.

Catie stared out the car window as they drove home. She was getting sick of Antoine's indifference or worse, irritation, when she did something he didn't like. He knew who she was when they got together, and now he was complaining that she paid too much for things and worried too much about the store. She was a boss— literally, with her own clothing company—and that was never going to change.

Antoine put a hand on her thigh and glanced at her. "Look, I'm sorry," he said. "I really, really don't want to have another fight. It seems like that's all we do lately. If you want to buy the bed, Caitlin, please get the bed. It's just expensive and you know how I am, but I know you like finer things, so babe, just get it."

"It's fine," she said, but it wasn't. She didn't feel like talking to the man who had ruined her beautiful Saturday morning with nonsense. Antoine knew Target would never be an option for buying a bed. She continued to stare out of the window.

Antoine sighed.

Catie and Antoine had met as kids when Antoine's mom, Wanda, dated Anaya's uncle Riley. They fell out of touch when Wanda and Riley broke up but reconnected years later through Anaya. Catie had always been attracted to Antoine, and not just because of his model looks and perfect body. Antoine was kind and made up for his mediocre income with his genuineness and thoughtfulness. Once, Catie broke her heel at Anaya's birthday party, and Antoine had carried her to her car. Neither of them knew their fathers, they both grew up in rough neighborhoods, and loyalty meant everything to them. At first, it seemed unlikely that they would survive as a couple, but two-and-a-half years later Antoine was still the blue-collar yin to Catie's YSL yang.

Their differences had started to clash more openly after moving in together last year, and even more since Catie became pregnant.

"Are you hungry?"

Catie was never too upset for food, but she wanted him to sweat it out for a while. She eyed him with frosty calm before saying, "Okay." Then she asked, "Antoine, do you lie?"

Antoine furrowed his brow. "It's not my hobby or anything." He chuckled. "But I'm sure I've told a tale or two in my day."

She studied his face, unamused. Antoine's face was like an open book. "A tale or two?"

"Yeah."

"Do you lie to me?"

"Nope."

"So you always tell me the truth?"

"What is this about, babe?" he asked.

"What is *what* about?"

"I don't know. These questions. The attitude. Getting all mad about the bed. I just didn't expect this today. I thought today was going to be . . ." He didn't finish his thought and kept his eyes on the road.

"Well?" Catie narrowed her eyes and glared at him. "Do you tell the truth?"

"Catie, I do. I always tell you the truth." He looked at her seriously as he pulled into the parking lot of one of her favorite restaurants.

She folded her arms across her chest.

"Do you want to eat here or do you want to get food to go?"

"To go," she pouted.

Antoine got out of the car.

To distract herself, Catie scrolled through Instagram while she waited for Antoine. Instagram was great for her business—she gained a lot of customers from posting—but she got tired of seeing the same posts over and over from the same overexposed people.

Look at me in a bathing suit. I look great, don't I?

Look at my beautiful children and amazing husband.

Look at me, I don't know how to correctly upload photos, but I'm going to flood your timeline anyway.

Look at me pretending to be happy when I'm utterly miserable and uncomfortable in my own skin.

Look at me pretending to be empowering and uplifting when I'm indeed a hater.

She was over it. She checked Kensington Palace's latest posts. She adored Meghan Markle. Just as she zoomed in on a photo of Meghan and Harry, Antoine's cell phone buzzed in the cup holder between the front seats. She absently picked it up and looked at the screen.

When will I see you again? It's been too long.

Catie frowned and looked toward the restaurant doors where Antoine had disappeared.

FOUR

S ophie pushed her hair out of her face in blissful reverie as Jabari hugged her from behind as they snuggled on her Taiwanese chaise. He had brought Italian take-out, but they hadn't stopped cuddling and canoodling since he arrived an hour ago.

"You hot." He kissed her welcoming lips.

"So are you." She ignored the trivial grammatical error that would make her cringe coming from anybody else. She grabbed his face and kissed him again. She was falling for him much faster than expected, even by her impulsive standards. Jabari said all the right things—though not necessarily in the right way—and revived her in places that had been dormant for months. She liked staring into his penetrating brown eyes, which were currently ablaze with desire. He smelled like wheat toast and his leathery hands assured her of what was coming next.

As he rubbed his finger across Sophie's cheek, she watched his gaze drop to her voluptuous curves. Sophie had gained a few pounds since leaving rehab, but no one except her mother Carmen would ever consider Sophie overweight. She wore outfits that worked best with her small waist and wide hips. Tonight, her black t-shirt dress shrouded her curves, and she opted for no bra. Her ringlets were pulled into a high ponytail, and she wore nude lipstick.

It was their tenth date in six weeks. This was a record for Sophie, but she stopped short of picking out a wedding dress. For now at least.

"You want to eat?"

"Nah, I actually gotta get outta here pretty soon."

Get out of here? He'd only arrived an hour ago, and she hadn't seen him in over a week. They hadn't even eaten yet. And they hadn't really talked.

"No." She wrapped her legs around him and squeezed.

"My aunt been ridin' me about movin' that stuff out of her garage."

"Can you do it another time? You helped her last week." It was late and dark. Who moved furniture in the dark?

"I know. I'm almost finished though. She wants it cleaned out for her birthday party next month."

Next month? Surely he could miss one Saturday night.

She moved closer to him and looked into his enticing long-lashed eyes. "Please stay." She started kissing him on the neck, and he made a low, throaty sound and pulled her closer.

"Ooh, girl, you don't play fair. If you keep kissin' me like that, I ain't goin' nowhere."

"I'm not trying to play fair," she said, kissing him more. "Stay."

"Yes, ma'am."

Jabari was Sophie's future husband. He didn't know it yet, but she did. He was almost what she was looking for. In high school, her requirements for a life partner included a six-foot frame and post-graduate education. He had to be spiritual (not religious), emotionally mature, and commitment-ready with beautiful teeth, no baggage, a Caesar haircut, and no more than three tattoos. However, after countless dates and an equal number of disappointments, she had altered her preferences a bit. Who cared about tattoos? And haircuts—including hair—were now negotiable. And college . . . well, not everybody was college material. So long as he was motivated, Sophie could work with that.

Jabari didn't speak the King's English, and he dressed like a cast member from *Love & Hip Hop*, but personal style was negotiable. She could work on that later. As long as the essence of him was acceptable, she didn't worry about the little things. She wanted a garden wedding. No more than fifty guests. Anaya and Catie would be her bridesmaids, and she might even invite her mom. It was going to be perfect.

They kissed until Jabari slowly reached beneath her shirt. Then Sophie pulled away.

"Let's talk." If they were going to be married, they had a lot to discuss.

He stiffened and she kissed him on the neck again. Jabari had proven not to be the best at communication, but he wasn't going to weasel his way out of talking this time.

"Do you remember that conversation we had last week?"

He looked confused. Did he forget or did he not want to talk about it? Probably both. These men and their inability to appreciate profound, emotional dialogue. She'd never get it.

She looked into his brown eyes and reminded him. "We talked about the equity theory and the importance of reciprocity."

"Oh yeah . . . How about we talk about the equity of lovemaking and neck kissing?" He kissed her neck.

Sophie pulled away again.

"Okay," he acquiesced and leaned on his elbow. The chaise was big enough for three people to sleep on comfortably. "We can talk, but let me ask the questions for a change."

"Okay," she said, sitting up. "Shoot."

"Why didn't you tell me who your dad was?" His gaze searched her face.

She had expected that question at some point. She used the greatest discretion online because she didn't want guys to know she was Terry Beat's daughter. Being the child of a famous music producer who was a judge on a primetime talent show always complicated things, and she didn't want anyone dating her because of her father's fame. Granted, she should have told Jabari by now, but she hadn't.

"I don't tell anyone that. Not until I'm sure."

"Sure about what?"

"That someone wants to date me, not my dad."

"You think guys wanna date your father?" He sat up.

"You know what I mean." She sighed. "I don't want guys trying to date me to get close to my dad."

"I feel you," he said. "But I've been to your house like five times. Seems like you would've said something. I mean, I see his pictures on your mantel every time I come over, and my aunt watches his show." He gestured towards the photo of Sophie and Terry in Dubai on a desert safari. "But it's cool. I hold no grudges."

"Okay," she said. She was used to asking the questions, but this was interesting too.

"Why don't you drink?"

She swallowed a few times. This was tougher than she thought, but she was game. They had to get past these things. "I was in a rehabilitation center for alcohol and cocaine abuse. I've been clean and sober for almost four years and I do not and will not ever drink again. I love my sobriety and my sanity and have found other ways to stimulate myself when necessary." She looked at him expectantly. His questions were hard, but she had put it out there. He could take it or leave it.

To her surprise, he nodded. "I understand. I don't drink either."

"No?"

"Nah. My parents are Muslim."

Her eyes widened. She couldn't wait until Ava heard that. "Muslim? I wouldn't have guessed. So, you don't eat pork? And you pray throughout the day?" That threw a wrench in her plans. Could they still be married by a minister? Would he expect her to fast during Ramadan? Why didn't she know this before?

But he was shaking his head. "I don't practice like I should, but I keep some of the tenets, and keepin' my body pure is one of 'em. So, no alcohol for me."

"I see," she said slowly, processing the news. The fact that Jabari didn't drink actually fit quite well into the life she had imagined for them. "So what do you think about us? I mean, this is the critical development time of our relationship—the time to set the stage for where we want to go."

Jabari leaned in for a kiss, and his hand wandered as she kissed him back. Every time she brought up the topic of their relationship, he tried to distract her. She knew he'd rather kiss her and rub her booty, but tonight they were going to talk.

"Stop." She giggled and pulled his hand from beneath her t-shirt. "I'm serious."

"Me too." He tried a different distraction. This time it worked.

Ten minutes later he was dressed and on the veranda talking on his cell. It had been kind of anticlimactic for their first time, but Sophie wasn't opposed to trying again another day. He had been gentle and passionate, so she didn't regret it. Wearing only her t-shirt, Sophie went into the kitchen to put the uneaten take-out in her fridge. There wasn't much space next to the food she had prepared for brunch with the girls the next day.

"I said no!" she heard Jabari hiss. "I'm on shift!" She stood close to the kitchen door so she was within earshot of his conversation, but the wind and passing cars stopped her from hearing more than a few unintelligible whispers before he returned. She moved to the sink, pretending to be washing a glass.

He tried to smile, but it was more of a grimace. "Thanks for a cool time," he said, and his expression softened as he looked at her. "I wasn't expectin' that."

"Wait. Are you leaving?" Sophie asked, her mouth dropping open in surprise. What the hell kind of hit-it-and-quit-it game was he playing?

"I told you I had to go help my aunt."

"But it's almost eleven." *And we just had sex.*

"I know." He kissed her forehead. "My aunt be buggin'. You don't wanna get on her bad side."

Sophie frowned as Jabari kissed her softly again and left the apartment, closing the door quietly behind him. She didn't care about his aunt's bad side. She wanted to know why all of a sudden, he couldn't spend the night. She wasn't the suspicious type, but something was up, and she intended to find out what it was.

FIVE

Sophie put a platter of fruit and some gourmet cookies on the table in preparation for Anaya and Catie's arrival. After Catie's clothing store had taken off, the trio had gone from hanging out most nights to Sunday brunches and group texts. Anaya's new work project meant they spent even less time together.

After last night's shenanigans with Jabari, Sophie was happy to hang out with her girls. Her newly remodeled Rockridge townhouse looked zen with triple-hued accent walls, Middle Eastern tapestries, and mandala wallpaper. She preferred cushions to chairs, and her new rug pulled it all together perfectly.

Sophia Inez Mondrágon Beat had ninety-nine problems, but money wasn't one.

As she stepped out of the kitchen with some glasses, Catie walked in the front door. Her short bob was pulled back into a ponytail, and she wasn't wearing makeup. She was a glowing mix of hormonal fluctuations and expensive facials.

Without even looking around, Catie said, "Your place looks great. But you need to keep your front door locked. There are crazy people out there."

"Yeah, one just walked in," Sophie joked. "It's nice to see you too." Sophie closed the door behind her and pecked Catie on the cheek. "And you should smile more, it's good for the baby."

"Smiling is useless. Can you put this CD in?" Catie waved a disc in Sophie's face, and Sophie popped it into her stereo.

"What is this?" Sophie asked at the first strum of a cello.

"Expand your horizons and give Kendrick Lamar a break, will

you?" Catie said. "It's Bach. I read that it's good for the baby's brain development. This baby's going to Yale." She rubbed her stomach.

"Do you actually believe that?" Sophie asked.

"Sure do," Catie said. "Just like you believe you can find lasting love on the World Wide Web." She picked up a cushion from the chaise, then looked around the room as if seeing the newly decorated space for the first time. "Dang, Sophie, it looks amazing in here."

Sophie brought out the appetizers while Catie took photos of the new decor. While taking photos, she started scrolling through her phone. "Oh my goodness. Have you seen Janet Jackson's baby? He's getting so big!"

"You know I haven't seen anybody's baby."

Catie rolled her eyes. "Will you puh-leeze get an Instagram account? Step into the new century, Sophia."

"Nope. Not interested." After growing up beneath the watchful cameras of the paparazzi, Sophie had no desire to electronically embalm every facet of her life.

"Oh, you're interested. You're just interested in those dang-blasted sites that have men plastered all over them."

"Sad, but true." Sophie laughed and carefully arranged the cucumbers on a deep blue ceramic plate before looking up at Catie. "And it might have paid off."

Catie's reaction was predictable. "The one? *Again?*"

The last time Sophie found *the one* it was Luke the math teacher, who was double jointed and chain-smoked. Then *the one* had been Tyrone, the saxophone player with double chins. And who could forget Adrian, the real estate agent with four kids by four different women? And finally, there was Brian who was born Brenda and didn't wear shoes. All four of them had been *the one*, and none of them had lasted longer than a week. That's why Sophie promised herself not to tell the girls about the next man until they had sex, and, well . . .

"For real, for real," Sophie said. She decided not to say anything about the differences between real-life Jabari and online Jabari. Online Jabari quoted E. E. Cummings and preferred soft jazz. Real-life Jabari favored underground rap. Online Jabari was cerebral, and real-life Jabari thought cerebral was something you ate with milk.

Catie dramatically put her hand over her heart. "Where did you get this rug?"

"India." Sophie loved collecting art pieces from her travels, and it was fairly easy to do since her dad bought whatever she wanted.

"It's beautiful. And how was that trip with your dad? I know we texted about it, but I need details. But first, spill on Uncle Terry's new girlfriend. Is she nice? Is she a gold digger? Is she ugly in person?"

Sophie shrugged and poured Catie a glass of ginger ale. "She looks the same in person as she does on television." She decided not to comment further.

"Well, Terry seems happy, so good for him," Catie said. She snapped another picture of the wallpaper. "Sophia, you have to decorate the baby's room for me. You have a real eye for décor. Why did I never know this?"

"Stop calling me Sophia. You sound like my mom."

"That's what I was going for." Catie sipped her ginger ale. "Maybe if I keep sounding like her, you'll call her. It's sad that I talk to your mom more than you do."

Sophie went to check on the garlic shrimp in the oven. She was used to Catie and Anaya pushing her to fix things with her mom and had accepted that her friends didn't understand why their relationship was strained. "I do call her. I have actually invited her over a few times to see the remodel."

"And?"

"And she's always busy or out of town."

"Well, keep trying," Catie said. "Can you do the room or not?"

"Of course. As long as it's okay with Antoine."

"Make sure it's okay with Antoine?" Catie stared at her friend with narrowed eyes. "What the hell? I'm not making sure anything is okay with him."

Sophie held up hands in surrender, surprised by Catie's outburst. "Catie, you're part of a team. Don't think of it as asking for permission. Think of it as being a team player. It's about respect."

"I don't know what you're talking about." Catie waved her hand as if to wave Sophie's comment away.

"You have to compromise, communicate, and connect in a relationship," Sophie said, enumerating each action with her fingers. "The three C's. We talked about this before. I have a workbook that you and Antoine can use. You need to release that anger, Catie. I don't know all the stuff you're holding onto, but you need to let it go so you can love Antoine and your baby unconditionally."

Catie groaned. "If I had known I was gonna get psychoanalyzed, I would've stayed home." She reached for the bowl of grapes and pulled out a bunch. "You know how hard it is for me to put on clothes these days?"

"Catie, I'm serious."

Catie pointed at Sophie. "See, that's why you can't get a date. You get too deep at the wrong times. Look, nothing is consuming me except this growing baby, who won't let me be great and wear Chanel."

"Fine. If you're not ready to acknowledge your issues, I can't make you. Anyway, let me tell you about Jabari."

But Jabari would have to wait, because Anaya burst through the door with apologies and a beautiful bouquet of flowers. "Ladies! I'm sorry I'm late. I got tied up with a work issue, had to drop something off to Aunt Deb, then as I was headed out the door, Daddy got to talking. You know how he is, and as my luck would have it, I got a flat and had to Uber over, but here I am!"

"Anaya, thank God you're finally here. Sophie's was just about to tell me about her new man. I need you." Catie put the back of her hand on her forehead and sat down on Sophie's recliner since the cushions were too low to navigate in her second trimester.

"Well, I'm here, and . . ." Anaya looked around the room with wide eyes, "your place looks amazing, Sophie Beat! I see why you kept us away until you were finished decorating."

Sophie beamed at her. "Thanks, girl."

"But what is this music?" Anaya crinkled her forehead and sat down on the chaise.

"I don't know. Ask Catie." Sophie shrugged.

"Bach. Cantata number 79. It's the Mozart effect. I read that it's good for the baby's brain development. Babies who listen to classical music, particularly Bach, have higher IQs and get into better colleges."

Sophie was pretty sure the Mozart effect had been disproved, but she held her tongue. She wanted to tell her girls about Jabari. "So Jabari . . ."

Half an hour and several hundred arpeggios later, Sophie finished telling Catie and Anaya all about Jabari, even admitting the part about the birthday candle she bought for his aunt two weeks ago.

"Have you met his aunt?" Anaya asked with wide eyes.

Sophie shook her head.

"Well, why in the heck did you get her a birthday gift?" Catie propped her feet on the mustard-colored leather ottoman.

"If you must know, I wanted to take the lead on exemplifying kindness. I thought it would bring us closer so we can overcome the typical trust issues couples have when one member has emotional problems. This becomes particularly important if that person has a history of abandonment or disappointment, and they have a hard time reciprocating love and kindness. It is sometimes one sided but is not to be confused with a parasocial relationship. Also, past trauma increases the chance of frontal lobe dysfunction, so social behaviors get mixed up."

"True." Anaya nodded vigorously.

"I hate it when you talk like that," Catie said, exasperated.

"It's like fatalism versus coincidence."

"Yup, pretty much." Anaya nodded.

"You know what that stuff means, Ny?" Catie looked confused.

"No, but it sounds good, doesn't it?" Anaya shrugged.

"Sophie, please just tell us in clear words why you bought a friggin' gift for someone you never met, and do so without the persnickety psychobabble."

Anaya held up a hand. "Hold up. Catie, why are you talking like that?"

"Like what?"

"Persnickety? Friggin'? Are you on curse-word probation or something?"

"I noticed that too," Sophie chimed in. "She said 'dang-blasted' before you got here."

Anaya leaned back in mock shock.

"Well if you must know," Catie relented. "I'm turning over a new leaf. I don't want to be using foul language in front of my baby. I want to use mom words like persnickety and dang-blasted. What's wrong with that?"

"I guess my mama didn't know that rule, she was always cursing when I was a kid," Sophie said.

Anaya shook her head, smiling. "I think it's great, Catie, that you want to be the best mommy you can be. It's just weird to hear you talk that way because there are curse words out there that you invented. But I digress. Sophie, you were saying?"

"I was just trying to be supportive and dependable." Sophie said calmly.

"Supportive of what? Are you guys in a relationship?"

"I don't like labels." Sophie avoided eye contact with her friends. She and Jabari certainly acted as if they were in a relationship, but despite her best efforts, they still hadn't exactly talked about it.

Catie's face turned red. "Are you kidding me right now, Sophie? Do you want me to eat this entire bag of gummy worms and give my baby gestational diabetes?"

"Wait, gummies? I don't have those in my kitchen."

"I keep a stash in my purse." Catie pulled out the candy, but not before a shower of receipts, gum wrappers, and a small book fell from her purse. "But that's not the point."

Sophie picked up the book to help her bending-impaired friend. "Wow, Catie, you still carry this tiny blue Bible in your purse? You've been carrying that thing since I've known you."

"That's not the point either. Stay on topic," Catie fussed, grabbing the volume and stuffing it back in her bag.

"Maybe I trusted him too fast," Sophie said, resigned. "There's something different about him, though, I can feel it. We match on a level that is unfounded in practicality and inexplicable by conventional definitions. We just match. And his teeth are gorgeous!"

"Now I know you didn't understand that." Catie looked at Anaya.

"You're right. I didn't."

A timer rang in the kitchen. "Time for garlic shrimp. Gather round the table." Sophie got up to retrieve the main course.

"Now you're talking," Catie said, struggling to stand up.

Sophie had just popped the first shrimp into her mouth when Anaya dropped the bombshell.

"Jeff wants to see me. Can you pass me a plate, Catie?"

Anaya's tone was so nonchalant, that it took a moment for Sophie to register what she'd said. When it did register, the shrimp fell from Sophie's mouth.

"Jeff who?" Catie pulled the plate she was previously going to give Anaya out of reach. "We don't know anyone named Jeff."

"You know who I'm talking about," Anaya said, trying to grab it out of Catie's hand. Catie was too quick. "Jeff Jackson."

"Don't try to sneak that in, Ny," Sophie said, still shocked.

"That's how Ny is. She's sneaky." Catie squinted her eyes. "Privileged people are always sneaky. You can't trust them."

"Wait," Catie held up a hand. "Is this all because of that girl you and Carl saw at breakfast the other day?"

"Who, Zendaya? No, that wasn't even a big deal." Anaya's tone was defensive.

"Seemed like something to me when you sent the text," Catie said.

"Word," Sophie said. "But this seems a little suss."

Anaya crossed her arms. "No. One thing has nothing to do with the other. Jeff wants to see me and I'm considering it." She shrugged like seeing Jeff would be harmless.

Sophie considered her friend for a moment, who was refusing to meet her gaze. "Anaya, I keep telling you that you should consider third-eye chakra healing. Your emotional senses are off. You're working too much and not taking enough time for self-care. As women, we need that, or it leads to imbalance. Imbalanced senses can have side effects that morph into physical symptoms like headaches and weight gain, and we all know how you feel about your weight."

"Really? I have been having these headaches lately." Anaya put her hand on her forehead.

"See?"

"Hold up, Deepak Chopra. Can you let Ny finish before you diagnose her with death by obesity? And Ny, stop being so gullible. You don't have imbalanced senses, and you barely fit a size two. Now tell us everything about Jeff." Catie gobbled down a mouthful of noodles.

"That's it, really," Anaya said. "He sent me an email yesterday saying he wanted to talk."

"Talk about what?" Catie leaned in towards the table.

"Is he still married?" Sophie asked.

"I don't know. I'd imagine so. I haven't talked to him since . . ." She trailed off and focused on heaping salad onto her plate.

Sophie nodded. "Good."

"Wow," Catie said slowly. "So what are you going to do?"

"I don't know."

"What I'm hearing is that you are willing to jeopardize your loving and committed relationship with Carl, a man among men, to meet with some old boyfriend who broke your heart and made you question your moral values. This feels bad to me, Ny."

"Can you lighten the hell up, Sophia? What's wrong with you tonight?" Catie glared at Sophie before turning to Anaya. "Wait. Ny, you are still in a loving, committed relationship with Carl, right?"

Finally, Anaya looked up from her plate and looked squarely at Catie. "Yes. I am. I love Carl. Nothing will ever change that. I'm not worried that seeing Jeff will make me suddenly fall back in love with him. I guess I'm just curious to know what he wants after all this time."

"Booty!" Catie laughed.

Anaya folded her arms and pursed her lips. "Can you be serious for a minute?"

"I don't think you should see him," Sophie said decisively. "Nothing good can come of it. It's self-serving and self-destructive. Neither of which is beneficial to your relationship with Carl."

"Maybe you're right," Anaya said, cutting her spinach into tiny strips. "I was just wondering what he wanted."

"It doesn't matter what he wants," Sophie said. "Forward, my friend. Not backward. Never backward."

"You know I'm all about figuring things out." Catie said through a mouthful of noodles. "But I don't know about this one, Ny." She slurped up a piece of shrimp that had been hanging out the side of her mouth.

Sophie stared at Catie. "You are disgusting right now—you know that, right?"

"Be quiet, Soph-ee-uh, I'm feeding my baby," Catie said before gulping down some water.

"Then feed your baby now and talk later," Sophie said, frowning. "But don't do both at the same time. It's gross." She turned to Anaya. "I say let it go. Let him stay in your past."

"You guys are right. That was my past, and there's no reason to look back." Anaya sighed.

"Good for you," Sophie said. "It's always good to self-assess because, in the end, you have to make healthy choices. Besides, you don't want that bad karma following you if you sneak around on Carl."

"That's true."

Catie wiped her mouth with a napkin. "That reminds me, are you guys working on my baby shower? You know it has to be fabulous."

Anaya groaned. "Catie, I sent you an email weeks ago about getting the names of people you want to invite. No party can be planned without a guest list."

Catie waved her hand dismissively. "You know I don't have anybody else to invite other than the people you already know. I don't have any family except you two, so my list is complete."

"Aw, we love you." Sophie threw a grape that bounced off Catie's belly.

"I love you too. Now make sure my baby shower is the bomb so I don't have to disown you."

SIX

Anaya sat at the back of the council chambers as Jayde Merrick—the county clerk and a good friend of hers—brought the weekly Board of Supervisors meeting to order. The County Board of Supervisors was primarily responsible for exercising administrative and executive authority throughout County government. Week after week, board members sat behind the grand dais, pontificating and providing lamentable responses to public outcries of dissatisfaction. Sometimes the board managed to conduct business like a Fortune 500 company—they made decisions and quickly moved forward through the agenda items. Other times, the meetings resembled the Jerry Springer Show with occasional chair-throwing and unhappy protests.

Meeting attendees represented all walks of life from each of the county's fourteen cities. Last week, a young woman had chained herself to the podium, saying she would only unlock herself when the board removed the tracking device from her brain. Glory days of public service.

Get ready for the circus, Anaya thought. She hoped her presentation wouldn't be too late on the agenda—she owed Carl some quality time. She was supposed to see him yesterday after brunch at Sophie's, but she had needed to finish the presentation.

Jayde sat at the dais with the five Alameda County supervisors, the county counsel, Sue Garcia, and the county administrator, Wendy Woo. The dais was a raised platform at the head of the room, located directly below a huge projection screen. A semi-circle of folding stadium seats, where members of the public sat, faced the dais. More seats were available in the balconies above. A large podium to the right of the dais provided the platform from which county staff and consultants presented information to the board, and members of the public addressed the board from a smaller podium in the center of the room. The faded industrial carpets, cathedral-coffered ceilings, and incandescent lighting preserved the historic nature of the chamber, which was built in 1910.

"Good evening," Jayde announced to the nearly full chamber. "The Board of Supervisors welcomes you to the meeting and your interest is appreciated." She read out the proposed agenda for the evening, and Anaya groaned when she heard that her naval base presentation would be last. Not only would she miss spending time with Carl, but the board would be grumpy and tired by the time her presentation began.

"If you would like to speak on an agenda item, please submit a presenter card before the item is called for discussion. When addressing the board, please give your name for the record before speaking. On roll call for this meeting: Chair Memphis, Supervisor Buckingham, Supervisor Abramson, Supervisor Fernandez, and Supervisor Harris."

Over the next two hours, Anaya sent several apology texts to Carl, listened to the various presentations, reports, and ceremonial items, and observed the supervisors, who she had come to know quite well. Eventually, Jayde called the final item, which was Anaya's preliminary report on the proposed development agreement for the naval base site. A development agreement was a contract between the company who would redevelop the naval base and the county, who owns the land. Anaya took a deep breath and walked up to the county staff's podium. *Let's do this.*

She had presented before the board plenty of times and knew what to expect. Supervisor Fernandez would ask questions that gave creed to the popular notion that he had absolutely no idea what was going on. Supervisor Harris would ask impossible questions because she didn't trust Wendy Woo. Supervisor Buckingham would smile the entire time. Supervisor Abramson would make empty statements that brought disgrace to her Harvard Law degree, and Chair Memphis would either sigh in boredom or cheer audibly when he reached the next level of Candy Crush.

"All right, looks like we saved the best topic for last." Chair Memphis cleared his throat and sat up in his seat. "Ms. Goode, you may proceed with your report." He stroked his mustache and put his hand on his phone.

"Good evening, Mr. Chair and members of the board." Anaya spoke clearly and slowly into the microphone. "My name is Anaya Goode, Director of Housing and Community Development. Tonight I will present you with a—"

"Excuse me, Mr. Chair," Wendy interrupted suddenly. "Just a point of personal privilege. I'd like to say something."

Anaya yielded, trying to keep her annoyance from showing as Chair Memphis gave what sounded like a murmur of consent. Anaya saw Jayde glare at Wendy from across the dais.

Wendy Woo had a penchant for several things, and being at the center of attention topped the list. She didn't care about making friends or hurting feelings. She once said that all she wanted her staff to do was fall in line and follow her direction. Being the top administrator of a county on the verge of a fiscal cataclysm didn't stop her from occasionally checking her make-up during public meetings, donning the finest couture or receiving quarterly Botox treatments that prevented her from demonstrating genuine facial expressions. Developers loved her, the unions hated the ground on which her red-bottomed Louboutins walked, and most of her staff and the Board of Supervisors could take or leave her.

Anaya was definitely of the "leave her" opinion. As county administrator, all department directors reported directly to Wendy, who was tougher on her staff than necessary. She was particularly hard on Anaya who wasn't afraid to stand up to Wendy like most of the other directors were.

"I'd like to express my gratitude to everyone for their support." Wendy cleared her throat and spoke as if she were reading from a script. "As you all know, this project has been a long time coming. I'd like to thank my staff for their long hours and dedication, and my husband for allowing me to work the extra hours on top of the long hours I already work. Should the board decide to approve the contract and move forward, my intention is to assemble a small task force to streamline the process. I am determined to make this project work, and now here we are." She gestured around the room. The only thing missing was a curtsy and a patent leather one-piece.

Anaya stared at Wendy in disbelief. She had spent the last three weeks creating and fine-tuning this preliminary report with her staff, and now Wendy was trying to take over? And who was part of this alleged task force? Why hadn't Wendy discussed it with Anaya?

"Um, excuse me, point of personal privilege," Supervisor Harris said with measured spite. Anaya looked expectantly at the small woman. Maybe those mandated anger management classes were starting to pay off. This was the third meeting this month and Harris hadn't used the F word once. It was definitely progress.

"First of all, Ms. Woo, I know you didn't contribute a single word to the report." Harris looked over the top of her purple-framed glasses. The tension was thick and Supervisor Harris could be unpredictable. "Secondly, you aren't receiving an Oscar; your department is delivering a preliminary report. *Pre-lim-in-ary.* We still have a lot of work to do. Get on with it already." Supervisor Harris did not receive quarterly Botox treatments, and contempt wedged between her over-sculpted brows like food particles in Chair Memphis's mustache.

"Thank you very much for that passionate rhetoric, Supervisor Harris," Wendy said with a pageant smile. "As I was saying, I appreciate and recognize everyone's hard work. Ms. Goode, you may proceed."

Anaya stepped up to the podium again.

"Good evening, board members. I will present a slide show with my report, and upon conclusion, I will take any questions."

Before the naval base closed ten years ago, the area had boomed because of the military families who lived there. When the government announced the base would be phased out and started transferring naval families away, businesses began to close and houses were eventually boarded up. Now the space was overgrown with weeds and the abandoned homes and businesses looked more like a scene from a zombie apocalypse movie.

More than a dozen investment groups had approached the supervisors over the years with different ideas of what to do with the base, but the board had never been able to agree on a development plan, and the idea was lost in legislative purgatory. In a final attempt to make progress, alongside rumors of his retirement, Chair Memphis had recently resurrected the idea of redevelopment.

All county development fell under Anaya's purview, so it was her responsibility to determine what type of development—business, housing, or retail—would be most beneficial to the county and recommend an agreement moving forward. The final agreement was usually reviewed by Wendy's office prior to submitting to the Board, who had final decision-making power. As administrator, Wendy could technically overrule Anaya's decision, but that typically didn't happen since Anaya was the subject-matter expert and department director. The Department of Housing and Community Development had determined that the naval base could generate approximately sixteen million dollars in property tax revenue alone. Additionally, there would be seventeen hundred housing units, with six hundred of those being affordable housing. Ten thousand potential new jobs could also be created.

Anaya expertly walked the board through her office's recommendations that had been her air and water since the board decided to consider reopening the naval base three weeks ago.

After Anaya finished her presentation (during which Chair Memphis had only visibly nodded off once), she tried to gauge the reactions of the supervisors. If the board approved the draft language, she would be even busier than she had been during her preparations for this meeting.

Chair Memphis opened his eyes looked down his nose at her. "Ms. Goode, thank you for your presentation. You've given us a lot to consider. You may be seated." Anaya nodded and took her seat near the podium.

"Madame County Clerk, how many speakers do we have on this item?" Chair Memphis asked, referring to members of the public who had signed up to comment.

"Twenty-five," Jayde replied.

"Twenty-five?" He sighed loudly. Whenever there were more than three speakers, Chair Memphis complained. The zeal that came with being an elected official had disappeared with his hairline and ability to stay awake during meetings.

"All right, I want to see if these members of the audience actually want to speak," he said. "Because if they don't feel like it, they don't have to." State law required that the public was allowed to speak without discouragement. Jayde reminded Chair Memphis of this at every meeting, and at every meeting he ignored her advice.

"So what is the pleasure of the board?" Chair Memphis asked the other members. "Do you want to deliberate or hear the public first? Either way, it's going to be a long night."

What a class act, thought Anaya, although he was right. Each speaker was given three minutes to speak, so they would be there for a while.

"I think we should listen to the speakers," Supervisor Buckingham said in her lilting voice. "Why would we put the cart before the horse?" she sang. Buckingham was married to the CEO of a company that produced keyless entry systems, and her father was a retired state senator. She was the only person in the county who matched Wendy's fashion sagacity.

"No, we should have questions first." Supervisor Harris was a former grassroots activist and she and Buckingham didn't agree on anything.

"Why would we deliberate before hearing public comment?" Buckingham smiled. "Isn't that the way the process works? Or do we not care about the public process anymore?"

"We care about the public," Harris's forehead furrowed with displeasure. "What we don't care about is you pretending you care so much. These people are the 99 percent; you are the 1 percent. How can you possibly relate?"

"Really, Miss Harris?" Buckingham sustained her smile. "Are you going to go on a tirade about my finances *again* when we have a room full of people who need our help? I mean, you're the one who wants to make a decision before we even hear public comment."

"I never said we would decide before hearing public comment." Supervisor Harris' voice carried the weight of their many disagreements. Harris' feistiness was one of the reasons that the unions and her constituents loved her. "I said we could ask questions. You *do* know the difference between asking questions and making a decision? Or do you not discuss such things in the Hamptons?"

"Hush," Buckingham said, pursing her lips. And that was the reason the unions hated Buckingham.

"Hush?" Harris was caught off guard. "That's articulate, Phyllis. Did you learn that in Pilates class?"

"Look," Chair Memphis interrupted. "We can hear the speakers first, it's fine."

"I suggest you tell that to Miss Good Government over there," Supervisor Harris said.

"All right, Madam Clerk." Chair Memphis tried to speak over the murmurs of the crowd. "Call the names."

"As I call your name, please step forward to the podium and state your name for the record," Jayde directed.

For more than an hour, the board listened to the public, union members, contractors, and gadflies. Their concerns ranged from whether local business would get an opportunity to bid on the project, to questions about the hiring of local workers. Another speaker approached the podium.

"Good evening, my name is Keith Hung. I want to say that you all need to pay attention to what's going on here. You have people here from all walks of life trying to help you navigate through this process. It's difficult. It's convoluted, and it's incumbent on you, our civic leaders, to make the right choice. We built this city on rock and roll. The rock and the roll and the roll and the rock. Get it right, or you will get it wrong. I have come from a place far away to deliver a message of peace and understanding. I made my point, so take my point. That's a 10-4, good buddy." He slammed the palm of his hand on the podium before walking away.

The audience and staff—all familiar with Mr. Hung—laughed. Chair Memphis was not amused and sighed loudly. Board meetings attracted the civic-minded, the business-minded, and the half-minded.

"Was that the last speaker?" Chair Memphis made no effort to conceal his impatience.

"No. Mr. Killian, please approach the podium." Audible groans circled the room. Clinton Killian was the gadfly from gadfly hell. He came to every board meeting and insisted on speaking on every item. Sometimes he made relevant points, but most of the time he just tried to stick it to the board, whom he deemed corrupt and unworthy of their paychecks and pensions.

"Well, here we are again at another meeting where Chair Memphis is discouraging members of the public from speaking. A clear violation of the law. But clearly, rules don't matter in this organization. You do as you please with no repercussions for your unlawful and thoughtless actions. The base should be reopened, but the oversight should come from elsewhere because this body is incapable of following simple local laws, let alone overseeing a multimillion-dollar development project." He went on about other violations, using fifteen seconds more than his three minutes speaking time.

"All names have been called," Jayde said when Mr. Killian finally finished.

"Good. It's time for board comments. Ms. Goode, please return to the podium."

Anaya stood and stepped up to the microphone again.

Supervisor Harris was first.

"I want to say the report was well presented, so good work to you and your staff. And while I agree with the recommendations, there's been a lot of talk about big developers coming to town and not using local contractors. We need to make sure the communities receive benefits from this deal. How will we know for sure that locals will get these jobs? We've been here before. How can we be sure there will be local hiring?"

Supervisor Harris peered over her glasses. She was a barracuda, but she was a well-informed barracuda. She read every report that was given to her, no matter how long, and when she had questions, she wanted answers.

Anaya opened her mouth, but Wendy cut in. Again, Anaya tried not to look irritated.

"First of all, that is one of the most unyielding stipulations in the contract. We would not have gotten this far in the negotiations if it wasn't."

"That doesn't answer my question," Supervisor Harris said. "I will repeat myself for the hard of hearing, like Ms. Woo. We've had these kinds of deals before with similar stipulations, and local contractors did not get the jobs. And as I look at this proposed agreement, I don't see a specific stipulation for the developer to hire local contractors"

"She might be able to answer you if she weren't looking on fashionbombdaily-dot-com," someone yelled from the audience.

Anaya looked up at the balconies. The individual who had called out was sitting in the perfect position to see Wendy's laptop screen.

Busted.

The audience booed, but Wendy's face didn't move. It couldn't.

"All she cares about is clothes and makeup," someone else yelled.

"Yeah, and her hair!"

Chair Memphis hit his gavel against the dais several times. "Order! I want order in this chamber or I will clear it out," he shouted unconvincingly.

"Seems to me that Ms. Woo is too busy expanding her wardrobe to be bothered with our little meeting," Supervisor Harris added, egging on the jeering crowd.

"We don't need the sarcasm, Ms. Harris," Chair Memphis said. "It doesn't help."

Wendy's disapproving glare meant nothing to Supervisor Harris. In fact, if hurling a chair was a socially acceptable thing to do in these chambers, Wendy would be in trouble.

"We also don't need an overpaid Video Vixen to sit on the dais and play with her hair and makeup." Harris's voice was like ice. "We have serious issues before us, and we need the full attention of everyone, including Posh Spice over there."

"That's an insult to Posh Spice!" someone yelled, and the audience jeered even louder.

"Please," Supervisor Harris said. "Now, I asked a question about local hiring, and I have yet to receive an answer. I'm not looking for smoke and mirrors. I'm looking for real solutions and real jobs for real people."

The crowd jeered again.

Chair Memphis rattled his gavel against the dais. "I want order in this room!" he yelled. "Now Ms. Woo, are you prepared to answer Supervisor Harris's question about the jobs policy?"

"There are stipulations in place to ensure local hiring and contracting," Wendy said. "We are looking at residency and education, as well as hiring individuals at both the apprenticeship and journeyman levels."

"Sounds good, but is it true?" someone yelled from the chamber.

"If there is one more outburst, I will clear this chamber, and there won't be a meeting at all!" Chair Memphis said, raising his voice again. He glared out at the crowd, then looked at Wendy. "I have also looked through the proposed agreement and I agree with Supervisor Harris. Admittedly, it's a huge document and I may not have read every single word, but I didn't see any stipulations in place to ensure local hiring."

Anaya saw her chance to clarify. "There is nothing in the—"

Wendy immediately cut her off. "We, uh, did notice some provisions were missing. We have an amended agreement that includes local hiring stipulations."

Anaya raised her eyebrows. There was no amended agreement, and Anaya knew for certain that the current agreement didn't include local hiring provisions. When Wendy had reviewed the draft, she had cut those provisions, saying they weren't necessary. Anaya had fought her on it, but according to Wendy, strict provisions frightened prime developers off. Anaya knew better but decided to let it play out with the board.

"Well, where is the amended version?" Chair Memphis asked, shuffling through the papers before him.

"It didn't make it into the agenda packet," Wendy responded, seemingly unmoved by the constant jeering from the public.

Chair Memphis looked down his nose at her. "So what you're telling this board is that for this multimillion-dollar project that we've been trying to get going for over a decade, you left out one of the most important components of this agreement that you've presented to us? I don't think I have to remind you, Miss Woo, that as a governing body, our job is not only to ensure that development is fair, but that our local residents get jobs from these big development deals. That is an essential part of this entire agreement."

"I have to agree with Ms. Harris and Mr. Memphis," Supervisor Buckingham said. "We need to see every piece of this deal. It's very careless to leave out such an important provision."

"Unless you're trying to hide something." Supervisor Harris said sharply.

After Wendy dodged the board's bullets and the verbal bashing from the crowd for a few more rounds, Supervisor Fernandez spoke.

"Enough about the local contractors. What I want to know is what we are going to do about prostitution on the base. There's nothing in the agreement about that." He had campaigned on cleaning up prostitution in the county and was relentless in his pursuit to make good on his promise—even at the expense of an agreement that was primarily focused on housing and jobs. "We are trying to use this base as a place to generate revenue, and there is prostitution going on over there. There are johns picking women up all the time. Everybody knows it's going on, but no one wants to talk about it."

"Supervisor Fernandez," Wendy said like his name was acid. "We are not aware of any prostitution being committed on the base at this time."

"Well, I have heard from many of my constituents that there was prostitution on the base. I don't see anything in this agreement that provides funding to eliminate the problem. Who are the johns? Are they members of the service? Random men off the street?" He slammed his hand against the dais.

"Ms. Goode, can you please respond to that?" Wendy asked.

"Yes." Anaya spoke into the microphone. "There have been no reports of crime in recent history, including prostitution. Since the military and all of the businesses moved off the base, the facilities have mostly been used for recreational soccer practice for children. As far as we know, there is no illegal activity occurring on the base and the police and sheriff departments have not received any complaints."

Fernandez gazed off in confusion for a moment before leaning into his microphone. "Thank you."

Anaya survived the next hour and a half of discussions, and in the end, the board directed Anaya to return in sixty days with a final revised agreement for them to approve that included the local hiring provisions. Anaya was also directed to move forward with putting out the request for proposals to all the contractors in the county, assuming the revised agreement would include local hiring provisions.

After the meeting, Anaya returned to her office with the four senior managers who had been present at the meeting and did a quick debrief. They had all worked tirelessly on this agreement and this was a significant win for them.

"All right, guys, so we got the green light," Anaya said. They sat around one end of the long conference table that could seat twenty. Each manager had a pen and notebook ready. Anaya didn't mess around, not at eleven o'clock on a Monday night. "We have to get this RFP out to all the registered contractors in the city. Tom, your team will be responsible for making sure the lists of contractor addresses we have is up-to-date. Nancy, get your people to start setting up community meetings within fifteen square miles of the base to get community input. Becks, tell your team to brush up on our local hiring provisions because we will start to get questions. Everyone will come to you for answers when they have questions about local hiring. Andrew, help the others but be prepared for those bids to come swarming in—a lot of folks will want a piece of this pie. Your group will be responsible for coming up with a system to keep the bids organized and categorized."

The group fell silent as their pens scribbled. Anaya looked up and saw Jayde walk into the conference room. Anaya held up a finger, and Jayde nodded and took a seat in the back of the room.

"I need you to anticipate calls from the press," Anaya told them. "Please forward the calls to me if you don't have solid answers to their questions. I do not want line staff fielding those calls." When each manager had finished writing, she met their eyes one by one. "We have to be careful with this one, guys. This base hasn't been open in over a decade. It's big local news. And all eyes are on us." Anaya sighed and leaned back in her chair. "That's it. I'll answer any questions you have tomorrow. Thanks for staying tonight."

The managers shuffled out, and Jayde followed Anaya to her office.

"What the hell is wrong with Wendy?" Jayde seethed when they were comfortably seated on the couch in Anaya's office with the door closed.

"Girl, I have no idea. She's nuts."

"I thought we were all on the same team. How did you guys forget to send the amended agreement to my office to put in the agenda packet?"

"We didn't forget, Jayde. There's no amended agreement," Anaya said in a low voice, even though everyone was gone.

Jayde's eyes were as wide as saucers. "What? She lied?"

Anaya confirmed Jayde's charge by folding her arms and pursing her lips.

"That bitch is crazy. I think she's up to something, Ny. Forgetting an amendment like that is too much, even for her."

Anaya sighed. "I don't get it. Wendy is a lunatic but she has a reputation for being above board. What could she be up to?"

"Are you joking? This is a huge project. If Wendy is messing with contractor negotiations, it sounds to me like she has a *preferred* contractor for the job—one that'll give her a cut of the profits."

Anaya started to laugh but saw Jayde was serious. She shook

her head. "I don't know, Jayde, Wendy has enough money, and her character means everything to her. But listen, I'll think on what you said. I gotta get over to Carl's house before it's too late."

"Well, don't let me hold you." Jayde grinned.

"I'll see you for lunch on Friday, right?"

"Not this week. Nick and I are going to Mexico for the weekend. We leave Thursday and get back on Sunday."

Anaya cocked her head. *Again? Didn't they just get back from Paris?* "Well, have fun, girl. I'll have Natalie put something on the calendar for next week."

On her drive to Carl's house, Anaya thought about Wendy's lies. She was starting to have a bad feeling about this project. She couldn't put her finger on it, but something wasn't right.

SEVEN

"**A**untie Ny!"

"Hi, sweetie." Hezekiah grabbed Anaya around the knees. His Spider-Man t-shirt was too small, and he proudly wore a milk mustache. He locked the door after Anaya stepped inside and followed her into the living room. Anaya yelped as she almost scraped her Prada pumps on a fire truck.

Large plastic bins were everywhere, and a stack of laundry lay untouched on the couch. Family pictures lined the walls, including one of her mom above the fireplace. Ava's house was lovely—when it was clean. The eggshell colored molding, large bay window, and high ceilings made the place feel much bigger than it actually was.

Anaya made her way carefully over to the couch. "Who said you could open the door, sweetie?"

"Mommy said I could." He was a miniature version of Joe except much, much louder. His piercing green eyes were bright behind the eyeglasses Anaya had bought him last year.

Anaya sat down on the couch and immediately jumped up again. "Ouch!"

"Dino the dinoswaur!" Hezekiah tripped in his rush to get to his beloved toy. "I've been wooking ebywhere for him!" Anaya wondered if his sessions with the speech therapist were helping.

Hezekiah's older brother, Jeremiah, swooped into the living room and grabbed Dino from Hezekiah.

"Give him back, we were tawking," the smaller boy cried.

"You can't talk to a dinosaur, that's dumb."

"Don't call me dumb!"

"Well, if you can't say 'dinosaur,' you are dumb."

"Hey!" Anaya took Dino from Jeremiah. "Dino and I are going to chill for a bit, so why don't you two go and play in your rooms."

Jeremiah ran off, but Hezekiah looked at her with big eyes. "Will you give him back to me?"

"Yes I will. When I leave."

Hezekiah pouted for a moment but eventually picked up a red car and began talking to it.

Ava walked into the living room and wiped her hands on an apron that read "Jesus is My Homeboy." Her reddish-brown coils were piled high, and her skin was bright. Ava was a free spirit who didn't conform to traditional ideas of eating, fashion, or health care. She preferred all-natural foods, holistic remedies for illnesses, and talked about homeschooling the boys because she didn't want "secular influences." Anaya didn't care about secular influences, but homeschooling the boys meant Ava couldn't get a full-time job, and that was a problem.

"Hezekiah, go and play with your brothers," Ava directed. No response. Hezekiah was having a conversation with his red car about the sun and how it made everything warm. *Ebwything.*

When he didn't leave, Ava didn't push. Discipline wasn't high on Ava and Joe's list of priorities. In fact, discipline lived in the sunken place with gainful employment, aspiration, and good housekeeping. Ava let the boys have their way so she didn't have to deal with tantrums. Anaya disciplined her nephews on occasion, like when she babysat, but it was becoming harder to get them to listen, especially Jeremiah. She had told Ava more than once that the boys were getting out of control, but Ava refused to take advice from someone without children. Instead, she always had an excuse for why the boys didn't listen.

Ava and Anaya tried to talk, but it was nearly impossible because whenever one of them spoke, Hezekiah yelled "yogurt truck!" at the top of his lungs. He followed them into the kitchen and back into the living room, continuing to disrupt anything they said.

"Hezekiah, Mommy asked you to go to the room with your brothers," Ava repeated firmly. Hezekiah didn't even seem to hear her.

After he ignored Ava three more times, Anaya grabbed Hezekiah by the arm and pulled him to his feet.

"Your mom said go to the room with your brothers, didn't she?" Anaya looked him in the eyes. He nodded. "Then go on."

Hezekiah ran off while Ava busied herself with the laundry on the sofa.

For a moment, Anaya reveled in the newfound silence. Then the smell hit her. "What are you cooking?" Everything Ava cooked smelled awful.

"Tofu meatballs."

It didn't smell like tofu or meatballs. Anaya hoped Ava wouldn't ask her to stay for dinner. If she had any chance of getting out of there, she would need to leave soon.

"There is no such thing as tofu meatballs."

"Sure there is. You staying for dinner?"

"If you put some turkey meat in there, I might." Anaya preferred turkey and fish for her protein.

"Turkeys are friends, not food, Ny."

"Turkeys are your friends, not mine."

"Can I get you anything else? Tiger nuts? Kale chips?" Ava asked brightly.

"No thank you. I prefer food with flavor."

"Okay. Just keep consuming animal flesh and industrially produced foods. I'm sure your body just loves it."

Anaya's bag buzzed, and, she instinctively pulled out her work phone.

Ava made a *tsk* sound. "And staring at that phone screen all the time. I'm telling you, that's how brain cancer develops. Do you know how many new cases of brain cancer are reported each year?"

"No." Anaya kept her eyes on her phone.

"Can you at least try to be present for five minutes, sister dear?"

Anaya ignored her sister, typing out a quick response to fix the wording on the development agreement. It needed more emphasis on the local contractors.

"I see you are working yourself to the ground again. You won't take your eyes off that thing. And why don't you have an iPhone like everybody else?"

"The Blackberry is more secure." Anaya still didn't look up.

"Whatever. The evening news reported the board wants to reopen that navy base. Not a good idea, Ny. One of my church members has a cousin whose nephew got robbed on that base years ago. They need to keep that Sodom and Gomorrah shut down."

"Sodom and Gomorrah, Ava?" Anaya looked up briefly. "You are so dramatic sometimes. If the base is reopened, it would generate revenue and create jobs. That's pretty far from Sodom and Gomorrah, I would say."

"Dramatic? I'm not dramatic, but you, my dear sister, are easily swayed. Do you know why God destroyed Sodom and Gomorrah, Anaya?"

Anaya hit send and put her phone away with a sigh. "Ava, please. Not tonight."

"I want an answer. Do you know why God destroyed Sodom and Gomorrah?"

"I said not tonight."

"That's because you don't know why."

"Yes, I do."

"Then why?"

"What? You don't believe I know?"

"I believe you, I'm just trying to make a point."

Anaya paused briefly, wondering how she got herself into this conversation. "God destroyed Sodom and Gomorrah because of vileness."

"Exactly! And the things that went on at that base were vile." Ava said vile like she could taste it. "Anyway, that base should stay shut down. It's not your fault if the project doesn't move forward."

"Of course it wouldn't be my fault. Why would you say that?" Now Ava had her attention.

"Well, it was on the evening news that your department is responsible for doing the research and that the county is so focused on revenue that they aren't considering the atrocities that happened on the property. I told my Bible study group that my sister has a conscience and would only give the board good information."

Anaya hadn't heard the news story, but she wasn't surprised. Since the board resurrected the idea of reopening the base, everybody wanted a piece and rumors abounded. Anyone who had even a small part in the redevelopment would make a ton of money. There were three new tech companies looking to build in the area, and the base would be a prime spot for development.

Anaya shrugged, realizing she wouldn't get the answers she was interested in from Ava. "It's going to be okay."

"You always downplay everything. If you're overwhelmed, just say it. It's okay to admit it. Dad told me you were stressed."

"You know how he sometimes embellishes when he is worried," Anaya said dismissively. "I'm fine. When did you talk to Dad anyway?"

"Don't call Dad a liar, Ny. It's disrespectful," Ava said.

"I didn't call him a liar."

"Yes you did. Anyway, do you know why he has so many plants in the garage? He can't possibly use all of those."

"I was wondering the same thing," Anaya said, grateful for the change of subject. "He visits the nursery at least once a week. He gives half the stuff he buys to Miss Grace."

"Probably just trying to keep busy. He misses Mom. And I think it's good for him, as long as he stays away from those insecticides. Do you ever wonder about the breast cancer rates in Marin County? It's because of the insecticides they use on those redwoods out there. Did you know . . ." And Ava was off, lecturing Anaya about increased cancer rates in areas that used large amounts of insecticides.

Anaya fell silent as Ava continued. She studied the room, which was bursting at the seams with five people's stuff. *This place is big enough for now, but they will need more room soon. But who will pay for it? Not me.*

"And that's why it's been so hot." Ava finally came up for air. "Ny, you aren't listening to me."

"You're right, I'm not. You're talking about too many different things. Besides, global warming and cancer are depressing to talk about. I'm not in the mood. I was actually thinking about mom. Do you ever miss her?" She looked at the picture of her mother.

"Of course. I miss her every day, and I hate that the boys never got to meet her. She was such a wonderful person." Ava paused. "Are you okay?"

"I'm okay. I just miss Mom sometimes."

"It's okay to miss her. She's always with us. You know that, don't you?"

"I do," Anaya said, standing. "I have to go. I need to get some work done. I just wanted to get this check to you."

"It's Friday night. Who works on a Friday night?"

People with jobs. Anaya thought.

"I'm just really busy. I also need to get to bed soon because I'm going for an early run tomorrow."

Ava frowned. "Girl, you are already too skinny. Stop running and exercising so much."

"Okay, Ava." Anaya reached into her purse. "You know what I need far better than I do. Please forgive me." She pulled out the envelope with Ava's check and handed it to her sister. That would shut her up.

Ava's eyes lit up. "Thank you so much, Ny. You're always so helpful. I promise Joe and I will pay you back."

On cue, Joe walked in and dropped his gym bag by the door.

"Sis!" he said, grabbing Anaya in a huge embrace.

"How are you, Joe?" Anaya's voice was muffled beneath his massive arms.

"Chitty chitty bang bang! Life is good," he said huskily, still holding her tight.

"That's good, Joe." Anaya's face was smushed into his bicep.

"Joe, let her go before you squeeze her to death." Ava chuckled. "How did it go today?"

Joe released Anaya, swept Ava into his arms, and gave her a wet kiss on the lips. Anaya cringed.

"Went great. I think this thing is really going to happen." Joe put Ava back on her feet and began to pace, his face bright with childlike excitement.

"Did I tell you Joe is going to make an exercise video?" Ava asked proudly.

"No. No, you didn't." *Sweet Lord, help these people.*

"He is. Tell her about it, babe. Ny, are you staying for dinner?"

"I can't, I need to get some stuff done," Anaya said.

"Let me tell you about this video I'm in before you go!"

"I'm all ears." Anaya couldn't help but appreciate Joe's big smile. He was under-unemployed and clueless, but he was easily one of the nicest people she knew. She was intrigued about how this exercise video had come to be.

"I met this guy at the gym a few weeks ago, and we just started talking. He asked me if I was a trainer, and I told him I was. I started helping him with his routine, and you know, we bonded while working out and got to know each other. One day, he asked me if I had ever thought of doing an exercise video. Said he was part owner of a production company and he thought we could make a lot of money."

Oy vey. "Wow, that's incredible, Joe."

"Yeah, we should start shooting in about a month at his house, so I'm working on the routines for the video now," Joe said, practically jumping with excitement.

"That's great, Joe."

It would be cruel to burst his bubble with reasonable questions like whether he would get paid, if he had signed a contract, or why this guy had randomly chosen him. If they asked for her help, she would give them her opinion, but if they didn't, she was not going to interfere.

Ava gushed. "Isn't that wonderful news?"

Anaya just nodded.

"Are you sure you can't stay for dinner?" Ava asked.

"I can't," Anaya said, inching towards the door.

"Do you need me to do anything for Dad's party?" Ava asked.

Anaya did, but she knew she couldn't count on Ava. "No. I got it. That's why I gotta go." *For the thousandth time.*

"Ny just doesn't have time for us anymore with that big fancy job she has," Ava told Joe sadly.

That big fancy job pays your bills.

"Love you, bye." Anaya hugged her sister and left.

EIGHT

"Yeah. Just out doing some work. Okay, Antoine. I will. Okay. Yes. Bye."

Catie hung up with a groan. She had just left the house, and Antoine had already called to ask where she was. It was okay for Antoine to be concerned, but he was taking the "concerned father" thing too far. Catie had told him she'd be home in an hour, so why was he calling? All his "where are you?" and "make sure you check in" requests were getting on her nerves. She had always come and gone as she pleased. Being pregnant wasn't going to change that.

She called Ny to gripe, but got her voicemail and then a text that said she would call back after she left Ava's. She was probably loaning her sister money again. Anaya was a good person but man, she was overworked by her family.

Catie drove through her charming Piedmont neighborhood. Initially, she had reservations about moving into the exclusive community, but it had grown on her. It was the best of living in the Bay. Comfortable twentieth-century homes in a bucolic setting that felt like the suburbs but was only steps away from the urban life.

She drove past her store, FastLane, and made a mental note to have the exterior power washed. She hopped on the freeway and headed west on Interstate 80. Thirty minutes later, she entered North Richmond. North Richmond was a forlorn community chock-full of low-income housing, multiple liquor stores, and insufficient social services. The first thing one noticed upon crossing the railroad tracks to enter North Richmond was two churches on opposite sides of the street, an inoperable RV, and blight. Unkempt lawns hid discarded beer bottles and other litter. Some houses were barely standing with broken windows and shoddy frames. A stray dog walked in front of Catie's car, sniffing for food.

Catie parked her Cayenne in front of a small, neat-looking house with dull yellow paint and bright blue trim. It needed a paint job and new stairs but was still one of the nicer homes on the block. Next door, a little boy with platinum bangs tried to dribble a basketball between his legs.

She rolled down the window and felt the sunshine on her face. After a few minutes, she pulled out her phone to schedule a fitting and confirmed an appointment to style a fashion blogger for an upcoming photo shoot. She'd be a happy woman if she could do onsite styling exclusively, but the store brought in the most revenue so that was her priority for now.

Catie looked at the small yellow house again, and then read a few more emails before getting out of her car. She didn't like coming here, but she felt obliged. She told Antoine she was working and technically she hadn't lied. She was working, just not at the store like she had implied. Some things were better left unsaid.

As she walked up the stairs and across the porch, she remembered the face of Amelia Govan, her childhood best friend and neighbor who would sit with her on these porch steps, eat chips, and dream about the future. Sometimes they played in the yard waiting for their moms to call them to dinner. If they got too hungry, they walked around the corner and stole chips from Gunny's corner store. Old man Gunny had been in the neighborhood for over fifty years and knew all the families. He fussed and shooed Catie and Amelia out of the store, but there was never a real consequence beyond a wag of his crooked forefinger and a threat to tell their parents. Back on the front steps of Catie's house, they would crunch the salty treats and talk about how much food they would buy when they got older. Catie always said she was going to be a zillionaire and buy a room full of sour cream and onion potato chips. Before going home every night, they did their secret handshake and wished each other sweet dreams.

For a long time, Amelia had been Catie's only friend. The other kids at school didn't want to be friends with Catie because of her knotted hair and tattered clothes. Amelia was a compassionate but quick-tongued scrapper from the south side of Chicago, and she defended Catie when Catie had been too afraid to speak up for herself. Their friendship blossomed beyond the school yard and sometimes they ventured around the neighborhood, but none of the other kids gave them the time of day. No one wanted to play with the kids of dope fiends.

One afternoon, Amelia went to Gunny's alone to get chips. But Old Man Gunny's daughter had sold the store to a new owner. The new storeowner saw Amelia stealing and told her to put the chips back. Amelia ran. The storeowner shot Amelia in the back. Amelia died in the hospital the next day.

Nosey Ms. Grier, who had nothing to do but meddle and feed her thousand cats, told the police that Amelia and Catie always stole from the store because their mamas were too busy using dope to mind their kids. She also added that the electricity was often off in Catie's house. This was all true, but it wasn't her business. The police called child protective services, and though the electricity was on when they arrived, there was no food or running water in the house. Catie spent two weeks in foster care until her mother could prove that there was sufficient food in the house. A year later, when Catie was six, her mom lost her parental rights, and Catie entered the bottomless depths of the foster system until the Johnsons adopted her when she was seven years old.

Catie shook her head and pushed the bad memories back to the dark corner where she kept them buried. There were some things she had never told anyone. Anaya and Sophie knew some things about her past, Antoine even less. They thought that Catie had been in foster care because she didn't know her father and her mother had died. Catie didn't correct them, as that would lead to talking about the other stuff.

The inside of the house smelled like olives. Catie struggled to pick up the mail from a small basket on the floor. An unopened Amazon box sat near the basket and she struggled to remember what it could be. The baby kicked and Catie realized that she wouldn't be able to come as often once the baby was born.

"Hi Miss Catie," a sturdy woman with white hair called from the kitchen at the end of the hallway.

"Hi, Stella. How's everything?" Catie waddled into the living room and sat on the flower-patterned couch with matching cushions. It needed to be reupholstered—or better yet, replaced. The mirror above the fireplace was old, the frame cracked on the side. She made a mental note to buy a new one.

"Everything is good," Stella said, entering the living room. "Been quiet around here."

"Okay. I'm just going to catch up on the mail," Catie said to the round woman in the yellow sunflower tunic dress. "I won't be here long."

"I see." Stella sounded disappointed but sat down on the matching chair next to the sofa. She pulled her red strands behind her ear and looked expectantly at Catie. Stella was nice and Catie didn't mean to be rude to her, but sometimes Stella forgot that she was responsible for the domestic duties of the house and nothing more.

Catie scanned each piece of mail before throwing it onto the floor. She was sure she filled out something to have all the junk mail stopped. She could feel Stella staring and tried not to indulge, but Stella wanted to indulge.

"Look at you, your little *niño* is growing." Stella reached over to put her hand on Catie's belly.

"I know. But I'm not sure it's a boy."

"Has to be. Look how low your stomach is," Stella said, imparting her Dominican cultural beliefs about pregnancy.

"Either way, I'm excited." Catie looked instinctively toward the back of the house before returning to the stack of mail. She added a few more junk letters to the pile on the floor; the bills went in her bag. The hardwood floors were scheduled to be buffed next week. Once that was done, she would replace the dingy throw rug in the front hall that was as old as Catie.

After glancing at her phone, Catie struggled to her feet. She was late for her appointment with Dr. Rhonda. "See you next week, Stella." She walked out to her car, remembering that tomorrow would have been Amelia's twenty-ninth birthday.

✳

"Have you talked to Antoine about your struggles?" Dr. Rhonda asked after Catie had settled into the oversized recliner. Catie sat on a blue couch with her hands folded. She didn't like coming to see Dr. Rhonda but it was necessary. Especially if she was going to deal with the demons that increasingly haunted her lately.

You already know the answer to that question, yet you ask me the same thing every time I come here.

"I haven't." Catie sighed, examining her cuticles. She had tried the new dip powder and liked it much better than gel polish. She looked at Rhonda expectantly. She wanted to heal, and she thought she was ready to do the work, but the process was difficult. All the recounting and pain and accountability. It was hard stuff.

"Why not?" Dr. Rhonda tilted her head to the left and squinted her eyes.

Catie racked her brain. There had to be a legitimate reason. "I get mad at Antoine a lot and I need a peaceful, calm atmosphere to talk about this. I can't remember the last time there was peace or calm in our house." Catie pursed her lips and crossed her ankles.

Dr. Rhonda nodded. "Okay, and why isn't there peace? You guys talked about the text message, correct?"

"Not yet."

"Why not? That was one of your assignments."

Yes it was one of her assignments—the one she avoided. "Same reason," she found herself saying. "I just don't want to have a big blowup right now. If Antoine wants to canoodle around with some floozy, more power to him," she tried to hide a wince. "Right now, I need to make moves to make sure I'm okay, and then I will talk to him." It's funny that the text messages didn't bother her until she started talking about them. How could he?

Catie had too many things on her plate to be derailed by flirty messages between Antoine and this mystery woman. Catie had heard that pregnancy enhanced emotions, and she was emotionally fragile. She worried about failing as a mom and felt she was already failing at being a girlfriend and a friend by keeping secrets. She worried that her business would suffer while she was on maternity leave and was scared that if she confronted Antoine about the texts, he would leave her. There was too much stuff for anyone to stomach, especially a pregnant woman. She'd have to deal with it later. Now wasn't the time.

"You treat your relationship like a stock option," said Dr. Rhonda, leaning on her right elbow. She was a big-boned woman with square glasses and a natural fro. "Do you realize that?"

Of course she did. Catie was strategic. After everything she'd been through in her life, almost everything she did was calculated. She was a boss with too many things to juggle, and Antoine's mystery fling wasn't on her urgent list.

"I know. I have a few things to take care of before I can talk to Antoine about the text message."

"And in the meantime?"

"What do you mean?"

"In the meantime, what happens to your relationship?"

Catie shrugged. She was accustomed to the silence now. Most evenings she came home, took off her shoes, and started working on her laptop. She wanted to get the new LA store up and running within a year. "We co-exist pretty well. We don't fight."

"Not fighting is not a solution. It's complacent."

Thank you for the prognosis, Dr. Obvious. "I'd say we are coping, and that works for now."

"And your secret?"

"What about it?"

"When are you going to tell Antoine and your friends?"

Catie glared at Dr. Rhonda. "I'm not ready for that. I'm not sure anybody is ready for that."

NINE

S omewhere between preparing for her father's birthday party and a boss named Godzilla, Anaya found herself going to work three hours early to catch up on the mounds of paper piled on her desk. It had been a week since the board approved the draft contract for the navy base with the assumption that local contractors would be given precedence in the development bids.

Anaya didn't mind starting so early as she could be more productive when no one was in the office. Even though she didn't get as much done as she wanted, she felt good about the paper shuffling and sending canned email replies. She read Carl's first text message of the day, which yielded her first real smile of the day. She responded with a promise to stop by after work, then dived back into editing a grant.

At nine o'clock, Anaya popped a Zantac, finished her second cup of coffee, then picked up her phone to call Jayde. The navy base project had propelled her stress range to level orange, and Jayde was always Anaya's voice of reason. Anaya had managed big projects before, but there was a lot at stake with this one, and as Anaya's mentor and friend, Jayde was good at helping Anaya put things in proper perspective. Although Jayde should've been back from her weekend to Mexico, her secretary answered and said Jayde was still on vacation.

Anaya hung up, frowning. Jayde must have extended the trip.

Natalie waltzed into Anaya's office with her phone by her ear and a coffee cup in her other hand. Her tight, cheetah print skirt only allowed her to take small steps, and her perfume filled the room.

"Yes, girl, people are a trip," Natalie flapped. "I gotta go." She hung up and slipped the phone into the bag hanging from her arm. Besides being the office cad and self-proclaimed "internal communications coordinator," Natalie managed Anaya's calendar and fielded phone calls with the gravitas of an army general. If you didn't have a scheduled appointment with Anaya, you wouldn't see her, and if you didn't announce yourself on the phone correctly, you wouldn't talk to her.

"Good morning, boss lady," Natalie chirped.

"Morning, Natalie."

"Here's your coffee." Natalie placed a coffee cup on Anaya's desk, then smoothed down her curly cropped hair.

Anaya sipped the coffee and closed her eyes. Although Natalie wasn't especially diplomatic and dressed like she was the chair of the Sexy Secretary Convention, she always brought an extra cup of coffee for Anaya.

"Thank you. How are you?"

"Good, if I can get this deadbeat to help me with these kids." Natalie had four children and was going through a divorce. She was a good mom and managed life stress and work duties in skin-tight skirts, high heels, and rotating wigs.

Natalie pulled dead leaves off of Anaya's ivy plant and straightened the books on the shelf while she talked. "How are things going with the project? I heard Wendy isn't making things easy on you. If she took more time to do her job instead of yours and spent less time at the MAC counter, she might be able to get something done."

"Yeah, I'm not sure what's going to happen. The board basically approved the contract as long as we include the local hiring provisions. We will have to see how it goes," Anaya said.

"Hopefully everything will be fine. Did you see how much

makeup Wendy was wearing at the last meeting? Where did she think she was going, prom?" The same question could be posed to Natalie, who looked like she and Wendy could have left the same MAC counter arm in arm.

"Thanks, Natalie, that's all for now." Anaya glanced back at her computer screen.

"Okay, okay," Natalie said. Anaya was grateful that the woman knew when she had gone too far. "Are you ready for your meeting with her?"

"As ready as I can be."

Anaya met with Wendy every other Monday since Anaya started working on the project. While sometimes she had no idea what Wendy would want to discuss, this week, she had a fairly good idea. Since the Alameda County supervisors had directed Anaya to move forward with the RFP, her staff had been working full speed ahead. They had already drafted an RFP and sent it to Wendy's office, as per protocol. Wendy had sent it back with a big red X and a note that read, "I'll fix this for you." It wasn't Wendy's job to fix, but Anaya already had enough on her plate and wouldn't miss it.

A few hours later, Anaya walked up one flight of stairs to the county administrator's suite where Wendy's office was located. She took a deep breath outside the dark wood door, knocked, and entered at the high-pitched "Come in."

"Good morning, Wendy." Anaya sat down at the edge of the chair across from Wendy's desk with a notepad in hand. Wendy's Ivy League education and self-touted competence didn't assuage her selective amnesia, so Anaya always took notes of their meetings and conversations in her work journal.

Wendy leaned back in her leather chair and rested her index fingers on the bridge of her pug nose. Anaya admired her vintage Chanel dress and heavy eyeliner. If Wendy weren't such a bitch, she would be mildly attractive.

Anaya had recently heard from a reliable source that Wendy was planning to apply for a position in the governor's administration. Wendy had been in county administration for a long time and claimed to have managed a project twice the size of the navy base in Ventura County. If this development agreement was approved, it would look incredible on Wendy's resume. So why was Wendy delaying the RFP with the wording about the local contractors?

Anaya frowned, thinking about her conversation with Jayde a week ago. Could Wendy's heavy handedness be an indication of some ulterior motive?

"The problem with young, inexperienced executives is they are scared to think outside of the box." Wendy stared at Anaya. "Sometimes the only way to make things happen is to think strategically."

That's an odd opening, Anaya thought, but she stayed silent.

"I'm trying to figure out the fastest way to move this process along, Mizz Goode." Wendy clipped her words dramatically. Sources around County Hall said that she lived in Manchester for six years after grad school. Others said she used a fake accent. "It's been a week and I want to support you any way I can. My office took on the responsibility of reworking the RFP process for you, and I'd like you to read it and sign it now."

She pushed two packets of paper toward Anaya. A glance at the title pages revealed that one was the RFP and the other was the development agreement. And this is why the project was delayed—a power-hungry administrator who micromanaged with a heavy hand to try to make a name for herself at the County's expense.

Anaya was familiar with both documents. She scanned the RFP first and immediately noticed that Wendy had changed the requirements to a restricted bid, which would drastically reduce the pool of contractors who could bid on the project.

Next, she looked at the development agreement. Anaya's office had amended the development agreement to include the requirement for a fifty percent minimum local hire provision like the board requested. The legalese of Wendy's revised agreement revealed a change in the local hire number to twenty percent. *This is why we can't get anywhere.*

Anaya tried to keep her voice calm and reasonable while she held the papers in her hand. "The numbers for the local hiring have been reduced, which is the opposite of what the board requested. The standard for local hiring requirements has always been at least 50 percent. There is absolutely no reason to change that. And what is this language about a restricted bid? I haven't seen any information to indicate that this bid should be restricted."

Wendy narrowed her eyes. "Many of the local contractors are too small to handle such a huge project. Not everyone will qualify to bid."

"I think it's fine to indicate that the main contractors for certain aspects of the project, such as the housing units, need to have proven experience with similar projects and have a certain number of employees. But we have plenty of large local contractors who would qualify. Why would we deviate from the standard 50 percent? This project could generate hundreds of jobs in our county," Anaya said evenly.

"We can't always go with the county's standard. Sometimes we have to think outside of the box and do what's best for the county and its residents."

"I think that having the opportunity to bid on a multimillion-dollar job would be a great benefit to our residents, not to mention the creation of new jobs. Please enlighten me on how hiring outside contractors would benefit our county more." Anaya spoke through gritted teeth. She was getting angrier by the second. Wendy's background was in finance and land use, not development. She was overstepping.

Wendy stood up abruptly and tapped her forefinger on her top lip. "Twenty percent is industry standard when there's a special need in the RFP, or did you not read that far? The base needs to be demolished, which means explosives. I will not have blood on my hands if some small-time local contractor blows himself and his crew to smithereens because he has no experience with explosives. We do care about the safety of our contractors around here, don't we, Mizz Goode?"

Anaya rubbed a hand over her eyes. Now Wendy was just being ridiculous.

"I understand your desire to get this project going. The community needs it. But since the demolition will likely be subcontracted out to a company that is experienced in explosives, I see no need to exclude some of our good contractors. Again, my concern is—"

"Why can't you just do as you are told?" Wendy stood up and paced the room. "You, my dear, and the rest of your millennial generation will be the death of us all with your illogical reasoning, desire for fair play, and bleeding hearts. You should be concerned about following through with the board's direction and looking out for the safety of our community."

Wendy stopped in front of Anaya. "I'm counting on you. I know you're a smart girl, and I know you want to do the right thing. We can't take our good jobs and lucrative salaries for granted now, can we? Slurping from the public trough of fully-funded pensions and lifetime medical benefits while other people barely skate by." Wendy began pacing again. "You are well-dressed and articulate. I can tell someone at least attempted to raise you properly. My concern is advancement. Yes, you're green and a little slow to understand basic concepts at times, but I see potential and budding wisdom that transcend your naïveté. Do the right thing. Not only for yourself, but also for the citizens of this county and your co-workers."

Anaya studied the woman thoughtfully. She could not make sense of Wendy's decision to limit the contractor pool except the sheer joy of a power struggle. And since Anaya's was the final signature needed on the agreement, Wendy would have to work a little harder to cooperate.

Anaya rose to her feet. As far as she was concerned, this conversation was done. "I won't sign it until the local hire is at least fifty percent, Wendy. If not, I can't make any guarantees that the contract will get out of my department anytime soon."

"Well, you might want to think about making some guarantees," Wendy said calmly. "You are in this position because someone thought you could handle yourself when things got tough. Don't give me reason to believe otherwise."

Anaya moved toward the door. She had her hand on the doorknob when Wendy spoke again.

"Your reputation will precede you no matter where you go, Mizz Goode. And believe me, if you have a bad reputation, you won't get far. Being insubordinate to your superiors will also not get you very far. I'm not asking you to reinvent the wheel or do the stanky leg in front of the entire Board of Supervisors; I'm asking you to do your job." Wendy's voice was steady, and her face didn't move, so it was impossible to tell how she was really feeling.

"When were you going to tell me about this task force you mentioned at the meeting?" Anaya asked suddenly.

"Well, that was the other thing I wanted to talk to you about before you got all hissy. It's nothing spectacular." She waved her hand. "Just four individuals with different areas of expertise to ensure we stay on track. The task force will include you, Sue, Will from finance, and I've handpicked a highly qualified legal consultant to help the three of you."

Anaya had never needed a separate team to help her do her job, but she was starting to care less by the moment. This was Wendy's way of controlling the project. It didn't make sense to spend county money on a consultant, but Anaya had bigger fish to fry. If Wendy wanted a task force, so be it.

"If that's all, I have work to do," Anaya said, turning the knob.

"I have guest passes to hotbox yoga. Would you like one?"

"No, thanks."

"It's guaranteed to burn nine hundred calories in an hour."

"No."

"You sure? You're looking a little, I don't know . . . hefty? You shouldn't let yourself go. Don't you have a boyfriend? Or perhaps a girlfriend?"

"I'm not signing the agreement unless you change the provisions." Anaya walked out.

"We'll see about that," she heard as the door closed. Tyranny in Chanel.

TEN

A naya left Wendy's office and went straight to one of her favorite restaurants for lunch. She scrolled though Instagram and fumed over what she could have said to Wendy. Ten things sprang to mind, nine of which would have cost her job, but how sweet they would have felt rolling off of her tongue. She switched to email and thumbed through message after message about cantankerous citizens, rising pension obligations, Sanctuary City resolutions, and something about gender-neutral restrooms.

She switched back to Instagram; she had put out enough fires for one day. She politely declined a follow request from a gentleman with a white beard. *Not today, boo.*

"Hey, little lady."

She looked up. Instead of plotting verbal revenge on Wendy, Anaya should have been mentally preparing for this moment. Though she had agreed with Catie and Sophie that meeting Jeff was a bad idea, curiosity had gotten the best of her. Seeing Jeff wasn't a big deal. She could handle a simple lunch with an ex-boyfriend.

"Hey there." She flushed in surprise, not recognizing her own voice. Her hands began to sweat as she stood and gave him a quick hug.

"It's great to see you." Jeff smiled. He was just as handsome as the day she blocked his number from her cell.

"You too." *Sweet baby Jesus, he grew a beard.*

"You look amazing." He took the seat across from her with a grin, and she knew he was happy to see her. It was unseasonably chilly that day, but suddenly Anaya felt warm.

"Thank you," she said, shrinking beneath his gaze. As her stomach fluttered nervously, she suddenly remembered this feeling. But how?

"Thank you for coming today." Jeff sat back in his seat and examined her face. Anaya held her breath as she admired him in silence. *Had he always been this handsome?*

"So, how've you been?"

"I'm good," she answered in a voice she didn't recognize. "Just working hard."

"Still working hard. I've always liked that about you."

"How, um, about you? How have you been?" *This is awkward. I shouldn't have come.*

"So much has been going on." He smiled again, but there was a hint of sadness in his eyes. "It's been a long time."

"Yes, it has."

He stared at her for a moment. "Let's see. Where to begin? Uh, work is the same. Taylor moved on and started her own firm, but we are still managing a heavy caseload. It's good though."

"I always knew she'd go out on her own. She was always a boss." Anaya would much prefer Taylor as a boss over Wendy.

"Let's see, what else?" He rubbed his chin. "My parents are getting older so I have to figure out how to manage all of that. The kids are growing up on me. It's bittersweet."

She cleared her throat. He had never mentioned his kids when they dated. *One of many things that went unmentioned.*

He paused when the waitress brought them water and asked to take their order. Jeff took a moment to study the menu, but Anaya just picked the first salad she saw.

"I know you said you didn't have a lot of time today, so I won't keep you too long with boring stories about me," Jeff said as the waitress walked away.

She had only told him she had limited time because she didn't know how things would go. Now she cursed herself. "It's okay, I have a little time." She rested her chin in her hand.

He snapped his fingers. "You know, something else has changed. I started running. I learned from a very wise young lady that running is one of the best forms of therapy."

"Ha, I'm surprised you remember that."

"I run twice a week now. That's how I keep my weight down." He leaned back in his seat. "But enough about me. What's up with you? You're all over the news, running the entire county. What happened to psychology?"

That was an excellent question, and she might tell him some day why she had decided to ditch her college major for county bureaucracy. But she wasn't ready to regurgitate the last few years of her life during a one-hour lunch. "Hardly," she replied. "The county is running me."

"That's not what I hear." He studied her face. She could tell by his measured stare that he was trying to figure her out. "But that brings me to why I reached out."

Finally.

Jeff told her how Wendy asked him to serve on the task force as a contract attorney with the county on the navy base project. It wasn't uncommon for the county to contract outside council, but they normally did so when county attorneys were stretched thin or subject matter was unfamiliar to the county attorney's office, neither of which applied to the navy base project. Sue Garcia was one of the best attorneys in the county, was on hand to answer any legal questions, and had already offered her input on the RFP. Anaya would be working closely with Sue as the details of the project were finalized. Although this was a great opportunity for Jeff, Anaya couldn't figure out why Wendy would need him on the project.

Jeff is the highly qualified legal consultant Wendy was talking about? Holy hell. "Wait. I missed that last part. What did you say?" Anaya shook her head as she tried to re-focus.

"I taught transactional law and procurement for a few years and have had an ongoing contract with the Port for the past nine years," he repeated. "So I have experience." He paused. "You weren't listening."

"I'm sorry," she said. "This is a lot to take in."

"If it's a problem, I can decline the offer. I haven't accepted yet."

She responded too fast. "No, it's not a problem. It's just such an odd coincidence."

"I know. I wanted to jump at the opportunity, but I was worried about your response, which is why I wanted to see you before accepting. I was on the verge of rejecting it when I got your reply about lunch. If you have reservations, I will back out. Just say the word." He held his hands up in retreat.

"No. Don't be silly. Take the opportunity. It's just such an odd coincidence."

"You said that already." He studied her face again. She could probably relax more if he stopped staring at her so intensely. It made her uncomfortable and want to hug him at the same time.

"I know. No, it's okay. Congratulations." She held up her water glass in a mock toast.

"Are you sure about this, Miss Goode?"

"I am. Really. Take the job. It's fine." *Oh boy. What am I doing?*

"Okay, I'm going to take your word and presume you're being honest with me. I'm supposed to start August first, so this is your last chance to change your mind."

She nodded her approval, water glass still in the air. As if on cue, the waitress came back with their food, and they moved on to lighter topics about mutual acquaintances and running shoes. For a few minutes, it felt like old times.

As Anaya wiped her mouth with her napkin, Jeff leaned forward.

"Now, can I ask you another a question?" His face was ripe with resolve.

"Cool," she said. Anything would be easier than talking about them working together. And the flutters in her stomach had mostly calmed. "Shoot."

"Why did you break things off the way you did?"

Anaya's heart pounded in her throat. "Wow. You went there."

Jeff shrugged. "You don't have to answer. But I've always wanted to know. Why the abrupt cut off? You didn't respond to my texts or emails. You just disappeared off the face of the earth."

Anaya stared at her water glass. This day was bound to come. She couldn't hide from him forever. "That was the best I could do. I was grieving my mom and grieving what was left of us, and I just needed to get away."

"With no good-bye? No explanation?"

She met his eyes. *Are you kidding me? Do you know the hell I went through?* "To be honest, I went to your office one day to talk to you, but I chickened out in the parking lot." She lowered her eyes. "I thought if I saw you, I wouldn't have the nerve to break up with you."

"I see." He ran his finger around the rim of his glass. "I never expected you would run off like that."

"It was hard, but that's what I needed to do."

"You hurt me," he said.

"I know," she said quietly. "But I did what I had to."

"You hurt me," he said again, and she saw the pain in his eyes.

"More water here?" The waitress refilled their glasses and left.

"Did I ever hurt you?"

He was full of loaded questions today. She stared at him for a minute. The Jeff she had dated was good to her but had never openly talked about such intimate feelings. It was one of the things that drove her crazy. She always felt like he was hiding something.

"Yes. You did."

"How?"

She took a deep breath. After all this time, she finally had the opportunity to tell him the truth. "Do you know how it feels to love somebody so much and not be able to have them when you want or how you want?"

"It wasn't one sided, Anaya," he said readily.

"But I was hurting, and the more time we spent together, the worse it got." She felt her phone vibrating.

He leaned in closer to her. She could smell his cologne. "I loved you and I risked a lot to spend time with you."

She tilted her head, feeling an ember of anger ignite. *You risked a lot? I can't wait to hear this.*

"I was late to meetings, I missed events. I even cancelled classes to spend time with you. Did you know that?"

And how would I have known that? "You never told me anything. Why didn't you tell me any of this?"

"I didn't want to lose you."

"Why didn't you just say that?"

"Because I didn't know what I was doing." He sat back, exasperated. "I was in a bad place when I met you. I had a failed marriage with a crumpling façade of happiness. I just did things based on my feelings. I did everything I could to spend time with you."

She nodded slowly but didn't speak.

"At the expense of everything else in my life."

"And I left you hanging."

"And you left me hanging," he said.

"I'm sorry. I guess we both had to do what we thought was best."

"I suppose. Are things better for you since you left me?"

Another loaded question. But just because he was being so open didn't mean she had to be.

"Things are good. How about for you?"

"Things are great," he said, self-assuredly. "I stopped focusing on the wrong things. Yes, people know my marriage failed, but I'm free. Free to be happy and free to enjoy my children and my success."

Anaya choked on her water. *So he's divorced.*

"Yes, she got half of my money and is now spending it with someone else, but the façade is over, and I'm a better person for it," he said. He shrugged. "It's over."

"Any regrets?" Her curiosity was getting the best of her.

"One."

"What's that?"

He looked at her. "That I didn't do it sooner."

Holy hell.

ELEVEN

Anaya had been planning Roscoe's sixtieth birthday party for months and when it was time to finalize the venue, she decided there was no place like home. Thanks to a great local catering company, the Goode dining room looked nothing short of amazing. No detail was left unattended. Dimmed lights and soft jazz set the mood in the dining area, and the DVR was queued up in the living room for Ava's boys. The rented gold tapestry from ZayZay's draped the dining room entryway and gave an elegant but warm feel, and the décor was festive but not fussy. The guest list included the pregnant, the hearing impaired, and the ill-behaved. With that many people sitting at the table, Anaya wanted to keep it simple. She also did her best to place the name cards strategically to avoid too much conflict, but there was no such thing with this family. The first to arrive was her mother's younger sister, Marie.

"Well, Anaya, look at you!" Marie gushed as Anaya opened the door. "Stunning."

"Thank you, Auntie," Anaya replied, taking Marie's jacket. "Where is Uncle Allen?"

"Allen will be along later," Marie said dismissively, scanning the room. "Where's Roscoe?"

Anaya pointed up the stairs. "Finishing getting ready, I guess. He'll be down soon."

Aunt Deb and Cousin Marguerite arrived next. The doctors said it was a miracle Aunt Deb survived the car accident last year. She had suffered inner ear damage and a head injury that caused rapid onset dementia. Now, the fiercely independent former world traveler had to outsource even the smallest tasks. It took some convincing to get her to move from her own home in Healdsburg to the luxury independent living condo complex in Walnut Creek, which was much closer to the rest of the family. However, she didn't let her injuries stop her from keeping a close eye on her finances and telling salacious stories.

"My sweet Anaya." Deb grabbed Anaya's face and kissed her cheek. Anaya cringed. Deb was notorious for leaving make-up stains, and Anaya's tan sheath was in danger.

"Marie." Deb hugged Marie with noticeably less enthusiasm. Anaya knew her mother had been Deb's favorite niece, while Marie was her least favorite. Aunt Deb was the younger sister of Marie and Anita's mother who died when Anita and Marie were young. Aunt Deb stepped up as a grandmother figure through the years and didn't hold back on giving money, or her unsolicited opinions to her nieces. Among many other things, Deb never approved of Marie's nose job and lip fillers.

"Hey, Auntie." Marie wasn't such a great fan of Deb either. She always resented that Deb took a greater liking to Anita and Anita's children.

"Hi, Cousin Marguerite," Anaya said. "Thanks for picking up Aunt Deb." Marguerite only picked up Deb if Deb's driver wasn't available, which was becoming increasingly common lately. Her driver was one of the kids from their neighborhood, who took her on errands after school, on weekends, and sometimes to evening events. But he was a senior now, and his social calendar was filling up.

"Of course," Marguerite said. As she hugged Anaya, she whispered, "You owe me."

"I read my charts the week before my car accident." Deb took off her cape, sending her salt-and-pepper dreadlocks swinging. "And it said something was going to crash. I reinvested some of my tech stocks thinking it was going to be the stock market, not my car!" She floated into the living room in a colorful robe and clinking jewelry, leaving the scent of incense behind her.

Marguerite followed Marie to the wine, and Anaya was about to head back to the kitchen when Deb grabbed her arm.

"I'm feeling wonderful vibes, Anaya. Anita would be so pleased. Venus reigns tonight, and this decor—*c'est magnifique!* You are going to make a wonderful wife to Carl. Just like my sweet Anita was to Roscoe." Deb looked at Marie and frowned.

Anaya nodded and smiled, then headed to the kitchen. Deb followed, and Marguerite and Marie appeared a moment later, with glasses of red wine in hand.

"Auntie, I heard what you said. Don't set women's suffrage back by letting this girl think she has to be in the kitchen to keep a man." Marie scowled.

After checking to make sure the oven was preheating, Anaya leaned against the sink and watched the three women.

"I didn't say that, Marie. But you make a good point. These young gals like to think cooking and cleaning ain't important, but it is. Men don't want to eat out all the time, and they don't want to live in no nasty house."

"That's why there are housekeepers, Auntie."

"Well, Marie, we see how well that served you, huh? Where is Allen, anyway?" Deb looked around the kitchen theatrically, as if trying to spot Allen.

"I don't know if Allen and I are going to make it." Marie's tone was casual as she flung back her braids.

"Say what now?" said Marguerite. She popped a mini cheese quiche in her mouth and spoke as she chewed. "You and Allen are the perfect couple. If you guys don't make it, there's no hope for the rest of us."

"Marguerite, there's no hope for *you* because you won't stop eating," Deb said. "Now Marie, what's going on with you and Allen?" She sat down at the breakfast table.

"We've grown apart," Marie admitted, sipping her wine.

Marguerite's eyes widened, and she popped another quiche in her mouth. Deb sat on the edge of the chair, looking outraged, and raised her forefinger high in the air.

"Check the charts? I'll have you know I check the charts every single day. Don't talk to me like that."

"Grown apart, Aunt Deb. I said, we've grown apart," Marie repeated in a louder voice.

"Grown apart?" Deb repeated in shock. "Lord, Marie. You are going to lose a good man. There's always someone prettier and smarter out there who is looking for what you have. Don't let your husband go. Y'all remember your Uncle Farley, don't you?"

Everyone remembered Uncle Farley; Aunt Deb wouldn't let them forget. Anaya saw Marie roll her eyes.

Marguerite excused herself to pour more wine, and Anaya went to the fridge to pull out more appetizers. At the rate Marguerite was going, the quiches would be gone soon.

"He was a good man, that Farley," Deb said even though she'd lost most of her audience. "Gave me anything I wanted. But I was young and thought I was fine with my big legs and little waist. All the men flirted with me, and I flirted right back. Yes, I did. Deb ain't gonna lie to you. But one time, I took the flirting too far." Deb looked into the distance. "Farley found out and moved on. Married Glenda, that hefty virgin from across town who made lemon pies with the lightest, crispiest crust I've ever tasted. But I didn't care because I was having fun and living my life. Farley was nice, but he was boring. Same old routine, same old moves in the bedroom. You know what I'm talking about when they put your legs—"

"Yes! Aunt Deb," Marie interrupted. "We get it."

"Well, I dated a little after that, but nothing permanent. Nobody I could marry. Men play a lot of games, you know. They will use you if you aren't careful. Just want to get in your panties and lick on your breasts." Deb nodded and Marie gagged. "And all that time I thought I was living, I didn't think about the time I would get old. Now I'm all alone. Went through breast cancer alone, knee surgery alone, and now I'm living my golden years by myself. Farley and I were supposed to travel the world. Now he's traveling with big-boned Glenda, and I'm over here recharging my bullet batteries every couple of weeks and looking at Marie make the same foolish mistake. Your lunar house is in shambles, Marie, I can feel it. Has anyone seen my purple fingernail file? I brought it over here right after Clinton's inauguration." Deb walked out of the kitchen.

Marie finished her glass of wine. "She is the most inappropriate person I know, but that freaky old ham might be right. Maybe I've got some thinking to do." She helped herself to more wine.

Anaya heard the sound of the door opening and went out to the front hall again. There was Uncle Riley, looking like a million bucks in a three-piece navy suit, and his girlfriend Troy, looking like a buck fifty in a plaid skirt, knee-high socks, and a green beret. Troy was a good four inches taller than Riley and had a peculiar fashion sense. It was a cross between Hannah Montana and Grace Jones, but somehow Troy made it work. Riley and Troy were going strong despite early speculation from her family that Troy was going to be a short-term fling, like most of Riley's female friends.

"Uncle Riley, Miss Troy." Anaya took Troy's coat.

"Hey, niece. It's looking good in here."

"Yes it does," Troy said, holding on to Riley's arm.

"Thank you, guys. I wanted it to be nice. Help yourselves to anything you want. Daddy will be down shortly, and the food will be out soon."

She turned to put Troy's coat in the hall closet and saw Roscoe coming down the stairs. "Good timing, Daddy! Almost everyone is here."

He smiled and kissed her on the cheek. "Everything looks perfect, baby." He went into the living room to calls of "The man of the hour!" and "Happy birthday, Roscoe!"

Just as Anaya had finished hanging up Troy's coat, the door opened again and Catie waddled in three steps ahead of Antoine and Carl, who was looking absolutely scrumptious in a maroon cashmere sweater. He was carrying the bottles of wine Anaya asked for. Anaya's heart fluttered, even after all this time. *Handsome and compliant.*

"Hey girl. Where can a pregnant woman find a place to sit?" Catie and Antoine were color coordinated in black and white. She looked around appreciatively at the decorations. "And dang, you dressed this place up nice! You and Sophie can start a business in décor."

Anaya laughed and ushered them in to the living room. When she returned to the hall, Carl was waiting for her.

"Hi beautiful." His lips tasted like marshmallows.

"Hi yourself, handsome man. Thanks for bringing these." She took the bottles and he followed her to the kitchen. By some miracle, it was empty, and as soon as she sat the bottles on the counter, Carl hugged her from behind.

"You look beautiful in that dress," he whispered in her ear. She turned and kissed him slowly, and he pulled her closer.

"I love you," he said. "You're doing a good thing tonight. Your mom would be proud of you, you know that?"

"Thank you, babe. And thank you for coming by earlier to help. I couldn't have done this without you."

"Anything for you."

She gave him another kiss. "Now, go mingle with my family. I've gotta start bringing out the food." She wiped lipstick from his lips and sent him on his way.

Anaya heard the front door close and walked out to see Sophie and a guy she'd never seen before. He was exotically handsome, if a bit nervous looking.

Just as Anaya was about to walk over and introduce herself, Aunt Deb bumped into her, asking about a bottle opener she'd lost.

By the time Aunt Deb finished with her detailed description, Sophie and friend were mingling with the rest of the family in the living room. Anaya would have to meet him later—she needed to start serving the food.

The moment she placed the last dish on the table, Ava and her brood poured through the door like a flood. Hezekiah and Jeremiah were tugging at that same toy dinosaur from the other day, and Joshua dangled on Ava's hip like a luxe bag. Joe held up the rear carrying a diaper bag, a plastic bag, and a rocker for Joshua. Anaya thought about helping, but where would she even begin? She stood back and watched the madness unfold.

While everyone else mingled, Ava tried to stop the boys from wrestling for the dinosaur and set Joshua on the floor to roam around. Joe gave hugs all around until his cell phone rang and he walked outside to answer it like he was single-handedly solving world problems. When he returned, Ava called him to handle the brewing fistfight over the innocuous dinosaur, but Joe didn't hear her—at least, he pretended not to as he talked with Troy.

As Ava untangled Joshua from Deb's robe, Hezekiah finally snatched the toy from Jeremiah and took off, running straight into a side table and knocking over a vase. Joe looked up briefly from his seat on the couch, but he didn't say anything. Anaya walked over and righted the vase, which luckily, had not broken. Hezekiah continued running around the living room with Jeremiah on his heels.

"All right, boys," Ava said with the authority of Tinkerbell. "That's enough. Pop-pop's gonna get you for running in the house."

Anaya rolled her eyes but hid her smile when she noticed Catie storming over as fast as her pregnant body would allow.

"*Hey!* Cut it out!" Catie barked like an army sergeant. The boys stopped immediately and stared at Catie.

"Let's turn on a movie, Ava," Anaya suggested, handing her sister the remote.

Ava smiled approvingly as the boys piled on the sofa. Looking at her serene smile, you'd never know her kids were behaving like monsters.

Not wanting to gather everyone for dinner just yet—Uncle Allen still hadn't arrived—Anaya went over to meet Sophie's friend. Aunt Deb was gesticulating wildly at something as she talked to Carl in the dining room. He caught her eye and she winked at him.

She found Sophie and her friend listening as Roscoe talked military. *Oh boy.*

"That F-22 Raptor is no joke. Ooh-wee! Have you ever seen one?" Roscoe looked at Sophie's friend expectantly, but the man didn't respond. Roscoe was undeterred. "And that's just for airstrikes. If you are talking about ground strikes, that XM25 CDTE will tear something up." He made a sound like a broken speaker.

"Hi, you guys." Anaya interrupted the military lesson.

Sophie beamed at her and nodded at her plus one. "Jabari, this is my best friend, Anaya."

Oh, so this is Jabari. Very interesting.

"Sophie said a lot of nice things aboutchu," Jabari said. The compliment couldn't be reciprocated. Sophie had left out critical details about Jabari's exotic handsomeness. Two large cornrows hung past his shoulders, and his blazer was as baggy as his jeans. Though the hip-hop attire was questionable, Anaya was a sucker for a beard.

"Well, that's nice to hear. I'm glad you could make it."

"Wouldn't miss it."

Sophie latched onto Jabari's arm. "Did you do all this yourself, Anaya?"

"I did." Anaya smiled proudly. "With a little help from the caterers."

"Wow," Jabari said.

Sophie beamed again. "Anaya has always been super creative. She's also good in the kitchen."

Anaya shrugged under the praise. "I learned a lot from my mom."

"I see. Cool," Jabari said.

A man of few words. Okay, Sophia, I see you.

The front door opened and shut, and Anaya glanced over to see Uncle Allen holding a bottle of Roscoe's favorite cooking oil. She looked back at Jabari.

"Jabari, it is a pleasure. I hate to run off, but I have to get ready to serve. Help yourself to whatever you want to eat and drink. Dinner will be served soon."

"Look at you," Sophie teased. "Miss Hostess-with-the-Mostess. Dinner will be served soon."

Anaya waved her off and went over to greet Allen and take his coat and gift. He was far more reserved than usual, and Anaya couldn't help but watch him hesitantly approach his wife. Marie spoke to him briefly as Aunt Deb and Marguerite watched her every move with pursed lips.

Anaya hung up his coat and went into the dining room. She checked over her list one last time to ensure everything was perfect and called everybody to the table. Ten minutes later, they were all finally seated, including Ava's boys at the breakfast table Anaya had set up for them. Roscoe sat at one end of the table closest to Riley, Troy, Uncle Allen and Marie. Aunt Deb sat at the other end next to Cousin Marguerite, Sophie and Jabari. Anaya and Carl sat in the middle of the group next to Ava and Joe and across from Catie and Antoine. When Roscoe asked Joe to bless the food, Anaya cringed. By the time he thanked God for the food, family, the gift of life, the great weather, those getting ready to eat the food, and those who had prepared it, Anaya was sure the food was cold. She was ready to punch him.

So was Catie.

"That was some prayer there, Joe," Catie said sarcastically. "You sure you covered everything?"

Carl hid his laugh behind a cough into his napkin.

"I try," Joe gushed. Anaya didn't know if Ava had learned to be so peppy from Joe or vice versa. "God is merciful, and I try not to miss an opportunity to thank him." Ava beamed like he had just made the inaugural address.

Catie watched in fascination as Joe pile food on his plate. Her jaw dropped lower with each serving he scooped.

Anaya caught Catie's eye and raised her eyebrows. *Stop staring*, she mouthed.

"I've been thinking about investing in more property," Deb was saying at the other end of the table.

"That's a great idea," Marguerite replied, chewing loudly.

"Are you going to eat all of that, Joe?" Catie's eyes were fixated on Joe. She didn't seem to care about Aunt Deb or her property interests.

Anaya shifted her attention back to Catie with a warning glare.

"Yeah, I'm hungry." Joe laughed. He didn't seem to realize he was being insulted.

Anaya took a deep breath and a long, slow drink of water.

"That's the same question I was going to ask you, Marguerite," Deb said loudly. "Do you think you should have any more of that bread? You had about twenty of them quiches in the kitchen earlier."

Marguerite ignored Deb and grabbed another roll. Deb started muttering to herself about the car accident, and then about a ring she lost during the Civil Rights movement. Anaya had heard her stories a hundred times before, and it was easy to tune her out.

"Catie, I'm excited to hear about the baby! Do you want a girl?" Marguerite asked between bites. Enthusiasm poured from her pretty, chubby face.

"We just want a healthy baby," Catie replied. She didn't acknowledge Antoine, who appeared focused on his food.

"When are you due?"

"November."

"Ah, that's my birthday month," Marie said, sipping more wine. *How many glasses had she had?* "Hopefully you'll have the baby on my birthday."

The conversation at Roscoe's end of the table was all basketball.

"I ain't trying to make excuses, but every team goes through a transition period, ya know?" Riley said to Uncle Allen and Roscoe.

"Now that's true," Uncle Allen said. "One year you can be in the championships, and two years later you can be trash."

Marie leaned towards Allen and nodded enthusiastically. "Yep. I remember when I did my first Spartan Race. The first one was great but the following year, my time was awful. I could hardly get over some of those obstacles. It was burpees all day for me." She chuckled at the memory. Uncle Allen rolled his eyes.

"I knew something was going to crash, but I thought it was the charts, not a car," Deb said from the other end of the table.

"So how many more rolls do you think you can eat, Joe?" Catie feigned an innocent, interested expression.

Joe was about to reply through a bite of roll, but Anaya interrupted.

"Catie, can you help me in the kitchen?"

"I'm pregnant." Catie waved her hand. "Ask Sophie or Ava. I'm too big to be running around the kitchen." She leaned on one elbow. "So, Joe—"

"I'd still like you to help me," Anaya insisted.

"Why do you feel incapable of helping with the food, Catie?" Sophie asked.

"What the heck?"

"I'm just asking. What about food service gives you negative thoughts or feelings? Ny simply asked you to help her."

Catie would prefer to cook the entire meal from scratch in an itchy bathing suit rather than engage Sophie in one of her psychobabble conversations. Anaya mouthed a *thank you* to Sophie as Catie got up and waddled behind Anaya into the kitchen.

"Not tonight," Anaya said, ushering Catie into the pantry. "Not at Roscoe's birthday dinner."

"What are you talking about? No one is trying to ruin Roscoe's birthday dinner."

"You know what I'm talking about. Do not assassinate Joe tonight. It's not the right time."

Catie crossed her arms. "Anaya, I'm not trying to assassinate anybody. I'm carrying life, fool. He's the one out there praying for world peace and cures for the incurable instead of the meal. And why does he have to eat so much food? Isn't gluttony and greed a sin? Thou shalt not eat more than a football squad in one sitting? And those poor kids, have they ever been disciplined? They are awful."

"Catie, stop it," Anaya hissed. "I don't want any drama. Be nice to Joe!"

Catie pouted, and Anaya sighed.

"I agree Joe needs a job. But we aren't going to talk about that tonight. Maybe you can invite him to lunch or something if you want to talk about this so badly."

"I can't afford to take him to lunch. You see the way he eats."

"Catie!"

"I'm just trying to keep it real."

"Catie, mind your own business and carry this bread out to the table so we won't look suspicious."

"But Marguerite is gonna eat it all up," Catie said.

"Shut up and take it."

"Wait. Before we go, can we talk about how fine Jabari is?"

Anaya smiled. "Right? Now I see why Sophie gave him so many chances."

"He looks like the prime minister of Dubai. But he needs to stay off his phone."

"You noticed that too?" Anaya asked.

"Girl, I notice everything. I notice you undressing Carl with your nasty little eyes too. Y'all need to just move in together." Catie frowned as Anaya pushed the pan of bread towards her again. "I'm not carrying that."

"Catie, take the stupid bread."

"Ny, I'm wearing Marchesa. Read my lips, *Mar-ches-a*. I'm not carrying buttery bread in this ensemble. Call someone else to do that."

"Fine. I'll just get Sophie to come in here to help us figure out why you are incapable of carrying bread."

"Ugh. You don't play fair." She grabbed the bread.

"Never said I did."

Catie held the bread at arm's length and dropped it in the center of the table. Marguerite reached across Carl to get a piece, and Joe picked up three slices. Aunt Deb rolled her eyes. Anaya slid into her seat and gave Carl's hand a quick squeeze.

"Ooh, this bread is delicious," Marguerite crooned.

"Chitty chitty bang bang. Even better warm." Joe took a huge bite.

"All right," Troy said. "Game time!"

"Not now, love muffin." Riley put his hand on hers. "Let's play a game later."

"Fine. Then let's talk." She said in her baritone and pushed back her chair. "Who thinks it's okay to keep secrets from your partner?"

Her question was met with initial silence. Anaya felt a pang of guilt. She hadn't told Carl—or the girls—about her lunch with Jeff last week. *Oh boy. How is this going to play out?*

"I'd rather play the game," Catie mumbled.

"Me too," Ava said disapprovingly. "That's not a fun topic."

Sophie was in the gleeful minority. "Now that's deep right there." Her eyes brightened and she pointed an approving finger at Troy. "Deep, my friend. Deep."

"Yeah. Too deep," Marie said into her wine glass.

"How did crickets get into the carpet?" Deb asked, standing up to examine her feet.

"*Secrets* from your *partner*, Aunt Deb," Marie said loudly. "Is it okay to keep secrets from your partner?"

"Well, I know all about keeping secrets. I'll tell y'all about it right after I find my passport. I left it right on that table over there." And off she went into the living room.

Riley seemed resigned to letting Troy talk about what she wanted. At one previous family gathering, her game had caused a serious dispute. Hopefully this time would be different.

"I don't think it's good," he finally said. He seemed hesitant to participate in the discussion.

"I agree," Roscoe said from his end of the table. "Anita and I never kept secrets. It's not necessary."

"Okay, okay," Troy said, nodding her head.

"Under certain circumstances, it might be," Marie said suddenly. All heads swiveled in her direction, and she sipped more wine.

"I don't know," Sophie interjected, sighing dramatically. "Secrets create barriers and can be poisonous. They destroy the fabric of a relationship from the inside, and it is difficult, if not impossible, to rebuild trust once it's destroyed. Eventually the secret will come out, so it's best to either tell your partner or just not do anything that you have to keep secret."

Anaya and Catie exchanged looks. Sophie lived for these relationship topics, and it would be hard to stop her now.

"It's not always that simple," Marie sniffed, gulping more wine.

"Oh no?" Allen said, folding his arms and sitting back in his chair. "And why isn't it?"

"Well," said Troy, oblivious to Marie and Allen's rift. "Sometimes you keep secrets to protect a person or surprise a person or even to prevent an argument. It's not always bad to keep secrets unless you are doing something wrong."

"It certainly is always bad," said Allen, staring at Marie.

And cut. Anaya jumped up. "I think it's time for cake!" she declared. She almost ran into the kitchen and quickly returned with the three-layered double chocolate cake that she knew Roscoe would love. When everyone had a slice, Uncle Allen lifted his glass in a toast to Roscoe.

"You've been through a lot and you are still standing. You are a good father and a good friend. Happy birthday, man."

"Here, here!" They all toasted Roscoe, and Marie led them in singing "Happy Birthday."

Roscoe glowed from the praise and attention. He didn't like a lot of attention, but he was always happy to be surrounded by family and friends. This was the first time he'd celebrated a birthday since Anita died. Joshua jumped on his lap. Roscoe thanked everyone for coming.

"Life is nothing without family," he said, holding his water glass in the air. "To family."

"Here, here."

After another round of tea and coffee, the boys were falling asleep in their plates and Aunt Deb recalled another Uncle Farley story and asked for green olives. Ava and Joe packed up the boys and left with Riley and Troy right behind them.

"Good night, niece. Everything was beautiful," Riley said. Anaya hugged him goodbye and waved to Troy.

"This was the most beautiful dinner ever, Anaya," Deb gushed as she fastened her cloak around her shoulders then whispered, "I hope Marguerite didn't eat too much and you have something for tomorrow."

"No, Auntie, it was fine," Anaya said. When she hugged Marguerite, she whispered. "I'll make it up to you."

"Drive safely, you two," Anaya called after them as the pair departed.

Roscoe and Allen went into the living room to watch Sports Center while Catie, Antoine, Jabari, and Marie sat at the dining room watching Anaya, Carl, and Sophie clean up.

"That was fun, Ny," Catie said, swirling her ginger ale.

"Yeah, babe. I'm impressed," Carl said, balancing several dishes on his arm as he walked to the kitchen. "Is there anything you can't do?"

She smiled and kissed him carefully on the lips as he passed by.

"Nope," Marie slurred, standing up for a refill. "She's like her mama. She can do anything."

"Thanks for all of your help, you guys. I couldn't have done it without you." Anaya bumped Catie gently with her hip as she gathered the last dishes off the table. "I have one more party to plan, and then I'm done for the year."

"Yes ma'am," Catie said. "My shower and I know it's going to be bomb-dot-com. Just like this party was. Roscoe looked so happy."

"Bomb-dot-com, huh?" Anaya laughed. She deftly replaced Marie's wine glass with a glass of water. Enough was enough for one night. "That's a pretty high standard."

"Well," Marie said, "if anyone . . . *hic* . . . can do bomb-dot-com . . . *hic* . . . it is my niece. Because she . . . *hic* . . . is the bomb." Marie plopped into a chair and almost fell into Antoine's lap.

"Uh, Ny." Catie raised an eyebrow and nodded towards Marie. "Get ya auntie."

"She's okay," Antoine said, helping Marie into her own chair. Marie sat back with her eyes closed.

Catie turned to glare at him. "Oh, she is? So you like women falling all over your lap? Probably like them rubbing all over your body, too, huh?"

"What? No." Antoine protested. "I'm just saying she's okay. It's Aunt Marie. I know she had a few glasses of wine. Chill."

Anaya and Sophie exchanged a glance.

Marie sat up, took a sip of water, then looked at the glass

morosely. "I gave Allen . . . *hic* . . . two beautiful children. I made mistakes, I know I did, but I didn't mess up all by myself. He hardly . . . *hic* . . . ever looks at me anymore, you know? I work out every day. I look damn good, and every compliment I receive comes from someone other than my husband. Can . . . *hic* . . . you imagine?"

"Nope," Catie said quickly. Anaya shot her a glare.

"Affection . . . *hic* . . . and attention should come from my husband, not someone else," Marie moaned.

"Auntie, I think that's enough. You want some coffee?" Anaya turned to Sophie. "Can you make some coffee?"

"Anaya," Catie said, putting her feet up on a chair. "You sure do know how to throw a party."

TWELVE

The morning after Roscoe's party, Anaya made omelets. She barely touched hers but drank two cups of coffee while Roscoe talked about the logistics of airstrikes. She had stayed up late putting the house back in order and thinking about her lunch with Jeff. The idea of working with him made her nervous. She didn't know if they could just move forward like they didn't have history. She nodded intermittently, only half-listening to her dad.

"I guess I've probably already told you about the F-22 Raptor," said Roscoe, sensing her distraction.

"What?"

He smiled. "I said I've already told you about the F-22. What's going on baby girl? Talk to me."

Anaya wasn't one for complaining, but she needed to get this off of her chest. "My boss Wendy makes me sick. Sometimes I just want to go off on her. Or smash a pie in her smug little face." Anaya sipped the last of her coffee. "She tries to make my life miserable because she doesn't have one. "

Roscoe nodded. "You ever see a stealth bomber?"

Oh Lord. Where are you going with this? "Nope," she replied honestly. It sounded like an ugly jacket.

His eyes lit up. "See, the B-21 stealth bomber is designed to perform at low altitudes to be effective against low-frequency radars." He put his hand near the floor. "This woman Wendy can only fly so high, but you aren't limited like that. Never allow yourself to be effective at low altitudes. Keep it high level, baby girl. Always keep it high level."

Ah. Okay. "Thank you, Dad."

The front door opened and closed and Anaya frowned. She wished her father would let her confiscate Ava's house key. This was the second time in two weeks her sister had shown up unannounced. Ava was up to something.

"Good morning, family." Ava walked into the kitchen wearing a colorful caftan and headdress, demonstrating her latest preference for Afrocentric outfits.

"What are you doing here? Where are the boys?"

"Stop frowning, Anaya, before your face gets stuck." Ava sounded like their mom. "Can't I have breakfast with my father and sister without interrogation or suspicion? And the boys are with Joe. He's their parent too, you know." Ava sat down but did not touch the omelet Anaya slid toward her.

Anaya tried not to be annoyed with the early morning drama, but if it walked and talked like a dog, then it was probably a poodle, and Ava's early morning visit reeked of canine. Anaya knew her sister well enough to know Ava had something up her Kente cloth sleeve.

As Ava launched into a list of her problems and the latest cancer statistics, gesticulating wildly as she did, Anaya noticed something. "Where is your wedding ring, Ava?"

Ava looked at her in surprise, then smiled smugly. "It doesn't fit."

"What do you mean, it doesn't fit?" Anaya asked.

Roscoe stopped chewing his food and looked from one daughter to the other.

"It doesn't fit because I've gained a little weight. I'm pregnant!" She put both of her arms in the air as if she was going to give birth to baby Jesus.

Please, God, let this be a bad joke. "You're what?"

"I'm pregnant." Ava tightened the loose fabric over her middle until the little bulge became obvious. "You will have another little niece or nephew in about five months. And Daddy, you will be a grandfather again. We are hoping for a girl this time."

Instead of hoping for a girl, Ava should be hoping for a job. Or to win the lottery. She didn't want to bond over breakfast, she wanted to drop her pregnancy bomb on them. Anaya sat back and tapped her fingers on the table. She calculated the numbers in her head.

"Wait. You are *four* months pregnant?" Ava appeared much smaller than Catie, who was five months and looked as if she were carrying twins, but it explained why Ava had been dressing like a tribeless princess lately with the wide dresses and overalls.

Ava giggled. "Look at you with that quick math. You should have graduated summa cum laude like I did."

"Ava, don't play with me. This is not funny."

"What's wrong with you? You should be happy, but you are over there acting all mad."

"Whatever, Ava." Anaya shook her head.

"Don't shake your head," Ava said. "Speak your mind. Do you want to judge me? Let he who is without sin cast the first stone, sister dear."

Anaya slammed her hand down on the table. "Do *not* come over here early in the morning quoting scriptures and dropping pregnancy bombs, Ava."

Roscoe put his hand over Anaya's. "Calm down, Ny."

"Don't bridle her words, Dad. Let her speak her mind and get it out," Ava said.

"Ava," Anaya warned with a wave of her index finger. "You don't want me to speak." Anaya stood, sat back down, and then stood up again. She was livid. After all the loans and support she'd given Ava and Joe over the years, the best her sister could do was to get pregnant. Again.

"I do, Anaya. There's tension between us, and I want it gone. Please tell me what's bothering you. You are obviously not happy about my pregnancy, and I'd like to know why."

"Ava." Anaya spoke slowly as if English was Ava's second language. "I've told you before, and I'll tell you again. I'm concerned that you and Joe already have three boys that you can't support financially." She took a long pause to make sure Ava was still with her. "Another baby will make things even harder for you. Daddy and I love you, and we support you, but I can't keep writing checks to support your family. It's not fair to me, and frankly, it's not fair to the boys."

"I see what you are saying," Ava said. "You have been a big help to us, Anaya, and I appreciate you more than you know. I didn't realize things would get this tough for us, but I know God has a plan, and I know that our breakthrough is coming. As soon as Joe gets this DVD out, I believe things are going to get better for us."

Anaya almost fell out of her chair.

"What DVD?" Roscoe asked.

Ava filled her dad in on the exercise video. Roscoe looked genuinely confused.

"Ava, why would people buy Joe's exercise DVD?" he asked. "Does he have a following I don't know about? Experience in making exercise videos? Why would this guy choose him?"

Ava waved a dismissive hand. "I don't know about his following, but he's in great shape, and I believe this is his calling." When Roscoe and Anaya looked back with blank expressions, tears filled Ava's eyes. "I just need to have your support. I'm not talking about financially. I need you to approve of me and love me. I can't live without that."

Give me a break.

Roscoe stood up and hugged his youngest daughter. Anaya sat in her seat and stared at her sister and father. She was still processing the news.

"Honey, it's going to be okay," Roscoe assured Ava as she sobbed. He gently rubbed her back.

"Daddy, you know it's been tough on us, and with this new baby coming, we are going to need to save our money even more," Ava said.

"I know, honey, and you know I will help you in any way I can," Roscoe said.

"You will?"

"Of course I will," Roscoe exclaimed.

Ava lifted her head from his shoulder and looked at him through her tears. "Well, I was wondering if maybe we could stay here until after the baby is born. That way we can save and get a bigger place."

Anaya choked on her coffee. She started coughing, and Roscoe reached over and raised Anaya's hands above her head like he had done when they were children.

"Breathe, baby girl."

Anaya finally caught her breath. With her eyes still watery from her coughing spell, she looked up at Roscoe and waited for his response to Ava's request. They had just gotten the house comfortable for the two of them. Andrew's room was cleaned out and everything was in order. They didn't have space for Ava and her entire family to move in. *Say no, Daddy.*

"Please, Daddy," Ava begged. "Joe and I can sleep in my old room, and the boys can take the extra room. I will put bunk beds in there."

Anaya couldn't keep quiet any longer. "Excuse me, that extra room is now my office, and there will be no bunk beds in there."

"I'm not talking about your precious office, Anaya." Ava turned her top lip up. "I'm talking about the small area between our rooms. We don't use it, and there is plenty of space for bunk beds and the boys' things."

"That's the media room."

"We don't use it. We don't even need a media room."

"Who is this 'we' you speak of? You don't live here anymore,

Ava. You have a family, and now you are trying to move your family into the space that Dad and I use. It's not a good idea. You and Joe need your privacy as husband and wife, and parents."

Ava clasped her hands together. "It's what we need right now. Until we find better jobs, we need to save as much money as we can."

Anaya knew how Roscoe was going to respond. He was going to let Ava stay. His baby girl needed help, and nothing would stop him from helping her. This was a battle Anaya wouldn't win.

She put her dishes in the sink and walked out of the kitchen.

THIRTEEN

A naya flicked through her *InStyle* magazine with her feet perched on her desk. It was impossible to get any work done with the barrage of protesters outside her office window yelling and blowing whistles. Another day, another protest in the name of social justice and reform. It didn't matter that county administration had no authority over the school district's budget that the group was protesting, nor did it seem significant that the state office that actually had jurisdiction was just down the street. County Hall had turned into the de facto landmark for protests, complaints, and quests for fairness, and the county staff simply had to deal with it. When she could no longer be distracted by couture, she closed her window.

Her phone beeped and she picked it up to see a text from Jayde saying she was going to stop by. Anaya hadn't seen Jayde for the past two weeks; recently, her friend always had an excuse for why they couldn't have their weekly lunch. She'd have to ask Jayde what was going on.

Anaya tried to read through a report for a new children's center but kept getting distracted by the chants, barking dogs, and the hovering police helicopter. Her eyes drifted back to the open magazine, and she tried to ignore the green, knotted sandals that were screaming her name. Through her open door, she overheard some staff at Natalie's desk chatting about the RFP for the naval base contracts. She walked to the door to eavesdrop a little.

"These developers are going to make a ton of money off the naval base and won't even hire the local contactors so they can get a piece of the pie. It's not fair," a male voice commented. It was followed by murmurs of assent from others.

Not what I was expecting to hear, but still interesting.

"Yeah, but you can't force them to hire folks if they don't want to. Just like you can't force people to pay child support or pick their children up from swim practice on time." That was definitely Natalie.

There was a long pause before someone said, "True, but that doesn't make it right."

Anaya stepped out of her office and addressed the group. "Actually we can kind of force them to hire who we want. To an extent."

"What do you mean, boss lady?" Natalie asked.

"Developers can't come in and make money off our backs without a contribution. The supervisors won't allow it. In the case of the naval base, we have included many community benefits but one of our conditions is local hiring." She leaned against her doorway and folded her arms.

"I agree," a woman said. "My husband has been living here for over thirty years, and he's a plumbing contractor. It would be nice if he were at least given a chance to bid on some of the work on that base."

"Didn't he qualify to submit a proposal?" Anaya asked.

The woman shrugged. "He didn't receive a request to submit for the job. When my husband called the county, someone told him it was a restricted request, and he didn't receive the submission information because he didn't qualify."

Anaya shook her head slowly. "But the request for proposals went out to all registered contractors. Is your husband registered with the county?"

"Of course."

"I'm confused," Natalie said. "Boss lady, what's the difference between the requests for proposals and the development agreement? I thought it was the same thing?"

"Well," Anaya said moving closer to the group, "the development agreement is the overall plan for the navy base that details how many units will be residential, commercial, and so on. It also sets a benchmark of how many local developers need to be involved, what green spaces will be created, and other community beneficial projects. The RFP is what the county sends out to potential developers to see who has the capacity to do the work and who will charge us the least. Does that make sense?"

"Now it does," Natalie said. "But if the RFP is supposed to go out to all registered contractors, why didn't some people receive it?"

Anaya fumed. Someone from Wendy's office sent out the RFP with the restricted terms, despite Anaya's objection. That was a shrewd move, but not totally unexpected. Wendy had made it clear that she wanted the list of contractors to be restricted because of the use of explosives and was not above sneaking behind Anaya's back to do so. And while Wendy needed Anaya to sign off on the final development agreement, she didn't need Anaya's approval to send out the RFP.

When the unions find out, Wendy will have hell to pay.

Jayde entered the office and broke up the party before Anaya had a chance to respond. She was happy for the interruption. She didn't want to let on that there was a hole in the process until she figured out how to patch it. She had become accustomed to Wendy's micromanaging, but this was going too far.

"Hey everybody," Jayde said, looking regal in a dark purple skirt suit that looked like it cost more than Anaya's monthly salary.

Anaya led Jayde into her office and closed the door. She decided not to mention the RFP right away. They hadn't gotten together in a long time and she didn't want to start off by griping about work. Not yet, at least.

"What's up, short-timer?" Anaya teased Jayde regarding her pending retirement. It was still two years away, but Jayde didn't let Anaya forget it was coming.

"That's right. Just two more years and I can leave this hellhole that sucked up three decades of my livelihood, my integrity, *and* my schoolgirl figure."

Anaya was taken aback by Jayde's bitter tone. She knew Jayde had been passed over for a couple of promotions, and didn't agree with everything the administration did, but she had never spoken in such a hostile manner about the county. Jayde was well respected among her peers, the supes, and the community at large. Her extensive institutional knowledge and no-nonsense compliance monitoring earned her a reputation as the de facto Ethics Police. Jayde held everyone—including Wendy and the board members—accountable. She had worked her way up from receptionist twenty-nine years ago. She didn't bend the rules, extend deadlines, or tolerate gifts of public funds. She was an asset to the county and Anaya admired her work ethic and her ability to stand up to Wendy.

"So where have you been? I've been calling and texting about lunch."

Jayde sighed. "I know. Things have been crazy. My office is getting ready for the ballot measures coming forward in November, so I'm just stretched."

Of course, the ballot measures. "Well, I know the meaning of stretched, trust me."

"Well," Jayde looked across the room, "I only have two years until I retire, but you have much longer. Why don't you consider going someplace that appreciates you?" She looked around Anaya's office and chuckled darkly. "Get out of this forsaken place."

Although she was again taken aback by Jayde's hostility, Anaya slowly nodded. This was a familiar question, and the simple answer was that she wasn't ready to leave yet. But she didn't think Jayde was expecting an answer. There was something in Jayde's eyes that Anaya hadn't seen before—something distant and determined.

Jayde suddenly snapped back to the moment and grinned at Anaya. "Anyway, I came here to check on you to see how everything is going with the project. Did you guys select a contractor yet?"

"I haven't received any of the bids yet."

"It's probably going to happen soon." Jayde glanced at her cell phone then dropped it back into her large leather tote. "Well, hang in there. And be careful with Wendy. She's all about herself. All that talk about organization cohesiveness and team player excellence is a bunch of bull. This project will bring out new things in her."

"Don't worry," Anaya said looking at Jayde as if she were trying to see her thoughts. "At first, I was excited to work on it because it's a good opportunity, but now I just wish it had never crossed my desk. I can't get anything done. Wendy is always breathing down my back and trying to insert herself in places where she doesn't belong. I know she's trying to make a name for herself for that position in the governor's administration, but she's taking things too far." Anaya was getting angry. This wasn't the first time she and Wendy butted heads, but this was the first time that it seemed like Wendy's motives appeared to be personally motivated.

"Wait. *Wendy* sent out the RFP?" Jayde looked shocked.

Oops. "Yes. Well, I mean, someone from her staff did, but she was in the mix."

"That's interesting. What kind of county administrator steps on her community development director's toes with such a huge deal at stake?"

"You got me on that one." Anaya shrugged her shoulders, relieved that she wasn't the only one who thought this entire thing was nuts.

"Do you think she's up to something?" Jayde frowned.

Anaya waved a tired hand. "No, I thought about what you said last time. Wendy is too concerned about getting that promotion with the governor's office to jeopardize this deal. If she's guilty of anything, it's being a horrible manager."

But Jayde was shaking her head. "Not that, Ny. Who's her biggest threat right now? Who makes her look like a sideshow?" She pointed at Anaya. "Maybe Wendy is trying to set you up."

"Huh?" The thought had never even crossed Anaya's mind. How one would even go about trying to throw a wrench in someone else's career by needlessly delaying a massive county project was incomprehensible. "I don't think so, Jayde. The only thing she is up to is micromanaging and getting on my nerves."

"Oh, okay." Jayde snorted. "How is everything else? You and Carl good?"

"Yes." Anaya blushed as she always did when anyone mentioned Carl. "We are good. How about you? How are Nick and the kids?"

"Nick is fine. Working hard like always. The kids are great. My oldest starts Oakland College Prep in a few weeks, if you can believe it, and the other two are in middle school."

"Wow, Oakland College Prep. Nick's new job must be giving him pretty nice bonuses."

"Well, we do okay," Jayde said, shrugging.

Anaya raised her eyebrows. "I would say being able to pay for Oakland College Prep is better than okay."

"We want the best for our children," Jayde said adamantly, if a bit defensively. "Nothing is going to interfere with that."

Anaya tilted her head. "Of course you do," she said slowly.

Jayde stood up abruptly. "All right, Ny. Time's a wastin'. Those ballot measures won't write themselves."

Anaya stood up and hugged her friend. "Thanks for stopping by, Jay. I'll call you next week."

Two seconds after Jayde walked out of Anaya's office, Natalie entered. Anaya thought she could see Natalie's gossip alarm ringing.

"Is Jayde okay?" she asked.

Anaya got up from the sofa and walked over to her desk. "Yes, why would you think otherwise?" She sat behind her computer and typed in her password.

"Well," Natalie said sitting in the seat across from Anaya. "I heard she applied for the deputy director position."

"Of the recreation department?" Anaya asked, raising her eyebrows.

"Yup." Natalie smacked her lips as if she'd eaten something tart. Then she leaned in and whispered dramatically, "I heard she didn't even make it to the interview stage."

Poor Jayde. "When did this happen?"

"Now, boss lady, you know I don't get in people's busi—"

"Natalie," Anaya cut her off. She was not in the mood. "When?"

"I think they received rejection letters yesterday."

So that's what was bothering Jayde. Anaya wanted to call her to say something, but Jayde hadn't mentioned it, so she wouldn't press.

Just two more years, Jayde. Hang in there.

FOURTEEN

W endy's task force included Anaya, Senior County Attorney Sue Garcia, the county's Assistant Finance Director Will Bresnan, and Jeff. Anaya had worked with Sue and Will on other county projects in the past. Jeff and Sue were responsible for reviewing and finalizing the legal aspects of the development agreement and reviewing judgments from previous civil suits and compliance issues to ensure such issues were preventable under the new agreement. Will ran all the financials and Anaya managed the community benefit portion. Given their already tight workloads, the group agreed the best meeting times were evenings and weekends. Anaya had worked on big projects before so she was okay working extra hours temporarily. She didn't appreciate Wendy's overstepping, but with so much on her plate, she had to choose her battles wisely. If nothing else, the Task Force offered extra sets of eyes.

They met in an office reserved for consultants on the ground floor of the administration building. It was a small room that felt very full with four desks and boxes from previous projects piled high against the walls. There was a large whiteboard in the center of the room and an old printer that produced when it wanted to. Jeff sat at the desk near the wall, furthest from Anaya, who was near the whiteboard.

At first, Anaya had felt awkward about working with Jeff, but he had acted nothing but professional. Since Sue and Will didn't know their romantic history, it was relatively easy for Anaya to act like she and Jeff were just getting to know each other. She had never seen Jeff's professional side, and it was like getting to know him for the first time.

"Ho-lee shit," Sue said.

Anaya looked up from an insurance report from one of the contractors. The task force had started working early that Saturday morning and it was almost six in the evening.

"What's up, Sue?"

Sue's eyes were bright as she met Anaya's curious gaze. "I just got an email from a friend at the DAs office. Keep it in this room, but it looks like there is going to be a grand jury investigation into the RFP process and the contract negotiations with the base."

Anaya's jaw dropped. "No way! Someone from Wendy's staff issued the RFP a couple of weeks ago, and I overheard my staff talking about it, and I told Wendy I thought it was unnecessarily restricted. But how would the DA get wind so fast?"

"Why is the county administrator's office sending out RFP's?" Jeff frowned.

Anaya sighed. "That's a whole other story. We don't have time to go into Wendy's power hungriness."

"Yeah," Sue agreed. "I am familiar with that."

"Well, if you heard your staff talking about the RFP, other people are probably talking about it too," Jeff said. "Which is how the DA probably got wind of it."

"Exactly," Sue confirmed, her eyes moving across her computer screen as she reread the email. "The tip came from a whistleblower. And since it's an active RFP, the DA had to make it a high priority."

"Does Wendy know?" Anaya asked.

"Oh, she knows," Sue hissed.

"Wow," Jeff said.

Anaya nodded, thoughts in a whirlwind. After hearing the rumors from her staff, she had tried to get hold of Wendy to figure out what had happened with the RFP, but Wendy had ignored her calls, emails, and office visits, citing that she was "too busy to talk". Anaya had eventually given up, resigned to seeing how it played out. But if the DA was looking into the RFP and found that it was inappropriately restricted, the blame would fall on Anaya's office. "Trying your best" didn't usually hold up in a court of law.

"So what are you guys thinking?" Will asked. "Does the DA's investigation change anything for us?"

Jeff looked at Anaya and said, "Anaya, I know you won't like this, but you need to bring Wendy's belligerence to the board's attention as soon as possible so they can force her to give you the database code and we can reissue that RFP if we need to."

Anaya had thought about this option as well, but it was basically a death sentence for her career. No one would want to work with someone who went over their boss's head to tell the board about a mistake. If she spoke to the board, she would never be promoted again.

But she didn't want to explain that to Jeff, who was looking at her like she could save the day.

"I don't know, Jeff. I don't think the supes would appreciate me breaking the chain of command to complain to them about my boss."

Jeff looked at her incredulously. "You have to. That's what we are here for. We can't let Wendy get away with keeping a project of this magnitude from local, qualified bidders."

"I agree," Anaya nodded.

"Anaya, isn't there a closed session coming up in a couple of weeks?" Jeff asked.

"Yes." Sessions closed to the public included sensitive topics like potential litigation, personnel issues, and real estate purchases or development. Closed session meetings were attended by the board, the county attorney, and any department heads who were presenting.

"Make the announcement then."

"Let me think about it. For now, we just keep doing what we're doing. Missing our deadline won't make anything better."

The room quieted as everyone returned to sifting through documents or typing away on their laptops. Anaya breathed a sigh of relief, actually glad to have the insurance report to distract her.

✳

Three hours later, Sue stood up and stretched. "I need to get out of here. Anybody want tea? I'm going stir crazy."

"Me too," Will said. "Can I go with you?"

"Sure," Sue said. "Anaya, Jeff? You guys wanna come, or do you want anything?"

"No, thank you," Jeff said. "I'm going to rough it out."

"Nothing for me," Anaya said, yawning. "I'm going to plough through these community benefit reports."

"All right, you two masochists, if you change your mind in the next twenty minutes, give me a call," Sue said on her way out.

After Sue and Will were gone, Anaya buried her face in her hands.

"I'm so tired," she sighed. Her phone buzzed. Carl had texted her to see if she'd be able to come over.

The knot in her stomach twisted a little tighter. She still hadn't told Carl and the girls that she was working with Jeff. She sent Carl a quick text back saying it would be another late night. It was the second time she had turned down an invitation from him that day—she had already declined a lunch date with him. Anaya had been busy with the task force; she wasn't trying to avoid Carl to spend time with the bearded attorney she was alone with at the moment.

She looked up and saw Jeff looking at her expectantly.

"I'm sorry, what did you say, Jeff?"

He gave her a look. "I said, yeah, it's a lot of work, but the good news is we're in the home stretch." Jeff rubbed his palms together.

Bless your heart. His optimism was darling but terribly illusory. She didn't want to crush his vibe, but they were far from the home stretch. Even if they managed to make sense of the numbers and reports, Anaya had a feeling that this was going to be tougher than they thought. There was too much history with the base. The public would want assurances of safety, and the supes would want assurance of jobs. It was doable, but it wouldn't be easy.

"I really just wanna go for a run." She rubbed her temples. Her head pounded and she could use a Zantac. Between the long hours, Ava taking over the house, and planning Catie's baby shower, she hadn't had a chance to run. She felt like a chunky biscuit.

"That sounds good," Jeff said. "You know, I didn't believe you when you told me that running was relaxing." He wagged a finger at her. "Now I'm a believer." She used to like it when he wagged his finger at her that way.

"Told you." She threw a paperclip at him. "You should've listened to me the first time."

"Yeah." He looked at his hands. "You told me a lot of things I should have listened to."

Oh, Jesus. Anaya stretched her arms above her head, trying to be casual. "How are you feeling about working together? Are you okay with it?" They had to talk about it eventually.

"The truth?" His eyes danced as if he'd been waiting for her to ask that question.

That's why I asked. "Please."

"It's hard," he said, then paused as if he were thinking about what to say next. "I respect your job. It's nice to see how successful you have become. It's actually pretty incredible to watch you morph from one of my students to this boss. Sometimes when I look at you, I see this pint-sized shot-caller. Other times, I see the woman I fell in love with years ago, and I just want to wrap my arms around you and—"

What the feezy?

"Wait. Whoa." She made the timeout signal with her hands.

"Too much?"

"I'd say so. I thought we were going to keep things professional and leave the past in the past. I wasn't expecting . . . all that."

"My bad. You said you wanted the truth."

"Yeah, let's start with small doses of the truth."

"Fair enough," he said. "I like working with you, and Sue and Will are great." He smiled. "Better?"

"Much." She sighed, trying to process the fact that Jeff still thought about her like *that*. It made her feel warm and tingly, and that made her even more irritated. She didn't want to complicate things even more. It was nice seeing him again and getting to know him in a different way, but she was in love with Carl. At least, that's what she told herself. "I just want this project to be over."

"I know. Just hang in there, old soldier."

"My mom used to say that."

"I know."

"I'm surprised you remember that."

"I remember everything about you," he said tightly.

Too much, too much, too much. Back to work. She picked up a report. She didn't care if it was rude. He crossed the line one too many times tonight, first with the love confession, then recalling notable memories of her mom.

"Does it bother you?"

She continued staring at the report. "Does *what* bother me?" Irritation glazed her tone.

"Well, at first I was gonna ask if working together bothers you, but now I'm wondering if it bothers you to read legal contracts upside down."

Crap. She shook her head. "Nah, that's okay," she lied. "I mean, sometimes people have good memories." *Sometimes people have good memories? What kind of bumbling response was that?*

"And you're okay working with me here?"

He moved closer and perched on the edge of Sue's desk directly in front of her.

"Yes, you are here," she said, avoiding his gaze. "We are working. Together. It's fine."

"You're lying." He smiled. "Don't forget I know you."

You won't let me forget. "Okay." She finally looked up. "It was a little awkward at first. I mean, I haven't seen you in so long, and then you show up, and . . . it's just different."

"I know. We got this though, right?" He walked over and tilted her face toward him. "We can do this together. No more awkwardness. No more reading upside down reports and walking into doors trying to avoid me." His half smile told her he was teasing.

"Wait, you saw that?" She groaned, wanting to disappear. She had been talking to Carl on the phone last week and Jeff came walking down the hall. She had swerved into what she thought was an open doorway to avoid Jeff, but it had actually been closed. Luckily, she had only damaged her pride and wasn't seriously injured. She was certain Jeff hadn't seen her. Wrong again.

She pulled her chin away, slightly embarrassed, but he caught it again, ever so gently.

"I see everything you do."

She held his gaze, then pushed her chair back to make some space between them. It was getting hot. "I just want this to be as normal as possible. I work with Sue and Will, and I don't want drama. And I want to see this project through."

"Gotcha. No drama. I promise. And this is strictly professional. I have no motivation other than getting this project done as well."

"Okay, cool. Let's keep it profesh."

"Profesh." They shared a fist bump.

They heard Sue and Will talking in the hall, and Jeff returned to his desk. The group worked another hour before Will heaved a huge sigh and pushed away from his desk.

"We've done enough. Let's call it a night." He glanced at Anaya. "You still need a ride home?"

Anaya nodded. Ava had asked to use her car, and she had reluctantly agreed. "I do actually, but I can take an Uber. It's out of your way."

"I'll take you," Jeff quickly offered.

Anaya inhaled slowly and thought fast. *Serenity now.* She didn't want him to take her home because that would make things murky. Trying to keep things profesh meant not driving her home. But then there was a part of her that *did* want him to take her home. There were still so many unspoken words between them. So much history and hurt. It could be worth salvaging the friendship, but at what cost? This could be her chance to try build a platonic friendship with him that wasn't based on attraction or their past. He looked at her with those bedroom eyes that once drove her crazy.

"Um, I can take an Uber. Really."

"Come on," Will said. "There are three people with cars here. We are not letting you take an Uber so choose one."

"It's on my way home," Jeff offered.

"Okay. Sure, thanks."

Will picked up his briefcase and waved. "See y'all tomorrow." Sue was right behind him.

Anaya and Jeff were quiet for the first part of the ride. Memories flooded like the Russian River. They had spent so many hours in the car together and had so many conversations. Many that left Anaya in tears. She shrugged off the memories and felt guilty about not telling Carl that she was working with Jeff. Jeff's car smelled like jasmine. Just the way it used to. She needed to tell Carl soon.

"Long day," he said when they were almost at Anaya's house.

"Yup," she said. "Turn left here."

"I remember." He looked at her from the corner of his eye and she concealed a smile.

He pulled up to the curb in front of her house and she didn't get out. Memories engulfed her of all the times they had sat in this same spot, talking for hours. The way he made her laugh. How she missed him five minutes after he left.

Jeff turned toward her. "Thank you for letting me take you home."

"I should thank you for taking me."

"It was my pleasure."

"Good night," she said.

"Hey," he put his hand on her arm. "We got this, okay? It will be fine."

"Okay," she said quickly getting out of the car before she said or did something she would regret.

She opened the front door carefully, as Joe fell asleep on the couch sometimes. She took off her shoes and almost jumped out of her skin when she sensed something moving in front of her.

Ava was learning against the wall with her lips pursed. "You aren't living right," she said. Even with her crazy hair and nighttime dashiki, in that moment, Ava's tone and bossy demeanor reminded Anaya of their mom.

Anaya put a hand to her chest and let out a slow breath. "Ava, you scared me."

"Since when is somebody standing in a room scary? You aren't living right, dear sister. Who was that man?" Ava said "man" like it was the plague.

"Ava, Mom died, and Dad is upstairs minding his own business like you should be doing. Don't question me. I'm an adult." Anaya walked past her sister and started up the stairs.

"Adults don't creep around, Ny." Ava was right on her heels. "I happen to know that wasn't Carl who dropped you off. It was some other man."

"That's true. Good night." Anaya closed her bedroom door and reached for the Zantac she kept by her bed. There were too many adults under one roof.

FIFTEEN

S ophie didn't typically have dinner so late in the evening, but her dad had come to town just to see her, so she gladly obliged.

She was studying the menu when he arrived. She had wanted her mother to join them, but Carmen had declined.

"Baby girl!" Terry said, excitedly grabbing her in a bear hug.

"Hey, Daddy. Look at you." He was wearing jeans and a t-shirt with a graphic on it and looked ten years younger than he did the last time she saw him. She wasn't one hundred percent sure about his new girl, but she definitely had an effect on his wardrobe. "You cut your hair!"

"Aw, baby girl, just trying to keep up." He rubbed his palm across the top of his head and slid into the booth. He ordered lemonade— one with extra ice for him, and one with no ice for Sophie. He always ordered for Carmen and Sophie when they went out. Carmen hated it, but Sophie didn't.

"Well, you're doing a good job." She poked out her lip. "I guess what's-her-face took you shopping."

"I took myself shopping," he said, poking her nose with his fingertip. "Thank you very much. And her name is Tiffany."

"I know her name." Sophie didn't have any real issues with Tiffany. She just liked to give her dad a hard time. "I think everybody knows her name."

"I guess that's true." He smiled.

Before Tiffany, Sophie could have never imagined her dad dating a reality TV star. Sophie had met Tiffany a few times, and Sophie had been surprised that although Tiffany lacked common sense, she wasn't pretentious, seemed thoughtful, and, according to Terry, was smart and had graduated from USC with a BS in biology.

Despite Sophie's reservations, her dad was happier than she had seen him in a long time and for that, she was pleased. She wished he'd file for divorce already. It wasn't fair to keep leading her mom on.

"So, is she the one?"

"She's the one for right now." He rubbed his goatee pensively.

"I mean, is she legit?" Sophie hadn't been able to tell if Tiffany was yet another opportunist.

"You want to know if she's using me," Terry said matter-of-factly. They had been here before. Whenever Terry dated someone, they always seemed to want something. Her dad deserved true love.

"I wasn't going to say that, but the idea did cross my mind."

"So you don't think your old man is capable of pulling a hot young thing like Tiffany? I still got moves, don't get it twisted. And have you seen these abs?" He pretended he was going to pull up his shirt.

Don't get it twisted? Sophie frowned. "Daddy, don't talk like that."

Terry laughed. "I've been in this game for a long time, baby girl, and I won't let anybody play me," he said soberly. "Tiffany is fun and beautiful, and one of the things I like about her most is that she's got her own thing going on. Never asks me for anything. Never asks to use my connections. I think she really likes me."

"You think so?"

"I do. And if she doesn't, there will be no love lost. I'm not looking to get remarried, I'm just looking for companionship."

"Um, you can't get remarried," Sophie pointed out. "That would be illegal."

He hung his head at the familiar criticism. "You and your mama won't let me forget that."

"Daddy, if you don't want to be with her, then get a divorce. She is holding on to the false hope that if you don't divorce her, you guys are getting back together."

"It's not that simple, baby girl." He rubbed his goatee again.

"And why isn't it?"

"This is California. The laws don't favor me." He spun his glass on its coaster.

"Daddy, are you seriously making this about money? You have plenty of money. You and Mom need closure to move on. Dating someone doesn't give you closure."

"I know."

"I won't go deep on you today," she said, cutting him some slack. "I just want to put it out there."

"Good. I can't deal with deep today." He smiled and she noticed how happy he looked. He was a handsome man with slightly graying hair on the sides.

They ordered food and she talked about her classes and the renovations to her townhouse. Sophie had always gotten along much better with her dad than with her mom. Terry took a call near the restaurant lobby and Sophie wondered how the evening would have gone if Carmen had decided to join them. She'd surely be picking apart what Sophie was eating and wearing. Sophie had never been able to be enough for her mom, even as a little girl.

Sophie looked down at her sparkly red dress and remembered another time she had worn red . . .

✻

Sophie ran into the styling room with her long pig tails flailing behind her. It was December 1997 and she was wearing a red pleated jumper and a crisp white button-down shirt. She knew Mommy would be with Sara getting her hair and makeup done, because that's where Mommy always was after the driver dropped her off after school. Sophie loved watching her mom "put her face on" and talk about her roles in movies, but today, Sophie had exciting news of her own. Her mommy would be so proud.

"Mama! I got the lead in the play," Sophie shouted, holding a pink Tamagotchi in her hand.

Her mother slipped a yellow pill between her full lips before smiling. "Oh my goodness, Sophia, *mi corazon*. That's amazing! But I thought you were going to be a tree."

"I was, but Tammy Decker got the stomach flu, and I was the only one who practiced, and I know all of her lines, so I'm playing the lead! And guess what? I get to wear the new dress you bought me in Hawaii last year. And guess what else? They want me to straighten my hair. Can I get my hair straightened, Mama, please?"

"Whoa, slow down, *mija*." She closed her eyes as Sara applied some kohl. "Of course you can get your hair straightened. Anything for you." Carmen opened her eyes and batted them at herself in the mirror. She was undeniably the most beautiful person Sophie had ever seen, with flawless almond skin and silky black hair.

"Yay!"

"Look at you." Carmen shooed Sara away and opened her arms to Sophie, who jumped into her lap. "So much ambition like your father."

"My play is on Friday." Sophie wiggled around in her mom's lap, excitement bursting out of her.

Her mother held her firmly by the shoulders. "*Un momento, mija*. Don't mess up my makeup."

"Can you and Papa come to my play, please, Mama?"

"Ah, *mija!* Friday is the American Music Awards, and your dad's new artist has been nominated for an award. We are leaving tomorrow night."

Sophie already knew about the American Music Awards, but she had hoped that becoming the lead instead of just being a tree would make her mommy change her mind. Her parents had missed her last play and her dance recital because of other events.

"But, Mama, I'm the lead in the play." Sophie's face fell. How could they miss her debut as the star of the show? She'd finally be a star like Carmen and everyone's parents were going to be there. The teacher had even reserved front row seats for the parents of students with lead roles.

"Don't worry. I can make sure Irma makes it."

"I don't want Irma to come," Sophie pouted, her face turning from sad to dark. "I'll be the only kid with her nanny there instead of her parents." She jumped out of her mother's lap and turned to face her with arms crossed.

Carmen bopped Sophie's nose with a French-manicured finger. "I will also talk to Miss Anita and see if she and Mr. Roscoe will bring Anaya and Ava to see you."

Sophie's face brightened some. She loved the Goodes. They were like family . . . but she wanted her parents there for a change. The Goodes were always there for her. She kicked Carmen's chair.

Carmen rolled her eyes. "*Mija*, please. You know your papa's artists are important. We have to support them. That's how we take you on all the nice trips and pay for that school you love so much, huh?" She pulled Sophie's chin up and tried to kiss her, but Sophie jerked away.

"And when we get back, we are taking you to Disneyworld, and we are going to see Jurassic Park!" Carmen called as Sophie slowly walked out of the room with her shoulders and head down. Just before the door swung shut, she heard her mother say, "Not too much cat-eye. I don't want to look overdone."

Sophie ran to her room and picked up her American Girl doll.

"Beatrice," she said, holding the doll close. "When I grow up, I'm going to have my own family and I am never going to be alone. Never."

SIXTEEN

The morning after Ava had accused her of not living right, Anaya came downstairs early to clean up before brunch with Catie and Sophie. It was her turn to host this month, and she hadn't realized the house would become so uninhabitable once Ava and her family moved in. No matter how many flowers she put in the vases or how many candles she burned, the house looked and smelled a mess. Although Ava and Joe were broke, their kids had a lot of crap.

When Anaya heard the doorbell, she kicked a toy beneath the staircase and rushed to the door.

"What died in here, Ny?" Catie frowned as she entered the house.

"Hi to you too," Anaya said closing the door behind Catie and Sophie.

"I'm sorry. Hi," said Catie. "I know I have a sensitive pregnant palette, but something stinks in here. I hope that's not what we are eating."

"Hey girl" Sophie scrunched up her nose and kissed Anaya on the cheek. She was carrying a fruit salad in an ornate blue glass bowl as she maneuvered down the toy-strewn hallway.

"I'm so sorry." Anaya led them to the kitchen. If these weren't her childhood best friends, Anaya would be embarrassed out of her mind. "Ava cooked dinner last night and the smell just seems to linger. By the way, I invited Ava to brunch too."

"Cool," Sophie said.

Catie sighed and paused to inspect the grimy fish tank—a recent addition to the toy-infested living room. "Are you sure it's not that nasty-looking thing that smells?"

Anaya sighed. "That's possible."

"What did Ava cook last night?" Catie's face seemed stuck in a perpetual frown.

Anaya just shook her head. "You will have to ask her about that."

"How long are they staying again?" Sophie asked.

"Just a few months," Anaya said.

"Yeah right," Catie said, rolling her eyes. "More like a few years."

"Don't say that!" Anaya pleaded. "Give the candles a few more minutes. That might help with the smell."

Anaya had set up the dining table with white orchids, various teas, pastries, and omelets.

"Nice spread, Anaya. This looks beautiful," Catie said, plopping down in the nearest seat.

"Yeah, chica. Impressive," Sophie said, setting her bowl down next to the orchids.

Anaya sat down next to Catie.

"Good morning, ladies." Ava floated into the kitchen wearing a flowery caftan with matching head garb.

"Hey Ava." Sophie hugged her. Catie waved.

"This looks lovely, ladies. Thank you for letting me join you."

"I have a question for you, Ava. What is that awful smell?" Catie ignored Anaya's elbow. "Anaya said it was something you cooked."

Ava beamed at the insult. "Ah. It's kale, tofu, and natto quiche, silly girl. It's delicious too. I made it last night. Natto does have a pungent smell, but it's very high in protein. You should try it." Ava stepped toward the fridge as if to take out leftovers, but Catie held up a hand.

"I'll pass. I'm pregnant. I can't have all that crazy smelling food in my system. It upsets the baby."

"I'm pregnant too, and it doesn't bother me," Ava said innocuously.

Sophie gasped and looked at Anaya with an open mouth. Anaya just nodded. She hadn't told the girls because it was Ava's business.

Catie stood up and walked over to Ava. "Did you say you love eggplant too? Because that's what I hope you said."

Ava filled a glass with water.

"Don't try and ignore me." Catie insisted.

"I said, the smell doesn't bother me," Ava repeated.

"What else did you say?" Catie leaned in towards Ava.

"I'm pregnant." Ava turned and faced her.

Catie stared at Ava and then looked over at Anaya and Sophie and then back at Ava. Eventually, she waddled back to her seat at the table. Ava glided in behind her and sat next to Sophie, who gave her a quick hug and a quiet "Congratulations."

Anaya breathed out a sigh of relief. *That could've gone a lot worse.*

"How far along are you?" Catie asked with her chin in her hands. She was like a kid asking her teacher questions.

"Twenty weeks." Ava looked at her hands. "I'm due in December. I think I'm right behind you, right?"

"Yeah. I'm due in November." Catie paused, then snapped her fingers. "That's why you guys moved in. It all makes sense now." She reached for a pastry but was interrupted by Ava hastily saying grace.

"Now you can eat." Ava took a plate. "I suppose you are going to judge me about being pregnant too?"

"Nope. I'm going to keep it real and admit that I'm not in a position to judge anybody at any time." Catie scarfed down a bite of pastry. "Lord knows I've done my bit of damage in this world. No room for judgment here. No, ma'am." Catie helped herself to an omelet and slid another pastry onto the plate.

"Good," Ava said. "Thank you."

"But I am wondering what the heck you are doing having another baby when you can't take care of the three you already have." Catie's gaze was steady and piercing. It was more intense than disapproving. Like she really expected a profound reason for Ava's predicament.

This ought to be good, Anaya thought. She'd love to know Ava's thought process in all of this.

"It wasn't planned. It was an accident," Ava said defensively, spooning fruit onto her plate.

"Ava, you are grown. If you get pregnant, then it's planned," Catie said, shaking her head. "There is birth control for this type of thing."

"Those hormones cause cancer. I'm not putting that stuff in my body."

"I will ask again," Catie said. "How are you having another baby while you can't take care of the three you have? Where are Shadrach, Meshach, and Abednego anyway?"

"Roscoe took them out so I could enjoy girl time with you guys." Ava smiled, already recovering from Catie's frankness. "And their names are Hezekiah, Jeremiah, and Joshua."

"Same thing." Catie waved her hand. "Seems to me like you and Joe need a little planny-plan."

"The prayers of the righteous availeth much," Ava said self-assuredly.

"As do the struggles of the jobless. What's your point?" Catie shot back.

"I love this white tea, Anaya," Sophie interjected.

Anaya smiled at her, grateful Sophie didn't pick fights. "I knew you would."

Anaya and Sophie served themselves and sat back to watch the show.

"I just believe God's word," Ava was saying. "He's a provider.

Jehovah Jireh." Ava waved her hands and closed her eyes briefly as if a sudden peace had come over her.

"And you should. But let me share something with you, my dear sister. You have to put in the work. Faith without work is dead," Catie said.

Ava raised an eyebrow at Catie.

"Oh yeah, I know you thought I was a total heathen. I've been to church a couple of times in my life. I know a few things."

"Doesn't exactly make you an expert," Ava retorted.

"That's not the point. The point is that Anaya has been holding you up long enough. It's time for you to get out there and make something out of yourself. And not just for you—for your boys."

Anaya avoided eye contact with her sister. She had said almost the same thing to Ava herself a few weeks ago.

Ava straightened in her seat and lifted her chin. "This is only temporary until we can get on our feet. I definitely have a plan."

Anaya looked in surprise at Ava. *Now this I have got to hear.* But Ava didn't divulge any more.

Catie smiled and nodded. "Oh, then I take it Joe found another job since you two are popping out babies like Jay-Z pops champagne bottles. Jobs *must* be part of the plan."

Sophie kicked Catie beneath the table.

"Ouch!" Catie glared at Sophie.

Ava slid out of her chair. "I will be right back."

"Don't look at me like that," Catie said after Ava was out of earshot.

"That was cruel," Sophie said.

"It's all fun and games until it isn't, and the fact that Ava is having another baby is a big deal. Anaya is too darn nice. Y'all know I love Ava like a sister, but the girl needs to hear some truth, and who better to tell her than a friend? It wasn't cruel, it was necessary."

"You hurt her feelings," Sophie said.

"I didn't say anything to Ava that wasn't true. Ny, you *have* been telling your sister that her thick beefcake of a husband needs a steady job, right?"

Anaya played with the grapes on her plate. "Not in the same way you would, but yes, I have told her that she and Joe should get some employment."

"She needs to understand that this is not a game. You and Uncle Roscoe can't be taking care of her and the tribe of Canaan. You know your mom would not allow this madness in her house. For goodness sake, the girl has a turtle in Miss Nita's living room, Ny! What the kerfuffle!"

Anaya found herself unexpectedly defensive. "First of all, I need you to stop talking like a second grader. Say a curse word already. It won't kill your baby. Second, it's not so bad. She's family and family is always welcome." She tried not to think about how annoyed she had gotten when Ava rearranged all the photos in the living room.

"Right. About as welcome as the German occupation." Catie scoffed.

Sophie sighed. "You can be really unpleasant sometimes, you know that, Catie?" She frowned for a moment and turned to Anaya. "I don't agree with Catie's delivery because it stifles communication and feels like an attack, not to mention it brings to memory an awful time in history. However, I agree with her underlying message. Ava has been living off you since she got married. Why can't she get a full-time job like everyone else?"

Anaya shrugged. "She needs to be home with the boys during the day."

"So does every other mom in America, but unfortunately things don't work that way for everyone. Ava needs a job, and so does Joe. I have a couple of self-interest workbooks I can share with her. I also know a life coach I can put her in touch with."

Catie rolled her eyes. "I don't think Ava needs a questionnaire;

she needs to get online and start looking for a job. And where is Joe anyway? He doesn't have a job, so he should be home with all of his seeds." Catie sipped her tea.

"Enough." Anaya was eager to change the subject. She didn't agree with the way Ava managed her life, but she didn't like to see Ava's feelings hurt. "What's going on with you, Catie?"

"Hmph, that's a conversation for another day. We'll be here until next week if I start talking about what's going on with me."

"Try us," Anaya said, biting into a slice of cantaloupe. They hadn't been together since Roscoe's party, and they probably hadn't shared the full details about their lives in their group texts. She certainly hadn't.

"Well, I'm growing wider by the day, trying to run an empire from home, opening a second store, and living with a man who doesn't appreciate my ambition or my swag. So I'd say, same old."

"Aw, chica. That's a lot," Sophie cooed.

"Yeah, and the worst part is that I don't think I'll ever be able to wear Victoria Beckham again. You know she has those slim cuts in her line." She sighed. "And my hips will be doomed after this baby. But I digress. Anaya, you know that you are welcome to stay with Antoine and me for a few days if you ever need to get away from Romper Room. Having you over will give me somebody to talk to since Antoine and I hardly speak."

Catie's casual delivery didn't throw Anaya off. She knew it was serious. "What's going on with you two, Catie? I thought something was off at Daddy's party. You two hardly spoke that night."

"Yeah, and you guys are usually all over each other," Sophie added.

"Well, those days are gone. I know I'm not perfect and I can be a little challenging sometimes—"

"A little?" Sophie broke in.

"Okay, maybe more than a little. Whatever, Sophia. The point is, I don't have the energy like I used to. I'm getting tired, guys.

And the more I try to improve, the farther apart we become. I will only say this once, but . . . I have some issues to work out and growth is hard."

Ava walked back into the room, interrupting Catie's moment. "The best thing you can do is pray and ask God to change you," she said, sitting down.

"I said I have issues to work out. I don't need to change."

"Sure you do." Ava said matter-of factly. "We all do. That's how you make a relationship work. If you stay the same, you won't grow individually which means you can't grow together. It's simple."

Sophie snapped her fingers. "Yes!"

"Oh wow, now I got these two teamed up against me." Catie sighed. "There's no hope."

Anaya laughed. "It's a tough team to argue against."

"Yeah. Joel Osteen and Julie Gottman. I'm in trouble."

Joe walked into the kitchen.

"Babe!" Ava jumped up and hugged him. He spun her in a circle, and beamed at the ladies.

"Aw, all my favorite sisters! Chitty chitty bang bang!" He began to lift Catie in one of his bear hugs, but seemed to think better of it and settled on a normal hug.

That's a first, Anaya thought, trying not to laugh at Catie's horrified expression.

"It is good to see you," Joe gushed.

"Yes, yes, you too." Catie's voice was muffled in Joe's massive chest. *He's dopey but it's hard to be mad at him.*

"How's the baby?"

Catie mumbled a response.

"What?" Joe asked.

"Let me go," she said, breaking away. "You are crushing my baby and me. What do you do, lift trucks as weights?"

Joe laughed heartily. He was big and pleasant and clueless. "You are funny, Catie."

"Babe, what are you doing here?" Ava asked.

"I was at work and I knew your dad was taking the boys for the morning. I figured we could steal a couple of hours for ourselves. I feel bad about breaking up the sister brunch though." He gestured toward the table.

"No, it's fine. I think Ny was just letting me crash anyway. Where do you want to go?" Ava asked excitedly.

"That's a surprise." He put a finger on her nose and Catie made a fake gagging sound.

"Well ladies, that's my cue. This has been fun, let's do it again," Ava said as she followed Joe out of the kitchen.

"Yeah, it was fun," Sophie waved.

"Bye," Catie called.

As soon as the front door closed, Catie leaned toward Anaya. "I don't trust him, Ny. He is up to no good."

Anaya raised an eyebrow. "Come on, Catie. He doesn't have his priorities in order, that's for sure. But he loves Ava and the boys. He just needs to be a little more ambitious."

"That's quite the understatement. That John Cena double needs a job and he needs to be home with his family. There is all kinds of stuff he can do. Pull up trees from the roots, or act as a stunt double—hell, he can find a job."

"It's not my business, Catie, and it's not yours either."

"Do you think it's because he's slow?"

"Slow? What do you mean?"

"Come on, Ny. We all know Joe is on the spectrum. Always in a good mood. No real facial expressions. Doesn't laugh at jokes. And why doesn't he use contractions? Talking to him is like having a conversation with Worf from Star Trek."

"Joe is not slow, Catie! What's wrong with you today? He just has a different sense of humor, and where is the rule that people have to use contractions?"

"It's in the behave-like-a-normal-person rule book," Catie said matter-of-factly. "I love Ava and the boys just as much as you do, and I want her and her marriage to succeed. But Ny, that slow brawn spawn is up to no good. Mark my words."

Sophie chimed in. "I don't know if he's slow, but he's definitely a little sus, and it does sometimes take him like five minutes to laugh at a joke."

"And *chitty chitty bang bang*?" Catie hunched her shoulders. "Like, who even says that?"

"You guys are trippin'." Anaya was over the conversation. Joe had his faults, but he wasn't mentally challenged. *Was he?*

"I'm tired." Catie yawned.

"Yeah, judging folks can take a lot out of you," Sophie said as she filled up the teapot with hot water. "Probably should take a break from that."

"Speaking of judging, how's it going with the new boo, Sophia?"

Sophie rested the back of her head on her neck. "It's not."

"What? Already?" Catie declared. "But I thought he was *the one*?"

"I don't know," Sophie whined. "I thought he was too. We were chillin'. Hanging out. Making plans. And now he's always busy and doesn't return my calls."

"Dang, that's kinda soon to get ghosted, Soph," Anaya said.

"I know, right?"

"He's got another woman," Catie said decidedly.

"Don't say that," Anaya warned.

"Then where the hell is he?"

"He says he's helping his aunt and he's busy with work," Sophie said, pouting. She clearly wasn't buying Jabari's excuses, and Anaya didn't blame her. But there was pain in Sophie's eyes, and Anaya didn't want to push her.

"I have an idea. What are you guys doing tonight?" Anaya asked, changing the subject.

"I'm having dinner with my mom," Sophie said. Anaya could see nervousness and excitement warring on her friend's face.

"That's awesome," Anaya said, squeezing her hand. "Good for you."

"I don't have plans," Catie said. "What's up?"

"Do you and Antoine wanna go to dinner with Carl and me?"

"Sure."

Anaya bit her lip and then added in a rush, "And Faven and Darren and the rest of Carl's friends."

Catie shot her an are-you-kidding-me look. "Nope."

"Come on," Anaya pleaded.

"No. Why do you hang out with those people, Anaya?"

"They're Carl's friends. They aren't that bad."

"Please. Faven is about as interesting as a phone charger. I have no desire to be around her or her alcoholic husband, ugly kids, and Stepford wife friends that follow her every move."

"They don't follow her every move," Anaya was defensive again.

"Wait. Did you call her kids ugly?" Sophie asked.

"Yes, I did. They look like Martians."

"Come on, Catie, just come to dinner," Anaya wheedled.

"No." Catie yawned. "I'd rather take a nap. Or lick a window. *Anything* but hang out with her."

"You can't call people's kids ugly." Sophie's comment fell on deaf ears.

"Fine," Anaya said. "You don't have to go."

"What I will do is help you clean up this mess before Uncle Roscoe comes back with the boys."

Anaya sighed. "I'll take that."

After they had tidied the kitchen and put the extra food away, Anaya walked Catie and Sophie to the front door, stepping over toys and shoes along the way. Anaya kicked a stuffed animal as hard as she could.

"You need a vacation," Catie said, laughing.

"You're probably right." Anaya hugged each of them. "Love you guys."

The two girls waved as they walked out.

SEVENTEEN

A naya put in her earphones to drown out the sound of the boys' screaming. She picked out two dresses and opted for Carl's favorite. She piled her hair at the top of her head and pasted the baby hairs down. Work had been keeping her and Carl apart more than either of them liked. Since Roscoe's party, she hadn't spent any real time with him besides the occasional lunch date and she was going to make up for it tonight. After the party, she planned to spend the night at his place, and there would be no sleeping.

She carried her shoes in her hand and closed her bedroom door behind her. The new status quo at home had taught her not to put on her heels until she had navigated the toy minefield outside of her room and office. From the top of the stairs, the house looked like a garage sale. Anaya spotted a new ugly lamp near the base of the stairs, next to a half-dead plant. *More crap. And where is the money to buy it coming from?*

Anaya stepped over a Tonka Truck, a study Bible, and a pair of ankle weights as she descended the stairs. Hezekiah, crying uncontrollably, stood in a corner of the living room wearing pajama bottoms and a white t-shirt with a greenish stain near the collar. A crusty milk mustache blended with the snot pouring from his nose. He wore only one sock.

Anaya had learned that crying didn't necessarily mean Hezekiah was in distress, but since Ava was nowhere in sight, she snagged a tissue from the table in the front hall and walked over to him.

"Honey, why are you crying?" She kneeled in front of him and swiped at his messy nose.

"Him was wooking at me," Hezekiah bemoaned, rubbing his eyes, which meant he needed a nap. He smelled like he also needed a bath. Him was Jeremiah, and apparently looking at Hezekiah was now enough to bring him to tears.

"Well, let me tell you something." She rubbed his back gently. "People will always look at you because that's the way life works. And if you are going to cry every time someone looks at you, people will start to tease you."

He stopped rubbing his eyes and stared at her. "But, but, if someone wooks at me, do they wook at others too?"

"Of course. Now remember, crying isn't the solution, but a haircut might be." She ran a hand across his ringlets and kissed him on the cheek. "Run along."

He pounced on a nearby dinosaur toy and started growling. She had this auntie thing in the bag. She walked into the kitchen where Ava stirred a pot filled with a revolting green concoction. *Please don't let the smell linger in my hair.* Joshua sat in a highchair next to her, receiving an occasional spoonful of the glop. Jeremiah ran by, halted next to his mother with his mouth open, and was given a big spoonful of the stuff himself. Then he ran off.

Anaya wanted to sit him down in a chair with a plate and his own utensils, but Ava started talking before Anaya could speak her mind.

"Wow, you look gorgeous," Ava said approvingly. Anaya begrudgingly noticed that Ava did as well, but she didn't return the compliment. She was one incident away from calling CPS.

"Ava, Hezekiah needs a haircut. He looks like a baby Bruno Mars. And why aren't they sitting at the table eating?"

"Stop fussing so much. You look much too pretty to be so catty right now. Now where are you going? Not with that *man*, I hope." Ava hissed the last sentence as if she were trading federal secrets.

Anaya took a deep breath and then wished she hadn't. Her tongue felt coated with the smell of Ava's dinner. "I'm going to a party with Carl. Not that it's any of your business. What's up with the boys?"

"What do you mean?"

Are you kidding me right now? They are still in pajamas at 5 p.m., haven't been bathed in Lord knows how long, and are running around like hooligans while eating dinner. Anaya decided to keep it simple. "Why aren't they eating at the table?"

"Those boys won't sit still for a minute." Ava giggled and fed another bite to Joshua. "They just have a lot of energy and need to run it off. And I'm too tired to chase them. This baby is taking a lot of my energy—that's how I know it's a girl."

Anaya frowned. "They can run it off after dinner. Right now, they need to sit at the table and eat like civilized children."

Ava stopped feeding Joshua and smiled at Anaya. "I appreciate you, sister. We all know it takes a village, but your experience with kids is limited to being an aunt. You are a professional, not a mom. I'm not trying to be rude, but you don't have children, and you don't know what you're talking about."

For someone who wasn't trying to be rude, it was a pretty rude thing to say.

"I don't have to have children of my own to know that kids need to sit down and eat instead of running in and out to take bites of whatever *that* is." Anaya pointed to the food. "They need discipline, Ava. I don't have to have kids to know that."

"Well good for you. And, yes, I know children need discipline. The Bible says, 'Do not provoke your children to anger but bring them up in the discipline and instruction of the Lord.'"

"The Bible also says that a child left to himself will bring shame to his mother!"

Ava looked like she had been slapped. "Ny!"

"What, Ava? The boys are running all over the place and all

over you, you are having another baby, Joe is never here and still hasn't found a better job, and this is not your house." There, she said it. She felt awful, but she said it.

Ava crossed her arms. "Is that what this is about? Us living here? Do you think that gives you the right to speak ill of my husband? My husband is a man with vision, and the Bible says, 'Without vision, the people shall perish.'"

Anaya didn't understand the context and didn't bother to ask. When Ava was on her spiritual high horse, only John the Baptist could bring her down. All Anaya wanted was for Ava to acknowledge that she had ungraciously taken over the house. Surely Ava knew how her family's moving in had affected Anaya's and Roscoe's lives, yet instead of being humble and grateful, Ava acted as if she were entitled to it all.

Hezekiah and Jeremiah ran into the kitchen, and Anaya grabbed both of them by the arms and firmly sat them down at the table.

"Eat your dinner. After you finish eating you can go and play. Do *not* get up until you finish. Do you understand?" Anaya commanded. She got two bowls from the cupboards, ladled green goop into them, and set them down forcefully in front of the wide-eyed boys. Then she got two spoons and stuck them into each bowl.

Jeremiah's forehead furrowed. "I want to play now!"

"Well, you can't play now. You have to eat. Once you finish, you can play. Understand?"

Jeremiah nodded, and Hezekiah followed suit. They started eating.

"See?" she said to Ava, who never looked up from feeding Joshua. "Discipline."

"That's great," Ava chimed. "Can you babysit for me tomorrow? The women's auxiliary is having brunch, and I'd like to go. Just for a few hours. Please? I mean, since you know so much about kids."

Smart ass. "I'll think about it. I have to check my calendar."

"Thank you."

Roscoe walked in wearing jeans and a t-shirt. "Well now, it looks like most of the gang is here." He rubbed the boys' heads and kissed little Joshua's forehead. Anaya knew she looked like she had just eaten a lemon, and Ava had her chin lifted in that holier-than-thou stance that Anaya found so infuriating.

"Hey, Daddy." Anaya tried to lighten her mood in front of Roscoe.

"Hey, Daddy. Would you like something to eat?"

"No, I don't want anything, Ava. I'm going to go out and grab a bite in a minute." Anaya knew Roscoe ate out to avoid Ava's cooking. He usually cooked at home before the move-in, but Anaya suspected that he couldn't stomach the smell of the kitchen any more.

"If you change your mind, there is plenty left." Ava kissed Roscoe on the cheek, then turned to her boys, who had turned the table and floor into a green Jackson Pollock painting. "Come on, boys. Time to get ready for bed."

"Ava, are you planning to wash these dishes?" Anaya asked. She frowned at the gluey green substance hardening on the counter. If she had to clean up one more time behind Ava, she was going to scream. Ava only did half-cleanups. She would put the dishes in the dishwasher but wouldn't put them away. She also didn't wipe the counters or sweep the floors.

Ava waved a dismissive hand, then pulled Joshua from his high chair. "Of course. I will do it after I put the boys to bed."

"Probably best to do it before you put them to bed," Roscoe said easily.

"Probably best to wipe the counters too," Anaya added.

"Okay, Daddy. I will."

"And probably best to always clean up after yourself in general," Anaya said.

"Come on, boys," Ava said. The sound of Hezekiah crying faded as the group tromped up the stairs.

"Ah, the quiet is nice, huh?" Roscoe asked once the door shut upstairs.

Anaya looked at her father in disbelief. "What quiet, Daddy? It's not quiet. It's always messy and noisy. There are too many people in this house."

Her father seemed disappointed. "Your family is here, Anaya. What's going on with you? Why are you so negative toward your sister?"

So I'm the bad guy? "The house is turned upside down." Anaya refused to feel guilty about Ava taking advantage of their dad's hospitality.

"I know the dynamics in the house are different, baby girl, and I know you are used to more privacy, but try to appreciate this time we have together. And this time with the boys. Don't take it for granted. You know your mother would let Ava and her family stay here if she were alive. Let's honor that and support each other. Life is short. You never know when it might be your turn to need somebody to lean on."

Anaya pursed her lips. If Anita had allowed Ava to stay, there would have been rules, and the turtle would not be a part of the agreement. Neither would the vegan Armageddon. Anaya's resentment was growing as quickly as Ava's stomach. But Roscoe had a point. Family was family, and no matter how irritating they were, she needed to be there for her sister and her family. *Suck it up, buttercup.*

"I know you're right." She sighed. "I just feel like Ava is taking advantage. She doesn't clean up behind herself and she lets the boys run around the house like wild animals. And then there's Joe. What exactly is his purpose?"

"Well, now let's be thankful that Joe isn't our business—he's

Ava's problem. We're here for Ava and those boys, that's it. But I've had a few talks with him. He knows it's urgent that he get another job." Roscoe put a hand on her shoulder. "It all comes out in the wash, baby girl. You focus too much on your expectations of the world. You are like an M40A5 sniper rifle, all set up for your target. The problem is, the target isn't yours, sweetie."

"You and Mommy taught us to be independent. All Ava does is go to church and run after the boys. She doesn't have any ambition to do anything else."

"Why is that your business?"

The question surprised Anaya. "What do you mean? She's my sister, and I want the best for her."

"The best according to whom? You? Let me tell you something. Those who do not look back to where they came from will not reach their destination."

Roscoe was trying to be a good father, and Anaya loved him for it. It didn't matter that she didn't always understand what he was talking about. After years of suffering through her dad's alcoholism, she was just happy to have her dad back again.

"I just want her to be okay, that's all."

"I know. And I want you to be okay. The hardest thing you can do is to live day to day. Try not to add problems to what's already a daily struggle. I watch you taking care of everybody, and doing everything for the family. Don't forget about you." He pointed at her. "You're just as important as everybody else. Your happiness matters too."

She couldn't remember the last time she thought about her own happiness. Did it even matter any more? She felt stifled by her family, resentful toward Ava, and a little disappointed that her dad wasn't seeing her side in this.

Instead of saying how she really felt, Anaya gave her father a hug. "I know I have a lot to be grateful for, Daddy. I just have to be patient. Work is busy, and coming home to the house like this really sets me on edge. You are right though." She didn't want him worrying about her.

"Don't let work run your life. You gotta have balance. Are you and Carl all right?"

Anaya nodded, then checked the clock and gasped. She would be late to their first date in two weeks if she didn't run. There was no sense in talking about it more. Ava would get her way and that was it. "I gotta go, Daddy! Carl and I are going out tonight! Love you!"

She slipped on her heels and checked herself in the hall mirror, then smoothed out the blue bandage dress that Carl loved. *Would Jeff love it too?* She pushed the thought from her mind and rushed out the door.

EIGHTEEN

L eave it to Faven to throw a party at the Marriott Convention Center the same night as a Blacks in Tech Conference, a Jack and Jill fundraising event, and the Charles Houston Bar Association gala. After wandering around for fifteen minutes looking for the Lauder room, Anaya accepted a free glass of champagne.

Mmmm. Veuve Clicquot.

"Can you point me to the Lauder room?" she asked the waiter passing out drinks. She squeezed through crowds in the direction he pointed. How was she supposed to find anything in this mayhem? Carl wasn't answering his phone.

A painting of a sunset over the Bay, set up for a silent auction, caught her eye. She paused to admire it.

What a beautiful painting. Too bad I don't have anywhere to put it. The boys would scribble all over it in crayon. But it seems like something Jeff would appreciate—

"Anaya?"

She spun around. Jeff and a tall man with thick glasses were standing in the crowded hallway. Anaya blinked a few times to make sure she wasn't hallucinating, but all six-foot-three of him stared back at her, looking dashingly handsome in a black tux.

"Hey, what are you doing here?"

"Just here supporting a good friend." Jeff patted his companion on the back. "Anaya Goode, meet Gerald Marshall. Gerald, this is Anaya Goode."

Anaya put a finger to her lips in thought, then snapped her

fingers. "I know you. You were the keynote speaker at the public administrator's conference in New York last year. You work for the governor." She was already feeling the champagne.

"That's right."

"I still have the notes from that speech. Great job."

"Well, thank you. I especially appreciate it coming from you, Ms. Goode. Since I've been in town, I can hardly turn to any news outlet without seeing your name. You are handling this naval base project brilliantly."

Anaya smiled. "Thank you. I really appreciate that."

"Jeff, I'm going to go grab our seats. Ms. Goode, it was my pleasure."

"Great to meet you as well."

Jeff gave a low whistle when Gerald was out of earshot and leaned close to talk to Anaya over the hubbub. "Wow, your fan base extends all the way to the East Coast. I knew there was something special about you."

"That's nice of you to say." *Why does he smell so good?*

"I know you don't want me to say this, but you are the most beautiful woman I've ever known." He looked her up and down from her curly updo to her black strappy heels. "I don't know what great deed I did to get to see you in this dress, but I would do it a thousand times over."

She frowned. He wasn't keeping it very profesh. But part of her wanted him to keep going. "I have to admit that I'm trying to entice someone tonight." She threw profesh out of the window as well.

"Wouldn't be me by any chance, would it?"

She bit her lip. "No. I didn't expect to see you."

"Ahh, so I'm just collateral damage?" He put his hand over his heart.

"Basically," she teased.

"Well, I don't know who you wore that dress for, but he is the luckiest person in the world." He leaned in and their lips met. It took her a second to process that she was *kissing* Jeff, and she pulled away with a small gasp.

Jeff's eyes were sparkling and serious. "My bad. I didn't mean to do that." He licked his lips.

"I gotta go." What was she thinking, gulping down champagne and kissing Jeff? She straightened her dress and headed down the hall with his gaze following her like a drone. When she turned the corner, she finally saw a sign for the Lauder Room.

Carl was standing outside the room down the hall. As soon as he spotted her, he strode toward her and grabbed her tightly around the waist.

"I'm glad you made it," he murmured in her ear. "And I'm so glad you wore this dress." Her kissed her long and slow, and everything that had felt wrong with Jeff felt right with Carl. She never wanted him to let go, but he pulled away.

"Is that champagne I smell on your breath?" he teased.

She giggled. "I needed one to find my way to this room! It's a madhouse in here." She wiped lipstick off of his lips.

He led her into the Lauder Room, crowded with guests milling around round tables. Anaya would have gone for black tablecloths rather than white, but the colorful woven baskets made great centerpieces, and everyone looked beautiful. A group of girls who looked like runway models were in the middle of the floor dancing Eskista. Anaya had always loved the bold shoulder dance. Traditional music, endless injera, and quality honey wine made the party a hit with Faven's guests.

Carl led them to the buffet table, and Anaya helped herself to doro wat. There were a few things Anaya broke her dietary rules for, and East African cuisine was one.

"There you are," Faven roared when Anaya and Carl made it to their table. She looked lovely in a white zuria with green, purple, and red trim. Next to her, Darren was oblivious to their arrival. Anaya suspected he had started drinking honey wine early because he was laughing loudly and stuffing his cheeks with Injera bread. At the table sat Bobby and Ricky and their wives, and Sam and her husband.

"You guys look beautiful," Anaya said to no one in particular. Each of the women wore traditional clothes even though Faven was the only native in the group. Anaya had missed that memo as well.

"So do you. I see you are eating tonight!" one of the women said.

Anaya ignored the dig. "Yes, I love Ethiopian food."

Faven stared daggers at her. "Eritrean."

"Excuse me?"

"Eritrean. My family is Eritrean. Not Ethiopian." Faven dismissed herself before Anaya could apologize.

"Faven is super sensitive about the Eritrean-Ethiopian thing. There was a civil war for like thirty years or something. It's just a culturally sensitive issue," Carl quietly explained.

And therefore she's allowed to be rude? Anaya just nodded and focused on her food. It wasn't her first time at the Mean Girl rodeo, and she knew no matter what she said, Faven would find an issue. The women around her—all soccer/dance/volleyball/girl scout moms—discussed private schools and minivans. The guys talked football across the table, and Anaya mentally checked out. She didn't know the difference between a fumble and a tackle and thought you got a tight end from doing squats.

Faven returned as Anaya finished eating, and turned her dark eyes on her.

"So, Anaya, long time no see. Where have you been?"

"Just working mostly," Anaya replied.

Darren spilled water on the table and laughed loudly.

"No more tej for you, Darren," Carl joked.

"No more anything for Darren," Faven said dryly.

"Uh oh, Darren, you hear that, man?" Ricky laughed.

Darren grinned. "I hear it, man, she's just saying that. Ain't that right, poo?" He rubbed Faven's forearm, and she quickly jerked it away.

"I have to make a speech in a few minutes," Faven said. "I'm so nervous, and I can't have you distracting me."

"You will be great," Sam said. "You are great at everything."

Anaya stifled a gag and pulled out her phone. They treated Faven like she was the Duchess of Sussex. *Oh, Faven your hair is perfect. Faven, you are so funny. Faven, it's okay that you treat your husband like crap, we still worship the ground you walk on.*

She liked a few photos on Instagram, sent a text to Roscoe, and added a meeting to her calendar. She got absorbed in work emails until Carl bumped her elbow gently and looked at her, then down at the phone.

Sorry babe, she mouthed, and put the phone back in her purse. *What else am I supposed to do if, even after an eighty-hour week, work emails are more engaging than the people around the table?* After a few minutes of hearing about Faven Jr.'s exceptional coloring skills (Faven had modestly named her daughter after herself), the difference between a nanny and a mommy helper, whether LeBron could bring another championship to the Lakers, and the tenets of toddler poop, Anaya excused herself to get more wine.

I know why Catie declined my invitation to this mess.

When she sat down again, she looked across the table at Faven talking loudly to some of her other guests. Faven was actually attractive with typical Ethiopian—er, Eritrean, features—caramel skin, large eyes, prominent forehead, and mounds of curly hair. It was her insides that were ugly.

Carl stood up and stretched out his hand. "I've been wanting to dance with the most beautiful woman in the room all night."

Anaya let him pull her to the dance floor. She smiled seductively and wrapped her arms around his neck. "Let's go back to your place," she said in his ear.

He kissed her. "Soon. Is everything okay?"

"Yes, I just miss you," she said, and rested her head on his chest while they slowly rocked.

After two more songs and a few group pictures, they were saying their goodbyes.

"Bowling party next week," Bobby called out. Anaya cringed.

Faven hugged Carl, and then Anaya. "Good night, guys," she said.

"Good night, Faven," Anaya said automatically.

Once they reached the lobby, still bustling with activity, Carl stopped. "Did you have a good time tonight?"

"Always with you."

"Good, I'm glad to hear that." He looked serious. "When you first got here, it felt like you would rather be somewhere else, with someone else."

Someone else? Where did that come from? Anaya took his arm. "Don't be silly. I want to be with you, Carl. Doesn't matter where."

"Good." He hugged her, and they walked out to his car.

Anaya fell asleep on the way home. The next morning, she woke up to the smell of coffee and eggs. Her blue dress had been replaced with one of Carl's tees, and one of her lashes was on her cheek. She had veiled memories of the evening, mostly from mixing champagne and honey wine. She pulled her phone out of her clutch and ignored a text from Jeff asking if she found her party last night.

She followed the smell of bacon into the kitchen where Carl stood over the stove.

"Good morning, sleeping beauty. Sit down. Breakfast will be served in a few." She gave him a quick kiss then walked blearily to the table. A moment later, Carl was bringing her a cup of coffee and an egg white omelet. He sat down next to her, and she nuzzled his neck, trying to remember last night. She remembered Faven's dress, dancing, and seeing Jeff. Something else happened with Jeff . . .

She looked up from her plate and found Carl examining her with a smile.

"You look good in my t-shirt."

"Oh, do I?" She smiled.

He nodded. "Yep. There's only one thing I like you in better than my t-shirts."

"And what is that?"

"When you wear nothing." He leaned in and kissed her, then began to lift the shirt over her hips.

The doorbell rang.

The disappointment of stalled intimacy hit Anaya hard, and her words came out harsher than she'd intended. "Are you expecting company this early?"

Carl glanced at the clock on the wall. "Shoot, I forgot. Zendaya wanted to drop off some papers." He looked back at her. "Hold that thought."

Anaya escaped to the bedroom while Carl went to the door. She threw on a pair of sweats. *What is Zendaya doing at Carl's place at this hour?* Anaya was trying to straighten her hair in the mirror when she heard Zendaya warble, "Good morning."

"Hey. Thanks so much for bringing these by. I forgot you said you were coming this morning. I could have picked them up from the center."

"Don't be silly. That's out of your way, and I was going to be over here anyway. I'm sorry I forgot to remind you I was coming."

Is she making her voice that husky on purpose? Anaya moved toward the bedroom door. One more step and she'd be in the hall that led to the front door.

"Still, you didn't have to do that, Zen."

"It's the least I could do. You've done so much for Tyrell."

Anaya stepped out of the bedroom and cleared her throat.

Zendaya's eyes widened in surprise before she plastered on a smile. "Oh, hi Anaya!"

"Hi, Zendaya." Anaya waved.

"I'm sorry. You two are trying to relax and I'm intruding. I know you don't get to spend much time together. I just wanted to drop off these papers."

How does she know how much time we spend together?

"Will you stop apologizing?" Carl said gently. "I told you I'm going to do everything I can to help you get custody." He put his hand on her shoulder. "We got this."

"Yeah," she said, putting her hand on his and clutching it. "Thank you."

Anaya cleared her throat again. "Have a good day, Zen," she said, smiling sweetly.

"Yeah, um, you guys have a good day too."

Carl closed the door and turned to her. "Now, where were we?"

Anaya folded her arms across her chest. "Does Zendaya come over here often?"

Carl cocked his head in confusion. "What? No, this is the first time. I know the director of this camp she wants to get her nephew into, and the deadline is tomorrow, so she brought the application over."

"To your house?"

He furrowed his brow. "She felt bad about it being so close to the deadline and didn't want me to have to travel to the center. She was being nice."

"That's awfully nice."

"Yeah, she's nice." Carl said the word slowly as he studied Anaya's dangerous expression.

"I'll bet. I mean, she comes over here early in the morning smelling like a Victoria's Secret factory, smiling all hard and hand delivering something she could have mailed. Very nice."

"Ny, the deadline is tomorrow. She would miss it if she mailed it—that's why she brought it over. Didn't you hear me say that?"

"Yeah, I heard you. I saw her face too."

"I'm not sure what you mean," he said, and his expression looked hurt.

Anaya felt her indignation melt a little. Surely Carl couldn't have a thing for this twenty-two-year-old girl trying to get custody of her nephew. Anaya was probably overreacting because she'd been hiding her new working relationship with Jeff. Her guilt about that loomed large, and she leaned against the wall. *I can't go on like this.*

"Never mind." Anaya walked back into the living room and sat on the couch. She remembered what had happened with Jeff last night. They had kissed. She squeezed her eyes shut and curled into a tight ball.

A moment later, a warm hand rested on her knee. When she opened her eyes, Carl stroked her cheek. "Do you still want this, Anaya? Want us?"

"Yes, of course, I do." She sat up and looked into his eyes. What was he talking about?

"I will give you anything you need, Ny. If you need time, I will give it to you. I want to make you happy, so I'm asking you to tell me what you need. I love you and will be whatever you need me to be, but we have to be honest with each other."

Anaya shoved away her thoughts of Jeff and let her heart fill with the safety and love she felt whenever she spent time with Carl. "I agree. I love you, and this is where I want to be. This is it. I'm sorry about the Zendaya thing. I know you better than that."

And she meant it. At least, she did until Carl pulled a small box from his pocket. She wanted to be here with him, but as boyfriend and girlfriend. She stopped breathing for a moment.

When Carl tilted the open box toward her, a diamond pendant glittered up at her. She exhaled in relief.

Carl tilted her chin up so they were looking at each other. "This is my commitment to making our relationship work. I know you aren't ready for marriage, but I'm committed to making sure we get there." He removed the delicate necklace from the box and fastened it around her neck.

She looked down at it, then up into his trusting brown eyes. "I love you so much, Carl."

"I love you too."

NINETEEN

"**S**low down!" Catie called out, interrupting Anaya and Sophie's conversation about curl patterns and natural hair products.

"My bad," Anaya said, looking back at her pregnant friend. She and the girls were walking around the lake instead of having brunch. The trio looked like a Lululemon advertisement with Catie sporting the maternity line. "I'm used to running, so it's hard for me to walk at this pace. It doesn't feel normal."

"*It doesn't feel normal,*" Catie mocked as Anaya turned back to Sophie.

"My hair is always so dry," Anaya complained.

"You are a 4b, so you should try the LOC method. That way, the moisture gets locked in, and you will hold your curl," Sophie replied.

Anaya nodded. "I've heard of that! I'm going to try it."

"And don't forget to deep condition. That's the holy grail for keeping natural hair moisturized."

"Have you guys ever done Kegel exercises?" Catie interrupted, catching up to them.

Anaya had wondered how long it would take for her to change the subject. Catie's hair was straight, so she didn't care about co-washing or length retention. For the past fifteen minutes, she had walked behind them while replying to emails from her clients, giving Anaya and Sophie plenty of time to realize they both needed to drink more water and get their ends trimmed regularly. Curly hair was both a blessing and a curse.

"Yep," Anaya answered.

"No. What are those?" Sophie asked.

"They are exercises to help keep you tight," Catie replied.

Sophie scrunched her nose. "Ew. In your vagina? That's not exactly a civilized topic for morning tea."

"Yes, in your vagina, and it's a perfectly acceptable exercise, but it is completely different when you are pregnant. It's scintillating."

Anaya held up a hand. "No details needed. Please and thank you."

"I'm telling you guys. These Kegels feel good." Catie paused, and Anaya just knew she was doing a few. "If I weren't pregnant, I'd have a cup of coffee and a cigar afterward."

"TMI," Anaya said.

"They feel good." Catie looked satisfied. "Wait until you're carrying a little Carl—you'll see what I'm talking about."

"Yeah, I'll definitely wait on that."

"Speaking of Carl," Sophie jumped in front of Anaya and walked backward, "when are you two planning to get married?"

Anaya tried not to be defensive, but if she had a dime for every time someone asked her about marrying Carl, she could purchase two round-trip tickets to Senegal. If she said it once, she said it ten thousand times: she wasn't ready to get married. And Sophie knew it.

Anaya decided to throw them a curve ball. Besides, she wanted their opinions. Maybe talking about it would get the problem out of her head. "Do you guys remember I told you Jeff contacted me to meet him?"

Sophie stopped walking, and Anaya almost bumped into her. "That's an interestingly inappropriate segue." Sophie raised an eyebrow. "I ask about the love of your life, and you mention your former lover. Hmm." She placed a forefinger on her chin in an exaggerated way.

"I'm going to agree with the shrink-in-training," Catie said.

"But to answer your question, yes, I remember you told us he wanted to see you. And I remember you saying you weren't going to oblige."

"Well . . ." Anaya began. She finally admitted to the girls that she had gone to lunch with Jeff in July and how he had wanted to check with her before he accepted a contract position with the county. They'd been working together every week for the past two months. She left out the lingering, unprofessional conversations and how often she thought about him. They weren't quite ready for that part. Even Anaya wasn't prepared for that part yet. Most of the time she had to force herself to stop thinking about him.

"Are you trying to make me go into premature labor?" Catie sat down on a nearby bench and practiced the breathing exercises she had learned in delivery class.

"I'm sorry." Anaya stood next to her and rubbed her back. "Was that a lot?"

"Was that a lot?" Catie asked. "Yeah, that was a lot. And I'm in distress because my heart can't take it. The last time you mentioned this man, you said you weren't going to meet him. So not only did you not take our advice to not see him, but you met with him, found out that he's single, and you guys work together now! I'd say that's a whole hell of a lot."

"I agree," Sophie said. "And you're only now mentioning it to us, after two months! We talk all the time and you haven't said a word. That's a little suss."

"Have I ever told you I hate when you say that?" Catie said to Sophie. "Ima just put it out there. You sound like a middle schooler." She shifted back to Anaya. "But Sophie is right, Ny, even though her slang is ridiculous. All you ever talk about is Ava and Joe and work and your crazy boss."

"And the turtle in the living room," Sophie chimed in.

"And how Natalie talks too much."

"And how you are fat."

"But nothing about this dude."

"I'm so confused. Poor Carl." Sophie shook her head. "What does he think?"

Here goes. "He doesn't know," she mumbled.

"Did you say he doesn't do blow?" Catie leaned toward Anaya with one hand cupped to her ear. "Because that's what I hope you said. Cocaine is addictive."

"He doesn't know," Anaya repeated, looking at her feet. "I haven't told Carl about Jeff."

Catie exhaled deeply. "You are being super deceptive and secretive, Anaya Goode. What the heck? You don't tell us, you don't tell Carl. I mean, what's going on? Why all the secrets?"

Anaya held up her hands. "It's just a working relationship, you guys."

"I've heard that before." Catie rolled her eyes. "And if it was just a working relationship, you wouldn't have held on to a lie for *two* months."

"It's not just a working relationship." Sophie was in therapist mode. "You used to be in love with this man. This is a complicated issue which requires open discussion about your thoughts and feelings. And you kept it from us for a long time. Why are you keeping this secret? Why don't you feel worthy of love? You need to explore this, Ny. This is dangerous. I wish I had my notepad with me."

"Sophia, shut up." Catie said, exasperated. "I can't deal with that psycho-shiz this morning, okay? You don't even know the answer to those questions, but you always want other people to answer them. Do some Kegels and hush. Be a friend, not a therapist."

"I am a friend, that's why I'm telling her the truth and asking the tough questions. I'm not going to tell her what she wants to hear. She's sneaking around with this man and hasn't told Carl or us anything. Never mind that this is the same man who came between them before. Never mind that he was also married. Have we forgotten all of that? A good friend would not encourage her to go down that road again. And I'm not doing Kegel exercises. I'm already tight down there because despite my colorful dating life, I keep my legs closed!" Sophie stepped back from Catie.

"Bitch, if I could get up from this bench, I'd strangle you." Catie sat on the edge of the bench and reached towards Sophie's neck. "Dang it! Now look. You made me cuss in front of my baby again." Catie touched her stomach as if covering the baby's ears.

"Even if you could get up, you can't catch me," Sophie teased.

"Guys, stop it. Catie, you are hormonal and Sophie, you are clearly not happy about any of this. But nothing is happening with Jeff. And I just haven't gotten around to telling Carl." She shrugged, almost convincing herself it was no big deal.

"You haven't *gotten around* to telling Carl?" Sophie threw her arms in the air, and Catie's chin dropped. "This is not like forgetting to tell him you hired a new secretary or added extensions to your hair. For two months, you have been working with a man you used to be in love with. Why is that not resonating in that pretty little 4b curly head of yours? The fact you haven't told him *means* it's a big deal. We need to take a moment to breathe and assess." Sophie put her ring and thumb fingers together, closed her eyes and breathed through a tiny hole she created with her lips. It sounded like whipping wind.

"I agree, Ny," Catie said. "Sophie is as crazy as a caveful of bats, but that's a good point. Carl is going to be pissed."

"Thank you, I think." Sophie briefly opened an eye. "And I also agree that Carl is going to be very upset."

Anaya felt their words sink in and tighten the knot of guilt inside her. She had been wrong about not telling them or Carl about Jeff. She felt tension building in her gut.

"Are you still in love with him? Because you need to decide which man will be this baby's godfather since you're the godmother."

Anaya forced a chuckle. "No, of course I'm not in love with him."

But she definitely felt something. She had to tell Carl soon and get everything out in the open. But how could she when it would hurt him so much? She fingered the diamond pendant around her neck.

"I hate being in this dilemma," Anaya groaned.

Catie rolled her eyes. "See, there you go with that spoiled, little sheltered-girl crap. Having two successful, handsome men in love with you is not a dilemma, my dear heart. Choosing between cheesecake and red velvet cake is a dilemma. Deciding whether or not to claim tips on your income taxes is a dilemma. A dilemma, no; a great opportunity to get things right, yes. Now help me off this bench before I get hemorrhoids."

Anaya pretended to pull her hair out.

"Girl, stop that," Catie said, looking around. "Some of my customers run and walk this lake. Pull it together."

"I'm just frustrated," Anaya said, helping Catie to her feet.

"I feel for you, my friend," Sophie said. "But you brought this on yourself. We agreed that you wouldn't see Jeff again. You decided otherwise. Breathe and assess, Ny."

"Yeah, now you look like a fool," Catie said mercilessly.

"It's not my fault he works for the county!" Anaya said. *Even though I did tell him I didn't mind if he took the job.*

"There's more to it than that," Catie said.

"No, there isn't," Anaya insisted.

"Don't try and Jedi mind trick me. Just because I'm pregnant doesn't mean I'm stupid. There's more to it, and we all know it. If there wasn't, you would've told Carl by now. It all comes back to that."

"At least you two have men after you." Sophie kicked a rock in her path. "I have one who won't even call me back. He only texts."

"Jabari still hasn't called?"

"Not for the past two weeks. I really thought after the last time he came over and cooked me that delicious Italian meal and—"

Catie held a hand up. "We already got those details. That was enough." She tapped her lips. "Maybe he's dead."

Anaya hit Catie in the arm. "What did he say when you spoke to him last?"

"I mean, he texted and said he was busy and he would call me when he had time, but he hasn't."

"Has he posted anything on Instagram or Snapchat?" Catie asked.

"How would I know?" Sophie shrugged.

"I keep forgetting," Catie said dramatically. "You frequent every dating site known to mankind, but you're scared of Instagram. I don't understand you. How can you spy on your dude if you don't have social media?"

"I don't need to spy on him."

"The hell you don't. He's MIA, and you don't know where he is. He might be posted up at a Drake concert, and you will never know because it won't come up on the Match.com newsfeed."

"Anyway," Sophie continued, ignoring Catie, "I've decided he's not for me. If it takes him this long to call, then he's not worth my time. I'm sad and want answers, but I'm restraining myself because I know this is best for me and best for my sanity. Last week, I took a vow of silence for forty-eight hours to give myself space and time to figure this all out."

Catie rolled her eyes.

"Aw, friend, I'm sorry." Anaya hugged Sophie.

"Thanks, Ny. That's why it's so important for you to nurture the relationship you have. I know Jeff may seem exciting and appealing, but be careful. Make it work with Carl. Trust me, the grass is not always greener on the other side."

"But sometimes it is greener." Catie put up her index finger. "And stronger and longer." She did a body roll.

"Seriously, Catie. I'm giving her real advice, here."

"Me too, fool. Carl might be Mr. Right Now, but who is to say either one of them is for her? You certainly don't know, Soph-ee-uh. You don't even know what a hash tag is."

"Catie, stop it." Sophie shoved her playfully.

Anaya felt like she had gotten all the constructive feedback she could and was ready to change the subject.

"What's up with you and Antoine? Are you guys getting along better?" The last few times Catie had stopped by the Goode house, she had been flying solo. Anaya still couldn't understand how Antoine and Catie were living together but were barely talking.

"I don't even know anymore." Catie sighed, her shoulders dropping. "It's just not working."

Sophie wagged a finger at her friend. "Catie, I know you don't want to hear this, but relationships are like houseplants. They need constant attention. Sometimes they need sunlight, other times water. Or they may need to be re-potted. They need different things at different times to grow, or they will shrivel up and die. You need to give Antoine what he needs and let him give you what you need. Please."

"Well if that's the analogy we're going with, we are one of those crispy brown leaves that fall on the floor after the plant has already died. It's bad, you guys." Catie buried her face in her hands. "I know I talk crazy and act like I don't care about anything, but I thought Antoine and I would be forever. He understood me, and I was proud to be having his baby. After months of non-communication, I think we've come too far to make it work. I don't want to be with a man just to say I have a man. You know how some women will do anything just to say they have a man? That's not me. I want my relationship to mean something." Her serious expression turned into a smirk. "Look at you, Sophie. You haven't had a man since before Obama was elected, and you're fine."

Sophie harrumphed. "First of all, it hasn't been that long, okay? And second of all, how hard have you tried? If he's doing something you don't like, why don't you respond differently and see if that helps? It's easy to blame the other person when the solution can be as simple as changing your reaction. It's not just him, Catie. It takes two."

Catie shrugged, her face hardening as difficult memories crossed her mind. "I'm not compromising who I am. I'm independent and strong. I'm not reducing myself to June Cleaver for a man."

Anaya shook her head. "That's not what Sophie means, Catie. Kindness is about love, not reducing yourself. Antoine's a good guy who cares about you. Give him a chance." She smiled. "You can be scary sometimes, girl. Especially when you get mad."

"Oh really?" Catie threw her arms up in surrender. "Am I so scary that I caused him to go out and cheat on me?"

"What?" Anaya and Sophie exclaimed at the same time.

"Are you sure, Catie?" Anaya put one hand on her hip and the other on her forehead.

"As sure as I'm pregnant."

"I don't believe it." It was Sophie's turn to do some deep breathing exercises. "Who is it?"

"Believe it. She's some dime-hoe masseuse."

"A masseuse? How do you know? Are you okay? When did this happen?"

"Don't worry about how I know. And, yes, I'm fine."

"Well what did he say?" Sophie asked.

"He doesn't know I know."

"What do you mean, he doesn't know you know?" Anaya was suspicious. "That's not how you roll."

"He doesn't know I know. And actually it is how I roll. I didn't get this far in life by revealing my hand whenever I get hurt. I haven't said a damn thing."

"What are you going to do?"

"I haven't figured that out yet. But in the meantime, Antoine won't be seeing this sweet, Kegel-reformed vagina."

"No, no, no," Sophie said, pacing back and forth and still breathing dramatically. "You have to tell him that you know. You have to communicate!"

Catie scowled. "No, Sophia, okay? No. He disrespected me for some two-bit trick. I'm not giving him anything. Least of all the opportunity to lie to me again."

"So you are just going to go on and not say anything? How long can you do that?"

"Until I've figured out my next move." Catie started to walk again. "How's *that* for morning tea, ladies?"

TWENTY

The Board of Supervisors couldn't unanimously decide when to lower the county flag to half-mast, so naturally, a project the size of the navy base development caused complete chaos. Most of the supposed leaders were rigid people-pleasers, so they balked at change and dodged accountability with the ease of swallowing a Tic Tac. Anaya would prefer to swallow rocks rather than sit in on yet another meeting about the navy base that would likely prove to be an unproductive waste of her publicly funded time. But that's how things went in the county.

The supes held a closed session to discuss the progress of the development agreement and the RFP. Anaya didn't want to be there and Wendy didn't want her there, but the supes insisted she come in case they had questions that Wendy couldn't answer. They all knew how Wendy liked to play the amnesia card occasionally. Anaya had invited Jeff along because he knew contract law, and she knew the contracts were going to come up. Plus, he smelled nice.

"I'm so happy you are at this meeting with me," she murmured to him.

The two sat in the back of the conference room while the board members sat in the middle of the room munching on Mexican take-out. Redundancy and ineptness didn't faze them, but heads would roll if there weren't enough tortilla chips. Supervisor Abramson devoured her beans and rice like it was the last supper.

Wendy sat at the end of the table with a direct view of Anaya and Jeff. Rather than engage with the supes or Sue, she touched up her lips with Dior gloss.

"Is it always like this?" Jeff whispered, leaning in. He looked striking in a cream merino sweater and slacks.

"Oh, God yes," she lamented. "They might be on their best behavior today because they don't know you well, but you never know with this group."

"Thanks for the warning." He nudged her arm.

The meeting was called to order fifteen minutes after the scheduled time. Chair Memphis gave opening comments while Anaya shopped for apartments on her phone. After catching Jeremiah coloring with one of her MAC lip liners yesterday, she realized somebody had to go. She was checking out an overpriced studio when Supervisor Harris asked a question.

"What's the status of the development agreement for the navy base?" she asked.

Here we go.

"We are on task," Wendy said.

Wendy didn't mention the RFP not getting out to all of the registered contractors. Anaya had heard from one of her associates that Wendy hadn't been offered the Director of Government Operations position for the governor's administration. But she was one of the final two candidates. In Wendy's warped mind, she probably hoped the project implementation would coincide with a job offer for the position. Her rationale was as off as her eyebrows.

Supervisor Fernandez looked at Wendy with his signature snarl. "I'd like to know the status of my requests as well. I've talked about the sex-trafficked, underage girls walking the streets many times and sent you emails, and nothing has changed. The girls are still out there. Every day, I see them. Supervisor Harris, you see them. Chair Memphis, you see them." He pointed around the room to each board member before coming back to Wendy. "And I know you do too, Miss Woo. All this talk and we're doing nothing. The other day, I counted sixteen young prostitutes on an avenue not too far from this building. Sixteen girls, and we aren't doing anything about it. All this talk and no action."

Supervisor Fernandez's familiar complaint was met with sympathetic nods but mostly silence. His concerns were notable but his lack of understanding was frustrating. Anaya and Jeff exchanged a glance.

"First of all," Supervisor Harris's agitation increased with each word, "I know there is a problem with underage prostitution in some of our cities, but this is not the forum for this issue. We are here to discuss the potential job loss for our community if this agreement goes through without the appropriate contractor stipulations in place. Second of all, why in the world are you driving around counting prostitutes?"

"Our cities are in a crisis, and we need to do something about it, that's why," Fernandez replied. "These pimps and johns should be arrested. Maybe you should count them too."

"Listen." Chair Memphis raised a hand. "We need to get a grip here. We are expected to approve the agreement, the public is restless, and we've run out of tortillas. Wendy, time is of the essence. What's the status?" He took a huge bite of his burrito.

Wendy ran her fingers through her pixie haircut. "I think there's a little confusion here. But that is what happens when we have inexperienced managers who don't receive direction well." The supes followed Wendy's pointed glare at Anaya.

Bile rose in Anaya's stomach, and she fought the urge to sprint across the room and karate chop Wendy in the throat.

"With all due respect, Chair Memphis and members of the Board," Anaya interjected. She was out of order but didn't care. "One of the perks of this project is that we will receive federal matching funds for some of our expenses. The requirements to receive those funds is that we begin the project before the end of the year, and since we are having issues with the RFP and it is already September, we are running against the clock. We run the risk of missing that deadline and losing the money." It was partially true, but Anaya wanted to put pressure for the supes to make a decision. If she didn't, they'd sit on this for weeks.

"Is this true, Ms. Woo?" Chair Memphis asked with his mouth full.

Wendy glared at Anaya again.

"Ms. Woo?" Memphis urged when Wendy didn't respond.

"What? I mean, come again?"

"Is that true? We can lose the grant money?"

"No, that's not true. I . . . um . . . We won't lose the money because we'll have all of this wrapped up well before the end of the year. The agreement language was amended like you requested and the RFP was sent out. The notion that we are going to lose funding is quite extreme." She tried to raise a micro-bladed eyebrow in Anaya's direction.

"Ms. Goode seems to be under the impression that we aren't on track," Chair Memphis commented.

"I think Ms. Goode is thinking about something different. We are right on schedule." She sounded like a parent who was getting ready to reprimand the heck out of their child.

"Ms. Harris, what do you think?" Memphis asked. Supervisor Harris was the only one who ever read all of the information presented to them.

"I'm not completely sure. I'd like to hear more from Ms. Goode."

"All right then. Ms. Goode, please explain."

A closed session was more informal than an open session, so Anaya stood and spoke from the back of the room.

"Against my better judgment, the RFP was sent out with a restrictive bid. We need to re-open the RFP so all registered contractors have an opportunity to bid and avoid further liability for the county. Secondly, while Wendy is correct that the development agreement was amended, we seem to have run into a disagreement about the threshold for local hiring. My understanding is that it is fifty percent, but Ms. Woo wants to hold it at twenty. I can't in good conscience sign off on that."

"Wait, hold on a minute," Supervisor Harris sat up in her seat and spun towards Wendy. "Are you telling me that you want to limit our local contractor pool to twenty percent? Why on earth would you want to do something like that?"

Wendy scoffed. "It's not that I want to, Supervisor Harris. This demolition and development project is huge. Tantamount only to the development agreement with the football stadium fifteen years ago. If we start telling the developers who to hire and how many, they might lose interest. I'm just thinking of keeping jobs here."

"If a developer isn't interested in hiring our talented local contractors, then we don't want them here. The local hiring provision should be fifty percent! We determined that at the meeting back in July."

"I agree," Chair Memphis said. Around the table, the supes were nodding.

"Fine," Wendy said. "We will make the change this week."

"No, you will make that change today and we will schedule a special meeting for Friday where we will approve the final agreement and put this damn thing to bed."

Anaya wanted to sing.

"And what is this about the RFP not being sent to all of the registered contractors?" Supervisor Buckingham asked.

"Nothing," Wendy replied too quickly.

"What does that mean?" Supervisor Harris's bracelets clanked as she scooted her chair closer to the table.

"Ms. Goode is incorrect," Wendy declared.

"Please," said Supervisor Buckingham, raising her French-manicured hand. Unlike Wendy, Buckingham's face made plenty of expressions, and her current one was of mild frustration. "Let us hear from Ms. Goode. Ms. Goode, please continue."

Anaya explained how the RFP process had been unnecessarily constrained by the requirement that the applying contractors be certified in the use of explosives, which was a service that was easily subcontracted by the winning contractor. Additionally, even taking into account only contractors who were certified in explosives, Anaya cited ten local companies that hadn't been included in the RFP, and after reviewing the files, she discovered that far less than the required fifty percent had been included.

When she finished, the room was silent. Then Abramson said, "I move that we re-issue the RFP and expedite the timeline for responses."

"Second," Buckingham said.

Memphis nodded. "Ms. Goode, make sure that new RFP gets out as soon as possible with a reduced closing date and report back in three weeks. And don't forget to get that amended agreement to us by morning. I want to get that approved and out the door this week. Meeting adjourned."

"Great job!" Jeff said as they walked out. He nudged her arm playfully and their arms linked briefly. "But how in the world will you do a three-week turnaround?"

Anaya held up a finger and pulled out her cell. "Hi. Bruce. It's a go. Yep. They approved it. Send them certified overnight mail just like we talked about. Great. Thanks."

She smiled mischievously. "Just like that."

"How did you know they were going to approve a second RFP?" Jeff asked, impressed.

"I know this board. They don't want to look bad. This is our second bite at the apple and I knew once they found out the requests didn't get to all of their beloved constituents, they would want me to re-send it. They don't want to deal with angry labor unions. I was a little disappointed that they didn't probe into why all of the contractors didn't receive it, because I would have loved to see Wendy splutter her way out of that one. But you can't have everything."

"So you already had the new RFP ready to go?"

"Yep. I had my people working on it all last week. Bruce was just waiting on the signal to go. Everyone will have them within three days. This RFP will be fair, the development agreement will have our standard local hire terms, Wendy loses, and we make the deadline for our federal matching funds. Boom."

"I don't know what to say. Very impressive, Miss Goode."

"Why thank you, kind sir," she teased.

He checked his watch. "The task force is meeting at four o'clock. You wanna grab a bite? I'm starving."

"I can't. I have to run a few errands during lunch. I'm, uh, meeting my boyfriend Carl." There, she'd said it. Her guilt was temporarily assuaged. *Now to casually mention Jeff to Carl . . .*

"Oh, okay." He awkwardly shoved his hands into his pockets. "I actually have a few errands to run myself. See you later."

Anaya was almost out of the building when she heard Wendy call after her.

"Ms. Goode!"

Anaya kept walking.

"Mizz Goode, slow down!" Wendy's heels clicked hard against the pavement.

"I'm off the clock," Anaya called over her shoulder after she had crossed the street. "I'm going to lunch." She was more agile in sensible three-and-a-half-inch pumps than Wendy was in five-inch fish cage sandals.

"You are never off the clock, Ms. Goode. You're a director."

"Today I am." Anaya walked faster until she thought she heard Wendy stumble. She finally stopped and looked Wendy square in the eyes. Wendy's makeup was overdone. The severe arch of her brows and overdrawn lipstick looked more like a Cirque du Soleil character than a top-notch government administrator. She could also tone down the spikes in her pixie for the sake of professional reticence.

Wendy glanced around before speaking and leaned in toward Anaya.

"This thing you are doing has to stop. You risk costing the county millions of dollars. Is that what you want on your résumé?"

Anaya wanted Wendy to fall flat on her face, but she had joined the public sector to help people, and if that meant she had to be cordial to a fire-eating dragon, then so be it. Professionalism was one thing, but being naïve was another. And Anaya was done with Wendy's bullying and scare tactics.

"I don't," Anaya said, not backing down this time. "Nor do I want it on my résumé that I participated in some shrewd coup. I spend a lot of time listening to you talk, Wendy. I watch you pat your face and use unflattering shades of lipstick when you should be paying attention. You mistreat people just because you can. I asked you for the full bid list, and you didn't give it to me. I also told you that the RFP needed to go out to all the contractors and to forget that restricted bid nonsense. I found out on my own that more than sixty percent of contractors didn't even receive the notice, and I told you we needed to resubmit the RFP. You decided to ignore me. I'm tired of sitting idly by while you intentionally derail this project. You only care about yourself and that job in the governor's administration, but as long as I'm here, you will never see another opportunity to obstruct this project."

She left Wendy staring open-mouthed.

TWENTY ONE

After the closed session with the supes, Anaya had planned on meeting Carl at the party store to get some final things for Catie's baby shower. She was excited to see him. It seemed like the only time they saw each other lately was when she was running errands. All of that would end when ground broke on the base before the end of the year. Soon, this would all be over and she could make things right between them again. She popped a Zantac before she got in her car.

Carl was waiting in front of the party store. He was wearing a cobalt blue t-shirt and had a fresh haircut. When he smiled, she remembered why she fell in love with him. He came over to open her car door and greeted her with a long kiss.

"Mmm," she cooed. "I've missed that."

"Me too, baby." He kissed her again.

They held hands like teenagers and walked through the vast warehouse filled from floor to ceiling with goodies. He tickled her, and she threw some sample confetti at him. When he wasn't dancing to the Mariachi music or trying on silly hats, he was staring at her. When she reached for a packet of silver balloons, he grabbed her around the waist. He was strong and warm, and she giggled as he kissed her neck.

"We're in the store, Carl."

"I'm fully aware of that. There's nothing wrong with spreading a little love in the party store. It's good for business." He kissed her neck, and she laughed out loud.

"Oh is it?"

"Absolutely. I'll tell you what else is good."

"Oh, what's that?" She gave in and let him kiss her.

"Don't go back to work and I'll show you," he whispered in her ear.

She longed to play hooky and spend the rest of the day at his place but the meeting with the supes only reminded her of how much work she still had to do. But she was in the final stretch. It was almost over.

She groaned as he kissed her ear. "I have to go back. I have so much stuff to do."

"I have some stuff for you to do too." He kissed her again. "I miss you, babe."

"I know. I miss you, too."

"I'm struggling, ma'am. I need some of that loving." He grabbed her booty.

"Boy, stop it." She laughed.

"Seriously, babe. I miss you. I need you. I don't like spending this much time apart. It doesn't feel right."

"I know. Once this project is over, you can have me all to yourself." She kissed him.

"You promise?" he asked in between kisses.

"I promise."

"You promise to do that thing I like too?" He held her again, and she giggled.

"Maybe."

"Well hello," a familiar voice said from behind them. *Holy hell.* The hairs on the back of Anaya's neck stood up, and she stepped away from Carl.

Anaya wiped her lips. If she were Spiderman, she'd weave a web and climb out of the building through the roof. She felt Carl's steady breathing behind her.

"Professor Jackson. How are you?" Carl's greeting was chilly. Carl and Jeff shook hands while Anaya focused her attention on a package of pink plastic sunglasses near the end of the aisle. *Maybe everyone can wear these at the baby shower.*

"I'm good." Anaya saw Jeff look past Carl at her and the sunglasses. She slipped on a pair.

"How have things been going with you, man?" Jeff asked Carl.

"Can't complain. Are you still teaching?"

"Nah, no time. How about you? Social work was your field, right?"

Anaya felt lightheaded.

"Yeah. Social work." Now Carl looked over at her, brow slightly furrowed. *He's probably wondering why I'm so far away . . . looking at stupid things.*

"Are you finding everything you need?" Jeff called over to her. She turned to them as if she had just realized they were there.

"Me?" She pointed to herself. "Oh! Yeah, I'm good. Just picking up some stuff. How are you?" She pretended as if she hadn't just spent the past two hours with him in a meeting or the past two months working with him.

"I'm great, since I last saw you a few minutes ago." Jeff chuckled. "Just came here to pick up some things for my daughter's birthday party. You're here for the baby shower supplies you were telling me about?"

Holy hell. It was a miracle that she wasn't visibly drenched in sweat because she felt it pouring from her armpits. The Zantac wasn't working.

"Yup," she said, staying at the end of the aisle. The distance allowed her to compare both men's physiques and expressions. Admiration lurked in the depths of Jeff's eyes while Carl's confusion was quickly turning to anger.

"Funny seeing you here."

"Yup." Jeff wasn't getting the hint. He was smart, but not smart enough.

"Better get your break in now. Tonight is going to be a late one.

I think Sue is calling in for Italian, but I told her to order a salad for you." He winked at her. "I know how you roll. Did you read that email from Wendy's secretary?"

Beads of sweat dripped down the back of her neck. She wanted to throw something at Jeff to get him to knock it off, but it wasn't his fault she had been deceptive.

"No, not quite yet, Jeff."

"Well, they are doing exactly what we talked about last night."

"Really? That's, uh, that's interesting."

"Yeah. Well, I got all my goods so I have to get back." He held up a roll of streamers and some pink plates. He turned to Carl. "All right, man, good seeing you."

"Take care," Carl said. Anaya could tell he was trying to keep his cool.

"I will see *you* shortly," Jeff said, pointing a finger at Anaya.

She wanted to break something. Anything.

"See you." She sounded like a wounded bird.

She had no memory of buying anything, and when she and Carl got outside, the walk to her car took a lifetime. She put her things in the trunk. Carl wasn't much for making a scene, and Anaya was grateful. But when she went to the driver's side where Carl was holding her door open, his eyes were narrowed.

"What's going on?"

"I, um . . . the county contracted Jeff to work on the naval base project. His, um, his firm is familiar with construction stuff and contracts," she said quietly. She wanted to leave and have this conversation somewhere else, but deep down, she knew that might just be her way of delaying this inevitable conversation.

"When?"

"Huh?"

"When did this happen?" He'd never raised his voice at her before, and she shrank back.

"Um, a couple of months ago," she mumbled.

"A couple *what*?"

"A couple of months ago," she repeated, louder. She couldn't look at the betrayal on his beautiful face. She had made a terrible mistake.

"And you were going to tell me about this when?"

"Eventually."

"Eventually when? Eventually in a few weeks? Eventually in a few hours?"

"V-very soon," she stammered.

Carl's fury rose with the volume of his voice. "So, you are working with your ex-boyfriend and you didn't tell me? Any other old boyfriends you have hanging around that I don't know about?"

She reached out a hand to him, but he stepped away.

"Carl, please. I'm sorry."

"That's the best you have for me, Ny? The man that you were in love with and left me for six years ago starts working with you, apparently with late nights and Italian food, and you decide not to tell me anything?"

She tried to interrupt, to explain more, but Carl kept going.

"I trusted you!" he said. "After what happened at my place, I was worried about what you might be thinking about me and Zendaya, and you were the one with the secrets all along!"

Without giving Anaya a chance to respond, he walked over to his car, got in, and drove away.

TWENTY TWO

Anaya had to admit that Catie's baby shower turned out more fabulous than she had expected. She had poured all her extra energy into the party in order to avoid thinking about Carl. And Jeff. The reality of life without Carl after the scene from the party store two weeks ago still hadn't settled in her mind. She kept wondering when Carl would call, and then she would remember. *How could I be so stupid?*

She turned her focus back to the party. Selected for its view, the room in the Ritz Carlton was arranged in lounge style with half a dozen bar tables along the wall, each holding hors d'oeuvres including tiny chicken and waffle sliders, bacon-jalapeno deviled eggs, macaroni and cheese cups, crudités, and cucumber rounds. The five ten-person tables had beautiful centerpieces of purple and white hydrangeas in tall crystal vases. The white chocolate fountain poured its never-ending decadence in front of a six-foot lavender and white rose wall that read *Catie's Fabulous New Addition*. The hotel didn't offer Tchaikovsky's Symphony No. 6, as Catie had requested, but Anaya ordered the music from Amazon.

Anaya was chic in a strapless, wide-legged jumpsuit with her hair pulled into a low bun with a middle part. With half an hour to go before the party started, she passed in and out of the main room making sure everything was perfect.

"Please move the fountain back from this walkway. I would hate for someone to get that on their clothes," Anaya said to one of the waiters.

"Can we center that photo of Catie and Antoine a little more?" Anaya tilted her head to the side. "It's off."

"Exactly who was in charge of folding the napkins? Do it over please."

"Anaya, where are the balloons?" Sophie asked as she put the satin and lace favors on the tables. "I think that's the only thing missing."

Anaya had delegated balloon duty to Ava, who had apparently delegated it to Joe.

"Joe is going to drop off the balloons when he picks up the boys." That was Ava's excuse anyway. As guests started to arrive, the boys played tag around the rose wall and had their way with the purple mini cupcakes. Joshua was napping in his car seat.

Catie arrived, looking radiant in a white, floor-length, off-the-shoulder chiffon gown with a lavender floral crown. As soon as she saw Anaya, she rushed over.

"Oh my God, Ny. I can't believe how incredible it looks in here. That rose wall! I feel like a Kardashian. And this view. It's perfect." Catie looked around in delight. "And you look gorgeous. I love your hair pulled back that way."

Anaya smiled, all the stress from hours of preparation melting away as she took in her friend's joy. "I'm glad you approve. Just enjoy yourself and entertain your guests. And no one is as stunning as you, my friend." Anaya hugged Catie and thought she saw a tear.

No way. Is she crying? Something is going on with her lately.

"Are you okay?"

"Yes." Catie blinked rapidly so as not to ruin her perfect makeup. "I just can't believe you guys did all of this for me."

Anaya grabbed her in another hug. "Girl, you know we love you. And we were not going to let your shower be anything short of extraordinary. You wouldn't let us." She winked.

"Yeah, I guess you're right. I underestimated you though. A chocolate fountain? Wow."

Anaya snapped her fingers and did a slight neck roll. "*White* chocolate fountain. Nothing less than the best for you."

London, Catie's only childhood friend that Anaya knew of, walked over wearing a huge smile and a tiny dress.

"What's this little love fest happenin' without me?" London said, hugging Anaya and Catie. "It's litty up in here."

"Just trying to get your girl to enjoy herself."

"Uh-uh, honey." London grabbed Catie's shoulder. "This party is for you. Get out there and enjoy thyself. No wallflowers, boo-boo. Mingle."

"Okay, okay." Catie paused, then smiled again. "I love you guys."

London dramatically put her hand to her ear. It was rare to hear such warm sentiments from Catie. "Say what now?"

Catie rolled her eyes. "Nothing. Just wanted to say thanks for the party."

"Thanks for helping, London," Anaya said after Catie walked away.

"Chile, please. Caitlin is my girl. Any celebration for her, I'm going to be there." London towered over Anaya in five-inch heels. "She looks great, doesn't she?"

"Yep. She'd look even better if she didn't have to dodge my nephews." Anaya frowned at Hezekiah and Jeremiah as they ran past. Sweet Jesus, why couldn't Ava control those boys?

"They're boys, that's how boys behave," said Troy, walking over to Anaya. It was hard to describe Troy's outfit. She wore suspenders, a newsboy cap, and a scarf that looked like it belonged to a train conductor.

"Boys or not, they aren't supposed to be here, and they aren't supposed to be behaving like . . ." Anaya searched for the right word.

"Savages?" London drawled.

"You are too hard on them," Troy said easily. "They are just having fun. No one's even noticed them."

"Yeah." London rubbed her neck and pointed. "Especially not that lady who just spilled wine all over her dress trying to step over the one that growls all the time."

Anaya gasped as the woman rushed off to the bathroom. That did it.

Troy caught her by the arm. "Don't stress. Everything is beautiful. The boys being here isn't that big a deal. Trust me."

"I hope not," Anaya said, exhaling deeply. She smoothed out her jumpsuit and smiled. It was nice to have the input of a levelheaded person. "Thanks for coming, Troy. Help yourself to the food. The games will start soon."

Someone behind Troy waved. It was Marie and Wanda—Uncle Riley's ex-girlfriend and Antoine's mother. They each carried a large bag.

"Hey aunties," Anaya said, rushing over to them and giving each a kiss on the cheek. Wanda wore a floral print dress and had her hair pulled back, while Marie was wearing a fitted pink jumpsuit with strappy heels.

"Wanda is all set with the games, and I have the prizes," Marie said.

Troy turned to look at Wanda at the mention of the woman's name.

"Great," Anaya said overly brightly before Troy could say anything. "There's a table over there where you can set everything up."

As Marie and Wanda left, Troy turned to Anaya. "*That's* the woman Riley was with for ten years? In those Clarke shoes? My grandmother wore those."

"Keep it civil, Troy." Anaya started to walk toward Ava to check on Joe's status, but Troy grabbed her arm.

"I could've done games, Ny. You know that's my thing! Why didn't you ask me?"

You could have, but you didn't volunteer. I've been working on this shower for months. "I didn't even think about it, Troy. And Wanda volunteered. Next party, though." Anaya excused herself. She saw Troy head in the direction of the game table where Marie and Wanda were setting up. *Please don't make a scene, Troy. Uncle Riley and Wanda are over and done.*

She found Ava standing by the rose wall. The party would be over by the time the balloons arrived, and now the boys were jumping around like frogs. *Sweet Jesus.*

"Ava, when is Joe getting here with the balloons and picking up the boys? They shouldn't be here."

"He will be here soon," Ava said calmly, examining a lavender rose. "He's going to take the boys to get Halloween costumes."

"You said that an hour ago and he's still not here," Anaya said between her teeth. *I don't care where he takes them as long as they're gone. And where did you get money for Halloween costumes?*

"He will be here, sister dear. Chill. It's too beautiful in here for you to be uptight." She strolled away without a care in the world, leaving Anaya shaking with rage.

This was typical Ava. There was no urgency whatsoever in her life. She had only been responsible for bringing the balloons to the party, and she couldn't even manage to deliver on that. And it didn't even bother her!

Anaya was arranging Catie's gifts when she felt a tap on her shoulder.

"Go and get your uncle's girlfriend," Marie hissed over Anaya's shoulder. "She's over there gushing about Riley to Wanda like somebody wants him."

"Oh my goodness," Anaya said exasperated. "Wanda and Riley dated eons ago. Wanda doesn't want him."

"Exactly. But Troy is over there acting like it's all fair in love and war."

"Wanda can handle her," Anaya said dismissively. "I'm not worried about it." She couldn't micromanage every relationship when she was the hostess.

Marie shrugged and walked to the bar.

"What's wrong, Ny?" Sophie walked by carrying a bag of extra favors.

Anaya sighed. "A lot, but my biggest concern is Ava. The balloons aren't here, and the boys are behaving like hoodlums."

"They're always like that."

"At home. This is not the place for it."

"Yeah, I noticed they were a little turned up. Where's Joe?"

"Who knows? At the gym? At church? Saving souls who don't want to be saved? Lifting things that don't need to be lifted? He's anywhere and everywhere except work or here."

"The games are starting now!" called Marie, getting the attention of the guests. Anaya smiled as she watched from a distance, doing her rounds of the food and drink tables to make sure everything was perfect. After the games, the guests mingled, munched on cupcakes, and took pictures in front of the rose wall.

It was only after the first guest left that Joe finally showed up with the balloons.

"Seriously?" Sophie whispered to Anaya. "Is he really just getting here with the balloons?"

"I can't even begin to address this because I will go off completely," Anaya fumed. "Please handle it, Sophie."

Sophie saluted and went to Ava and Joe near the door.

By the time most of the guests had left, Anaya could see Catie was exhausted. She had seemed far more emotional all day than Anaya had ever seen her.

"You all right, girl?" Anaya asked. Catie had propped her feet up on a chair and was fanning herself. Anaya pulled out a chair next to her. She could take a break from cleaning up for a moment.

The others who had stayed to help drifted over, as if Anaya sitting down gave them permission to take their own breaks.

"Yes, a little overwhelmed. I think this pregnancy is making me emotional."

"You were fabulous today." Anaya kissed Catie's cheek.

"This party was phenomenal. I can't believe how creative you are," Catie gushed.

Ava came over and sat next to Catie with a look of tranquility. "Next, we will be planning your bridal shower." She patted Catie on the thigh. "You didn't do it in the right order, but that's fine."

Anaya and Sophie exchanged glances. *Why must Ava always put her foot in her mouth? Why?*

"What is that supposed to mean?" Catie leaned away from Ava. Her tone was light, but her face had darkened.

"You know what I mean," Ava shrugged her shoulders. "People typically get married first and then have a baby."

"That's funny. I thought people typically do whatever the hell they want to do. Besides, what makes you think I'm getting married?"

"Well, you are already with child, so it would seem to me that the next Christ-like step is marriage."

Catie looked like she was about to spit fire. "And you are with three children and a fourth on the way, so it would seem that the next Christ-like step would be for you and Joseph to seek gainful employment."

"Fine," Ava said, shrugging again. "Just trying to keep you grounded in Christ."

London stood up. "Hell, y'all over here talking about Christ? That's my cue to go. I have a date, boo." She said her goodbyes and promised to call Catie later.

"Ny, I just realized Aunt Deb didn't come," Catie said. "Why didn't you invite her?"

"I did, but she said something about the North Node, so she needed to travel east."

"North Node?" Catie shrugged. "Aunt Deb and her astrology."

"She sent a gift though." Anaya pointed at a big purple bag on the loaded gift table.

"Aw, she's so sweet."

"She knows motherhood is a big deal. It takes some people a lifetime to get it right." Anaya reached over and rubbed Catie's belly.

"Antoine is going to make a great father," Marie said, and Wanda smiled at her. "He reminds me of Allen." She paused and frowned. "Twenty years ago Allen, not this new Allen."

"Auntie, what is happening with you guys?" Anaya asked. "You guys used to be so in love."

Marie sighed. "Girl, if I knew, I would fix it. Things just changed. Allen stopped being spontaneous and turned into someone I can hardly live with."

"That's what happened in my first marriage." Wanda sighed. "One day the fire went out, and we just couldn't get it back." She gazed off. "I used to blame it all on him, but I realize I had a part in it too."

"Why does that happen?" Catie asked. "Why are guys one way in the beginning and then they change?"

"I don't know." Marie swirled her wine. Anaya rarely saw her so contemplative. "It's like they get comfortable and forget that it still takes work to keep us interested." She stood up. "Look at me. I work damn hard on this body. I'm the same size I was when Allen met me *twenty-five* years ago. I keep this body tight. And look at him."

"Auntie," Anaya warned. It wasn't fair to bash Uncle Allen.

"Seriously," Marie said. "He drinks all that beer and carries that spare tire around. I don't like looking at that. What if I let my body go? He would be buying me all kind of Jenny Craig snacks." She plopped back down in her seat.

"It's not all about looks," Anaya said, trying to calm Marie.

"But it kinda is," Catie jumped in. "The same things that attract you to a person are the things they should keep. If you meet someone and they have a six-pack, they should at least try to maintain it. I think that works both ways."

"Excuse me?" Wanda said. "I am almost sixty years old. God bless you, Marie, and whatever genes you have, but this body will never look like it did twenty-five years ago. Whatever man that is lucky enough to get me better appreciate that. What you see is what you get. And while I don't have a six-pack, I have a heart of gold. I love hard and I make the best lasagna this side of the Mississippi."

"Word," Sophie said. "I get where you are coming from, Aunt Marie. Looks can change at the drop of a hat. Like, what if your face gets burned in a fire?"

"Or someone accidentally pours acid on your face." Catie smirked.

Ava giggled. "Or your eyebrows fall out."

"Or you get a thyroid disorder and gain uncontrollable weight?" Troy added.

Marie scoffed. "None of that stuff is going to happen. And it's not just the looks, it's the effort. Allen won't even try to go to the gym or eat right. It gets on my nerves." She frowned like she smelled something funky.

"You get no sympathy from me," Wanda said, shaking her head. "Allen is nice, he works hard, he takes care of you and those kids, and I never heard him complain or say a mean word to you—ever."

"Word," Sophie said again. "No one is perfect, but Uncle Allen seems cool to me. What I want to know is why a guy meets a good woman and it's not enough? Like, why do they still want to see other people? What are they looking for?"

"Someone better," Marie said matter-of-factly.

"What do you mean?" Sophie asked.

Marie sighed. "Men are always looking to see if there is something better out there. Women are different. When we like somebody, we will go to the ends of the earth to make that person ours. We will dress them, teach them new words, buy them teeth if we have too. We do what we can. Men aren't like that. They're always on the hunt for the next best thing, even if they aren't worthy. Men always want women who are out of their league. It makes them feel better about themselves. Think about how many unattractive powerful men you see with beautiful wives."

"I don't believe that," Anaya said, frowning. Carl was nothing like that. But he wasn't hers anymore. *Don't think about him now, you might start crying.*

"It sounds ridiculous," Sophie said. "But there may be some truth to it. Especially these Bay Area men. I mean, are they allergic to commitment? I'm a relatively good catch—"

"You are a damn good catch," Catie corrected.

"Okay, thanks," Sophie said. "But I can't meet a decent guy to save my life. And when I meet someone promising, he doesn't want to commit. Or he doesn't have a job. Or he's in the 'music business.'" She used air quotes.

"Or he has kids," Catie said.

"I just can't catch a break. Why do so many men have kids and are not married or in the relationship with the person they procreated with? What is that even about?" Sophie was exasperated. "I don't want to start a relationship with you and your baby and your baby mama and her son by someone else that you claim because his daddy isn't around. I just can't."

"Maybe you should stop looking," Wanda offered. "Maybe there are some other things you need to work out first. Life has a way of speaking to us and making us slow down."

"I keep telling her that," Catie said. "She definitely has some stuff to work out. A man will come eventually." Catie looked up at the ceiling. "Excuse the pun."

Sophie rolled her eyes.

"I think as hard as it is for us to figure out men, it's just as hard for them to figure us out," Wanda said sagely.

"Now that's a word right there," Marie said. "You better tell the truth, Wanda."

"We also have to remember to be accountable for our actions. It takes two people to make a thing go right." Wanda looked at Marie. "We gotta get our priorities straight, ladies. Can't say we want a good man and we aren't willing to be a good woman. We want a man in a Tesla but we are driving a broken down Prius with bad credit. We want a man with a good job and we are still over here trying to make up credits to get our degree. We have to be willing to bring something to the table as well. We also have to learn early on to read the signs."

"What do you mean?" Anaya asked.

"Well, if you meet a guy and catch him in a lie right away—red flag. If he won't let you visit his place and he's visited yours half a dozen times—red flag. Just don't set yourself up is all I'm saying. Check yourself before you catch feelings. That way, you can walk away easily. We can all have a man if we want to, the question is, do you want a good man or just a man?"

Anaya found herself lost in thought. Too many times Carl had told her his friends thought she was too good for him. She'd asked him the reason for their incorrect theory and he always shrugged it off with "You are different from other girls I've dated." She chose to take that as a compliment. She chalked it up to the reason they were so chilly towards her. In the end she tried to convince herself that it didn't matter if his friends didn't like her, but in fact it did. She was starting to wonder if maybe Carl was the one who was too good for her. He knew what he wanted, he was ready for commitment, and he didn't care what anybody else thought. Anaya didn't have the same emotional girth. And then there was Jeff. How could she be with Carl knowing Jeff was an option? She couldn't make Carl her second choice again—that wasn't fair. He deserved so much better. She rubbed her temples.

"Ny, are you okay?" Ava asked, bringing Anaya out of her thoughts.

"Yeah," Anaya said too quickly. "Just thinking about what to do with the extra food." It wasn't good to be such a quick liar, but sometimes it was helpful. "Catie, you stay right there. Everyone else, let's finish cleaning up."

TWENTY THREE

S ophie felt as amazing as she looked in a fitted cotton dress, strappy sandals, and flawless makeup. Her curls cascaded around her shoulders, the way she preferred, and she wore her favorite diamond studs. She circled the block four times before finding a spot within walking distance of the Yard House restaurant. Phil was from the South Bay, and she had agreed to drive out his way. If things didn't work out, she could always hit up Santana Row for some shopping.

She grabbed her wool jacket and checked her matte lipstick. Although she told herself this date wasn't about Jabari not returning her calls, it actually was. All of his talk about falling asleep and forgetting to call, working overtime, and helping out his family with chores was getting tiring. Wanda was right. If someone wanted to spend time with you, they made time. Regardless of whatever else was going on, Jabari would have made time if he wanted to. She wanted to text him and curse him out, but she didn't. She was going to be cool. If he didn't want her, fine. She couldn't force him. And if he wanted to go through his adult life lying to people and being disingenuous, then more power to him. This would be her opportunity to see what Phil was all about.

Sophie had met Phil online the same time she met Jabari, but brushed Phil off when she and Jabari connected. She was pleasantly surprised to see Phil was still available when she logged back into her account after Jabari went AWOL. She didn't typically allow face-to-face dating so soon after meeting online, but she was a woman scorned and a woman scorned was unpredictable and careless.

Yard House was full, as expected. She looked around the waiting area and saw only families and couples. She rechecked her phone to see if Phil had called. Maybe he was late or had changed his mind about coming. She moved aside to let a short man with a limp pass. She took a seat next to the door and pretended to be interested in the football game like everybody else.

"Sophie?" The stunted man had circled back and stopped. Sophie looked around. Perhaps there was someone else with that name. Maybe the tall lady in all black? Or the blonde with the thick glasses and Raiders jersey? *Please Lord, let him be looking for another Sophie.*

"I'm Phil."

Of course he was. As many times as she talked about the rules of online dating, she hadn't followed them this time. Phil, the six-foot ardent golf player and college basketball star, was nothing more than this diminutive dude with plaid pants and preferential parking privileges. His pasty hair was brushed to one side like Jidenna. His earrings didn't match, and his yellow-and-blue polka dot tie clashed terribly with his britches. His smile was crooked, he used a cane, and he had clearly embellished his height in his profile.

The waitress offered them a table near the center of the restaurant, but Sophie asked for a booth in the back, near the kitchen. Phil protested, but she was having none of it. She didn't owe him anything. Especially after tricking her. Getting through dinner would be her charitable gesture of the year. She followed the waitress to their table and prayed she didn't see anybody she knew.

Phil was a challenge on the eyes, but Sophie quickly found he knew a lot about psychology and therapy—two of her favorite topics. Apparently starting therapy had really helped him deal with his issues. Occasionally he said something that interested her, like how he used toothpicks to get over his social anxiety, but for the most part, she spaced.

When he started talking abut the new Warriors stadium, she stifled a yawn.

"It's going to be hard to get to that stadium. No p-parking and the prices are going to g-go up," he said.

Sophie raised an eyebrow. She only went to Warriors' games when her father was in town, and they always sat courtside. "Yep, I guess that's true. The only sports team Oakland will have is the As. The Raiders will be in Vegas soon too."

"That's right. Man. Oakland won't be the s-same."

"Well, it's not the same now. It's overpriced, has failing schools, and random white people feel entitled to call the police on black people picnicking."

"Oh, wow. Okay. Tell me how you really f-feel." Phil laughed and picked at something on the right side of his chin. "It's g-getting like that here in the S-south Bay. Gran-Gran and I live in Menlo Park right now, but we lived in East Palo Alto for years. They drove us all out. Built that huge Ikea and some other s-stuff. Offered Gran-Gran a lot of money to buy her house and she took it. Now when I go back, I hardly r-r-recognize the area."

"Yeah, I guess it's an epidemic," Sophie said. If she squinted, maybe Phil wasn't so bad looking. She opened her eyes again. *Yes, he was.*

When the waitress came to take their order, Sophie realized Phil had more than physical issues. She ordered a salad while Phil squinted at the menu for too long and finally asked about the enchiladas.

"We have pork, chicken, and cheese," the waitress said impatiently.

"What do you mean? Don't all enchiladas come with ch-ch-ch-cheese?"

Sophie hid behind the menu.

"That meat loaf looks good, but why do you put bleach on the vegetables? That could k-kill somebody! You should j-just use a vegetable wash like Gran-Gran."

"The vegetables aren't bleached, they are blanched." The waitress didn't hide her irritation.

Phil squinted at the menu again. "Oh, that's an 'n.' Oh, okay. I s-see. Blanched vegetables. Okay. And I see you have linguine. Cool, cool."

"Those are langoustines," the waitress said.

"I see." He rubbed the stubble on his chin. "You know this entire menu, huh, smarty-pants? All right, what is this right here?" He pointed.

"Tilapia."

"Ah, okay. That's some kind of steak, right? Probably a center cut. That's one thing about me, I know my b-beef." He wiggled his eyebrows at Sophie.

"It's fish."

Sophie felt no sympathy for him or his sub-par reading ability. After he finally ordered chicken strips, Phil took a dive into his life story and ventured to places Sophie wasn't interested in learning about. He had been in rehab like Sophie, never knew his father, and hated his speech impediment. The waitress brought over their food as he told her about his first colonic.

"I have to go back tomorrow," he explained. "They said for the cleansing to really work, I should come a minimum of three times." He didn't notice Sophie's subtle gag. He talked for another fifteen minutes before he came up for air. Whatever rapport they had established in the beginning of their dinner was now gone.

"Wow, you, uh, have a lot going on, Phil." Sophie wondered if he would stop talking if she stabbed herself with the butter knife on the table. *Probably not.*

"Yep," he said.

"Not much time for dating or relationships I'm sure." She took a bite of salad.

"Oh, no, I am def-definitely looking for a life partner," Phil said. He smiled flirtatiously. "T-two is better than one." He put up two fingers for emphasis. "Would m-my situation be a problem for you?"

"*Would your situation be a problem for me?*" She repeated, tilting her head curiously. Surely he was kidding, but she sought clarity just in case. "Are you talking about the fact that you live with your grandmother, your infertility, or the Hep-C?"

"Yes. I m-mean, would any of that s-s-stop you from pursuing a r-relationship with me?"

Yes, and about twenty-five other things, including your missing bicuspid, your right eye that refuses to comply with your left one, and your plastered-down hair.

"Yes, they would likely play a factor." She gazed down at a few grains of salt on the table.

He started on again about his life while Sophie slowly ate her salad, taking care to chew thoroughly. He had worked at a bank after high school and was on the VP track until he had an accident in a golf cart that disabled him. But he was a trooper and completed physical therapy. On and on he went. He talked so much that Sophie checked out for ten minutes and he didn't notice. The server came to refill their drinks, and he asked her to take a photo of them.

"My phone is dead. Can she take it on your ph-phone?" he asked. Sophie gave the server her phone and looked away as she took the photo. The waitress didn't offer a re-take.

"Be sure to send that t-to me."

Not going to happen.

Once she had finished her salad, it was time to get down to business. "Why did you misrepresent yourself online?" Sophie asked directly.

He rocked back like she had slapped him, then hung his head. "I don't know."

"Phil, you can't mislead people that way. When someone views your profile, they are looking for you, not pictures of your favorite athlete."

"I know I shouldn't have lied." He looked up pleadingly. "But if I p-post pictures of myself, I won't get girls like you to contact m-me."

"Maybe you don't need a girl like me. You don't even know me."

"I know you are beautiful."

"Well, thank you. But whether I'm beautiful or not, you tricked me into coming here, and that's not right. It's dishonest, and even if I were interested in you, you shouldn't begin a friendship with dishonesty. When you get home, you should write down ten reasons why you don't think you are good enough as you are."

He looked down again. "I-I don't know what to do."

"Be you. You are a great guy. You tell funny stories, and some woman out there will appreciate you for you, but you have to give them a chance. Today, you took my option of deciding if I wanted to be here with you or not because you posted a fake photo and false information."

"If I posted a photo of m-m-myself, would you have come?"

"No. And that's my prerogative. But just because I wouldn't doesn't mean other women wouldn't. You can't mislead people. It's not fair. And I don't think that is your personality." She gave him some exercises to do for self-exploration and open communication. "The key is to be consistent."

"Y-you know a lot about relationships, Sophie. Why is a beautiful girl like you single?"

Sophie thought for a minute, and then told him about Jabari. It was easy to vent to a stranger. Phil listened closely, picking at his chin.

When she finished, Phil nodded knowingly. "He is intimidated b-by you."

"You think so?" It was the first time she wanted to hear what he had to say.

"Yep. Or he's got another woman somewhere. L-look at you. Your profile picture doesn't do you j-justice. I've never even b-been in the presence of someone as beautiful as you. And you are nice. After all them l-l-lies I told you, you still s-sat here and talked to me. He's a fool and h-he is scared. S-scared you are too good for him, and you know what? Y-y-you are. If he treats you like that, you are too g-good for him."

"Thank you, Phil. That is the nicest thing anyone ever said to me."

"I'm sure it's n-not, but it's the truth."

She bid Phil farewell, deleted their photo, and got on the freeway. Forty-five minutes later, she was back in Oakland. Sophie decided to take the long way back to Rockridge. She passed through downtown where the hipsters lived. Cafes and bike shops populated every other corner, while murals and landscaping had replaced graffiti and blight. She was happy for progress but hated to see Oakland lose its history. Oaktown was now Oaklandish, and she didn't know how she felt about the San Francisco transplants making their mark in her city.

She called her mother, who was on her way to yoga. This was the third time they had spoken this week, and they hadn't had a single argument. Yes, the conversations had been less than two minutes long, but progress was progress. Sophie was okay with small victories for now. She knew that part of her recovery depended largely on repairing her relationship with her mom. Her dysfunctional relationship with her parents was part of the reason she had starting using drugs in the first place. Getting high helped to numb the pain so Sophie was able to deal with the disappointment of knowing her parents chose to fight rather than spend time with her or try to keep their family together.

She was driving up Broadway when her cell rang. She picked up, thinking her mom had forgotten something.

"Hey, you."

Ugh. She wanted to hang up in Jabari's face, but she also wanted to hear his reason for not calling. She decided to play it cool. She put J. Cole on mute so she could hear Jabari's excuses.

"Hey yourself. What's up?"

He said all the usual stuff: he'd been busy, he couldn't stop thinking about her. All the same crap he used to say to her, that she used to forgive him for, but no more. If he missed her, he would have called, and if he cared about her like he said he did, he would have made time to see her. She wasn't going to fall for his web of lies. She missed him, but she also missed the Obama administration. Sometimes you just had to let go, no matter how hard it was.

After his unconvincing apology, the line went silent. He was waiting for her response. Sophie waited. Let him sweat.

It didn't take long. "Can you come over?" he asked softly.

Could she come over? For what? For him to disrespect her some more and dream up more lies to tell her once she got there? So he could have sex with her and then tell her he had to go and help his aunt move? What did he take her for? Did he think she was some desperado who didn't have any other options than getting played by some hip-hop wannabe chef who couldn't be honest? No way.

But she'd never been to his place.

"What's your address?"

She hung up the phone and hit the steering wheel in frustration. She was weak. She put his address in her GPS and cursed herself all the way to his place. Why was her self-worth so dependent on his acceptance? Why did an invitation to his house suddenly make up for all the pain and confusion he had caused her? By the time she arrived at his apartment in Hayward, she still hadn't figured it out.

Jabari's apartment smelled like grilled salmon and peaches, and he greeted her at the door with a kiss, though she returned it stiffly. He was in jeans and had decided he didn't need a shirt.

"I gotta watch the salmon on the grill, babe, but make yourself at home."

Don't call me babe. Sophie stood in the center of his living room and turned around slowly. After all this time, she was finally in his space. Where he slept, cooked, rested, and talked to her on the phone when he bothered to call. It didn't look like she had imagined. The place was clean and well decorated, with beautiful artwork on the walls and a lovely ceramic centerpiece on the dining room table. A small figurine she'd given him sat on the mantel, and a book of poems she'd given him was on the coffee table. The brown sofa wasn't much to look at, but it was carefully masked by colorful throw pillows. There was no sign of any other woman in the living room.

She found the restroom neat, just like the rest of the house. She freshened her lip gloss and stared at herself in the mirror before doing the inevitable. There was nothing in the medicine cabinet except men's shaving cream, deodorant, some over-the-counter pain relievers, a little bottle of something for athletes' foot, and Band-Aids with Dora the Explorer on them. Nothing damaging in there. She blew a kiss in the mirror and went back out to the kitchen.

"Are you hungry?" Jabari asked, coming in from the patio with a plate of grilled salmon.

"Sure. It smells amazing, Jabari." Her mood was improving.

He moved around the kitchen like an expert, dicing, slicing, and smiling at Sophie. How could this be the same guy who didn't return phone calls and made her feel so suspicious? This man looked at her like he loved her. And when they were together, it didn't feel like there was any place he'd rather be. It didn't make sense, but she didn't want to ruin the moment with heavy discussion. She would ask the hard questions after dinner.

Dinner was delicious, and afterwards, they moved to the couch. He started kissing her lips and ears and neck. He pulled her dress over her head and caressed her breasts. She panted, filled with passion and happiness. This was it. They were going to be together and move past all the nonsense. When she reached down and grabbed him, she made a mental note to buy him new underwear.

"I want you so bad," he groaned.

The first time she heard the doorbell, she thought she was hearing things. Then it rang again. And again, followed by pounding on the door. She pushed on Jabari's chest.

"Jabari, is that the door?" She tried to sit up.

"Nah," he moaned.

"Jabari, I know you're in there!" The muffled voice was female.

"Someone's at the door! Who is that?" Sophie jumped up and pulled on her dress, grabbing her handbag.

Jabari looked guilty. "I dunno."

The pounding finally stopped, and his cell phone rang. Jabari put his fingers to his lips.

"Don't shush me!" Sophie rushed to the door, but Jabari got there first.

"Sophie, don't go out there. Please," he whispered.

"Then tell me the truth."

"The truth about what?"

Sophie reached around him toward the door.

"Okay! Wait," he said, voice still hushed. "I'll tell you anything you want to know. Please." He flinched at the voice on the other side.

"Jabari! I hear your voice. Open this door now!"

"Who is that?" Sophie demanded.

"My sister."

Sophie reached for the doorknob again.

"Wait. Okay. It's my friend." *What a persistent friend.*

Jabari wasn't capable of loving anybody. He didn't even love himself. Love is selfless and giving and kind. Love is not manipulative and deceitful. Once Sophie walked out, she would never come back. The guy she thought she loved and had been willing to do anything for a few moments ago was nothing more than a dishonest weasel.

The fear in his expression and his tight, white underwear didn't do anything to make him more favorable in her eyes. She pushed passed Jabari and opened the door.

A furious-looking redhead with balled fists stood at the door. She furrowed her over-plucked eyebrows and stared at Sophie, dragging on a Newport.

"I'm sorry," Sophie said to the thin woman.

"Who are you?" she demanded.

"Babe," Jabari said.

The woman turned to him with fire in her eyes. "Don't babe me, Jabari. You will pay for this."

Sophie stood there, frozen, watching the scene unfold before her.

"I'm not talking to you, Becky."

Becky? No way.

Becky took a long drag of her cigarette and continued to stare at Sophie.

"Put that cigarette out." Jabari's tone was venomous.

"Don't talk to me like that!" Becky countered. "You were nothing when I met you. Just a boy from the desert. You probably would have been recruited by the Taliban."

The Taliban? Sophie needed to get out of there. Why was everyone crazy today?

Becky dropped the cigarette and extinguished it with the point of her thigh-high suede boot. She made her way inside as Sophie brushed passed her and ran down the stairs as fast as she could.

After all the time spent examining her feelings and trying to offer him the opportunity to be honest with her, Jabari had been with another woman. The last thing she needed was to deal with some messy relationship gone wrong. She was done with negative headlines. The last time there was a story about her, she was high at Jack in the Box fussing about the French fries not being hot enough. Her parents almost disowned her after that episode.

Since getting clean, she had stayed out of trouble and out of the headlines. She wasn't going to allow Becky and Jabari to send her to blog hell. All of her emotional survival skills and training were out the window. Tears of outrage and humiliation temporarily blinded her vision, as she tried to decide what to do next, apart from punch him in the face and break his windows was illegal. She pulled out her phone.

"Hello?"

"Catie, thank God," Sophie said, power-walking toward her car. Then she changed directions. She was too agitated to drive.

"Sophie? What's wrong?"

Sophie took a deep breath and unloaded the entire story by the time she reached the front of Jabari's gated complex. She was talking so fast, she had to repeat herself several times. Catie could hardly keep up.

"Wait, wait, wait," Catie said after listening to Sophie rant. "Jabari wears tighty-whities?"

"Really Catie?" Sophie was almost hysterical. "After everything I just said, the only thing you comment on is the kind of underwear Jabari was wearing?"

"You're right. I'm sorry. I'm focused now. Okay. So where is she? Did you say her name was Becky?"

"She's in his apartment. And yes."

"Is she white?"

"Yes."

"Classic." She snorted. "Where are you?"

"At the gate of his complex. I'm just walking off my anger before I get in my car."

"Oh, you're not leaving. You finally get an invitation to his house after all this time, and while you are there, some white chick comes knocking on the door while you are making out and *you leave*?" Catie tore open a pack of something and started chewing loudly.

"Yes. I didn't know what else to do." Sophie kicked the wall.

Why was she feeling so helpless? She had notes, questionnaires, and books on this exact situation and she couldn't think of anything to do. *Stupid!*

"Look, I know I said I wasn't going to cuss anymore, but bitch, fuck that. Get your ass back in there. That son-of-a-bitch has been telling you lies all this time, and you have the opportunity to find out the truth. March your ass right back up there and find out what the fuck has been going on. And after you leave, get yourself tested because that asshole has probably been in prison. Trust me. Any man under seventy years old who wears tighty-whities has been in prison. Or he's mentally challenged. Either way, you don't want him."

"Can you please stop with the underwear?"

"Sophie, you have to go back and get answers. Having her in the room is the only way to know you're getting the truth because he clearly doesn't know how to be honest. And you deserve to know what's been going on. Go back up there and get your truth."

Sophie felt her resolve hardening with Catie's support. "Thanks, Catie."

"Girl, I gotchu. Call me when you get home."

"OK. Love you."

Catie hung up and Sophie walked back toward Jabari's apartment, thinking about all the times she watched Carmen waiting for Terry to get home. She thought about all their fights about him lying and all the times she felt responsible for her parents breaking up.

Regardless of our beginnings, we have the power to determine our ending.

Sophie repeated the mantra to herself. Just because Sophie's parents were dysfunctional and couldn't make their marriage work didn't mean that was Sophie's destiny. She couldn't fix Jabari, and she no longer wanted to.

Sophie walked in to Jabari's apartment without knocking.

Jabari had put on a shirt and was sitting in the chair across from Becky, who sat on the couch, biting her nails and spitting them out. They stopped talking when Sophie came in.

She sat down on the couch next to Becky. Jabari leaned forward with his elbows on his knees.

She glared at him. *Months of lies and excuses and you've been cheating on me with this redhead with over-filled lips and go-go boots. I'm so glad we used condoms.*

"Sophie, I didn't think you'd come back. Thanks." He rubbed a hand over his face. "I wanna apologize to the both of y'all."

He sounded as pathetic as he looked. The charm that once entranced both women had disappeared and most of the color was gone from his face. He lowered his frizzy hair in shame. "I've been lying for a long time, and I'm sorry."

"Ha, that's the understatement of the fucking year," Becky said, crossing one boot over the other.

Jabari looked up to meet Becky's gaze. "Becky, you cool and everything, but we both know our relationship's been over for a long time."

Sophie eyeballed the ceramic centerpiece and fought the urge to smash it across Jabari's head. She started counting. *I need to calm down before this gets ugly. Terry will never forgive me if I show up on some blog for beating this guy down.*

"I didn't know shit," Becky spat. "All I know is you been running around with floozies behind my back."

Sophie bit her bottom lip. *Floozies? One. Two. Three.*

"And you couldn't tell me that? I've been asking you for two years now if you want to break up and you kept saying no! And each time," Becky sniffled, "you said you wanted to fix things. All you had to do was tell me."

Two years, huh? Fifteen. Sixteen.

"I know, and I'm sorry about that. I didn't wanna hurt you. And I'm sorry to you, Sophie." He looked at her, eyes pained. "I didn't expect to meet somebody like you. I mean, when my cousin made up that dating profile, I knew I'd meet some cool people, but nobody like you. You threw me off with your travels and how cool you are. You never judge me. Then I started likin' you a lot, but I was already . . ." He trailed off and hung his head again.

"Finish your sentence, JB," Becky lambasted him. She moved to the edge of her seat and Sophie thought she was going to punch Jabari in the face. It would serve him right. "Because you were already what? In a relationship?"

"I wouldn't call it a relationship," he said bitterly.

"Oh, you wouldn't?" Becky tilted her head to the side. The entire thing was like a scene from a bad reality television show.

"But you spent so many nights with me," Sophie finally said. "How did you do that?"

"I'm a firefighter, Sophie," he said. "I spend three days a week at the station."

"You're a firefighter?" She let it sink in for a minute. "I thought you wanted to be a chef." *What a web of lies.* "So you were—"

"Lying about his shifts," Becky interjected. She turned to Sophie. "What kind of relationship were you in, girl, that you don't know your man's occupation?"

Fifty-seven. Fifty-eight.

"The same kind of relationship *you* were in not knowing where *your* man was for days at a time," Sophie said. "No observer bias here, please. We both suffer from a collective unconscious that most women experience at one point or another in their lives. Transferring your anger to me is unproductive and creates unnecessary tension. Let's not do that."

Jabari smirked.

Becky looked confused, but didn't keep quiet for long. "He just got this apartment a few months ago," Becky said with a side-eye towards Jabari. "Said he needed space, so I gave it to him. I didn't think he was over here cheating on me!"

Becky needed to learn how to communicate without screaming.

That's why Jabari never invited me over. "And your parents?" Sophie asked Jabari, though she was afraid of the answer.

"My parents are dead like I told you."

Whew. "Why couldn't you just tell me about the rest?" Sophie asked.

"Because he's a filthy, stupid liar, that's why," Becky said. "Wait until my father hears about this."

Jabari looked down at his hands. Sophie looked back and forth between Jabari and Becky. Something wasn't right.

"I didn't tell you," he said to Sophie, ignoring Becky's threat, "because I didn't think you woulda stayed around."

"It was my choice, Jabari, and you took that choice away by lying to me."

"Well, my dear, that's what he's famous for. Lying and using people!" Becky yelled again.

"It was a mistake." He paused pensively. "I didn't wanna lose you, Sophie."

"Don't you dare try and pretend like I don't exist. You wanted me!" Becky yelled, fighting for attention.

"Please." Jabari kneeled in front of Sophie and held her hand. "I'm sorry. I never meant to hurt you, Sophie. I swear."

"Blah, blah blah," Becky said, turning redder the longer she was ignored. "How many times have you said that to me?"

"Never," he said, finally turning to her. "You told me you were pregnant. Twice!" It was Jabari's turn to raise his voice.

"I had miscarriages. That wasn't my fault. If you weren't stressing me out, I could have kept our babies."

"I'm not saying it was your fault, Becky, but every time I talked about breaking up, you brought up the miscarriages and said you were depressed. I couldn't leave you like that. I'm not an animal."

"You tricked me too! You were cheating on me all this time," Becky screamed.

"Becky, please. I haven't touched you in over a year. You knew something was wrong. Stop playin' games. And stop yelling."

"You were a gangbanger when I met you." She stood and hitched one hand on her hip. "Trying to finagle your way into any hustle you could. You are nothing without me."

"I was never a gangbanger." Jabari clenched his jaw. "Never."

For some reason, Sophie believed this.

But Becky went on as if he hadn't spoken. "My dad's connections got you that job as a firefighter, and as soon as he finds out about this, you will lose it." She stormed toward the door but abruptly turned back to Sophie. "Good luck, sweetie."

Five hundred and three.

After Becky was gone, Jabari grabbed Sophie's hands again. "This is not who I am. Please believe me. I haven't touched that girl since before I met you, and I have never, ever cheated on her. I swear. I promise you." He gently traced her knuckles and spoke softly. "I dig you, Sophie. It was hard for me to do this—that's why sometimes I just didn't come around, didn't call. I'm all messed up in the head. Her dad helped me get on my feet, so I felt guilty about leaving her, but I don't love her. Please believe me. I'm not some cheating bastard. She was always holding things over my head and playing with my emotions, making me feel like I owed her my life. I was a hustler, but I wasn't no banger. I was never in a gang."

Sophie cocked her head. She felt strangely detached from what was happening. "But you are a cheater, Jabari. That's all I know you to be."

"All I ask is that you give me a chance. I want to start over."

She shook her head slowly. "No, Jabari. You lost that option when you lied to me. Excuse my lack of a clinical term, but this is a hot mess, and I'm not going to spend my time trying to make sense of any of it. Good luck."

She didn't close the door behind her, and she didn't go back. She wasn't perfect, but she was a good person and didn't deserve to be lied to. If Jabari behaved this way at the beginning of the relationship, it was undoubtedly a prelude of things to come, and that wasn't a part of the plan. Relationships were hard enough without that kind of drama. She had watched her mom pine over her dad for years, and she wasn't going to follow that path. She was sad, but she was also relieved. She stopped counting.

Unfortunately, she couldn't undo or un-know the events of the day: Jabari the liar, chain-smoking Becky, and Phil who needed Adult Kumon. The day would go down in history as one of the worse.

TWENTY FOUR

C atie was sad and angry. Lately, her days were overshadowed by vague depression. Her clients irritated her more than usual and she didn't have patience for cancellations or reschedules like she used to. She was worried about the kind of mother she would be. What if she were making a horrible mistake and ended up like her mom? She really thought she was making a breakthrough with therapy. But every once in a while, she got this haunting feeling of looming failure.

She had already talked to Dr. Rhonda about it and did all the textbook stuff she was supposed to do, but still she struggled. Success, money, and power were no solution for her insecurity and guilt. She had grown up as a foster child and had made her way through the system. She should be proud of herself. But it seemed that no matter the level of success, Catie still felt like the little girl who cowered in the corner at night. The little girl who nobody loved. With only a few weeks left in her pregnancy, she still didn't feel like she had resolved these issues. And she was scared.

Most of the time, Catie liked Dr. Rhonda Scott, but sometimes she regretted the day she scheduled that first appointment. Dr. Rhonda was no nonsense and insightful. She could spot a deflection a mile away and often called Catie out on them. Sometimes she knew Catie was going to swerve on an issue even before Catie did. There were multiple awards on the walls and on her shelves of her office.

Practice of the Year.
Award for Psychological Contributions.

Excellence in Diversity.

"Why didn't you tell your mom about the abuse?" Rhonda asked during their appointment one Tuesday evening.

"I did. I told her that he hit me sometimes."

"When you misbehaved, right?"

Catie nodded.

"I'm talking about the sexual abuse. Why didn't you tell her about the sexual abuse?"

Catie looked down at her manicured hands. She had told the lady at the nail shop that she wanted a design on her ring finger, but now she realized it looked like a dead flower.

"I didn't know how." Catie looked up at a black-and-white photo of a large dog with droopy eyes.

"You knew something was happening to you, didn't you?" Rhonda never took her eyes off Catie. Rhonda's cropped red hair was perfectly styled, just like her makeup and tailored pantsuit. She was probably the best-dressed head doctor in town.

"Yes."

"Did you know it was wrong?"

"Of course I knew it was wrong, but I think I was afraid to admit it. If I admitted it was wrong, it made me angry at my mom. I didn't want to be angry with her."

"And why not?"

"She was sick. She was always looking for her next hit of drugs, and telling her something like that wouldn't help. She wouldn't have been able to handle it."

"So you absorbed the pain and stress without telling anyone?"

"Pretty much."

"So, let's talk about how you move on." Rhonda shifted in her chair and crossed her legs. Catie saw the bright red on the bottom of her shoes.

Here we go with the stuff about forgiveness. Again.

"You are going to have to forgive. Your mom, Bill, and yourself."

"Bill is not my father. I don't have to forgive him."

"It doesn't matter, Catie. You have to forgive him so you can move on. You also have to tell your mom what happened."

"I know."

"Do you want to talk about ways to make that happen?"

"Not today."

Catie always felt heavy after these sessions, but it was good because she was working her way through the pain. She desperately needed to get through this so she didn't drag her baby into her trauma like her mom had done. If Leah had worked through some of her issues before becoming a mom, Catie wouldn't be so damaged because of her actions. Catie wouldn't make the same mistake. This baby deserved more.

On the drive home, Catie thought about the crowded bedrooms of her foster homes. The families were almost always low on cash and fostered multiple kids for the money. In every foster home she lived in, there was constant fighting among the kids for attention, clothes, food, or anything else they deemed valuable. She was teased mercilessly at school for her worn out garments. She would be crushed when she walked down the hall and the girls would whisper and laugh.

One day, she was in class and Demond Wilson randomly started taking inventory of shoes. He named all the different brands of shoes until he got to Catie's shoes and blurted out, "Salvation Army!" All the kids laughed and Catie wanted to disappear.

She was afraid to ask her foster parents for new clothes, so she got creative. She was the first person in her school to add rips to her worn-out jeans and cut the collars on her t-shirts and sweatshirts. Catie couldn't recall the exact day Evelyn Garcia brought an old Warriors t-shirt to school and asked Catie to cut it for her. But she did remember the day Jaycee Gordon offered Catie money to bleach and rip her jeans. And the time the cheerleaders invited her to help them style their spirit week outfits. That school year, she earned almost four hundred dollars, and Miss Anne let her keep all of it.

Miss Anne was the only foster parent that showed any interest in Catie for something more than a check. "You remind me of myself," Anne would say through smoke rings. Miss Ann was the smoke-ring master. In the evenings, she would sit and talk to Catie about men. Catie was beautiful, and although Catie hadn't told anyone about the sexual abuse, Miss Anne seemed to know.

"Men will tell you anything," Miss Anne said one night, wrapped in a blue satin robe. Her lips were dark and she never combed her hair, but whenever she had male company, she wore Dottie—her short, curly wig. Miss Anne had a sordid history with men and probably should've been the last person to render advice, but she doled it out anyway.

Miss Anne always had company after the kids went to bed, but that didn't stop the kids from sneaking to the bathroom to be nosey. One night, Catie went to the bathroom while Miss Anne had a visitor, and it was an act she would live to regret. When the social worker came to remove Catie, Miss Anne gave her a small blue Bible. "This will protect you," she said. Catie never saw Miss Anne again. Catie was moved five more times and abused twice more in her foster homes. She built an emotional wall of Teflon and vowed not to let anyone tear it down.

Catie parked her Cayenne and walked up the steps of the dull yellow house with bright blue trim. She typically visited earlier in the afternoon. But not today. She was a woman with a future and the only way to ensure that future was to lay her past to rest.

The young ghost of Amelia played on the porch, but Catie walked past her into the house. Pictures of young Caitlin with bushy ponytails and missing front teeth peered from frames in the front hall at adult Catie, who rocked a Brazilian blowout and veneers.

Young Caitlin was pretty but awkward; nervous and cautious.

In the living room, the glass coffee table smelled like Windex and the floral drapes that matched the sofa were closed. She had finally replaced the rug. A photograph of Catie's grandmother grimaced from a wooden frame above the fireplace across from a picture of the Last Supper and another of the Hollywood sign. Stella's excellent housekeeping skills were no match for the stench of cooking grease and cigarettes that had been part of the house for as long as Catie could remember. The new paint was nice, but in Catie's mind, the dark memories still overshadowed the puce colored living room.

Catie peeked her head into the bedroom. Leah lay beneath the covers. She smiled shyly when she saw Catie, but Catie didn't return the smile. Instead she filled a glass of water and put away a couple of shirts that lay neatly on the bed. Thankfully, Leah's inheritance was enough to outsource a nurse, food delivery, and cleaning service. The small bungalow was paid for.

Leah was Catie's birth mother, and rather than embrace her, Catie had spent years keeping this part of her life hidden.

Catie hadn't planned on being responsible for Leah, but she always found herself being called on to help her in one way or another. When she'd heard about Leah's stroke two years ago, Catie started visiting more. Leah didn't have anyone reliable to manage her affairs, and Bill was about as useful as a dirty mop. When it became clear that Catie had to take on more responsibility, Catie hired Stella and began doing small projects to fix up the house and pay Leah's bills. Catie only came around when she knew Bill wasn't there. The one time he had been there at the same time as Catie, he'd walked out of the house without speaking a word to her.

Catie looked at Leah from the corner of her eye as she closed the dresser. A few months ago, Dr. Rhonda challenged Catie to start talking to Leah during her visits instead of just managing logistics and talking through Stella. Catie managed to do so about every other visit. Leah's stroke left her only able to respond by blinking her eyes or through soft grunts.

"You look nice today," Catie would say. "Did you get enough to eat?" After a while, she began to share more. "I'm pregnant, you know? Antoine and I are going to be great parents. I'm trying to be a better person. I'm in therapy, and it's helping me see myself better. I want to be a good mom. I really don't want to blow this."

During Catie's last visit, Leah put her hand on Catie's stomach, and one side of her face smiled.

Leah hadn't always been so dependent and fragile. Unfortunately, drug addiction and bad decisions extinguished Leah's once burning ambition. Leah grew up in Napa with loving, supportive parents who never went to college and ran a small winery owned by Leah's grandparents. Leah was class president and captain of the cheerleading squad. She went to Oregon State after graduation and met a guy during her first semester on campus. He was a fast-talking, dark-haired trucker from Medford who said he was eight years younger than he really was and Leah fell in love. She started skipping class and was on academic probation by the end of her sophomore year. She had been academically disqualified for two months before her parents found out that Leah was hooked on meth. She refused her parents' help.

The trucker from Medford disappeared when he found out Leah was pregnant, and she got clean. Leah moved back to Napa with her parents. Shortly after Catie's second birthday, Leah's father died of a heart attack, and her mother succumbed to kidney disease. And then Leah met Bill. Bill worked security at the local appliance store. He was nice, but young Caitlin didn't like the way he looked at her. When Bill and Leah first started dating, Caitlin kept her distance from him.

Catie went into the tiny kitchen and warmed a bowl of soup and reminded herself to ask Stella to change the kitchen rugs. Glancing in the pantry, she frowned. She hadn't put beef jerky on the grocery list. That was one of Antoine's favorites. And why would Stella buy Frosted Flakes?

The front door slammed, and Catie jumped. A moment later, Bill walked in. He reeked of alcohol, and his beady eyes were red and swollen. A brown curl of hair fell into his eyes, and his yellow teeth peeked from beneath his mustache. He reminded Catie of the Brawny man but with bad hygiene. She stepped away from the counter and pushed her hand into her purse. She wasn't a child. She wasn't young Caitlin anymore.

Dr. Rhonda probably wouldn't agree with confronting him, but Dr. Rhonda didn't live in Catie's shoes. Catie had suffered a lifetime of abuse, insecurity, and pain caused by this man. For years, she had allowed her body to be used by men because she didn't feel worthy of anything more. She had always felt like she deserved that kind of physical and emotional abuse.

"What the fuck are you doing here?" Bill sneered in a low voice when his bloodshot eyes finally focused on her. He was different when he had been drinking.

There was one way out of the kitchen, and it was through him. It was the only way to get past her sexual abuse, through the first man who had touched her, the sick man who had hurt her.

Bill was the reason that Caitlin had been repeatedly placed in the foster care system. He would hit her, then tell her he loved her, and then rape her. Caitlin felt drunk after he kissed her. When Caitlin's teacher called Social Services after she saw marks on Caitlin's arms one day, Leah lost custody again. Leah was always too drunk or high to realize what was happening in her own home.

"Caitlin, are you sure you fell?" the social worker would implore. Caitlin never told, but that didn't stop them from removing her from the house. "If it isn't abuse, then it was neglect," they said. "Who falls this much?"

Caitlin was frightened of Bill. Catie was not.

Bill stumbled further into the kitchen, and Catie took a step back. No one knew where she was and for the first time, she felt like Antoine may have been right. No pregnant woman should be running around without anyone knowing her whereabouts. Particularly when she had planned a confrontation with her former abuser. She put her hand deeper into her purse.

"I am here to see about my mother. What are you doing here?" His stench made Catie nauseous.

"Don't come in here sassing me," he hissed. "This is my house. I take care of Le-Le. You just started coming around." After Leah's stroke, Bill helped out minimally, but he started sleeping in the spare bedroom. He didn't like the way Leah's mouth turned up on one side, and he said her slurred speech and grunts freaked him out. Both of them stopped using drugs years ago, but Bill still drank heavily.

"This isn't your house. This is Leah's house."

"Why are you even here? You ain't in control of nothing. Not even yourself." He leered at her. "You remember what I used to do to you, don't you? I saw you on TV, thinking you all sophisticated trying to dress people, and you don't even know how to dress. Look at you. That dress is ugly. You too light for that color. I know you, girl. You a hoe, always been a hoe, and always gonna be a nasty little hoe. I don't care how many clothes you try to sell."

Catie took a deep breath. She thought about all of her indiscretions with boys at school, all the name-calling she'd endured from the girls from good homes with "real" families. All of the nights she cried alone, the foster homes, all the men, the pain, the loneliness. She'd wasted time, and she'd hurt people. Hers was a past to forget, a story that should never be told. Her clients wouldn't understand, the industry wouldn't get it, and no one would respect her if they found out.

"I don't know who the hell was stupid enough to knock you up, but they don't know the truth about where you from and what you are."

Maybe this wasn't the time. She looked towards Leah's room, not sure if she wanted Leah to hear or not.

"I love Catie like she's my own," Bill used to tell Leah. "Those teachers don't know what they are talking about."

Catie clutched her bag closer to her chest.

"Where do you think you are going?" Bill took a step toward her. "How about a little fun for old times' sake?"

She moved away from him until her back was against the refrigerator. Bill looked down for an instant when he reeled into the chair, and the next thing he knew, Catie's pocketknife was at his throat.

"I will say *fuck no* to that offer, but how about I cut you into little tiny pieces?" She backed him into the wall with her knife pushed against his throat. Blood trickled down his neck and onto the collar of his shirt.

"No one would notice you missing because nobody cares about you." She pushed the knife harder, and the trickle became a stream. He whined like a kenneled puppy. She felt empowered and strong.

"Shut up," she hissed between clenched teeth. "Do you feel good about yourself for the nasty things you did to me? Are you mad that I made it out of this hellhole? Mad that you didn't break me? You are a disgusting piece of trash. No one would miss you if I killed you right now, you piece of crap child molester."

Bill didn't move, lest he lose his life. Catie's hands shook ferociously. Bill's tears mixed with the blood trickling down his chest.

"You tortured me as a kid. Why, Bill?" She clutched the knife harder. "Because somebody did it to you? Did somebody come into your room at night and rape you? Is that why you decided to hurt an innocent little girl who just wanted to go to school and dress her dolls? A little girl who thought you were a nice man who made her mama happy? A little girl who baked cookies for you, only for you to repay her by sticking your dirty fat fingers inside of her while she cried? Is that why?"

As quickly as Catie had brandished the knife, she pulled it away. Bill slid to the floor holding his neck and staring at her in horror.

"You're not worth it. Not worth my time or my freedom, and you're not worth my peace of mind. You lost then, and you lose now. Your life will always be hell, and mine is just beginning."

Catie knelt down to face him. She now knew that for as awful as he was, what happened to her wasn't her fault. She knew what she had to do. It was one of the hardest things she would ever do in her life, but she needed to be free. Free to love and free to parent the beautiful soul growing inside her. Free to love Antoine and allow him to love her. She needed to be free and in order to do that, she had to release her anger and relieve him of his power.

"I forgive you, Bill," she said to the pathetic man balled up on the floor. "You have twenty-four hours to pack your shit and get out of my mother's house."

✳

At home in Piedmont, Catie took a shower and changed her clothes. She drained spaghetti and took the garlic bread from the oven. She had made a critical breakthrough and she was feeling good. She still had a long way to go, but she was ready to regain control of her life, one day at a time.

She and Antoine had made mistakes, but Dr. Rhonda had encouraged Catie to think about whether she really wanted to end their relationship. It would be hard to peel back the layers of their long silence, but by compromising and communicating, she would be able to decide once and for all if Antoine was worth it. If they were worth it.

Shortly after dinner was ready, Antoine arrived home with an expression that Catie didn't recognize. He sat down at the table without greeting her and she immediately knew that something was off. He stared at her for a long time, tapping his finger on the table.

She stood directly in front of him and folded her arms across her chest. *What the hell could be bothering him now?* Catie opened her mouth to speak, but Antoine beat her to it.

"When were you going to tell me your mother was alive?"

All of her plans flew out of the window. *How did he know? When did he find out?* She sat down, feeling weak, her head spinning.

"I planned to tell you." Her voice sounded like straw. She grabbed her stomach. *Ouch.* It felt like all her problems were ripping their way out of her.

He got in her face. "What kind of person pretends their mother is dead? Huh? What kind of person?" He was yelling. She'd never seen him this way. He was always so calm and forgiving. His fists were balled and his face was contorted. She wasn't afraid, but she was uncomfortable. *Ouch!*

How could she have done this to him? He and Wanda always took special care with Catie on Mother's Day, and they even celebrated Leah's birthday each year in memory of her. Antoine had never questioned all the stories Catie told about her mom being dead. Why would he? She wasn't even sure why she lied. It just came out one day and it made her past seemed simpler, so she stuck with it.

"Antoine, I didn't know how to tell you. I was scared." She bent over as far as she could, cradling her stomach.

He snorted, a look of disgust on his face. "Scared? You're not scared of anything. Not the Great Caitlin Murphy. You walk around with a chip on your shoulder the size of South America, and now you want to claim you were scared? I'm not buying it. You are a straight-up fraud."

The rage that swelled inside her made her voice stronger.

"Antoine, give me a break. Do you think this was my plan? It just happened. People assumed she was dead, and I went with it. I know it was bad that I lied, but I was scared to tell you. To tell anyone." The pain was getting more intense. She did her breathing exercises.

"Wow." He laughed sarcastically. "So you can tell me that you've slept with half of North America, but you can't tell me the person who gave birth to you is alive?"

Antoine never brought up her sordid past of prostitution and bad decisions. It was an unspoken vow that he had just broken.

"Antoine, please. I'm sorry." Catie sobbed.

"I can't do this anymore." Antoine backed away from her. "I learned how to live with your extravagant tastes and stubbornness. I let you control what I wear and eat. I allowed you to make me look stupid in front of your clients and friends. But lying to me about something like this is different. This is bullshit!" He punched the wall. "Ouch. Fuck!"

"Antoine!"

"*What!* What, Catie?" He circled the kitchen table. "You told me your mother was *dead*. That is beyond unacceptable, Catie. Beyond!"

Catie couldn't stand the hypocrisy for another minute. "Antoine, seriously? Are you going to sit here and act all self-righteous while you have been fooling around with some trampy masseuse?" Her accusation didn't come out as strong as she would have liked. She knew it was wrong to deflect and throw daggers, but the old Catie was all about defending herself, no matter what.

His slack face confirmed her worst fears, but she plowed ahead, despite the increasing pain. "Yeah, I know all about it. How could you do that to me while I'm carrying our baby, Antoine? No, I didn't tell you about my mother, and I'm sorry, but I didn't disrespect our relationship either."

Everyone knows it's never a good idea to throw stones when you live in a glass house, and this crystal mansion was toppling.

"Wow." Antoine sat down again. "I have tried to be everything I can to you. In every way. All I wanted to do was to provide for you and our baby and make both of y'all happier than you could imagine. That's all. I'm simple. I don't need a lot of stuff. I just need to make my woman happy, and I can't even do that." He put his head in his hands.

"I guess not."

He stood up. "Fine. I'm out."

"Antoine!" Catie screamed as something insider her burst. "ANTOINE!"

He turned around. "Oh my God!"

TWENTY FIVE

P hone to her ear, Anaya watched the sunset from her office window as she listened to Ava talk breathlessly about Joe's new job. Most of her staff had gone for the day, so the office was quiet. Anaya was still relishing in the board's final approval of the development agreement. She looked up and was surprised to hear Natalie shuffling papers at her desk. Overtime wasn't allowed unless absolutely necessary, and there was nothing about Natalie's job responsibilities that required overtime. Not unless someone had added snooping to her job description without telling Anaya.

"Oh, and Marie says not to forget the sparkling Evian."

"She texted me three times about it already." Anaya sighed. Uncle Allen was away on a business trip, and a raccoon had come through Marie's dog door a couple of days ago. Now Marie and her yorkie Pinot refused to go home until Allen was back. *The joys of family.*

She heard someone clear their throat and looked over to see Natalie peeking into her office. Hopefully whatever Natalie wanted would be better than raccoon invaders and grocery store runs.

"Listen, Ava, I have to go, but I'll see you tonight. Bye."

She hung up and turned to her assistant, who was in full violation of the dress code in a tight leather skirt and low-cut blouse. Natalie had been peeking in and out of Anaya's office all day. That morning, Jayde had stopped by to tell Anaya about rumors swirling around that Wendy was out to get Anaya and that Anaya's job was on the line. Somehow, the whole office already knew about it, but it would take more than petty disdain to get rid of Anaya. Anaya knew her job, the board respected her and, at the moment, Wendy needed her. But she wasn't going to share any of that with nosey Natalie.

"Natalie, tomorrow when you get in, send a PDF of the Endless Opportunities for Youth report to the director at New Beginnings, make sure staff is set up for training for the new system upgrade, and please send a reminder email to those who need to attend. Also get the mailings for the library grant proposal out, and please schedule an appointment for me to tour the new library. I've promised Tina for weeks that I would be up there soon."

Natalie nodded from the doorway but didn't budge.

Anaya raised her eyebrows. "How can I help you, Natalie?" No matter what Anaya said, she couldn't give Natalie what she wanted. The Senate Intelligence Committee couldn't give Natalie what she wanted. Natalie's thirst for gossip was insatiable.

Natalie took that question as an invitation to sit down. "I didn't really want anything. I'm glad the board finally approved the development agreement. That was a big deal."

"Yes it was," Anaya agreed. She and the task force would be having celebratory drinks in a few weeks.

"You were the star of the show. Wendy tried to pretend she was in your corner, but we all know she's a hater."

"Was there anything I can help you with, Natalie?"

"I was just wondering if you were okay. You haven't been yourself lately. " She crossed her legs and leaned forward.

"I don't know what you mean."

"Come on, boss lady. You are different. I've been working for you for a long time, and this is not you."

"I'm fine except that I have a ton of work to do, as I'm sure you know. So if you don't need anything, can you close the door behind you please?"

"Man, it's just so crazy," Natalie said, completely ignoring Anaya's request and continuing the conversation. "Are you planning to leave the county?"

Anaya was ready to physically kick Natalie from the room when she looked up to see Jeff standing hesitantly at her door. He looked handsome in a navy suit and no tie. Sometimes she wished he would shave that beard just to break the spell he had over her. *Damn him.*

Anaya sat up straighter in her seat and mindlessly fixed her hair. Natalie looked back and forth between her and Jeff with curiosity.

"Hey," Jeff said lightly. "I rang the bell at the reception desk, but no one answered."

"Oh." Natalie giggled and looked at her wrist. "Deena is gone for the day. Most of the guys don't work past five around here." She gave Jeff the once-over and looked at Anaya again. Anaya hid her feelings behind a mask of professionalism and a barely there smile.

"Come in." Anaya waved Jeff inside her office. "Natalie, you've worked a long day. You can head home."

Natalie stood slowly. She watched the dynamics for a few seconds more before asking, "Can I get anybody coffee or water?" She looked back and forth between the two of them. "Or wine?" She laughed.

"No, thank you, Natalie," Anaya said. She tried to hide her irritation, but it wasn't working. This would come up in her review again this year.

Natalie reached the door, and Jeff stepped inside.

"Open or closed, boss lady?"

"Closed."

"Closed? Are you sure?" She raised her eyebrows as if Anaya should reconsider her answer.

"Yes, closed."

Natalie sniffed and closed the door, and Anaya was left in her small office, lit in rose by the setting sun, with Jeff. He sat down in Natalie's recently vacated chair.

Anaya was responsible for a multi million-dollar budget. She managed personnel issues, labor negotiations, and constituent problems, but somehow, her personal life had become too much for her. She knew how many floors to add to the multicultural center downtown, and how to revitalize an entire neighborhood, but had no idea what to do with the man sitting across from her. Why did he have to come back into her life, and why was he so damn handsome? She tapped her pen on her desk, hoping to distract herself from his cologne.

"How are you, pretty lady?"

She stopped tapping the pen and tilted her head to the side. That was a loaded question. *The pretty lady is tired, irritated, and confused.*

"I'm okay. I'm glad we are finally finished with the heavy lifting of the project."

"Yes," Jeff nodded. "I was holding my breath when the supes were voting on the final agreement."

"But they voted for it," Anaya reminded him. "And the RFP went out and our primary contractor is local and committed to seventy percent hire even though he's required to only do fifty." Once Wendy was out of the way, everything about the project had gone better than she could have hoped.

"You were amazing through all of this," he said. "You could have just let Wendy take the reins, but you fought for what you knew was right and a deserving, local contractor got the job. You changed a lot of people's lives forever, you know that?" Jeff was suddenly serious.

She waved a hand. "I don't know about all that. I'm just happy things were done the right way."

"Me too," he agreed. "So, how are you doing?" She didn't recognize his expression. Admiration? Pity? Lust?

She looked away and then back up at him. Now was not the time to tell him anything. "Oh, I'm okay, Jeff. Nothing I can't handle."

"You aren't okay. Don't forget I know you. Now that the agreement is signed, I know there's something else bothering you. I can sense it. I've sensed it from the day we started working together." He stood up and walked around the desk until he was standing right next to her. *Too close.*

"Yes, you know me." She sighed and slid her chair back a little to put some space between them. "You won't let me forget."

"Does that bother you?" He sat on the edge of her desk and put a hand on her arm. *Way too close.*

"No," she managed weakly.

"I don't know everything that is happening with you, but I know it's been bananas around here." He gazed intensely into her eyes. "You take care of a lot of people, but you gotta remember to take care of you. That's one thing about you that hasn't changed. Your nurturing spirit won't allow you to be selfish enough to take time for yourself even when you need it. I'm not here to take anything from you. I just want to know what I can do to make things better."

She smiled at him gratefully, then looked away and studied her hands. "That's nice of you. I appreciate that. More than you know."

"I love you," he said, and she looked up in shock. His eyes held her. "I wanted to tell you since the day I saw you at lunch. I can't stop thinking about you, and my life is incomplete without you."

Hold up. She stood up and took a step back, shoulders hitting the wall. She leaned against it for support. What kind of trickery was this? Coming to her office pretending to be supportive, then bam. *He loved her?*

"Jeff . . ."

"Let me finish." He held up a hand. "I also know you need something else right now. And that's what I will be. I will be whatever you need."

She shook her head, trying to process it all. First, he was her friend, then he was in love, and now he was just her friend again? She didn't know what to say.

"You are a special lady." He reached for her hands, and she cautiously let him take them. His hands were warm and a little rough. "You are wise beyond your years. But you also have to learn to put yourself first sometimes. At some point, you are going to do what makes you happy. Not what makes everybody else happy."

"I don't know what I feel anymore." She was bursting at the seams with uncertainty and fear. Fear of letting go, fear of holding on, fear of moving on, and fear of being herself. The naval base project had eaten all her time as she tried to do the best she could for the citizens she served. Now she was thinking about finding a new job and a new place to live. Her home was a disaster thanks to Ava, whom she loved dearly but couldn't live with. And her issues with Carl brought tears to her eyes regularly. Ever since they started dating, she had assumed he would be the one when she was ready for marriage. He was everything she had always wanted and more. Now they weren't even talking.

And what about Jeff? She had denied her feelings for Jeff as long as she could, but something was there. But what was it? Was she happy to finally get to know him in a way she never had before? Was it the undeniable physical attraction? His charm and intellect? She wasn't sure what it was, but she found herself thinking about him when she shouldn't, and wanting to talk to him when she should be talking to Carl.

But she loved Carl. He was her man, her companion, the person she had devoted her time and heart too. The person who supported her more than anyone. Maybe she didn't have real feelings for Jeff. Maybe the feelings were left over from the past, some kind of side effect of the rough ending of their relationship, and it would go away soon.

She started to cry. Jeff stroked her hair, and she surrendered to his arms even as his touch made her cry harder. In between sobs, she tried to pull it together. Her cluttered desk was evidence of her busy days and late nights. When she calmed down, he lifted her chin so she would look at him.

"Maybe it's time to start thinking about you."

"You might be right," she whispered.

"I will always do what's best for you, and right now, you need me to be your friend, and that's what I will be. Nothing more, nothing less. No pressure. I promise."

"Thank you, Jeff."

He wiped a tear away and kissed her on the top of the head.

"You are beautiful even when you are snotty and in distress." He handed her a tissue. She laughed uneasily.

Suddenly the door opened, and Anaya practically jumped away from Jeff.

Natalie stuck her head around the door. "Boss lady, Carl is here."

Holy hell. Anaya had told Natalie a thousand times to wait for a response after knocking, and after a thousand times, Natalie still didn't listen.

The door opened the rest of the way to reveal Carl standing right behind Natalie. It was the first time she'd seen him since the party store, and her heart hurt to see his cold expression. Anaya dabbed at her eyes with the tissue and straightened her back. Jeff stayed where he was behind her desk, face unreadable.

"Carl, come in. Thank you, Natalie. That will be all. Close the door behind you and *go home.*" Anaya took a deep breath.

Carl stepped inside, and Natalie slowly began to close the door, as if it weighed three hundred pounds.

"Natalie!"

"Oh, okay, boss lady."

With a click, the door closed.

Anaya felt literally and figuratively trapped between Carl and Jeff. She looked from one to the other, trying to decide how to proceed.

"I can go, Anaya," Jeff offered. Carl glared in his direction but didn't look directly at him.

Then Anaya realized what she needed to do. What she should have done a long time ago.

"I think that's a good idea, Jeff, but before you go, there's something I need to say." Anaya took a deep breath. "To the both of you." She should have asked Natalie to turn on the air conditioning. Suddenly, she felt hot.

She turned to Carl. "Carl, I know I didn't tell you about Jeff and I working together on navy base project, and that was wrong. I should have said something sooner. Much sooner. But despite my mistake, I remain committed to our relationship." She took a hesitant step toward him, wanting to wipe the icy expression from his face. "I'm sorry for not being completely honest with you, but I love you, and I haven't done anything to disrespect our relationship because you mean a lot to me."

Next she turned to face Jeff. She took another deep breath. "Jeff, I have tried hard to keep things professional between us, and I think I have succeeded. I like working with you, but we are co-workers only. I want that to be clear."

Jeff nodded, his expression stony. "Thank you for the clarification," Jeff said formally. "I respect your decision. And when you have a moment, get back to me on that last email from Sue." He headed toward the door. "Take care, Carl," he said as he passed. When he opened the door, Anaya heard Natalie squeal. She must have been standing right outside.

The door clicked shut once again.

"Babe, I'm sorry," Anaya said turning to Carl. She took another step toward him, wanting to see forgiveness on his face. But he just stared at her.

"All of our rushed conversations and you working late were because of him?"

"Carl, no. I mean, yes. I would've worked those long hours regardless of who was on the project. It just so happened we were working together."

"When did this all happen? When did we start having problems that made you run to another man? I thought we were good, Anaya.

I mean, you had been working a lot so we hadn't spent much time together, but I never suspected this. I never expected you to betray me this way. To betray us. I trusted you. When you said you were working, I believed you. Why, Anaya?"

She shook her head. Tears streamed down her cheeks, following the paths that earlier ones had carved. *This isn't the way things are supposed to be.*

Carl put a hand to his head as if it pained him. "I don't know what to do anymore."

"I'm sorry."

"You think apologies fix everything, Anaya? How many times can you apologize, and how many times am I supposed to forgive you?"

Anaya shrunk back from his venomous tone. She spoke softly, hoping to calm him down. "Carl, it's not what you think."

"Oh no? That's interesting because it seems like something is going on. You were crying when I got here, weren't you? That must have been some conversation."

"I don't know what to say." She felt defeated.

"You can start by telling me why you lied to me. How about that? You work with developers, lawyers, and politicians all the time. You've never lied to me about who you worked with before. Why now? Or have you been lying to me all along?"

"Carl, no. I never lied to you about who I worked with before." She didn't care that Natalie was probably listening at the door.

"Then why now? Why now? Why for him?"

"I don't know." She sobbed uncontrollably.

"Are you still in love with him?"

"What? No. I'm in love with you."

"I don't get you." He sighed and put his hands on top of his head. "I came here because I wanted to see your face. That's it. Seeing your face always makes me feel better. Sometimes it's the best part of my day. Can you imagine loving somebody like that?

Where just seeing that person's face can make everything alright? You have been everything to me, Ny. My mornings, my afternoons, my weekends. My entire life revolves around you, and I didn't have a single complaint about it."

"Carl, please," she sobbed.

"I won't compete for you," he continued. "I can't do that. Especially if I'm going to lose every time. I love you, Anaya. But I can't be second anymore. It's bad enough that I come after your work, family, and your girlfriends. But now, to come second to the same—" He took a deep breath. "Look. I'm sorry that we're having this conversation here. I know you keep work and personal life separate. Honestly, I didn't expect all of this to happen. Like I said, I just came by to see your face, but I guess things happen the way they should." He took a step forward and kissed her on the forehead.

She clutched at his arms desperately. "Carl, let's work this out. Please, I love you."

"I accept that." And he did. He accepted that she loved him in the way she wanted to.

"Thank you." She breathed a sigh of relief. "I love you so much." She put her arms around him, waiting for him to hug her back.

"Then marry me, Anaya Goode."

Maybe she didn't hear him right. She took a step back to see his face. He couldn't be proposing. That didn't make sense. Married? She couldn't get married. Not right now. Life was complicated. Ava was in the house. She didn't know if she was going to continue working in the county. Carl's place was too small. She could never live in a space with such a small closet. Things were too complicated to think about marriage.

"Marry me," he repeated, and his voice was full of love and pain and desperation all at once. "Marry me, Anaya."

She took another step back, shaking her head. "Carl, we aren't ready. Life is complicated. I can't—"

"That's what I thought," he said. "Exactly what I thought."
They both turned in shock as Natalie burst through the door.
"Boss lady, you have an urgent call on your line."

TWENTY SIX

For the first time in over a year, Carmen accepted Sophie's dinner invitation. In the past, Carmen had declined Sophie's invitations complaining of traffic, exhaustion, or wet hair. A low barometric pressure could be a solid excuse for Carmen. Until this beautiful October day, she seemed to have no interest in visiting Sophie's home.

"Hi, Mamá." Sophie hugged Carmen, who smelled like roses.

"Hola, mija."

"Make yourself at home. I'm so glad you came." Sophie turned to light three peace candles. She saw her mother look at a photo of Terry and Sophia in Spain, before picking up the most recent one of them in India. Carmen and Sophie hadn't traveled alone together since Sophie was in high school.

"Oh mi Dios!"

Sophie looked back to see her mother sprawled on the seating cushions. She rushed to help her sit up. "Are you okay?"

"These pillows are so low! Who likes to sit on these things, Sophia? Agua, por favor."

"Everybody likes them," Sophie called as she made her way to the kitchen. "I think it's a nice touch, no, Mamá?"

She came back with the glass of water to see Carmen nod with pursed lips.

Carmen studied the glass as Sophie handed it to her. "Sophia, did you take this glass from my home?"

"No. Daddy bought them for me as a housewarming gift."

"A housewarming gift? Do you know these glasses are Baccarat?"

She knew. She had picked them out herself. Sophie inhaled and exhaled five times. She was going to have a pleasant dinner with her mother if it killed her.

"So, do you like my place?" Sophie asked brightly.

Carmen frowned and nodded towards the pictures of Terry and Sophie. "I see you and your father are communicating more."

"Yeah, we have been taking trips."

"How can I forget? That's the reason he was late with my check last month. Can you believe it? I'm his wife, and I get an allowance like the help."

"It's been good spending time with him," Sophie said, putting tiny sandwiches on a plate.

Carmen snorted. "Well good for you. It must be nice to just take off without a care in the world while others have obligations."

Sophie didn't know what her mom was talking about. Perhaps she had met someone with obligations, because aside from manicure and day spa appointments, Carmen didn't seem to have an obligation or a care in the world.

"Did that varmint go to India with you?"

"If you are talking about Daddy's new friend, no. It was just the two of us." Sophie sighed. She didn't want to fight, but she had to find a way to tell Carmen to stop bringing her father into every conversation.

"And did your father ask about me?"

"No, Mamá."

Carmen snuffed again. "Fine." She looked off onto Sophie's veranda.

"Daddy is happy, and he wants you to be happy too."

"How can I be happy without my husband, Sophia? All the years of supporting him and putting off my own career. Now look. Who am I now? I am nothing!"

Sophie widened her eyes in surprise. She had never heard Carmen say anything like that; she always wore a proud façade of independence and happiness. It was the first genuine thing she heard her mom say in a long time.

"No, Mamá, you are something. You are a mom and an actress and a daughter and a friend." Sophie kneeled in front of Carmen and grabbed her hands. "You've done well for yourself, and when it was time, you chose your family over your career. That's admirable."

"Your father doesn't think so," Carmen said, disappointment lacing her tone.

"Does it matter what Daddy thinks?"

For a long moment, Carmen continued to look out the patio window. Then she turned to look at Sophie. "Your place is lovely, Sophia."

Sophie held her breath. Perhaps an evening of tea, conversation, and those little sandwiches would be the first step in repairing their relationship. Perhaps she could even invite her mom to the Goodes' for Thanksgiving next month.

Carmen looked at the floor and frowned. "This rug is nice, but a darker color would match better."

Sophie rolled her eyes. *Baby steps.*

"The rug is one of a kind. They don't make it in this pattern in any other color."

"I see," Carmen said. "I like your hair that way too, even though it's a bit frizzy."

Sophie dodged Carmen's criticisms like a black belt. "Yeah, sometimes the wind does that." Dodge right.

"Your hips look so wide, *mija*. Have you been eating paella again?"

"Nope." Duck.

"You remember the Johnson's daughter, Robyn? She's a forensic scientist. Why don't you do something like that?"

"Not interested." And dip.

"What are you going to do with your life, Sophia?" Carmen asked, frustrated by her daughter's responses. "Continue living in this fancy place that your father pays for? Where is your degree, Sophia Inez? Where is your job? Caitlin and Anaya have degrees and jobs. Good jobs. Why can't you?"

A few months ago, Sophie would have exploded as her mother systematically asked about each thing she thought was wrong with her daughter. It was like she had a mental list of Sophie's faults, and she could not see her daughter without addressing each one.

Sophie could either kick her mom out of the house or persevere with understanding and love. She decided to continue in love because while Carmen judged Sophie's lack of ambition, Sophie knew that her mom's lack of substance was one of the reasons Terry moved on from their marriage.

Continuing in love didn't mean Sophie wasn't affected by her mother's words. Sophie almost bit a hole in her lip trying to rein in her anger at her mother's assumptions. But she could do this. She had spent months in therapy and had mentally prepared herself for this moment. Ny and Catie didn't have mothers, and they always encouraged Sophie to make amends with Carmen. Sophie spent a lot of time making sure she was emotionally healthy, and mending things with her mom was important to her. Not just for recovery, but because she wanted a relationship with her mom.

She took a deep, cleansing breath. "I had a major setback in my life, and I wasn't healthy, so I couldn't finish school. Now that I'm moving towards being healthy, I will pursue my degree again." *For the thousandth time.*

Carmen flung her hands into the air, but Sophie spoke before she could. "Why are we like this? Why can't we just get along and love and support each other like other mothers and daughters? Why all the animosity?" Sophie struggled to keep her voice level. "I didn't use drugs to hurt you or embarrass you. I was having a hard time, and that's the way I dealt with it, and believe me, I'm paying for it. While all of my friends can drink wine and enjoy life, I have to be careful about certain triggers so I can maintain my sobriety.

I work hard to lead a normal life, and all I want is a little support. Why can't I get that from you?"

Her mother looked up with fire in her eyes. "We gave you everything, Sophia Inez! Everything!"

This was the moment. People always assumed Sophie had everything because her parents had money and celebrity status. But all the gifts and trips in the world didn't change how Sophie felt about herself. Money couldn't teach her life lessons and appreciation and all the things that parents helped their children develop. Sophie was self-made because her parents were too busy to raise her, and she had done a horrible job at raising herself.

She looked at her mom, whose lips were turned down in a frown. It looked like she had stopped with the lip fillers. They were still too big, but they weren't as bad as before. She had also ditched the false eyelashes.

"You and Daddy gave me wonderful experiences and all the tangible things anyone could ever hope for."

"Then why, *mija*?" Carmen yelled. "Why did you do this to us? To yourself? To our family?"

"I was hurting. Fancy trips weren't enough. I needed *you* there during my school plays and soccer games. Do you remember when I got bronchitis? Irma slept at the foot of my bed because I couldn't sleep. You and Daddy were there for me in some ways, but I didn't feel the love and guidance that I needed. I was hurting and desperate for attention most of the time. The drugs just numbed the pain. Don't you think I want to make you and Daddy proud? To make something great of myself like Anaya and Catie? The pain was eating me alive, and the drugs made me forget about all of it. They just made me numb." Her eyes welled with tears, but she blinked them away. "And now I'm starting over. I'm trying, Mama. I am."

Carmen walked over to the window and looked out for a long time before turning to Sophie.

"I wasn't the first person in my family to model. I had an older sister who modeled too."

Sophie almost choked on her coconut water. She never knew she had an aunt.

Carmen recounted how her older sister, Eliza, became a model and was represented by a large New York agency in the seventies. Eliza was discovered during a family beach vacation in Havana. Eliza had no modeling experience beyond the somersaults she was doing in the sand when the modeling agent approached Carmen's parents. Apparently, Eliza's cheekbones "would set magazine covers on fire."

Sophie listened intently while Carmen continued.

"At first, my parents refused to let Eliza go. They heard about the rumors of acting and modeling and didn't want Eliza exposed, but eventually, Eliza convinced them it would be a good way for her to pay for college and to help our family. They finally agreed, and Eliza started modeling." Carmen sat down near the window and looked out. "One day Eliza didn't show up for a shoot, and one of her roommates found her in a hotel room, dead from a cocaine overdose."

Sophie gasped and hurried to her mom's side. "Why did you never tell me any of this?"

"Ah, *mija*. My parents buried her twice. Once at the cemetery and again when they forbade me to ever speak of her again. My father saw Eliza's drug addiction as a betrayal. It brought shame to the family. My parents told everyone Eliza was hit by a car while she was on a modeling shoot."

"Mama, that's terrible," Sophie cried.

Carmen's normally stoic countenance dissolved into tears. "This is the first time I've cried for my sister in thirty years." Sophie knew they were tears for every day Carmen had missed her sister and for every time she was forced to deny Eliza's existence.

"When I found out that you, *mija*, were going down the same path as Eliza, it was too much. It was hard enough to lose my sister. I couldn't face losing you." She sighed bitterly. "So I pretend I don't care and cover my fear and concern with anger."

"Oh my goodness, Mama. *Lo siento*. Why did you never tell me this?"

"Ah, Sophia. I wanted you to have a life of a princess. Not a life of regrets and family shame. I wanted you to be something great. Much greater than I ever was. Not living in the shadows of the past or the hindsight of some man. You are much better than that. Much better than I am. *Te amo*, Sophia Inez, and I want you to be the best person you can be. That's all I ever wanted."

Carmen put her arms around Sophie for the first time in a long time, and for the first time, Sophie felt safe there. She held on tight. Sophie hadn't expected that her mother's attitude toward her would change overnight, but she understood Carmen in a way she hadn't before. And looking in Carmen's eyes, Sophie thought maybe Carmen understood her, too.

A buzzing in Sophie's pocket made them pull apart. Sophie pulled out the phone and rolled her eyes. It was Jabari. He had called three times since she had left his apartment two weeks ago.

Carmen didn't miss a thing. "Uh oh, who is that?"

"This guy," Sophie said casually.

"*Diga mas*," Carmen entreated.

Sophie shrugged. "Just this guy. He's nice, but he's a liar."

"Okay. And?"

Sophie sighed, not wanting to delve into the confusion of how she felt about Jabari after feeling so good about her relationship with her mom. "He tells me he cares about me, but he has an entire life that he hasn't shared with me." Sophie told her about the incident with Becky and the crucial parts of her short relationship with Jabari.

Carmen nodded. "Ah, that's almost the same thing I went through with your father when I first met him."

"What? He didn't call you when he was supposed to?"

"Never. And he had another girlfriend that he lied to me about. Ah, your father was a character, but I loved him." Carmen paused, frowning thoughtfully. "Sometimes people make mistakes, *mija*, and we all need second chances. You never know when you will be the one who needs another chance. You would want somebody to forgive you when you need it, no?"

Sophie snorted. "Are you telling me to forget that all that stuff that happened with Jabari?"

"Of course not. But I'm telling you to be forgiving and open your heart. People make mistakes, Sophia. It sounds like he made a bad choice, but from everything you said, I think he cares about you. And it sounds like you lied to him about your identity."

"I lie because I didn't want people trying to date me because of dad. That's a logical reason."

"According to you. What makes your lie better than his?"

Carmen was missing the point. Sophie didn't trust Jabari anymore. He had told her lie after lie.

Sophie shook her head. "Maybe you're right, Mama, but it will take me a while to forgive him, if I do. I gave him a lot of opportunities to tell me, and instead, he kept lying. I have to decide if I can move past that."

Carmen gave Sophie another hug. "I understand, *mija*. Now, let's eat! It smells *delicioso*."

Sophie was serving the garlic shrimp and thinking of Jabari, when she received an urgent call.

TWENTY SEVEN

Anaya sat in the waiting room at Mercy Medical Center, which smelled of antiseptic and worry despite the botanical photos on the walls that tried to convince her otherwise. Antoine sat across from her, nervously playing with the buttons on his cuffs. He stood up and paced down the hall toward the double doors leading into the ER.

Anaya watched him. Antoine hadn't been too forthcoming with the details, only telling her that they had been talking when Catie collapsed and started bleeding "down there." He had called 911 and she had been rushed into an emergency delivery. That's when Antoine had called Anaya, Sophie, and Wanda.

Surely there was more to it than that, but Anaya didn't want to press. Her eyes drifted to the TV mounted on the wall showing the national news. Across the waiting room, a man demanded to be seen immediately. Beyond him, the electric doors slid open to reveal Wanda, Sophie, and Carmen.

Carmen? She looked magnificent as usual in a fitted jumpsuit and pulled back hair.

Anaya rushed over to meet them, but Wanda headed straight to her son. Sophie gave Anaya a big hug.

"Mamá and I were having dinner when Antoine called. What happened? Is Catie in labor?"

"You'll have to ask Antoine, Sophie. I think she is in labor, but it's an emergency delivery."

"She still has two weeks before the baby is due," Sophie said, worry creasing her forehead.

"Two weeks isn't so early, *mija*, but an emergency delivery sounds bad." Carmen squeezed Sophie's arm, and the three of them walked over to where Antoine was telling Wanda what had happened.

"She fell down clutching her stomach, and I could see blood streaked on the floor where she sat." He rubbed a hand over his face and muttered, "This is my fault. The doctor said no stress and I stressed her out. I shouldn't have started anything."

That's new, Anaya thought. Maybe Catie had confronted him about the masseuse and it had started a fight. She and Sophie exchanged a glance.

"Blood!" Wanda cried "Oh, my *goodness*!" She sat in a padded chair and rocked back and forth. Antoine sat beside her and buried his face in his hands. Carmen sat on Wanda's other side, gently rubbing her back and murmuring in Spanish, while Sophie and Anaya sat across from them, holding hands.

It wasn't long before Antoine stood and started pacing again. Anaya studied him, then squeezed Sophie's hand and released it. She walked over to Antoine and took his arm. He looked over at her in surprise.

"She's going to be fine." She needed him strong for Catie and the baby. He couldn't fold now. "It's not your fault. Just calm down. You aren't any help to her in this state of mind. Calm down."

"I know," he choked. "I just feel so bad. I should have tried harder to accept her for who she is. She never lied about who she was, and who am I to throw anything in her face?"

What was he talking about? Was this about text messages Catie saw?

"It's hard to accept people completely sometimes. It takes time," she said. She turned at the sound of the doors opening and saw Carl walk into the waiting room. He spotted them and strode over.

Since getting the phone call from Antoine, Anaya hadn't had much time to think about Carl's proposal. She had insisted on taking BART because of traffic, and Carl had reluctantly agreed to drive his car and meet her there.

She moved away from Antoine as Carl gave him a solid hug and patted him on the back.

"Thanks for coming, man," Antoine said, wiping his eyes.

"Oh, for sure." Carl looked at Anaya. "Hey. Are you okay?"

"I'm good. Just waiting to hear something."

"They still haven't said anything?" Carl asked, looking at Antoine.

"Hell no, man. Just keep telling me to wait. This shit is frustrating." Antoine rammed his fist into the palm of his hand.

"It's all right," Carl tried to console him. Anaya sat down again.

"This is my fault," she heard Antoine repeat.

The doors leading to the ER swung open, and Antoine spun to face the doctor that entered the waiting room. Once he saw Antoine, he swiftly walked over to him. Anaya overheard him say something about high blood pressure, baby in distress, and C-section.

Wanda went over to stand next to her son. "Go on, son, we will be here waiting for you." Wanda wiped her face and sniffled.

The doctor shook his head. "I'm sorry, but Ms. Murphy asked for Anaya. Which one of you is Anaya?" The doctor looked at the group that had gathered a few feet away to listen without encroaching.

Anaya raised her hand.

"Ms. Murphy asked for you."

Wanda stepped between the doctor and Anaya. "Wait just a minute! My son is the father. He belongs in there!"

Antoine put his hand on her shoulder to calm her down. "Mom, please, not now. If Catie asked for Anaya, let her go. We don't have time for this right now."

Wanda mumbled something about ridiculousness and stormed off.

Before Anaya knew what was happening, the doctor led her through the doors and into the capable hands of a nurse, who rushed Anaya into a robe, took her to the scrub room, and sat her down by Catie's bedside.

Catie started crying when she saw Anaya. Anaya was shocked at how pale Catie looked, but tried to keep the concern from showing on her face. She squeezed her friend's hand and listened as the doctor mentioned something about the position of the baby's head.

"We got this," she whispered in Catie's ear.

"You're my best friend, Amelia," Catie mumbled. Anaya furrowed her brow. *Amelia?*

"Ms. Murphy, can you feel that?" one of the doctors asked. Catie moaned in response. Anaya tried listening to the doctors, but they could be talking about giving Catie a Brazilian blowout for all Anaya understood. The fetal heartbeat monitor echoed through the room.

Anaya remembered when Ava delivered the boys. It was nothing like this. Ava had opted for an all-natural delivery with a bunch of towels and a plastic swimming pool in her living room. Anaya didn't think it was safe, but Ava was determined, so that's how she delivered her babies. The painful way.

The next thing she knew, there was a sucking sound followed by a loud wail. Catie held her head up and smiled as much as the meds would allow.

"She's beautiful," Anaya murmured as the doctor lay the wrinkly baby girl on Catie. Catie touched the baby's cheek before the nurse took the baby away to clean, poke, and do whatever else they did to aggravate new babies. Anaya couldn't hold back her emotions.

"You did it. You are a mama now, girl."

A nurse tapped Anaya on the shoulder. "Ma'am, the baby needs to be dressed. Would you like to dress her?"

Anaya nodded in happy surprise. "Of course!"

An hour later, they had been moved to a recovery room that looked like a home nursery. Catie lapsed in and out of sleep while

Anaya sat in a rocking chair staring at the baby. It was impossible to tell who she would look like, but as she lay peacefully in Anaya's arms, Anaya noticed Catie's nose. She sang a song her mother used to sing to her.

She saw Catie open her eyes and asked softly, "Catie, what you are going to name her?"

"Amelia," Catie said groggily.

"Wait. That's what you called me when—"

"Ms. Goode?" A nurse had stopped in the doorway of the room. Anaya turned to the nurse. "Yes?"

"There's an Antoine in the waiting room. Says he wants to see the baby. He's being pretty insistent, actually."

Anaya looked back at Catie, whose eyes had closed again. Poor Antoine. His baby was born an hour ago, and while Anaya was in the room cooing and rocking, he hadn't even seen his child.

"Yes," Anaya said. "Please tell him to come in." Whatever happened between Antoine and Catie before they got to the hospital would have to wait. This beautiful baby came before everything else, and Anaya was not going to stop Antoine from seeing her.

She gave the baby to a nurse and left the recovery room. On her way to the waiting room, she saw Antoine walking toward her. He looked like he had been crying.

Anaya touched his arm as he passed, but he hardly looked at her. He was focused on getting to his baby.

When Anaya returned to the waiting room, Ava and Roscoe had joined the group.

"Is she all right?" Wanda asked anxiously. Her eyes were red and swollen.

Anaya didn't know if Wanda was talking about the baby or Catie but she nodded.

"Glory to the lamb that was slain," Ava said, raising her hands high above her head. Anaya walked past them all and sat down. She really wasn't in the mood. She half listened to Wanda and Ava talk about delivering babies while Carl and Roscoe made small talk. Carl kept shooting glances at her, but she couldn't deal with him right now.

"Why wasn't Antoine in the delivery room?" Sophie slid into the seat next to Anaya.

"I don't know." Anaya scooted away slightly—she needed space—and checked her cell. Jeff had texted an hour ago to see if she was okay. He didn't even know about Catie. She responded, *Thanks for checking. I'm okay. Talk later.*

"What happened?" Sophie asked in a whisper. Ava sat down on the other side of Anaya. She leaned close to hear Anaya's response but seeing Anaya's glare, she changed her mind.

"Sophie, I don't know," Anaya snapped, feeling penned in. They were getting on her nerves. "I showed up at the emergency room just like you did and found out she wanted me in the delivery room. Catie was in the middle of delivering a baby, so there wasn't much time to chat about Antoine."

Sophie sat back as if slapped. "Whoa there. Misdirected anger, much?"

"I'm sorry, Soph." Anaya put her head in her hands. "I'm just worried about Catie, and you're asking me a bunch of questions I don't have answers to."

"I'm glad you are releasing that energy, Anaya. It's healthy. Let it flow." Sophie breathed heavily and waved her arms. "Release some more and you will feel better."

"Antoine and Catie will be fine." Anaya didn't sound convincing. "This is just one of those things couples go through."

"Yes, it is," Ava swayed from side to side. "Jesus will fix this, and when the time is right, my Father will put those two together the right way. Not in the ways controlled by the flesh, but the ways ruled by the Almighty." Ava closed her eyes and raised her hands high above her head again.

"Ava, shut up," Anaya barked. Carl, Roscoe, and Wanda looked in their direction.

"Wait. Whoa." Sophie leaned away from Anaya. "Ny. Seriously? You can't shut people up when they are praying. I think its heresy or something like that. If nothing else, it's rude."

"No it's not," Anaya retorted. "What's heresy is interfering in other people's business when it doesn't concern you." Anaya glared at her sister.

"She didn't mean any harm, Sophie," Ava said serenely. "Anaya is stressed, but she won't admit it. But God is merciful, and this too shall pass." Ava kept her arms held high. Anaya wanted to slap them down.

"Stressed about what?" Sophie asked Anaya, but Anaya just shook her head. This day was about Catie having a baby, not about Anaya's problems. Anaya was stretched, not stressed. She wanted to strangle Ava. If she did, maybe a nice couple with jobs would adopt the boys.

"I'm fine." She saw Carl looking at her from across the room. She tried to avoid his gaze, but she wasn't quick enough. He started to drift toward them, and she bowed her head. She didn't want him to see her like this. Especially not after what happened in her office earlier that day. "Ava, mind your own business. Talk about something positive, like Joe's new job."

"Joe got another job?" Sophie sat at attention.

"Yes." Ava beamed. "He did. My God is yet on the throne." Another wave of the hand.

"That's great, Ava," Sophie said.

Yeah, now hopefully they can get out, Anaya thought.

"Yes it is," Ava agreed. Anaya felt a hand on her back and flinched away. "But that doesn't change the fact that my dear sister is stressed beyond measure."

She was so melodramatic.

"I'm fine, Ava."

"No, she's not," Ava said to Sophie. "That Wendy person at work is making her crazy, she's up until all hours of the night working, and she never goes to Carl's house anymore."

Anaya gasped in outrage and looked up at Ava. Carl, standing right in front of her, clenched his jaw.

"Ny, what?" Sophie furrowed her brow. "What's going on?"

"It's too much," Ava said quickly, like she was trying to say it before Anaya cut her off. "She can't fix everything. She wants everybody to think she can, but she can't."

"Yeah, she does take on a lot," Wanda added, walking over.

Slowly the family gathered around her in a circle. Why was everybody in her business? All of them had other things they needed to tend to, but instead they wanted to persecute her for handling her own life.

"She just needs a little rest," Roscoe said calmly.

"And Jesus," Ava added.

"Mindfulness Meditation wouldn't hurt either," Sophie said.

Anaya looked down, trying to breathe as her family babbled on around her.

"She's so skinny. That's part of the problem."

"Yeah, but you can't tell her that. She won't listen."

"She's stubborn just like her mama."

"But she's smart though."

"Oh, yes. Yes, she is smart as a whip."

"Just like me. That's why I graduated summa cum laude."

Suddenly she felt someone's hand on her knee, and she looked up, ready to shove whoever it was off her.

Carl's sweet face looked back at her as he crouched down at her level. "Do you want to get out of here?" Carl whispered.

She nodded, and the tears started to come.

"Hey, I'm going to take her to get some rest," Carl said to the rest of the group, helping Anaya to her feet. He parted the goggling family members, and they left them at the hospital trying to figure out what was wrong with Anaya and what happened between Antoine and Catie.

Good luck, Anaya thought, and broke into sobs.

TWENTY EIGHT

C arl drove Anaya to his place. They slept in late the next morning until he got up to make breakfast. She sat on the sofa in the living room while he moved easily around his small kitchen. Being at his place was just what she needed.

She sipped the coffee he brought her. He kissed her on the forehead.

"You take such good care of me," she said.

While Anaya's job offered her a high professional status, and her family put her on a pedestal just like they had with Anita when she was alive, Anaya still felt inadequate. Like something was missing in her life. She realized that for the past six years she had put everything and everyone before her own needs.

That's where Carl came in. He loved her unconditionally. No matter how crazy her world became, he was there, willing to give and be present and do whatever he could to make her happy. He gave her foot rubs and massaged her scalp when she had those awful headaches. He knew she was allergic to cinnamon and he never, ever offered her bread. He didn't seem to mind that she snored and gave her the extra time she needed in the bathroom. Why couldn't she love him the way he deserved?

He sat across from her on the ottoman and she put her socked feet in his lap.

"Have you heard from Catie?"

"Yeah," Anaya sipped her coffee again. "She sent me a text. She and the baby are resting. You talk to Antoine?"

"Yeah, while you were in the delivery room, he and I talked."

"What happened?" She leaned forward.

"I don't know all of the details, but he said something about finding a pile of bills for a house out in Richmond. Apparently he got suspicious and went to the house. I'm not sure what he found out because he left to see the baby before he got to that part."

"A house in Richmond?" Anaya frowned. Maybe Catie was helping one of her staff?

"Yeah, that's what he said."

Maybe that's what they were fighting about when Catie went into labor. Anaya shook her head and sighed. "Wow, I know Catie gets mad, but for her to want Antoine to stay in the waiting room, something terrible must have happened."

"Yeah, I'm sure they will figure it out." He rubbed her leg.

"Yeah," she said.

"So, yesterday." Carl sighed. She moved her feet from his lap and sat up.

"Yeah, I'm sorry. I don't know why I keep making stupid mistakes."

"Not that part," he said gently. "The part where I proposed."

She took his hands, so large and warm, and squeezed them. "I love you, Carl. And I want to spend the rest of my life with you. I just don't think I'm ready for marriage right now. We have something good, but I don't want to ruin it with marriage. Can we just be together for now? Can we just love each other?"

"I love you. You know that, right?"

"I do."

"And I will do anything for you. If you need time, I will give it to you."

She kissed him softly. Hopefully she didn't need too much more time.

TWENTY NINE

Anaya sat on the couch holding her niece. Miriam's birth was much less traumatic than the previous three since Roscoe stood his ground and would have nothing to do with swimming pool or a doula in his living room. Ava had delivered at a natural birthing center in Berkeley a week ago. Miriam was a six-pound, eight-ounce bundle of pure, dark, curly-haired joy. Ava and Joe were proud parents, and Anaya now had a goddaughter and a niece to shop for.

Anaya had taken a long-needed break from work when Miriam was born. County activity typically slowed down during the holidays, so she felt there would be fewer fires to put out while she was gone. Reveling in her time off, she mostly wore joggers and a ponytail and ran errands or lounged around catching up on her favorite podcasts.

This particular morning, she was feeding Miriam a bottle of Ava's breast milk while Ava wrapped Christmas presents on the floor in front of her. She vaguely listened to the local news until she heard the newscaster announce "breaking news about the grand jury findings of the county's bid processes for the navy base." Sue had warned Anaya before she took her vacation that the decision was forthcoming, but no one knew exactly when.

Anaya watched with growing amazement as the newscaster explained how the grand jury noted the county's "dysfunctional and inefficient" competitive bid process and an appalling lack of oversight by the administration. Her eyes grew bigger when the man outlined a plot by a county employee to extort the county during the process.

Jayde was right. Wendy is a crook!

According to the newscaster, the county clerk, Jayde Merrick, and her husband, Nick Merrick, had assumed other names in a business agreement with Nick's brother. The trio owned a print service, a landscaping business, and a painting business, all of which had won bids for parts of the navy base reconstruction. Jayde hadn't reported any of the interests as required by the county's Conflicts of Interest Code, and Jayde knew the requirements better than anyone. The Merrick family also had financial investments in DevCon Construction, a major winner in the bids. The report lambasted Wendy and the board for poor oversight and a severe lack of due diligence. They also noted specific deficiencies by Anaya's department including the re-issuance of the RFP, which they characterized as "clumsy" and an "afterthought." The report included numerous unrelated incidents when County directors were given full authority without sufficient feedback from Wendy.

Miriam coughed, and Anaya looked down to see milk flowing down the newborn's neck.

"Ny! What are you doing?" Ava stopped wrapping. "You are going to make Miriam choke, and you are wasting my breast milk!"

Anaya wiped the spilled milk from Miriam's neck with a burp cloth and moved Miriam to her shoulder, patting her on the back lightly with her eyes still glued to the television. The news reported no comment from the county, but Jayde's attorney gave a statement claiming it was all a mistake and his clients would be exonerated. A clip of Jayde and her husband entering their home flashed briefly, and Jayde covered her face while her husband demanded privacy and respect for their children "during this difficult time."

"Wait, isn't that woman a friend of yours from work?" Ava stood and walked in front of the television, blocking Anaya's view.

"Ava, move! I'm trying to watch that."

Ava went back to her wrapping while shaking her head. "You need to get a new job, Ny. Those people down at the county are corrupt. Illegal contracts? That's not good."

Anaya frowned to see the report had already concluded. She turned to her sister, who was piling her shoddily wrapped gifts beneath the tree.

"I will get a new job eventually, but I can't just pack up my stuff and leave." Anaya absently stroked Miriam's soft, round cheeks. The baby cooed at her.

"Why not? They don't deserve you."

Ava was probably right, but Anaya didn't tell her so. Instead she put Miriam in her bassinet and went upstairs to grab her Blackberry. She had sworn not to use her phone until she went back to work after Thanksgiving, but this was an emergency.

Sure enough, she had missed calls from Natalie, Wendy's assistant, and Sue. She sat in her home office and scrolled through emails. Wendy had announced the interim county clerk would be Marilyn Abrado, a twenty-year county employee, and there was a mandatory executive team meeting the following day. Anaya wanted to go into the office right then and see what was going on, but she decided to give it one more day before going back. She wasn't ready for the drama right now. She was enjoying her new niece and trying to make sense of her life again.

After finally making a decision about Jeff and Carl, she thought she would feel relieved and things would go back to normal. But Carl's proposal had thrown everything into perspective. He wanted a life that she couldn't offer: marriage, kids, and uncomplicated love. He deserved that. Why couldn't she give it to him? Instead of being excited about starting the rest of her life married to the man she had always thought she'd end up with, she was questioning her love for him. Again.

She got a text from Jeff.

Do you have time to talk? Just saw the news report.

She closed the door and called him.

"Hey," she said, unsure why she was whispering. It was a work call.

"Wow," he said. "Did you see the news?"

"Just now. I can't believe it. There must be an explanation. Jayde wouldn't do that." Anaya remembered all the accusations Jayde had made against Wendy. All this time, Anaya was starting to think Wendy was corrupt, but in fact, Wendy was just pompous and selfish. Jayde was the one with questionable intent. That might explain why she hadn't returned Anaya's calls.

"Yeah, I don't know the facts, but things don't look good. Have you talked to her?"

"No. I was thinking about calling her but figured she probably wasn't talking to anyone but her lawyer right now. I feel so bad—she must be going through hell."

"Well, hang in there and be careful, okay? I know that's your friend, but keep a safe distance right now."

She understood. "I will. Thanks. Are you working?"

"I am, but on some other stuff. You doing okay?" He sounded concerned.

"I am. It's been a crazy few weeks."

"It sounds like it. How's your new niece?"

"She's beautiful."

"Like her auntie, I'm sure." He paused. "I'd really like to spend some time with you in the near future. Just to unpack some of this stuff that happened. Is that going to be possible?"

She both loved and hated the butterflies in her stomach. "I will see. I kind of need this time with my family after how crazy work was the last few months." She laughed uneasily but she really wanted to cry.

"I understand. I'd really like to see you though."

Of course he would. She hung up without making any promises. She felt both giddy and guilty with Jeff. Why was there so much baggage associated with him? Was he right that she hadn't forgiven herself for their previous relationship? And if she hadn't, why not? She always put a lot of pressure on herself. Ava wasn't right about much, but she was right about that.

She rubbed her neck, and her fingers landed on the chain that held the diamond pendant around her neck. *Carl*. Sweet, loving, devoted Carl. He didn't deserve Anaya's indecisiveness. He deserved love and loyalty.

She opened her laptop and started to draft an email. "Carl, you don't deserve this," she began to write and then deleted it. She began and erased six more similarly worded emails. If she just got Jeff out of her system, then she could move on and make Carl happy. She'd go to all the bowling parties he wanted and even eat a slice of pizza. She just didn't want to hurt him anymore. Jeff was etched in her brain like a sleep line from a pillow. It would fade away eventually, but for now it was bothersome and obvious.

She and Carl had talked about her past relationship with Jeff. He felt intimidated by it, but more than anything, he felt betrayed, especially when Jeff being around meant she had difficulty committing to Carl. It brought up a slew of issues from when they first started dating that both Carl and Anaya thought they had moved past. Here they were again, with Anaya keeping the fact she was spending time with Jeff from Carl. Carl always said he didn't get Anaya's attraction to the father of two. Especially since she claimed that she didn't want children.

And she herself couldn't explain it. She couldn't tell Carl that everything she liked about Jeff was the opposite of what Carl was. Jeff was spontaneous and Carl was safe. Jeff was opinionated and Carl was passive. Jeff brought out a side in her that she didn't know existed. Their love was daring and forbidden, and she loved and hated it all. She knew early on in their relationship from six years ago that he couldn't love her in a long-term way. All the stolen moments and pretending they weren't in love in front of others and hiding her relationship from her family was all bad, and it was a feeling she'd never forget.

She stared at the blank email on the blank computer screen. She should have never let things go so far with Jeff. Not then and not now. It wasn't worth it. She had to make a decision. Jeff was her colleague, and she had to leave it there. And whatever issues or doubts she had about Carl, she could work through them. Couldn't she?

She walked over to the full-length mirror on her closet and looked at herself. Her bare face looked tired. *Months of work stress, love stress, and family stress will do that to you.* Her body looked good though. She turned around to look at her butt and rock-hard abs. Even though work had kept her from running as much as she liked, she had kept up with her workouts. Just last week she had gone to the boot camp near the lake and endured verbal bashing while doing plié squats and bicycle crunches. "Just because you are thin doesn't mean you are fit!" the trainer had yelled. She didn't know if he was talking to her, but she pushed harder anyway.

She pulled out her phone and texted Carl, "We need to talk." This time she hit send. She couldn't run from this decision forever, and she couldn't keep Carl in this limbo. They needed to figure something out. She slipped her phone back in her pocket when she heard a step on the landing outside the office door. She opened the door and Ava jumped back, Miriam in her arms. Guilt was clear on her face.

"Ava, what are you doing?"

"Walking Miriam."

"What?"

"And checking to see if you can watch her while I pick up the boys."

"Ava, you were spying on me. That's creepy."

"I was not! I was walking Miriam. She seemed gassy and I

needed to ask you to sit with her, so we walked up here. Why would I spy on you?"

"Um, because I have stuff going on and you don't have a life of your own beyond play dough and baby poop? Because I have a work scandal and you have to pump your breast milk? Because you are nosier than anyone should ever be? Because . . ."

"Okay, fine." Ava held up a hand. "You have a point, but I was *not* spying on you. So will you watch Miriam?"

Ava still hadn't learned how to mind her own business or properly ask for assistance. Anaya felt like her vacation had turned into being a live-in nanny, though it was still a relief to not be at work.

Anaya was about to nod and reach for the baby when Ava's voice reached a new whiny pitch. "You said you were going to help me with Miriam and the boys because Joe has to work a double shift tonight."

Anaya clenched her fists. Wasn't it enough that she helped support Ava, her now *four* kids, and husband? Now Ava wanted her to be the regular babysitter too? She smiled sweetly and shut the office door in Ava's face.

✳

County Hall was even more chaotic than usual. The camera crews and the feeling of uncertainty eclipsed the shiny holiday ornaments and the beautiful tree in the plaza. Anaya saw the county's communication director giving a press conference on the front steps. *Good luck to her.* Anaya entered through the back and kept a low profile in skinny jeans, a blazer, and a milk-stained t-shirt. She didn't wave to the security guard like she normally did, and took the stairs, two at a time, up to the second-floor conference room.

She snagged a chair at the back of the conference room and

watched as the team slowly piled in, choosing seats around the large oval table. Normally Wendy reserved this room for meetings with special guests, like when the lieutenant governor came to Wendy's presentation on rising housing costs or when the state assemblyperson wanted an update on the cannabis businesses in the county. Anaya felt out of place in the room, and she could tell the others did too by how they all sat toward the back of the room. Only the latecomers landed seats closer to the front.

Marilyn stood at the front of the room and acknowledged congratulatory remarks from her colleagues.

"Thank you for your support," she said. Her dark frames were perched at the tip of her nose, and her oversized suit jacket swam past knuckles. From the murmurs around her, Anaya gathered that most people were shocked about the accusations against Jayde. So many people trusted her. Some people were shaking their heads like they refused to believe it.

Anaya was so busy watching and listening to the others that she hadn't realized who had sat next to her until the woman started talking.

"Wow, so I see Tony Jones finally came to work. What does he average? One day a month? Oh, and looky-looky, the IT director bleached her hair *even more*. Now she looks like Storm from X-Men."

Anaya turned slowly and gave Emily Breslau, the library director, a weak smile. Rumor had it that Emily suffered from Asperger's or something similar. Her continued unsolicited opinion of every director who walked in the room confirmed that diagnosis for Anaya. And if Emily thought she were whispering, she was terribly mistaken.

"I normally don't come to these things as they are a waste of my time. Oh, my . . . someone's been eating too many of the free donuts from the lounge. Ah, and here is our fearless leader, looking like a female member of Public Enemy. This place is a zoo . . ." Emily folded her arms across her chest and leaned back in her seat.

Anaya looked up at the mention of Wendy. Emily was right about Wendy's outfit. Wendy wore a black jumper, a wide, patent leather belt, and black patent pumps. All she needed was an Uzi strapped across her chest to complete the look. Her pixie was at full height. The Botox was deceiving per usual, so it was anybody's guess what she was actually thinking. She stood at the head of the full table and looked each director in the eye. It was dramatic, but so was everything else Wendy did. If she weren't so good with finance, she could probably fare well in Hollywood.

"First of all, good morning," she said. The room quieted. "Thank you for being here. I know the meeting was last minute and may have interrupted your Thanksgiving plans. I won't prolong the issues and will get right down to business. I need each of you to send me a summary of your department's role in the navy base project. This will help me prepare for my press conference tomorrow. Next, I'd like to assure you that we will get to the bottom of these allegations. We hold high standards in this organization and will *not* tolerate such vile corruption."

"Now," Wendy said, running a hand through her hair, "there will be no talking to the media. Do not discuss even this meeting with your staff. I will be the spokesperson for the county, and that is more than enough. Direct all questions to me. I will not tolerate insubordination on this, and if I see a single quote from any of you to any media outlet, there will be a price to pay. Enough leaks and misinformation are floating around. We don't need additional cooks in an already full kitchen."

"Wendy, we cannot tell our staff what to discuss," the public works director said in his thick Nigerian accent. "That is not proper."

"Neither is his tie, but he makes a good point." Emily chuckled.

"Of course you can, Adedayo. You can do anything you set your mind to do; everyone is forbidden from talking about this issue. That's the direction to take from this meeting."

The IT director stood and cautioned everyone about sending emails. He was a kiss up and did whatever Wendy wanted him to do.

"I would also be careful about voicemail since it transcribes to email," he said huskily, looking for approval from Wendy. She didn't even look at him. "If it's important, take a trip to the person's office and speak to them directly."

"Ha, so much for transparency," Emily snorted. Wendy looked at Emily, but her Botox was unrelenting.

Wendy finished the meeting with an eight-minute video on risk management and conflicts of interest. The video was a waste of time, like the rest of the meeting. After the video, Wendy allowed time for questions.

"None of this would have happened if Jayde married within her race," Emily said in another failed whisper. Anaya moved her chair as far from the offensive library director as she possibly could.

"What happens to the project?" the HR director asked.

"Business as usual," Wendy retorted. "We aren't going to let one monkey stop this show. We are moving forward."

"Is there a plan for addressing the grand jury's allegations? There should be some damage control in the works." Anaya said to no one in particular. *And who is Wendy calling a monkey?* "People are already freaked out, and that report adds fuel to the fire."

"Is that you, Mizz Goode? I didn't recognize you in . . . that." Wendy ran her eyes distastefully over the stained shirt. "People are freaked out? Very articulate. You did attend college, right?" Wendy raised her eyebrows. "I will work with an outside consultant and the communications team to address the very flawed and inaccurate grand jury report. Does that answer your question, Mizz Goode?"

Anaya nodded, satisfied that she brought the grand jury report to light. Wendy wasn't going to mention it.

"Fine then. Any other questions?"

"What's going to happen to Jayde?" someone from the back of the room asked.

"Jayde will get what she deserves," Wendy said as if the words tasted rotten in her mouth. "Exactly what she deserves. Any other questions?"

Yes. *How did this happen? Is there any indication that Jayde was in violation prior to the navy base project? How long have they known? Were other employees involved?*

But no one said anything.

"Good. Thanks for coming, everyone. Enjoy your holiday." Wendy dismissed the group with a wave of her wine-colored acrylic nails.

Some directors lingered afterward, chatting among themselves about the scandal. Anaya overheard someone saying they knew Jayde was suspicious all along, and she brushed past the group. She didn't engage in the backstabbing banter.

Anaya went back to her office and called her staff together. Although she was officially on vacation, as director, she had been the only one from her office at the meeting, and she owed them the information she had. She was hoping for more details, but Wendy hadn't provided much, so she'd have to wing it.

Anaya tried to calm the accelerated beat of her thoughts as the group gathered. She took a deep breath and gave a brief statement about teamwork and due process and business as usual. She didn't believe half of what she said, but she needed to boost confidence and make sure people knew their jobs weren't in jeopardy. She didn't want to give creed to the nasty local headlines, but she didn't want to defend questionable actions either. She didn't know if Jayde was guilty, but that didn't matter.

"So are we going to lose our jobs?" was the first question. It didn't make sense for anyone on her team to lose their jobs based on something Jayde did, but Anaya understood fear.

"No. You will not lose your jobs."

"Are *you* going to lose your job?" That was a different story. Anaya never bent the rules and wasn't involved with Jayde. But this was Wendy's opportunity to tie Anaya and Jayde together. She would uncover every email and correspondence to figure out what had gone on. Although Anaya wasn't involved, Wendy would probably find another way to get rid of her.

"I don't think so," she said without skipping a beat. "Next question?"

"I'm tired of all the games and lying," Natalie said from the far end of the table. She'd been texting throughout the whole meeting. Probably giving somebody a blow by blow of their conversation. That was Natalie for you.

"I mean, if people are stealing from the county and aren't held accountable by our administrator, then how are we supposed to feel? I mean, can I start taking money from petty cash for my own needs? You know, people sometimes don't pay for their share of alimony to take care of their kids even though they can pay for trips to Vegas."

"No, you cannot," Anaya said. "And nor should you think that way. We will not let this situation affect our moral compass. We know the correct way to do things, and it is business as usual." Except it wasn't. Their county clerk had been indicted for fraud, misappropriation of funds, and some other illegalities that were too complex to explain.

Suddenly her staff all looked behind her.

"Well, hello everyone." Wendy's voice seemed to cast a pall over the room. Anaya turned and nodded to her.

Wendy spoke to Anaya with her back to everyone else at the table. "Mizz Goode, may I see you in your office please?" It was more of a demand than a question.

"I'm just doing a quick debrief with my staff. I will meet you in my office."

Anaya was annoyed at Wendy's interruption, but she took a few more minutes to wrap up with her staff—including the directive to not respond to any press requests or questions.

Wendy was pacing around Anaya's office. Anaya was annoyed. She was supposed to be on vacation and two meetings with Wendy in one day were two meetings too many.

"I appreciate you coming into work today. It shows that you are a team player. I like that." Anaya knew Wendy didn't care one way or the other.

Anaya held back her real thought of *who the hell cares what you think or what you like?* and said, "Sure." She looked at her nails. She needed a manicure.

"You know I'm not one to split words so I won't start now. Did you know what Jayde and her husband were up to?"

Anaya looked up, eyes narrowed. "No. How would I?"

"Are you sure?"

"Yes, Wendy, I'm sure."

"You two are friends, and so I just wondered if at some point there was anything that made you think something was amiss with her. I want to be sure there wasn't some collusion between you and Jayde. And since so many things fail under your tutelage, I need to ask the question."

"Collusion? There was no collusion and the bid process went through your office as well, remember? You insisted. Instead of allowing my staff to manage the process like it has been done for the last fifty years, you inserted yourself in the process, so nothing *failed under my tutelage*." The words came out harsher than Anaya intended, but the gloves were off. She had had it with Wendy.

"Yes. *Collusion.* You do know what that word means don't you?" It's like Wendy hadn't heard a single word Anaya had said.

"I know what the word means. There's no collusion, Wendy, and I am on vacation, so I'm leaving."

"Well, consider yourself warned. If I find out you knew anything about this, you will never work in government again."

Anaya's heart raced as she stared Wendy down. They were standing so close to each other that she could feel her breath. A lot of things crossed Anaya's mind to say and do, but she held her peace. Despite all of the problems Wendy had caused, Anaya had stayed calm. Whatever happened to the project would be revealed, and if Wendy were a part of it, she would go down as well. She might not have tried to circumvent money, but she tried to use the process to her advantage and to increase her marketability. Anaya wasn't above holding that against Wendy if Wendy took a shot at her.

Wendy was the first to look away. Anaya smirked.

"Wendy, I will not be threatened."

"And I will not be undermined. There is no way you are so close to Jayde and had no idea what she was doing. I'm not buying it."

Anaya was so angry she didn't have words. Anything that came out of her mouth at that moment would've been lethal. She tried to remember the mantra Sophie taught her to calm down. *Surrender to the moment? Let go and surrender?* She couldn't remember, so she clenched her fist and took a deep breath. *I surrender and let go.* That was it! She breathed deeply again. She was smart, she knew her job, she had a place to live, and she had family and friends that cared about her. If she lost her job, she wouldn't lose her life or her ability to find another job. Enough was enough. She took another deep breath.

"I would never do something like that, Wendy. That's not my character."

"Yeah, that's what they all say," Wendy said, unmoved. She rested her weight on one spiky heel. "Enjoy the rest of your vacation and tweak your resume while you are out. You will need it." She turned and stormed out of Anaya's office.

After a few minutes of fuming, Anaya left her office as well, closing the door behind her. This time she wouldn't come back until her vacation was over, if she came back at all.

She walked to the office the task force had shared for the four months and stood at the door. A solitary figure was looking through papers in a banker's box.

Jeff looked up when he realized she was there. "Well, hello." He beckoned her inside.

"Hey. Are you finishing up?" She walked in.

"Yep, pretty much," he said. It looked as if Jeff had his things packed in the small box near the door.

Anaya looked around the room, almost overcome with memories. The space was small, and it seemed even smaller with boxes piled everywhere. The four desks were covered in paper and office supplies. The team had spent a lot of time resolving issues in that room. The whiteboard still had notes scribbled on them, and the recycle bin hadn't been emptied of coffee cups. She spotted her pink umbrella that she forgot one rainy evening.

What had started as just another contract assignment had resulted in Anaya and Jeff reconnecting. They had worked long hours together, and there was an undeniable affection. They had fought it, but it was there. Real love doesn't die. It waits like a faithful dog. And it all happened in this space.

Anaya was in denial, but denial was safe. She didn't have to choose or make decisions while in denial. She pulled down a piece of paper taped to the wall. One night while working late, the team had a contest to see who could draw the best giraffe. Sue won, and she was rewarded with her giraffe posted on the wall.

"Ah, fun times," Jeff mused.

"Yeah," Anaya said, looking at the drawing. She folded it and put it in her purse.

"Well, great job." He stepped out from behind the desk. "We couldn't have done this without you. We had a lot coming at us, but I'm impressed with your tenacity. You'll run this county one day."

"Thank you."

"Thank *you*," he said, moving closer. "I noticed you didn't respond to the group text about drinks tomorrow."

"I didn't see it. I'm technically on vacation, so I've been trying to stay away from my work cell. Except for today, of course."

"Ah, yes. I remember. Good for you. My girls are away at their ski camp." He stared at her. "Are you all right?"

"Huh? Yeah. Your girls left last night, right?"

"Yeah," he said slowly. "And since you're on vacation, it's perfect. Celebrate with us," He grabbed her hands.

She pulled away and feigned interest in the packing boxes. Files from the project, both disposable and ones that needed to be hung on to, were piled everywhere. The records manager would have a conniption if he saw this room. Anaya and Will would likely be tasked with going over what needed to be stored and what needed to be tossed, and then whatever was left of this project that had consumed her life would be stored on a shelf somewhere.

She turned to see Jeff shut the door, his eyes locked on hers. He pulled Anaya to him. She turned her head away, but he held on.

Long work nights, stolen glances, moments of reminiscing and hours of longing culminated into that moment. She was finally in his arms again, and it felt right. The commotion in County Hall faded away, and she focused on nothing else except that moment. That's when Anaya realized that all of the accomplishments in life and love of family and good health didn't replace that feeling of fire and satisfaction that she hadn't felt since the last time he held her. He rested his hand on her cheek, and the room felt even smaller. Her stomach danced and she felt sweat prickle her scalp.

"Please. Don't pull away. This is happening." Yep, it was happening, right there in the consultant's office. "You don't feel anything for me?" He put her hand over his heart.

"I don't think what I feel matters." She pulled away, conflicted. "I can't do this. We both know I can't."

He let her go. "But you haven't tried. We can't live in the past. I want to move forward in life . . . with you."

She put a hand to her forehead. "Jeff, you can't just waltz into my life after six years like nothing ever happened."

"I wanted to talk to you and try to work things out six years ago. You left *me*, Ny."

"You were married!"

"I never lied to you."

"You never lied to me? So you think you were the paragon of honesty when we dated?"

"Please don't do that. It wasn't an ideal situation. I'm not blaming you for anything, and I'm not saying I did everything the right way. I'm a flawed man. I own it. It wasn't right. My marriage was over long before I even knew who you were. Should I have done things the right way before dating you? Yes. Did I handle it all wrong? Yes. But I didn't, and I have had to live with that. I lived with the guilt every single day when I got up to go to work, every day when I hugged my kids and when I looked in the mirror. But at some point, I realized it was time for me to forgive myself, and I did. Now you have to forgive yourself too. You can't move on until you do. Not with Carl, not with me, not with anybody."

Her jaw dropped. "Forgive myself? You think I'm holding on to guilt from our past?"

"I know you are," he said quietly.

For a moment, Anaya seethed. "You don't know me. You come walking in here professing your love for me, after all this time, like we are just supposed to go sailing off into the sunset with no regard for my life or my current situation. That's not fair."

"What's not fair? That I have taken the boldest step of my life to make things right between us? That I took a chance on pouring my heart out to a stubborn woman who won't accept the truth?"

She straightened, hands by her side. "Jeff, I'm glad we had the chance to clear some things up. I think it was good for both of us."

She had rebuilt her life without Jeff and didn't want to redo any of her plans. Their baggage and his kids weren't in her plans. She studied his face. He looked frustrated.

"And?"

"And what, Jeff?"

"That's it? That's all you have to say?"

"And I wish you the best of luck. With everything."

"Come on. It can't end like this. Not again. I need you to give us a chance. Please," he pleaded. He grabbed her again. This time she didn't resist. She absorbed his warmth, the tickle of his mustache, and his strong arms. It felt right, and neither of them wanted it to end. They didn't remember that they were at work or that the door was unlocked.

"I love you," he whispered in between kisses. "I always have and I always will." He ran his fingers through her hair.

"I love you too, Jeff. But I really should go."

THIRTY

Catie sat on one of Sophie's cushions devouring a plate of Thai food. After being pregnant for nine months, it was nice to sit on Sophie's plush seasonal pillows rather than being restricted to a chair. It was also nice to be out of the house without Amelia for the first time. Six weeks after giving birth, Catie's cravings were as vicious as ever, but the thirty-five pounds of baby and water weight she gained was gone except in one place.

"Dang, girl, look at your titties!" Sophie exclaimed.

"I know." Catie grabbed her chest. "The blessing and curse of breastfeeding. I kinda like them though. All my t-shirts fit *extra* tight." She pushed her chest out.

"They look like they hurt." Anaya frowned.

"Don't be jealous, Ny. Just because you are president of the Itty Bitty Tittie Committee doesn't give you the right to hate on my bodacious ta-tas."

"I'm not hating on you. I would fall over if my boobs were that big."

"I have no comment," Sophie said, looking down at her own DD-cup breasts.

It felt good to be sitting around and hanging out like they used to when they didn't have a care in the world. This was the first time the three of them had spent time together alone since Catie had Amelia. The calming, resort-like feel of Sophie's place was just what they needed.

"I still can't believe you're a mom," Sophie gasped and leaned back in her seat.

"Neither can I." Catie scooped more Pad Thai on her plate. "It feels weird. I'm responsible for somebody's entire life. It's weird."

"Scary," Anaya said, then winced.

"Yeah," Catie said with a faraway look in her eye. Then she started eating again. "So, gimme the gossip." She pointed her fork at Sophie. "Have you talked to Jabari?"

Sophie turned up her top lip.

"Should I take that as a no?"

"I'm not ready. I'm over Jabari for now."

"Wait. What?" Catie sat back in her seat. "I thought for sure Jailbreak Jabari's persistent efforts to get back with you would've worked by now."

Sophie sighed. "It is what it is. I'm just not interested in the games. I do still like him, but lies at the beginning of a relationship are a real red flag."

"Wait. Jailbreak Jabari?" Anaya looked from Catie to Sophie in confusion.

Catie burst out laughing and Sophie ducked her head in embarrassment. "Catie has this weird obsession with Jabari's underwear. I might not have told you that detail when we talked, Anaya." She shrugged. "Anyway, I'm over him. Anybody who tells that many lies has more issues than I know how to deal with. Today is my day of redemption and freedom from excess baggage." Sophie stretched her arms above her head and she slowly put them back down on her lap with a huge exhale.

"Good girl," Catie said. "And good for you for making things right with Auntie Carmen."

"Yeah," Sophie said proudly. "It's a slow process, you know? A lot of baggage to unpack, unchecked emotions to figure out. It's hard, but we are willing to do the work. She even cancelled her last Restylane injection appointment to go on a hike with me."

"Ha," Catie said. "F.O.B.—Family over beauty injections. I'm so proud of you two, girlie. I knew if you gave each other a chance, you guys would make progress."

Anaya sniffled. It was great that Sophie and Carmen's long-standing disagreements and petty fights might finally end.

"Aw, hell, here we go," Catie said.

"I can't help it." Anaya leaned over and hugged Sophie. "I was just remembering how you and your mom came to the hospital together when Catie had Amelia. I was so worried that she would stress you out, but you guys got along great!"

"Well, don't get all emotional too soon. It's still very early. We still have some things to work out, but things are definitely getting better. Watching you two struggle without your moms made me take a closer look at my relationship with mine. We only get one mom."

Catie choked on her tea.

"Are you okay, Catie?"

Catie nodded and waved her hand for them to continue talking. "I'm fine," she coughed again. "So, what's up with you and Carl, Anaya? When is the wedding?"

Anaya studied her nails. "There won't be any wedding. It's not working out, guys."

"What?" Catie sat up. "What do you mean, it's not working out? You and Carl are the poster couple for love. Y'all are like J. Lo and A. Rod, Michelle and Barack, Beyoncé and Jay-Z."

"That's not a good one," Sophie interjected.

"What?" Catie was annoyed at the interruption.

"Beyoncé and Jay-Z. That's not a good example. You know, because of the infidelity and all."

"Girl, bye." Catie dismissed Sophie with a wave of her hand. "Have you heard Lovehappy? The Carters are back and in love. They are the epitome of love. Anyway, Ny, if you and Carl don't make it, there's no hope for the rest of us."

"I slept with Jeff."

Catie shrieked and put her hand over her heart.

"I knew it!" Catie said. "That's why your cheeks are all rosy. Maybe there's nothing wrong with your little va-jay-jay after all."

Anaya threw a cushion at Catie.

"Wow, Ny. Are you okay?" Sophie scooched closer to her.

"I don't know. I feel horrible for doing this to Carl, but it just felt right. And then it felt right again."

"Wait. Y'all did it *twice*?"

Anaya sheepishly held up three fingers and Catie screamed again.

"I know that was hard, Ny, excuse the pun." Catie cleared her throat. "But you know what? You have to start doing you. You take care of everybody else. Since Miss Nita died, I never see you do anything for yourself. I know you care about Carl and don't want to hurt him, but I know you feel something for Jeff too. Don't deny yourself. See what it's about. You guys had a faulty break up. Give yourself a chance at happiness. And you finally got some of that Vitamin D!"

"Oy, chica," Sophie sniffled. "I'm going to have to agree with Catie. I am Team Carl all day, but I am Team Ny over everyone. If you are struggling this much to hold on to Carl, something's not right. Give yourself some time, and when you are ready, give Jeff a chance. I don't know him. I don't like him because of before, but I love you, and I trust your judgment. Think about it carefully, but your happiness comes first."

Catie wasn't sure how Anaya's tiny body was producing so many tears, but they kept coming.

"Maybe you guys are right," Anaya said quietly after the tears had subsided. "But enough about me. Let's see Amelia's new pictures."

"Yes," Sophie said, facing Catie with a wicked gleam in her eye. "And tell us about Antoine. Have y'all slept together too?"

Catie rolled her eyes as she pulled up the latest pictures of her sweet Amelia. "Ugh, Sophie you can be so annoying sometimes. The answer is no, okay." Catie passed her phone around and told them about her and Antoine's new co-parenting norm. It wasn't ideal, but it worked. He took time off from work to help her around the house; she didn't fuss as much and they got along. When she got her phone back, she smiled down at her tiny angel and put her phone away.

"So Catie, can we get the tea from you? What happened the day you gave birth? Why didn't you want Antoine in the room?" Sophie asked.

"It's complicated." Catie sighed. She knew this was coming. She could no longer pretend like it hadn't been a big deal. "Sometimes Antoine can be real nosey. He saw some mail on the console that had an address on it, and being his nosey self, he went to the address and then confronted me about it. It was a bad day, and everything came crashing down."

"That doesn't make sense," Sophie said. "What mail? What address? What came crashing down? What are you even talking about?"

"Yeah," Anaya said. "Something is missing."

"I, um . . ." Catie pushed back her plate and fiddled with the bracelet on her wrist. She twisted it around a few times and looked up at Anaya and Sophie. "I . . . have been paying bills for my mom and I hadn't told Antoine about it."

Anaya's mind did flip-flops. Did she just hear what she thought she heard? She closed her eyes and shook her head like she was trying to get something out of her hair.

The room was silent except for the sound of the small ceramic waterfall on Sophie's patio and some weird instrumental music. Then Sophie began to hyperventilate.

"Wait, wait, wait. Hold the phone," Sophie got out between breaths. "Are you saying your mom is *alive*?"

Anaya still couldn't formulate words. After more than fifteen years of friendship, Catie had never said a peep about her mom being alive. She had told them her mom was dead. Anaya had felt closer to her when her own mom had died. But now Catie's mother was alive? Had never been dead? It made no sense.

"Yes," Catie said slowly.

"How is that possible?" Sophie was still shaking her head, but much slower.

"I was embarrassed about who she was, and I lied."

Anaya couldn't handle Catie's nonchalance. Not about this. Not about lying to her best friends. Not about her mother.

"Embarrassed?" Sophie asked. "Uh, you've met my mom, right? The Botox queen? What could be more embarrassing than all those Botox and Restylane injections?"

"It's not the same. My mom is nothing like Aunt Carmen or Miss Nita. She's . . . different."

Anaya started to process what Catie was saying. Flashbacks of her own mom getting sicker from cancer crept into her mind. Losing weight, losing her hair, the fact that her nephews would never know their grandmother. How could Catie be so deceptive?

"I understand that you may have been embarrassed, but deceiving people who love you isn't healthy, Catie. We can move past this, but we have a long road of forgiveness ahead of us." Sophie's voice was hard.

"Unbelievable," Anaya said so low the others almost didn't hear.

Catie looked at her. Only now were her eyes sad and serious. "I know, Ny. I'm sorry."

"I have shared some of my greatest pains and embarrassments with you, Caitlin. I loved you like a sister and welcomed you into my home and into my family. My mom loved you like her own daughter, and all this time you've been lying to me? To all of us?" Anaya stood up. She couldn't believe her friend would do this.

Catie motioned for her to sit back down. "You guys don't

understand what I went through. My mom was a drug addict. How do you introduce someone like that to the Goodes or the Beats?"

"You watched my family suffer while cancer invaded my mom's entire body and killed her." Anaya couldn't stop the tears from streaming down her face. "You've watched us struggle to pull it together day after day, holiday after holiday, to make our family complete even though there is a hole inside that will never go away." Anaya realized she was shaking. Tears streamed down her already swollen face. "You have a mom that's alive and well, and you *lie* about her existence? That's the most fucked up thing I've ever heard of in my life."

"I know. I'm sorry," Catie repeated.

"You should be."

Catie's expression turned defensive.

"Wait a minute, Ny. You don't have to talk to me like that. I made a mistake, okay?"

"No, you did more than make a mistake. You lied, you disrespected your mother, and you broke our friendship."

"Ny, please don't get self-righteous on me. Everyone in this room has made mistakes."

"Don't you dare try and turn this around on me, Catie," Anaya yelled. She pointed an accusatory finger. "You lied. I'm not perfect, but I'm not a liar."

"Guys, this is getting bad," Sophie said in a calm voice, slowly standing to light a few candles. "Catie, as a rule of thumb, you do not bring up someone else's stuff when you are confessing or apologizing. It's disingenuous, and an ineffective attempt at distraction. And Ny, when someone bares their soul and asks for forgiveness, we don't stick a knife in an open wound. We are treading in dangerous territory with these accusations." She waved the scent of the candles around with her hands.

"Well, that's a lie right there," Catie said, ignoring Sophie completely. "You lied about Jeff for months."

Anaya gasped.

"Ladies, please," Sophie said. "Let's take a moment. Let's close our eyes and breathe."

"Shut up, Sophie," Anaya and Catie barked in unison.

"Yes, okay. I lied, but not to you guys. *Never* to my best friends." Anaya's forehead glistened. "And my lie is not even in the same hemisphere as yours. You don't *deserve* Antoine."

Catie had a history of bullying everyone and not being accountable for her actions. Since childhood, Anaya and Sophie always forgave Catie for anything she did, usually without Catie ever apologizing. This final deception, especially with how desperately Anaya missed her own mother, was too much. Anaya's reaction was strong, but it was too late to pull back.

Sophie had a hand on her arm. "Anaya. You are talking out of anger. Words are powerful, and you can't take them back"

"I don't want to take them back." Anaya glared at Catie.

"Sophie is right. You need to calm down, Ny." Catie pointed her finger. "I'm apologizing here, come on."

"Oh, and because you are apologizing for the first time in your entire life we are supposed to just bow down and forgive you like we always do?"

"I didn't ask you to bow down. All I'm asking for is a little compassion."

"Talk to your mom about compassion." Anaya grabbed her purse. "Or better yet, ask your man who has to find compassion in a massage parlor." Anaya stormed out.

THIRTY ONE

A naya's breathing quickened as she took a table at Lakeshore Café. She sat near the window with clammy hands and looked outside at the menagerie of hipsters, singles, and techies who seemed lost. It was a much different crowd from Saturday mornings. Anaya ordered an almond milk cappuccino and a bowl of fruit, and suddenly wished for wine instead of caffeine. She hadn't talked to Catie since their argument a few days ago and was still confused and angry about how her friend could lie to her for so long. Her stomach felt sour and she'd had anxiety about this meeting all day. She couldn't believe she was about to possibly sabotage her future with the man who had loved her more than she sometimes loved herself. Across from her table, a wall mirror reflected her image—minimal make-up, wild curls, and a black Notorious B.I.G. t-shirt. She sipped her coffee and played around with her fruit until Carl arrived.

She saw him before he saw her, and her heart throbbed with memories. She hadn't seen him since they had dinner at his place last week. It was nice, but they were both awkwardly quiet, which was unusual for them. He was casual in khaki cargo shorts and the Titleist cap she bought for him last Christmas. He couldn't keep up with her on the dance floor, but he held his own on the golf course. She stood and wrapped her arms around him. He smelled like lazy Saturday mornings and comfort.

"Hey," she said as he slid into the chair opposite her.

"Hey," he replied.

"Nice cap."

He nodded. "Thanks."

"Did you play golf today?"

"Nah. I was helping Faven and Darren move." He looked at his hands. "They bought a beautiful house. And all the kids have their own rooms now, so that's good."

Anaya nodded. Although they needed to have a serious conversation, a part of her just wanted to hug Carl and pretend like nothing was wrong. Now that he was here, couldn't they just work it out? She fought back the tears that had appeared far too often during the past few weeks. Then she took a deep breath.

"So I figured it would be good for us to get together and talk in person."

"Okay." He leaned in with his elbows on the table. "So, talk." He pushed his lips to the side the way he did when he was worried about something.

"Well." She cleared her throat. "Things have been hard for us lately. I feel like we haven't been connecting the way we used to."

"Agreed. Last week's dinner was pretty awkward."

"Yeah. It was. And I just want to know how you feel about us. I mean, do you want us to keep trying, or do you want to take a break, or—"

He held up his hand. "Whoa. Don't do that, okay?"

Anaya was taken aback. "Do what?" Carl's gruff tone was unexpected.

"Insult me. Let's not pretend like we need this grand gesture of a conversation while you try to make yourself feel less guilty about what you've been doing. I have never wanted a break from you. And I don't want to break up with you. I'm pretty sure you know that." He lowered his voice. "I love you and I have always been very clear about the fact that I want to spend the rest of my life with you. The answer is no, I don't want a break. So now what?" He folded his arms across his chest.

Well, damn. "Carl, I love you and no matter what happens, I want us to always be friends."

He laughed, but the warmth of it had turned to ice.

Anaya kept going. "We have a good time together and you mean a lot to me. I don't ever want us to break our bond."

"Our bond?"

"Carl, yes. Our bond. You were there for me during some of the hardest times of my life. When I was grieving for my mom and Andrew, and when Roscoe was drinking too much. You've always been right beside me. No questions asked. No regrets. Just supporting and loving me."

"That's what you do when you love somebody, Anaya." He looked into her eyes.

She took a deep breath. "Right now, I just don't know that things are working for me. I feel like there are too many other things that have come before our relationship."

"I saw you," he said quietly.

"What?"

"I saw you. The night of the anniversary party for Faven's parents. I saw you kiss Jeff in the corridor."

Holy hell.

"Carl, I—"

"You don't need to say anything. Actually it's probably better if you don't."

"It just happened. It didn't mean anything."

"Of course it didn't. A lot of things don't mean anything to you lately."

"Carl that's not fair. I'm trying."

"Trying to do what?"

"To give you what you need. To be what you need. To like your friends who hate me. To want to want kids, which I never have. I want to feel like you want me for me."

"Those things have never been an issue for me. I've always loved you for who you are and I've never wanted you to be any different. You know that."

"That's not how I feel sometimes," she said quietly.

"And whose fault is that?"

"It's no one's fault," she said. "That's just the way I feel."

Carl slowly shook his head. "And therefore what, Anaya?"

"Huh?"

"And therefore what? What are you trying to say, Anaya? That you don't want to be with me? That you love me, but you kiss other men? That you want to be with me, but you lie to me over and over? What is your point here?"

The thought of cutting Carl out of her life was like considering which vital organ to remove, but she had to get through this. Sleeping with Jeff meant that something wasn't right between her and Carl. You don't slip into another man's arms; you end up there after traveling a shaky road of uncertainty. It was awkward working with Jeff, but it was slow torture after they slept together. Now she felt like a hypocrite and it was hard to face him or Carl.

"I'm just saying that for right now, I don't think I'm ready for a relationship."

Carl hung his head, and when he spoke, Anaya had to lean in to hear him. "I can't say I'm surprised. And you are right, things have been different. I want to blame it all on you, but I had my part in this too. You've always been crystal clear about your priorities, and our relationship was always at the bottom of the list." He wiped at his eyes roughly. "I should have paid attention to that. You kept saying you didn't want kids. You didn't want to live together unless we were married, but you weren't ready for marriage either. Then you didn't want to spend too much time together. I guess this has been happening all along and I was too dumb to see it."

"No it wasn't, Carl."

"It was, but it's cool. You kept it real with me the entire time. I was the one who kept holding on to the hope that you would come around. I guess I thought I could love you into changing your mind. That was stupid."

"It's not stupid to believe in somebody. I love you for believing in me. I love you for loving me the way you do." She grabbed his hands.

When he looked up at her, his eyes were devoid of hope. "Yeah, and where did that get me?"

She knew she had hurt him and she didn't know how to make things right. "I love you."

"Don't say that." He pulled his hands from hers and covered his face. "This is hard enough. Please don't say anything nice to me."

Fair enough.

He was quiet for a long time. "I'm going to miss you, girl."

"We can still talk sometimes and—"

"No," he cut her off. "As of today, we are no longer a couple. I need to let that sink in. We will see what the future holds. No plans and no promises. That's the best I can do."

She nodded slowly in agreement. He stood up, wrapped his arms around her waist, and kissed her gently on the forehead.

They walked hand in hand to her car. As she drove away, she looked in the rear view mirror and saw that instead of waiting for her car to disappear like he always did, he had turned his back and walked away.

Anaya had to face her truth. Letting Carl go was hard and she would miss him, but if they were meant to be, they would get back together. In the meantime, she needed to figure out how to stop putting everything before her needs and truly be happy. But first, she had to figure out what to do about Jeff.

THIRTY TWO

O. J. Simpson was being followed on a Los Angeles freeway, it was hotter than normal, and Catie was hungrier than normal. She fanned herself with her hands and sighed so loud Amelia jumped.

"They will be out soon," Amelia said in her soft Tinkerbell voice.

Catie fixed her eyes on Amelia, taking in her dark skin. "You always say that. It's been four hours. When will they be out?"

"Soon." Amelia grinned. "Let's go to Gunny's."

"No," Catie snapped. Their moms had just gotten paid, and she wanted real food, not chips. Besides, Angela Parker from down the street told Catie that the new owner was a mean man from Saudi Arabia and that all the kids were afraid to go there, even if they had money. Someone said he hid a gun next to the register.

Amelia shrugged and picked up an old length of rope they used as a jump rope. Catie sat on the front porch and watched Amelia jump.

"Wanna jump in?"

Catie shook her head at Amelia's happy smile. No, she didn't want to jump in. She wanted food and she wanted her mom to come out of that stupid bedroom. She put her chin in her palms and stared at the street.

"Aren't you hungry?" Catie asked.

"Yeah. My mom said we are going to Wendy's for dinner! You guys should come with us."

There wasn't going to be any Wendy's for Catie. There was

never anything left over for her. No money, no attention, nothing. She continued to sulk. She hated her life.

"Everybody is going to the ballpark to watch the big boys play. You wanna go?" Amelia asked.

"No." Catie was sour. Sour at Leah and sour at Amelia for being so darn happy.

"Come on Catie-Cate. Cheer up!" Amelia sang to the beat of her rope hitting the sidewalk.

"Stop calling me that. I hate that."

"You love it." Amelia dropped the rope and darted up the stairs to try to pinch Catie's cheeks. Catie swatted her hand away.

"Catie-Cate." Amelia danced around Catie.

Catie frowned. "I'm going inside."

"Come on, Catie-Cate. I'll just run to Gunny's. You'll feel better when you have chips inside you!" And she was off, running at full steam down the street toward the corner store.

"Amelia, stop!" Catie cried. But Amelia just turned and waved and sprinted off again.

Catie ran after her, but knew she'd never catch up in time.

✸

After hearing Catie tell the story, Dr. Rhonda challenged Catie to make contact with Amelia's mom and to visit Amelia's grave.

"This is not your fault," Rhonda leaned forward as if she was trying to convince Catie with body language. "You have supportive friends and a family who care about you and you can't live the rest of your life feeling afraid that you will lose them. You lost Amelia, but you aren't going to lose anyone else."

"You can't guarantee that." Catie looked at Dr. Rhonda's awards. "No one can guarantee that."

"You are right," Dr. Rhonda sat back. "But I can guarantee that you will never be happy if you keep living in fear and regret. You have to let that go and free yourself. Amelia's death was not your fault. And you will not get hurt by opening your heart to your loved ones. You gotta trust, Catie."

"How?"

When Catie got home that evening, Amelia was asleep in her rocker and Antoine was on the couch watching television. She kissed her precious baby on the cheek. Whether she liked it or not, Amelia was a beautiful, curly haired rendition of Antoine.

Since Amelia's arrival, the formerly estranged couple had become a baby-rearing machine that managed feeding time, diaper changes, and the night shift without acrimony. They had become closer. They were respectful and honest and had conversations about things that mattered, not just logistical nuances. As Catie learned how far she could work her postpartum body, Antoine gladly volunteered for laundry duty, dinner duty, and anything else that involved bending or climbing stairs. For the first time in a long time, she let Antoine help her. She needed him, and she wasn't afraid to let him know she needed him. She knew that he wanted to be a part of her life in a meaningful way.

"You look beautiful today."

Surprised, Catie looked up from Amelia to see Antoine admiring her fuller curves. He hadn't complimented her in so long she almost asked him to repeat himself.

"Thank you. How was she today?" Catie sat down in the easy chair across from him.

Antoine shrugged. "She was fine. We missed you though."

"Oh?" Antoine missed her? Since when? Looking around, she noticed the dimmed lights and candles. Did he have company while she was gone? She would kill him if he did. He was supposed to be babysitting.

She remembered that just six weeks ago, he had called her a liar and thrown her past in her face. Catie knew that it had been bad to not tell Antoine about her mom. He seemed to have gotten over it quickly—at least, he hadn't brought it up again.

But they hadn't brought up the texts from the masseuse since that night, either.

"You wanna tell me about your day? How was Amelia? And why is it all dark in here?"

"My day was uneventful," he said. He couldn't seem to maintain eye contact with her.

Here we go. He wants to move out and ask for joint custody or something equally inconvenient. Maybe he's moving in with the masseuse.

She decided to cut to the punch. "Antoine?"

"Yes?"

"Tell me about the masseuse."

Antoine didn't miss a beat. In fact, he seemed relieved as he met her gaze.

"One of my jobs got cancelled while I was in the valley and I had three hours to kill, so I used the massage gift card that you gave me." He took a deep breath. "I booked a last-minute massage, and Melissa was the therapist. It was one of those weeks where you hadn't spoken to me, like, at all. She gave me her card after the massage, and I stupidly put her number in my phone."

"Did you like her?" Catie asked. Her voice was flat.

"I don't even know. Most of our texts were talking about our day or her asking me to book another massage." He sat on the edge of the couch and looked her in the eyes. "I'm sorry."

"How many times did you see her?"

"Three times."

"Did you have sex with her?"

"Absolutely not."

"Did you kiss her?"

"No way. It wasn't like that. She was just . . . easy to talk to. She listened to me and seemed like she needed me. I didn't—I don't feel anything for her. I haven't talked to her since before Amelia was born."

Catie studied him. She knew how it felt to pour out your heart about something you regretted only to be met with disbelief. She knew Antoine loved her. He had made a mistake. She didn't believe he was capable of intentionally hurting her. It didn't justify his indiscretion, but she finally acknowledged her role in the demise of their relationship. Hearing how neglected he felt and how he had just wanted to be heard by someone made her want to cry and hug him. She hadn't made life easy for him with her constant barrage of insults, making him sleep on the couch for no reason, and threatening to leave every time she got upset. Everybody needed to feel needed.

"I believe you," Catie said decisively, forgiving him without a second thought.

Antoine looked shocked. "Wait. You believe me?"

She nodded solemnly. "I do." She loved him, and she wanted to try to make him happy the way he had always tried to make her happy.

He scooted off the couch and knelt in front of her chair. "Then can I ask you a question?"

She laughed uncertainly. "Okay, but you don't have to sit on the floor! Get up, we'll—"

"Will you marry me, Catie?"

Catie froze. She remembered Dr. Rhonda's words. *You gotta trust.* Antoine grabbed one of her hands and pressed it to his lips.

"We aren't perfect, but we can make this work," he said. "I love you and I know you love me; you are just scared to show me. We can do this, Catie. We can love one another the right way. We can raise our family and we can be happy. We can work through whatever happened to us in the past. It's gonna be hard work, but I'm all in. We can even see a counselor. I just need to know that you are all in too."

"But—"

"Shhh," he cut her off. "No buts. Say yes."

"I don't know what to say. There's my mom to take care of, and my business, and—"

"She can move in with us." He kissed her softly. "Or she can stay in her home. I will support you in everything you do. Say yes."

For a moment, Catie wanted to say no. All her doubts about herself bubbled up from a dark place inside her. She didn't deserve this man. She didn't deserve to be happy. *You gotta trust.*

"Are you sure, Antoine? You know I'm crazy. And adding another person to the mix is a lot. Leah's still—"

He put his finger on her lips to stop her from talking, and it was like he wiped all her doubts away with a single touch.

"I've never been more sure of anything in my life. Say yes."

Catie nodded through tears. "Yes. Yes!"

THIRTY THREE

Anaya began to seriously look for a job outside of public service the same night that Wendy threatened to link Jayde's scandal to Anaya's reputation. By Christmas, she had accepted a position with public affairs conglomerate Timothy and Associates. They offered her a generous compensation package that put her county salary to fiscal ignominy.

She offered the county three weeks' notice and started wrapping up her projects in her remaining time. She handed off projects to her staffers, sent well-meaning emails to people in the community to announce her resignation, and met with Wendy more times than she cared to.

Wendy announced Anaya's resignation during the first board meeting of the new year. Wendy claimed to be "saddened to lose such talent" and while most thought it was another one of Wendy's deft pontifications in order to save face, Anaya knew it wasn't. Anaya *was* a talented professional who didn't go with the status quo, and Wendy had to respect the fire in Anaya. Unfortunately, that respect came too little, too late. The board was disappointed about Anaya's departure, and even Mr. Killian said a few kinds words about her "timeliness, courteous nature, and unfortunate inability to see corruption right before her very eyes."

Wendy showed up to Anaya's farewell soiree at Luca's dressed to the nines in a camel-colored wool coat and looking like she'd eaten a sour pickle. She made nice-ish comments about Anaya, which was more than anyone had ever received. Then she disappeared quicker than queso at a closed session meeting.

Anaya breathed a sigh of relief when Wendy left. She looked at her phone and reasoned that she only needed to stay another twenty minutes before she could make a graceful exit.

"Wow," said Will, who had had one too many whiskey sours. "Wendy came to your goodbye party—you must be pretty special." He downed another shot, then leaned in conspiratorially. "You guys hear about Jayde?"

Everyone had heard about Jayde. She had admitted to conspiracy, fraud, and other ethics violations cited by the Fair Political Practices Commission. She had sent Anaya an email with a promise to call soon. She couldn't imagine what Jayde was going through and had no desire to; Jayde made a terrible choice. However, she was Anaya's friend and Anaya would be there for Jayde whenever she called, just as Jayde had been for Anaya in the past.

Anaya simply nodded, not wanting to regurgitate her friend's fall from grace.

Sensing her reticence, Sue gave Anaya a side hug. "We will certainly miss you," Sue said. "No one else has stood up to the Dragon Lady."

"I will miss you all too," Anaya said sincerely. "The navy base project is going ahead thanks to us." They clinked glasses in cheers.

Anaya went to get more water. She smiled and said hello to a few familiar faces. She had met some genuinely good people at the county. Granted, most of them doubted her ability to perform her duties in the beginning and didn't miss an opportunity to let her know it, but over time, they had all grown and evolved. She wasn't one to hold grudges. Not usually.

"So, did Wendy make you quit?" Emily the library director cornered her by the bar and leaned in like they were discussing a secret mission. Anaya wondered who had invited her. "Do you have something on her? Does she smoke pot? Like porn? Eat small children?"

"No." Anaya tried not to gasp. How was this woman in charge

of children's programs? "I found an opportunity for growth and decided to pursue it. This has nothing to do with Wendy."

"That's a crock of crap," Emily spewed, sipping on an amber-colored drink with ice. "Wendy is a bitch and probably threatened your life. You don't have to lie to me, you are the victim here."

Should she be drinking?

"Emily, I'm not a victim and I am leaving because I want to." Anaya wished she hadn't engaged.

"Fine, keep lying to yourself." Emily downed her drink, spun on her heels, and walked away.

"What was that weirdo talking about?" Natalie came over to Anaya.

"Nothing," Anaya said, shaking her head.

"Aw, boss lady, I'm going to miss you so much!" Natalie embraced Anaya. "It's never going to be the same."

"I know. I'm going to miss you too. Are you going to be okay without me?" Anaya half joked.

"Oh, I'll be fine," Natalie said coolly. Then she blurted out, "I have officially given my two weeks' notice. Philippe and I are going to try to give it another go." She grinned.

"Wait, you guys are back together?"

"Yep." Natalie flashed her wedding band.

"That's awesome!" Anaya hugged her. "I'm happy for you. But why are you quitting?"

Natalie shrugged. "We figured I would stay home for a while with the kids. Five kids are a lot to handle, you know."

"Yeah, I guess that's true. Wait. You guys only have four—" Anaya stared at Natalie. "Wait. Are you—?"

"Fourteen weeks!"

"Oh my goodness, congratulations!"

Natalie beamed. "Thanks. So really, we're both leaving this godforsaken place."

Anaya was putting on her jacket as Jeff walked in. He still

looked handsome, and she felt vulnerable as his eyes drifted across her body.

"I love your hair," he said.

"Thank you. I rarely straighten it, but I needed a trim." *Why am I explaining my hair maintenance to him?*

"It looks good."

She studied his face for a moment. "I wasn't expecting to see you."

"Well," he said slowly. "If I didn't show up, I didn't think I'd see you otherwise."

Very true. She looked at her shoes. "I've been meaning to call you back."

"You don't have to explain," he said sadly. "I understand. I, um, I just wanted to see you, that's all."

How had they gotten back to this place? After he kissed her in the office that night, she went home with him and they'd made love all night. She'd even told him she loved him and it felt right. The next morning, that feeling had evaporated. She didn't want breakfast. She didn't want to talk, and she was dressed and out of the door before he could pour coffee. They hadn't spoken to or seen each other since. They'd texted a few times, but she had disappeared the same way she did six years ago.

"I think I do need to explain," she said slowly. "That night at your house was incredible."

"Anaya, please," he interjected. "You don't have to do this."

"I do. I have to do this. Please let me finish. That night was incredible and you were as gentle and loving as I remember. For that short time, I felt connected to you again and it reminded me of why I fell in love with you—your kindness, your thoughtfulness, how attracted to you I am. It also reminded me of how convoluted our past was.

"I know you don't think I've forgiven myself, but I have. I just don't think I can go back to a relationship that was once so painful. I wouldn't be able to live with myself."

"I think I understand," he said, clearing his throat and putting his hand on her shoulders. "I'm not asking you for anything. I just want you to think carefully about what you want." He stared deeply into her eyes. "It's okay if you don't know what you want, but don't turn your back on something until you have thought it through. Please don't give up on this without giving it a chance. Can I call you?"

"Please do." She smiled.

He kissed her on the cheek before leaving.

EPILOGUE

"I will see you guys in a bit," Roscoe said over his shoulder. "I'm headed to the nursery." He rushed out of the door.

"Bye, Daddy," Ava said, pulling out a large bin filled with clothes and placing it in the middle of the floor. Joe had been promoted to front desk manager at the hotel and he finally earned enough to move Ava and the kids into a place with enough space for all six of them.

The Carraway family had accumulated a lot of stuff in the six months they lived with the Goodes, so Roscoe had bought a bunch of boxes and grilled some chicken and burgers before he left. Anaya had called in the reinforcements. She, Ava, Anaya, Catie, Sophie, Marie, and Aunt Deb were sorting, folding and throwing things away in anticipation of Ava's big move.

"Is Roscoe still running up to that nursery every week?" Marie frowned at a stained t-shirt and threw it in the trash pile.

"Yes, sometimes twice a week. Hopefully he finishes the yard soon," Anaya said.

Marie laughed as if she had heard the funniest joke in the world. "Yard? Honey, your daddy isn't going up to that nursery because of the *yard*. He's going because of Delilah."

"The flower lady?" Ava asked, eyes wide.

"Girl, you say you know what's going on, but you're missing your daddy's love life and it's right under your nose. He's been crushing on Delilah for months."

Anaya scoffed. She could picture who Delilah was, but it was hard for her to picture her dad with anyone other than her mom.

She sat back and thought about it. She wanted her dad to be happy, and if happiness for Roscoe was Delilah, then that worked for her.

Marie was still talking. "He's been trying to work up the courage to ask her out for a while now. I think today is going to be the day. At least, that's what I heard him telling Allen."

"Good for him," Anaya said.

"Why wouldn't he tell us about her himself?" Ava was confused.

"He probably didn't think you guys were ready for him to date," Catie said simply.

"I want him to be happy," Anaya said.

"Me too," Ava said. "Is Miss Delilah a Christian?"

Catie threw a stuffed animal at her. "No, she's a vampire, and she's going to suck all of your daddy's blood."

"Not funny." Ava said. "Oh, Lord Jesus, what if she's a Methodist? That would never do."

"Is being Methodist worse than being a vampire?" It was Catie's turn to be confused.

"Ava, leave your dad alone." Marie tugged some sheets with cars on them out of a pile and tossed them into a box.

"Fine," Ava relented. "I don't have a problem with him finding a life partner, but this Delilah better be a God-fearing woman who believes in the Trinity and speaking in tongues, or there will be problems."

Anaya shook her head and started folding the bedsheets in the box. She was glad they could all come together to support Ava and help her move out. Even with their differences, Catie was still very much a part of Anaya's family. It was odd that Anaya was hardly speaking to her, but no none but Sophie seemed to notice.

"Ava, you are a hoarder." Catie held up a child's sock. "Where is the match to this?"

"I don't hoard," Ava said looking up from a dresser drawer. "I keep memorable things for my children. I will make them all scrapbooks one day, and I don't want to throw away anything important."

"Hmm, like this torn bracelet from the fair? Crucial memories right there."

"Okay, that doesn't count. You can throw that away. And the sock too."

"Ava, I'm excited for you and Joe," Sophie said while rummaging through a toy bin. Anaya noticed she threw most of the toys into the trash pile without asking Ava's permission. "I think this freedom is just what you need to get yourself centered and ready for the next step in life."

"I agree." Aunt Deb said. "Saturn enters Capricorn this week, my dear niece. You have perfect timing."

"Yep," Catie said. "I think that means that you can get a real job now."

"I'm grateful that dad and Ny let us stay here to save money, and the good Lord provided for us just like he said he would. God is so good."

"All the time," Catie chimed in.

"Yes, he is," Sophie exclaimed.

"You certainly are chipper today, Sophia."

Anaya had to agree with Catie—their friend was acting exceptionally cheerful.

"Life is good right now. I feel like my family loves each other again and my classes are going well." Sophie shrugged and beamed.

Anaya couldn't help but smile back. From what Sophie had told her, she was getting along with both of her parents, and for the first time since she was at middle school, they had gone out to dinner together as a family, with no fights. Both of her parents called her regularly, they supported her, and they acted like they cared. Sophie had even put online dating on pause for now, which Anaya could scarcely believe. She had told Anaya that Jabari was still calling and apologizing. She had forgiven him, but she wasn't sure she wanted to give him another chance. For now, she appeared content. Anaya couldn't have been more proud of her.

Catie narrowed her eyes suspiciously. "Classes? Are you seriously back in school? What exactly is your major, Sophia?"

"I didn't want to ask," Ava added. "Somehow I figured I should know, but I don't."

"None of us do," Catie said.

"Well, I think it's going to be sustainability," Sophie said proudly.

"Sustainability? Girl, you aren't going to finish that."

"Don't be negative, Catie," Ava said. "It has taken Sophie a while to make a decision, but sustainability is a growing field. She might actually finish."

"Wait," Sophie said. "What do you mean?"

Catie darted her eyes from side to side. "Um, I mean you won't finish. *No habla ingles?*"

"What you guys are trying to say?" Sophie looked around at each of them.

"Sophie, you change your mind a lot," Catie said.

"You don't always follow through," added Ava.

"You are inconsistent," Aunt Deb piped in.

"You always—"

"Okay, I get it," Sophie started sorting through the bin of toys again. "I know I've been a little scattered in the past. It's good to know y'all pay so much attention. Geez."

"We love you, Sophie," Anaya said fondly.

"Give her a break," said Marie. "We all make the wrong decision from time to time. Just make sure that you admit to your mistakes and move on. Don't linger over them like I did." She threw a coloring book in the recycle pile and sighed.

"Cheer up, Auntie." Ava reached over and hugged Marie. "All things work together for good to those who love God and are called according to his purpose."

"I'm fine." Marie folded and unfolded the same towel three times.

"You don't look fine to me," Catie said. Sophie threw a baby towel and hit Catie in the head.

"What?" Catie shrugged.

"You don't look fine to me either," Aunt Deb called. She was on her hands and knees looking under the bed. "You look sad. Pitiful actually." Anaya and Ava exchanged a glance.

"Auntie, it's going to be okay," Sophie said maneuvering carefully across the room. She pushed a box to the side, sat cross-legged in front of Marie, and closed her eyes. "Breathe and assess, breathe and assess." Sophie took deep breaths, but Marie just stared at Sophie.

"Things went wrong. It happens, but you have to let go now and move on."

Sophie made a whistling sound.

"Marie, you need to make a decision." Aunt Deb emerged from under the bed but her rimmed glasses were crooked on her nose. "You don't need to breathe to figure that out. If you had concerns about your marriage, you waited a long time to address them. I watched you take Allen for granted all these years. Years ago, I tried to tell you that you were making a mistake. Just like I did with Farley. You remember Uncle Farley, don't you?"

Marie nodded.

"Anita tried to tell you too. But you were out there thinking you cute with that new nose and them spinning classes. Well, you got the attention you wanted and now you are about to lose your husband."

"I don't want to lose my husband," Marie admitted.

"Marie, I'm going to make this plain for you okay?" Deb wagged her index finger. "I tried to be nice, but you are taking this too far."

"Oh, that was her being nice?" Catie whispered to Ava. Ava nudged her.

"Your failed marriage is largely your own doing," Deb continued. Marie opened her mouth to protest, but Deb silenced her. "Now, it's time to get real. You haven't had a job since Allen Jr. was in diapers, and you can't boil a potato. A man needs something to hold on to. Something to respect and be proud to call his own. Having a nice derrière isn't enough, honey." She paused before walking off. "I need to find that silk headscarf I gave Anita for her fiftieth birthday. It's purple. Has anybody seen it?"

"I tried to find a job," Marie called after Deb in vain. "Allen said I didn't need to work!"

"Give him time, Auntie," Anaya finally said. "It's all pretty fresh, but if you give him space, I'm sure things will get better. After all, 'to err is human, but to forgive is divine.' Alexander Pope said that."

"Yep," Catie said throwing another sock. "Sometimes you have to forgive and forget. 'Forgive them for hurting you and forget they exist.'"

"That's dope." Ava gave the thumbs up. "Who said that?"

"Kid Cudi."

"Okay. We need to be careful here," Sophie said, still breathing deeply. "We're quoting the laureates and rappers all in the same space. Let's just clear the air." She closed her eyes and fanned the air with her arms.

"Girl, please shut up," Catie said. "And finish going through those toys. We are going to be here all day at this rate."

Sophie frowned. "Okay, but don't say I didn't warn you."

"How did you guys do it, Catie?" Ava asked, dragging a full box across the room. "How did you and Antoine go from living in sin to being happily married?"

"Don't bring up her marriage," Sophie growled. "Catie deprived us all of seeing that event."

"Girl, hush. I didn't deprive you of anything. It was personal between Antoine, Amelia, and me. And it was perfect. I told y'all we are having a reception in July. And guess what? You are all invited."

"Oh, yay," Sophie said with sarcasm. "A reception."

"Back to my question," Ava said. "How did you guys get from sin to lovehappy?"

"First of all, who said we're happy? And second of all, who are you to say we were living in sin? You don't know my life."

"Catie, stop pretending," Ava said. "We know you are happy; it's in your eyes."

"What you see in my eyes is agony from all the hard work and compromise I have to do to keep peace in my house. You know I'm not used to keeping my mouth shut."

"Yeah, we all know that," Marie joked.

"It's hard, but I have to admit it's worth it. We wouldn't want to bring another baby into the world if we were still fighting all the time."

Sophie widened her eyes. "I guess Antoine has been allowed back into the Kegel reformed kingdom?"

"Girl, Antoine couldn't wait to get his hands on me once I reinstated his privileges." Catie stood up and twirled the fuller figure that Antoine loved so much. "Told y'all heffas to do those Kegels."

"Wow." Sophie was still processing. "I can't believe you guys want another kid."

"She's following in my footsteps," Ava said proudly.

"Um, *not*," Catie said. "We only want two. We don't need a basketball team. It's too much work and too expensive."

"But the Bible says—"

Catie held up her hand. "Ava, darling, I know the Bible says wonderful things all the time. I love God too, he heard *all* of my cries, but God also gives us wisdom and choices. And the Bible has no bearing on how many children Antoine and I plan to have."

"Fine. I'm just trying to help." Ava looked frustrated. " I don't know why you guys get so upset with me. I just want everybody to know how good God is."

"Then stop pushing people away with condemnation," Sophie said.

Ava furrowed her brow.

"I'm going to have to agree," Marie chimed in. "I know you mean well, niece, but sometimes your good message gets lost in what feels and sounds like judgment."

Ava stared at them with her mouth open. She looked over at Anaya, who was sifting through another box of toys. Anaya wouldn't get her out of this one; she wholeheartedly agreed with the ladies.

"Why do you love God so much, Ava?" Sophie asked.

"*That's* a silly question."

"No. I really want to know. Why do you love God so much?"

"Because he is merciful and he answers prayers, and when the world is crazy, he gives me hope that things will get better. He's my doctor, my healer, and provider."

"That's your message," Sophie declared.

"Huh?"

"If you want people to give your God a chance, Ava, tell them about the good things. About the things that bring you joy and the reasons you love him. Not all that other stuff. People are imperfect and make mistakes. We don't need to be reminded of them constantly. But everybody wants to hear about something that makes them feel good and that gives them hope."

"I never thought about it that way."

"Well, maybe it's time you do. Because if you judge my life once more in the name of the Bible, you might catch these hands." Catie raised her fists.

Ava ignored Catie and looked at Sophie gratefully. "Thanks, Sophie. I appreciate you saying that."

The women stood back and looked at their work.

The trash pile was massive, which meant they could probably move the full boxes to Ava's new place in one trip. As they stacked trash bags near the front door, Catie pulled Anaya to the side.

"I'm sorry about lying about Leah," she said. "I know I didn't handle it right, especially with all you've been through. I feel so bad, Ny. That was a terrible thing for me to do to you and Sophie. You guys have been here for me and I lied to you. Can you please forgive me?"

Anaya just nodded. She had forgiven Catie a long time ago, she just hadn't been able to admit it. She had let her pride get in the way of progress.

"I love you, Anaya," Catie continued. "You are my family, my sister, and I can't live without you in my life. Being here and hardly speaking to each other—it's weird and it's wrong. I will never lie to you again."

Anaya wiped the tears from her eyes and hugged Catie. Life was about owning mistakes and forgiving. And that's what she did. At some point, we all needed forgiveness.

"I love you, Caitlin."

"I love you, too."

"I'm sorry for not forgiving you earlier."

"Girl, please. There is nothing for you to apologize for. That was a massive lie I let linger. I understand where you were coming from. But I will never betray our friendship or your trust ever again."

Anaya nodded and attempted to stem the stream of tears.

"Now let's get Ava and her family out of this house before she changes her mind."

"Aw, I'm so happy!" Sophie ran over to Catie and Anaya. "Group hug."

Ava joined them. "Praise the Lord!"

"It's never too soon to change our minds when we are wrong about something," Anaya sniffled.

"And it's never too soon to make up our minds about things that have held us emotionally captive," Sophie said.

Catie nodded. "And it's never too soon to learn to let go of things that cause you pain."

"And it's never too soon to get to know Jesus, who is the lily of the valley," Ava said.

Catie reached out her hands like she was going to strangle Ava, while Anaya and Sophie pulled her back, laughing.

ABOUT THE AUTHOR

A Bay Area native, Tamika Christy began writing at an early age, prompted by the gift of a journal. She continued writing throughout college where she realized her talent for creating intriguing plots and multidimensional characters. Using words to paint vivid landscapes of the emotions, triumphs, and the madness of life, Tamika continued to nurture her love for writing while attending law school, where she gave birth to her first novel, *Any Time Soon,* which won the Next Generation Finalist Award for African American Fiction.

Now a practicing attorney, Tamika still devotes time to her love of writing. She describes her writing as urban prose—funny, warm, and soulful with blunt dialogue and familiar realism.

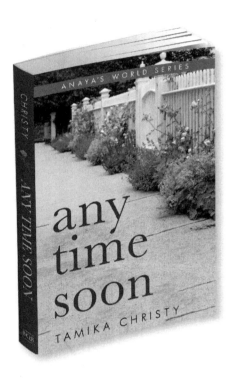

Book One in the
Anaya Goode Series

Frenzied. Overburdened. Stressed. Overwhelmed. These are just a few ways to describe college senior Anaya Goode's life. Add to this no career prospects following a looming graduation, and Anaya quickly finds herself drowning in the chaos of her own life. Her family and friends demand much of Anaya, and she's struggling to balance herself in the mire. Facing an onslaught of grief, complex relationships, and a life that is full of deafening noise, Anaya must find herself, and maybe even true love and redemption, amid old traditions and new beginnings.

Any Time Soon was a Finalist Award Winner in the African American Fiction category at the Indie Next Generations Awards in 2014.